# THE SECRETS YOU KEEP

TRACY LORRAINE

Editing by Pinpoint Editing

Proofreading by Sisters Get Lit.erary

Photographer - Wander Aguiar

Models - Camden, Sophie and Pat

# 1

# VIOLET

"Fold," Ella groans, throwing her cards down on the table before curling her legs beneath her and reaching for her drink.

"Ella," West whines. "You can't keep bitching out."

"My cards suck," she complains, taking a sip of her margarita.

"So? Everyone else's might too. You gotta play the game."

"I can't lie for shit, and you all know it. I'm better off just leaving you all to it. Watching your poker faces is so much fun. Vi always looks like she's taking a shit, she's so serious."

Brax and Micah snort a laugh at her comment.

"How do you know what I look like taking a shit?" I bark.

"From before you shower together," Brax pipes up, his eyebrows wiggling in delight.

"Ugh, are you still obsessed with that?" Ella groans, throwing a cushion at his head.

"Ow, fuck," Brax barks as the cushion knocks over his beer, soaking his pants, making it look like he just pissed himself.

"Karma is a bitch," I announce happily as he hops up, rips open the button and shoves the fabric down his legs.

"Dude, you better not be going commando under those," Ella shouts, faux horrified.

"You fucking wish," West snorts. "When was the last time you saw one up close, El?"

She sighs in sadness while Micah watches her closely, just like he always does.

That poor guy has got it bad. But he's also a rule follower, so I know that he'll never do anything about it.

None of us met until two years ago when we all began on the next chapter of our lives by starting at Maddison Kings University and found ourselves in a dorm together.

Safe to say, we were all nervous as hell. It was our first time away from home, and we were all starting over. But from that very first day, something just clicked into place for us.

It was like fate or some shit. Our ride-or-die friendships started from the very second we all gathered in the living area and lifted our beers to embark on our new lives.

Now, that's not to say it's all been easygoing. Especially when not only are the guys fucking awesome, but they're also smoking hot, too. Micah is rocking the sexy nerd look, while West and Brax are ripped football players who leave drooling girls in their wake.

There have been moments, especially when drunk, and never more so than the time we all decided it would be a good idea to play Twister and Brax and I... yeah, probably best not to even think about that. The miniskirt and the tiny panties were definitely an oversight on my part.

But we all made a pact. Any fucking going on under our roof would not include two, or more, of us. We had to solely look outside our new little family to get our kicks.

And by some fucking miracle—because the guys are actually that freaking hot—it's worked. And despite the odd fantasy here and there, I couldn't be happier. They are the family I was craving when I first found myself here, more lost than ever. Not that any of them are aware of that.

They saved me, dragged me from the darkness I'd been drowning in since my life imploded and brought me back to life. I'll forever be grateful for each and every one of them. And one day, I might even tell them.

"Thank fuck for that," Ella cries when Brax flashes us his boxer-clad ass.

"You love it. You know you want to sink your teeth right here," he says, pointing to his solid behind.

"Pfft, I don't think so. I'd need a hedge trimmer first."

"You know, it's a good job I love you," Brax sulks as he walks out of our new living room to clean himself up.

The second he's out of sight, West leans over and looks at Brax's cards.

"Motherfucker," he grunts, throwing them down on the table and letting us all see that the little shit was lying. His hand is even worse than mine.

"You still in, Vi?" West taunts, while Micah sits quietly in the corner, his face unreadable—other than his desire for Ella, obviously.

"Hell, yeah. You motherfuckers are going down."

But as I say that, the lights flicker and the music stops before we're plunged into darkness.

Panic grips me in its tight hold and I wrap my arms around myself in the hope they'll keep me together. The only bonus right now is that none of them can see what I can only assume is the unfiltered fear that is no doubt written all over my face.

As a kid, I wasn't scared of anything. I was shy as hell, but I wasn't scared.

I used to hide in the dark for longer than I wanted to admit when my older brother and I used to play hide and seek and he'd get fed up looking and abandon me in whatever place I'd chosen to hide.

All it took was one night to change everything.

"What the hell?" West barks before the flashlight on his

cell brightens the space, allowing me to at least see where they are.

Some of my panic fades, but still, I refuse to look at anyone for fear they'll see my reaction.

They know I sleep with the light on. We've all been living together for two years now, so I was hardly able to keep that a secret. But they think it's just my preference, not that I'm fucking terrified.

"See what happens when you get your ass out?" Ella shrieks in the direction Brax disappeared in. I focus on her voice, begging for the fear to leave me.

"Fuck you, El," he bellows back. "Someone go and find the fucking circuit breaker."

"Sure thing, boss," West quips before getting to his feet. "Come on, Micah. Maybe we can put your geeky knowledge to some use."

Micah scoffs but climbs to his feet to help. "IT geek," Micah grunts. "I know fuck all about electrics."

"I'm sure you can figure it out. You're smart as shit."

More light floods the room as both Micah and Ella put their flashlights on.

West continues ripping into Micah as they disappear from the room before Ella's light turns on me.

"Vi, are you okay?" she asks, concern obvious in her tone as she slides closer.

"Y-yeah," I say, hating that I stutter like a cowardly little kid. "I-I'm just not a fan of the dark."

"It's okay. They guys will have it back on in a flash," she assures me, finding my hand and squeezing.

Her warmth seeps up my arm and I latch onto her support.

She's right. Of course she's right. But that doesn't stop my brain from going back to that night.

Faster than I thought possible, the lights flicker back on, helping to banish my memories and allowing me to shove them all back into the box they are usually securely locked in.

Nothing good comes from thinking about that night and everything that came afterward. Or much of what happened before it, to be fair.

"See," Ella soothes.

"I-I know, I'm sorry. I'm just going to—" I hop up from the couch and turn toward the door as West and Micah's footsteps climb the stairs from the basement where the circuit breaker is.

"Whoa, Vi. Where's the fire?" Brax asks when I barrel into him before I hit the first floor.

"Sorry," I cry before bolting toward the second set of stairs.

"Vi, wait," he calls, but I don't hang around long enough for him to say anything else, and the second I'm on the top floor, I fly through my bedroom door, slamming it behind me.

So much for not letting them see me freak out.

Stripping out of my clothes, I make a beeline for the Jack and Jill bathroom that Ella and I share and march straight into the shower, turning the dial and blasting myself with ice-cold water for a few seconds.

My entire body trembles with both the cold and the lingering fear that those few minutes in the dark dragged up. Thankfully, as the water begins to warm, things start to settle down, and by the time the inevitable knock comes from Ella's side of the bathroom, I'm just about ready to face her.

"Yeah," I call. It's pointless, she'd let herself in even if I told her to go away. That's just how it is with us.

Family.

The word forces a sob to spill from my throat right as she steps into the room.

Concern pinches her brows as she finds me hiding behind the shower screen. The middle of it might be frosted, hiding my body from her, but honestly, we've both seen everything enough times over the past two years and right now, it's not my curves I'm desperate to hide.

It's my past. The broken girl who lives behind the mask of the confident, say-yes-to-everything woman that I am now.

"Violet," she breathes, coming closer and hopping up on the counter between our double sinks. "Do you want to talk about it?"

My eyes find her kind, honey ones. Eyes that have been there for me without question since the moment I stepped inside our dorm on that first day as a freshman.

I was nervous as fuck, but one look in her eyes and I knew she was too. It was the first thing that bonded us. Then the guys arrived, looking equally as overwhelmed and, well, the rest is history, I guess.

I shake my head. "It's nothing. Just some stupid childish fear."

My chest heaves as the water pounds down on my shoulders, giving me little choice but to let go of some more of the fear.

"It doesn't matter how childish you think it is, it's still scary," she says, empathy clear in every word.

I can't help but smile at her.

"What the hell are you scared of, El? You're one of the strongest people I've ever met."

"We all have our things, Vi. And they're nothing to be ashamed of." I stare at her, more than willing to dive into her issues rather than mine right now. "Public speaking," she confesses. "I literally have nightmares about it."

"I think that's fairly normal. Talking in front of people is terrifying."

"Just like the dark." She shrugs. "But it's the reasons behind them that are the bigger issues, right?"

Fuck.

I know about Ella's past. Her school years were less than desirable. She was bullied badly because of her weight, because she looked different from the cheerleaders that everyone wanted to be.

It's bullshit. All of it. Ella is the most beautiful person I've ever met, inside and out. She might have lost her baby fat now, but it's the confidence that has come with it that is the most stunning thing about her. That, and her smile. She can melt hearts and harden cocks from a mile off with that smile.

"M-my brother," I force out, falling back on the story I've perfected, ready for the day this was inevitably going to come up. Though I have to admit, I thought it would have happened before now. "He used to leave me in the dark for hours while we were playing as kids. A couple of times, he knew where I was and locked me in there."

"Sounds like a dick," Ella mutters, making my heart ache for that playful little boy.

"Yeah," I say with a laugh. "He was. I loved him, though."

Ella smiles sadly at me. They might not know the details of what I went through with my family, but they all know that I've lost them. My mom and brother through tragedy and my father through choice many years before that. Honestly, I'm not sure which is more heartbreaking when I think about it—to have people ripped away from you, or to have someone choose not to want you in their lives.

"You should come back down, get drunk."

The suggestion is tempting—more than tempting. But tomorrow is the first day of classes, and I refuse to turn up with a hangover, or worse, not turn up at all.

I shake my head. "I think I'm just going to head to bed."

She smiles sadly. "I think we should all probably do that. I'm not sure I'm ready." She pouts, thinking about classes starting tomorrow.

"Same."

We've had a pretty insane summer. All of us stayed in Maddison County, but it's been epic. We all volunteered with different kids clubs that the uni runs. The guys have trained with the rest of the team. And we've all just hung out and loved life without the stress of classes and assignments. That's all about to change, though. We're becoming juniors. That's some scary shit right there. Adult life and big decisions are looming, and I'm definitely not ready for those.

"This year is going to be insane, though. The guys are going to fucking kill it. They've been on fire all summer."

"They deserve to go all the way this year."

"They do, and we're going to watch every minute of it. Plus, they've got the added benefit of their new GA." Ella wiggles her brows at me, and I can't help but laugh at her goofiness.

"Why did I tell you about him?" I moan.

"Because you know how much I love a football hottie."

"Tristan's..."

"The hottest of them all."

"I was going to say off-limits."

"Jeez, girl. You ruin all my fun," she sulks. "It's like you want him for yourself."

My lips part to argue, but she beats me to it.

"Don't even lie to me, Violet Brady."

"It's not like that with us and you know it."

"You've tried convincing me that that's the case for the past two years, all the while watching every game he played, every interview he did and talking to him almost on the daily. Yeah, I totally know it."

Reaching behind me for the sponge, I launch it at her, spraying water everywhere. It smacks her right on the side of her head, soaking her hair and covering her in water and bubbles.

"Now that's what I'm talking about," a deep voice booms from the doorway.

I can't see them, but knowing they're hiding in Ella's room and have come to check on me fills me with the warm fuzzies.

"What are you waiting for? Retaliate. We want some naked wrestling," Brax shouts excitedly.

"You're a dog," Ella mutters, hopping from the counter and walking over to swing the door closed on them.

"W-wait. Vi, you okay?" West calls.

Poking my head around the shower screen, careful not to give them an eyeful, I find the three of them standing there, looking like lost puppies. "I'm good. Thank you."

"Is everything okay with—" Ella starts but is quickly interrupted

"Everything's good. Just one of those things. We've got you, girl."

"Thank you," I breathe, more grateful for them than I could ever put into words.

Happy that I'm okay, the three of them disappear, and after checking that I'm not going to freak out again, Ella heads through to her room as well.

I wash my hair and scrub every inch of my body while my thoughts linger on the Panthers' new graduate assistant football coach.

Tristan Carver has been...

Hell, he's been my rock over the past five years.

He used to be my brother's best friend. The boy who would spend every single waking hour possible at our house hanging out with Roman and, in turn, driving me insane.

They were three years older than me and thought they were so freaking cool.

I mean, I guess it was easy to tell themselves that when they were easily the two most talented players on our high school football team. They had girls hanging on their every word almost from as early as I can remember.

I literally thought he was the single most irritating person on the planet, behind my brother of course, until I was about thirteen.

Something happened then, because suddenly, his presence had a very different effect on me.

He was no longer an annoying and disgusting boy, and I no longer wanted to get as far away from him whenever he came to hang out with Roman as physically possible. I wanted to do anything I could to monopolize his time, to get his attention.

It's just a shame he didn't see me the same way. I've always been Roman's little sister. And I'm pretty sure I always will be.

I blow out a sigh as I turn the water off and reach for the towel.

But then, he became everything to me. Literally.

I have no idea how I would have survived everything if it weren't for him.

I wasn't his responsibility. I was just his best friend's little sister.

But he took his role seriously, and he's held me up and attempted to put me back together more times than I can count over the past few years.

Even while he was away playing during the past eighteen months, he was always at the other end of the phone when I needed him.

I pad through to my bedroom after cleaning my face and teeth and drop onto the edge of my bed still wrapped in my towel.

Unable to stop myself, I reach for my cell and find our conversation from yesterday.

**Violet: Are you all ready for tomorrow?**

# 2

# TRISTAN

I slouch back in my chair, my eyes burning from spending the entire day with my head in textbooks.

I knew becoming a student again after two years out was going to be hard work. And I'm not stupid—doing a graduate degree while also being an assistant coach for the Panthers was never going to be a walk in the park—but shit, classes haven't even started yet and I can't help feeling like I'm already behind.

An exhausted groan falls from my lips a beat before my cell buzzes against my desk.

Other than my bed, it's the only bit of furniture I have in my apartment. It seemed way more necessary than a couch, seeing as the only things I'm going to be doing while here are working or sleeping.

Reaching for where I left it face down in the hope I wouldn't get distracted by my notifications, I stare at the message, a smile twitching at my lips.

That is, until I catch sight of my background.

I should have changed it already. But I can't.

I might have made the decision to walk away from the

dream I'd had since I could barely walk, but it still pains me to know I have.

I had everything. Every little boy's ultimate goal.

Yet, here I am. A student at MKU once more, starting over.

I stretch my leg out. It still aches, and I fully expect it to for quite a while yet. There's nothing to say that I won't make a full recovery and that I could have stepped back out on the field and continued my career. But something just felt wrong about sitting around, waiting for the chance.

Home was calling, and so was a certain curvy brunette that really shouldn't factor into any of my decision making.

But even knowing that, she's always there, up in my head like she's always been.

I tell myself for the millionth time that it's because I made my best friend a promise. And at the beginning, that was true.

But all these years on... I'm finding it harder and harder to tell myself that lie.

Swiping the screen, I open the message. Just like always, I feel like a virgin schoolboy, not a twenty-four-year-old ex-NFL player when I stare at the little thumbnail of her profile picture.

My smile finally breaks free when I read her words, and I immediately begin tapping out a reply, wincing with a barefaced lie.

**Tristan: Yep, I'm more than ready. MKU doesn't know what's about to hit them.**

The little dots start bouncing instantly, and those dumbass butterflies in my belly only party harder.

**Pip: Good to know that your ego is as large as ever. We still on for lunch?**

I can't help but laugh at her comment.

**Tristan: Would I cancel on my best girl? I'm only going to manage about thirty minutes though, that going to be enough?**

A rush of adrenaline shoots through my veins at my innuendo. When I was away, our messages were a bit of fun to break up the monotony of traveling and all the less-than-desirable things that come with life on the road during a heavy season.

I should have reined them in when I made the decision to return to her life permanently and not just be this friend on the other end of the phone.

But then again, I probably shouldn't have done a lot of things I have. And a little innocent flirting with a girl I can't have doesn't seem all that dangerous in the grand scheme of things.

**Pip: I'm not sure... I do prefer having a nice, long, slow... lunch...**

"Jesus," I mutter, reaching down to rearrange myself when things start to get a little tight.

Yeah, so it's been a while, despite my reputation and the shit the journos like to spread about me. So long, in fact, I'm getting fucking hard over a text and a thumbnail picture.

Classy, Tris. Real fucking classy.

**Tristan: Oh yeah? I had you down as more of a quickie kinda girl.**

I regret it the second I hit send.

"Fuck. You fucking moron."

But not one to be deterred by my terrible game, she immediately starts typing again.

**Pip: I don't know who you've been talking to, but I can confirm that those stories aren't true... well... not all of them. Perhaps you shouldn't listen to anything the team has to say...**

The thought of any of the guys I've been training with over the summer touching Violet sends a surge of possessiveness through me that's so strong I find myself on my feet, pacing my bedroom.

**Tristan: Have you been a busy girl, Pip?**

"Fuck. Fuck." I don't want to know.

**Pip: Just enjoying college. You remember what it was like, right, old man?**

**Tristan: Watch your mouth, kid.**

**Pip: Why? Are you going to punish me?**

All the air rushes out of my lungs and my knees give out, sending me crashing back onto my bed.

Scrubbing my hand down my face, I try to drag my head out of the gutter and shove the image from my mind of her round little ass staring up at me with my glowing red handprint across it.

It doesn't fucking work, though, and before I know what I'm doing, my hand is inside my sweats, my fingers wrapping around my length.

**Tristan: You're trouble, Pip.**

**Pip: Just the way you like me. Think how boring your life would be if I were a good girl.**

**Tristan: I always thought you were. You're ruining the illusion.**

**Pip: Then you need to look closer.**

"Yeah, or run in the opposite direction as fast as you fucking can, Carver."

**Tristan: I'm gonna crash. Got a stupidly early class in the morning.**

**Pip: Boo, you're boring.**

**Tristan: I'm sure there are plenty of boys your own age who want to stay up all night talking to you.**

**Pip: What if I don't want to talk to them?**

**Tristan: Night, Pip. I'll see you for lunch tomorrow.**

**Pip: Can't wait. *winky emoji***

"Christ, Pipsqueak." *Do you have any idea what you do to me?*

Unable to leave it there, I send her a kiss emoji—because yes, my best friend's little sister turns me into a fucking teenage girl—and then I shut our conversation down and shove my cell under my pillow in the hope I can shove my cravings for her away with it.

Unfortunately, it's not that easy, and as I lie there staring up at the ceiling, all I can think about is her.

"Goddamn it, Violet."

Giving it up as useless, I shove my sweats down over my hips and do the only thing I can that will rid me of my boner. Well, the only thing I'm willing to do when it comes to her.

"Fuck," I hiss, jerking myself violently in punishment for once again having the image of her body in my mind while getting myself off.

There is something fucking wrong with me.

*"Promise me, Tris. Promise me that whatever happens after this, you'll take care of her. I need to know that she's going to be okay."*

"Fuuuuck," I groan, coming all over my hand like a pathetic douchebag who spends all his days locked in his room or watching a bunch of guys running drills and plays.

This time last year, I was getting ready for my second season as a Titan and living my best life.

Oh, how the mighty fall...

---

"Tris!" Her soft yet excited voice hits my ears as I stand outside the coffee shop where we agreed to meet for lunch, and when I spin around, I find her running toward me before she jumps into my arms.

"Oh shit," I grunt, stumbling back and colliding with the wall.

"Oh fuck. I'm sorry, did I hurt you?" she asks in horror as she fights to get away from me.

"I'm fine, Pip," I assure her, pulling her back for a hug when she tries to escape. "I missed you, kid," I say into the top of her head, enjoying the warmth of her body pressed up against mine way more than I should.

I might have been back on this side of the country for a few weeks, but with both of us moving into new places, and me spending all my time working, training with the team or doing my own physio, we haven't found the time to catch up in person.

Not that it really matters. As she pulls back from me and I look down into her eyes, it feels like no time has passed since she surprised me not long after I ripped my ACL by turning up at my front door to be my nurse. Sadly, she didn't come armed to be *that* kind of nurse. Didn't stop my overactive imagination though, as she helped me around my apartment and with the exercises I'd been given to build my strength back up.

"I can't believe you're really here."

I hold my arms out from my sides. "You missed me?" I ask with a smirk.

"Meh." She waves me off. "I'm starving, come on. We've gotta make it a quickie, remember?"

"I remember," I mutter, following her inside and trying—and failing—to stop my eyes falling to her ass in the almost indecent shorts she's wearing. "Decided against real clothes today then, huh?"

"Dude, you're letting your age show. All the boys love them, right?" she asks loudly, looking over my shoulder at two unsuspecting guys who are innocently waiting to order food.

Both of them turn beet red as they run their eyes down her body, finally landing on her ass when she flashes them.

"Jesus, Vi," I hiss, placing my hand on the small of her back and pushing her forward.

"What? It's not my fault if the freshmen can't handle it."

"What happened to that sweet little girl who blushed the second someone said a bad word?" I whisper, barely able to believe that the firecracker with curves for days standing before me is the same person.

"She grew up, Tris. That girl is long gone. Poof," she says, making a little explosion gesture with her hand. "Up in smoke."

She might say it lightly and with a smile on her face, but I see the dark shadows in her eyes those words drag up.

Unable to stop myself, I drop my eyes down the length of her as my thumb brushes along my bottom lip. "So you have, Pip. How many guys do I have to warn off you in the next two years?"

She places her hands on her hips, her eyebrows jumping up. "Um… none. I am a strong, independent woman. I am more than capable of fighting off the guys who don't give me the flutters."

"The flutters?" I ask, but when her eyes alight with mischief, I realize my mistake. "No, don't answer that."

"Tris," she says. Her brows pinch as she steps closer to me. "Are you blushing?"

"N-no, of course—"

"Next," the guy behind the counter calls, thankfully rescuing me from whatever the hell I just walked into.

*She's just that annoying little kid,* I tell myself. Roman's irritating little sister… who now has a spectacular ass and a great rack. But still his little, off-limits sister.

Fuck. Why did I think coming back here was a good idea?

---

"What?" I ask, lifting my hand to wipe my mouth, assuming I've got a giant blob of mayo somewhere as Violet stares at me.

"Nothing. You look… happy," she says with a soft smile.

"I am," I confirm. "Being back here, it feels… right, I guess."

"I was worried," she confesses.

"Aw, Pipsqueak. You don't need to worry about me."

She glares at me, lifting one brow in the process.

"Tris, you're my…" She sighs, seemingly unable to come up with the correct term.

"Friend?" I offer, although the word tastes bitter on my

tongue.

"That seems a little weak after everything, don't you think?" Reaching across the table, she squeezes my hand.

My initial reaction is to pull my arm back. Not because I don't welcome her touch—quite the fucking opposite, in fact. Sparks shoot from her innocent contact, making my blood heat and my heart race.

I stare back at her, wondering when the hell my body decided to betray me.

I made a promise. One I fully intended to keep after her life imploded. And it was fine, to start with. I was just there for her, my parents too. But somewhere along the way, my need to protect her and follow the request of her brother has morphed into something I shouldn't be feeling. Something that was not part of what Roman asked of me.

Finally, I do what I should have done the moment she reached out, and I tug my hand free of hers in favor of lifting my sandwich.

Hurt flickers through her green eyes, although the second she blinks, she manages to hide it.

"I was just worried that you'd get here and realize you made a mistake," she explains. "What you left behind, it's... it's huge, Tris. Most people wouldn't walk away from that willingly."

"I'm not most people," I say with a smirk.

She chuckles. "Oh, don't worry, I'm more than aware of that."

"I did the right thing," I confirm confidently.

"What if your leg heals and you can play again?"

I shrug. "I did it, Vi. I got there. I played almost two seasons for the NFL. It was incredible, everything I'd always dreamed of, but—"

"But it was ripped away from you. When I came out to Tennessee to see you, you were so—"

"Angry? Yeah. I was pissed. We were on our way to the

best season in the Titans' history, and I'd just fucked myself up, possibly forever. But things change.

"I'd rather be here doing something, making use of my life than following a team around while watching games I can't play in from the sidelines.

"Here, I get to make a difference. I get to help train the future stars of the NFL, and hopefully, I can do that for years to come. Football is my life, it always has been. But it doesn't just have to be about playing it. There is so much more to it than that."

She nods, accepting my explanation. "I'm just worried you'll heal and then you'll regret being stuck here."

*With you?* "Never."

"How is it?" she asks, nodding to where my leg is hiding beneath the table.

"It's getting there. Everything happens for a reason, right?" I ask, but I regret the words instantly as pain crosses her features.

"If you say so."

My cell buzzes on the table, alerting me that my next class is starting in ten minutes and it's on the other side of campus.

"I'm sorry, Pip. I've got to head out."

"Wow, it really was a quickie, huh?"

"I'm sorry, things are crazy, my schedule is—"

"I know, Tris. I get it. You don't need to explain yourself to me," she says sadly.

"I'll find some time, okay? We can hang out. You can come check out my new place, not that it's got anything worth showing off."

"Oh, I don't know. I hear it's got a pretty kickass pineapple plant," she teases, reminding me of the housewarming gift she sent. I'm not sure who she's trying to kid, I can barely keep myself alive, let alone a freaking plant.

"Hey, now. You leave Penny out of this."

She stares at me for a beat as if she's trying to figure out if

I'm being serious or not before she falls about in a fit of laughter.

"P-Penny? Tris, tell me you didn't name the plant?"

"What?" I argue. "It gets lonely sometimes."

"What, you mean your NFL fame doesn't have jersey chasers at your door every second of the day?" she teases, although despite trying to cover how she really feels about that statement, there's no hiding the way her top lip peels back in disgust.

"Oh yeah, they've all been flocking to me every night of the week to welcome me to town and massage my knee." I shouldn't say it, but I can't stop myself. My need to see that she's as affected by me as I am her is too much to ignore.

It's a dangerous, dangerous game but one I can't seem to stop playing.

"Tell me you're kidding," she begs, trying to keep her tone light and teasing.

"Of course. The only people I've seen are the coaching staff, the team, and now you."

"Living the high life, huh?"

"You know it," I say, throwing my bag over my shoulder and gathering up my trash. "I'll message you."

"Wait," she calls behind me, making my body freeze. "I've got like an hour until my next class. Can I walk you?"

"You sure you want to risk your life like that, batting away all the jersey chasers?"

"I'll take the risk. I'll point out the ones you really need to stay away from, unless of course you want your dick to rot off."

"Can't say it was on my to-do list, Pip," I confess as we walk out of the coffee shop.

"Do you have to keep calling me that?" she whines. "I'm a college student now. The childish nickname can go at any time."

"Nah, I think it's cute. You'll always be my little pipsqueak."

# 3

## VIOLET

"Great," I mutter to myself as I trail behind Tristan after dumping my trash.

I don't want him to see me as cute. I want him to see me as a sexy woman, not an annoying little child.

Was that the reason for the slightly obscene booty shorts that I'd never usually wear to class? Yeah, there's a very good chance it was.

And they might have worked for a beat. He checked me out while we were standing in line for lunch, sure, but it was only once. I certainly wasn't getting the 'I can't keep my eyes off you, you're so hot' vibes that I was hoping for.

"So where are we going?" I ask.

Really, I should be heading to the library, but my need to have more time with him is too strong to ignore.

"Augustus Building."

I fight to school my reaction. He wasn't kidding when he said he was heading to the other side of campus.

Instead, I flick my hair over my shoulder, thread my arm through his and set off on the hike through campus, soaking up his warmth and strength like a junkie craving her next fix.

We barely make it twenty feet when I spot the first group of jersey chasers, obviously headed up by fucking Clara.

"Look out, desperate skanks at three o'clock," I murmur as the three of them push from the bench.

I can't help but roll my eyes as each of them adjusts their clothing and pouts their lips.

With their eyes laser-focused on Tristan, they saunter our way, with their hips swaying.

"Tristan Carver, to what do we owe the pleasure?" Clara purrs. Her voice is so high-pitched and squeaky that it makes a shiver of disgust run down my spine.

Despite not wanting to show my clear distaste for these hussies, I can't help my top lip from peeling back and my brows rising.

"Ladies," Tris drawls. It's polite at best, but the fact he's even addressing them sends a wave of jealousy through me so strong it almost knocks me off my feet.

*He is not yours, Violet,* I chastise myself.

"I could hardly believe it when I heard you were coming back. It's so good to see you," Clara continues, batting her lashes while playing with a wavy tendril of hair.

"Oh, have we met before?" Tristan deadpans, and I can't help but snort.

"Oh, I'm sorry, I didn't see you there, Tulip."

*Oh no she fucking didn't.*

I don't realize the growl that rings in my ears comes from my own lips until Tristan's fingers twist in the back of my tank as I lunge toward Clara.

"It's Violet," I hiss.

"Oh yes, that's right. One half of the duo who follows the team around, waiting to be thrown crumbs of attention like desperate little—"

"Pot calling the kettle black, much? Have you looked at yourself in a mirror recently? You've practically got 'desperate' tattooed on your forehead."

"Okay, Vi. That's enough," Tristan growls, pulling me into his body and wrapping his arm protectively around my waist, much to Clara and her bimbos' horror.

He steers me away with nothing more than a nod at the three of them.

"We'll see you soon," Clara sings, needing to have the final word.

"Calm the fuck down, Pip," he growls in my ear. And fuck, if it doesn't give me flutters between my thighs.

"She called me Tulip. *Tulip*," I spit.

"Yeah, to rile you up. And look how well it worked," he smugly points out.

Despite the fact I want to burrow into his side and never leave, I force myself out of his hold and smooth my hair back.

"How do you do it?" I shoot over at him.

"Do what?" he asks innocently.

"Put up with the likes of Clara and all the other jersey chasers who are only interested in bouncing on your cock for bragging rights."

"Well, you either ignore them or just suck it up and give them what they want. If you're lucky, you get a decent lay. If you're not, well... mostly, it's still better than your own hand, so..."

"Fucking hell," I mutter. "You did not just say that."

"You're right. Some are fucking terrible. I'd probably take my hand over the ones that screech like I'm trying to cut their vag lips off with a blunt knife."

"Why was I so glad to have you back here?" I mutter as we cut across the main quad that will lead us to the other side of campus.

"What? You asked," he says, glancing over at me with a smirk.

"I guess it's a good thing your schedule is so full. No time for entertaining the whores of Maddison Kings."

"Oh, I don't know. There's always time for that."

"You're a dog," I mutter.

"And what about you?" he asks, forcing me to look up at him.

"What about me?"

"Clara just implied that you have a little habit of following the team around so..."

"If you're implying that I'm one of them, then you'll be the one losing your genitals with a blunt knife," I warn.

"It's always the sweet ones who are secretly the kinkiest," he mutters to himself.

My lips part to respond but no words come out.

*Is he really thinking about how kinky I might be in bed?*

No, probably not.

"You know I live with two guys who are on the team. That means we're usually at the parties and shit. Plus, Letty, our old housemate, is engaged to Kane Legend and BFFs with the Dunn twins. I can't really get away from them even if I wanted to."

"And now you've got me too."

"Have I?" I blurt like an idiot, making his brow shoot up as he must hear how those words sounded.

"Uh... to hang out with, yeah."

"You'll squeeze me in with your busy schedule and harem of chasers, huh? I'm honored, truly."

"You're an idiot, Pip."

Yep, got something right. An idiot with a stupid crush that I really need to get over.

"This is me," he says, interrupting my internal battle with my hormones.

My brows pinch, but when I look up, I find the sign for the Augustus Building emerging in front of us.

"Right, well. I hope you have a good afternoon," I say, my voice lacking any of the excitement it had when I found him waiting for me earlier.

He comes to a stop, his fingers brushing my wrist before they tighten and tug me in front of him.

"What happened? Did I do something to piss you off?"

"What? No, of course not." I lie. And when his intense stare begins to make me a little uncomfortable, I end up rambling instead of jumping into his arms and kissing him like a horny teenager. "It's just them," I say, waving my hand in the direction Clara and her bitches were. "I just get so fed up of them thinking they own any guy who wears a Panther jersey around campus. They're entitled little—"

"Whoa, Vi. You need to calm down." He steps a little closer, forcing me to look up into his dark eyes. The warmth of his body seeps into my skin, making certain body parts react a little too violently to his proximity.

I just have to hope that he's so firmly little-sister-zoned me that he doesn't let his eyes drop from mine to see my nipples trying to fight through my clothing in their need for his touch.

"I'm sorry. They just make me a little—"

"Batshit?"

"Y-yeah, if you want."

"You don't need to worry about girls like them. All the guys see them for who they are. And I can assure you, they don't own any of us." I can't stop my eyes from rolling. "Okay, so I can't speak for the whole team, but I can tell you without a doubt that they don't own me. I haven't come here to hook up with immature undergrads."

*Ouch.*

"No, of course not. You're like, old now," I tease, hoping like fuck he doesn't see how deep that comment cut me.

He glares at me. "Well, I've done my time being young, dumb, and reckless."

"What are you trying to say?"

His knuckles brush down my bare arm, and my entire body shudders at the innocent touch.

"That you're in college and meant to be enjoying yourself, not walking me to class."

I shrug. "There's only so much fun to be had on a Monday."

"I'm sure you'll find some if you look hard enough."

"In the library?"

"You never know. It was good seeing you today, Pip."

"You too, Tris. It's good to have you back."

"I'll message you. We can hang out, yeah?"

"Sure thing, whenever you're free. I know you're swamped already."

"Come here, Pip." He tugs me into his hard, strong body, and I have no choice but to wrap my arms around his wide torso and breathe in his scent.

Everything about the embrace is too comforting, too comfortable, too tempting.

"I should go. Gotta go and be young and dumb." I wink teasingly, but I don't feel it.

Mostly, I just feel sad. And that was the opposite of what I was hoping my time with Tristan would be like.

"You're a good kid, Pip. See you soon." He gives me a little salute before turning on his heels and marching toward his class.

With a heavy heart and my head full of memories I really don't need to be dwelling on, I quickly walk in the opposite direction in search of another coffee and somewhere I can sit in peace to get on with some work.

I look back over my shoulder when a shiver of awareness runs down my spine. But to my disappointment, Tristan isn't watching me.

---

The rest of the day dragged, not helped by the fact Clara and one of her bitches were in my last class of the day. West also happened to be in it as well, and they practically spent the entire time snarling at me for spending more time with their beloved players.

"What the actual fuck is their problem?" West growls when our professor brings our class to an end after delivering one meaty assignment to complete on the first day back. Ugh.

"They've got their panties in a twist because they caught me hanging out with Tristan earlier. Their possessiveness knows no bounds."

"So, he's your brother's best friend. Jesus. It's not like you were fucking him out on the quad. You weren't, right?" he asks, amusement dancing in his eyes.

"What? No. Of course, I wasn't." Sadly. "Why would you even say that?" I pretend to act horrified by the suggestion, but I'm pretty sure West sees right through it.

"It's no secret that you're going through a bit of a dry spell, titch."

"West!" I screech.

"What? We live in the same house. I hear things... or not."

"Fucking hell. I'm not having this conversation right now." I stuff all my things into my bag and push to stand.

The auditorium is almost empty already with everyone else's need to escape. I get it, the first day back is hard. But I fear that the second I head home and lock myself away in my room to work, my mind is going to wander, and I know exactly the direction my thoughts are going to go in.

"You know," he purrs, cluing me in as to where this is going, "I could always offer a hand."

"Seriously?" I snap.

"We wouldn't even have to tell the others. It could be our little secret." I look up just in time to see him wink. "I'm good, I promise."

"With an ego like that, how could you possibly not be?" I deadpan.

His smirk only grows wider. Weirdo.

"Thanks for the offer and all that, but I think I'll pass. I've got a perfectly good vibrator that will do the job just fine."

"Pfft."

I stand there with my hands on my hips as I wait for him to follow that judgmental scoff with something. "Spit it out. I'm all fucking ears."

"You just deserve better than your pussy blaster, is all." He shrugs like this is just an everyday conversation. Although, in our fucked-up little family, I guess it is.

"Okay, firstly, most of the guys around this campus are fuck boys wanting a good time, and trust me when I tell you, they do not do it better. And secondly—"

"You're not going to win this argument," West calls over his shoulder as he descends the stairs ahead of me, ready to escape for the day.

"And secondly," I call, ignoring the fact there are still a few people milling around and the class GA, "you have no idea just how mind-blowing a decent vibrator can be."

My skin prickles with the attention of the eyes in the room.

"Give me one over a guy with noodle fingers and a flappy tongue any day."

Someone barks out a laugh behind me, before a female voice calls, "amen," but I don't turn to look.

"If you say so," West murmurs, holding the door open for me.

I'm still on a rant about the benefits of a battery-operated boyfriend and the lack of bullshit, lying and cheating that comes with one when we find Ella waiting outside for us, having finished her class a few minutes ago.

Her brows pinch as she studies us.

"And do you know what else?" I bark.

"It makes you breakfast in bed the next morning?" West asks with a smirk.

"Now you're just being ridiculous."

"What's going on?" Ella asks, looking between the two of us.

"Violet has turned convincing me that a vibrating plastic imitation cock is better than the real thing into a competitive sport."

"It's not," she replies bluntly.

"Ella," I complain, hoping she would be on my side with this. With all the drama she had recently involving he who shan't be named, I thought she would have been more than on my side.

"What?" She shrugs, grabbing her bags from the floor and walking toward the parking lot with us. "It's true and you know it. Nothing compares to getting good and railed by a guy who knows what he's doing."

"Thinking of anyone specific there, El?" West asks. "Ow, bitch," he hisses when she smacks him around the back of the head.

"Do you remember our deal, Rogers?" Ella growls.

"Yeah, yeah," he mutters, popping his trunk and dumping his stuff in. "I should leave your ass here for that."

"But you won't," she says, smiling sweetly at him. "You love me too much."

"I'm such a dumbass," he quips before pulling open his passenger door and allowing her to climb in.

"I'll take the back then, shall I?" I tease. But before I get a chance to open the door, my skin prickles with awareness as if someone is watching me. But a quick scan of the parking lot tells me I'm being ridiculous and I climb into the car.

"I thought you only needed plastic, vibrating friends these days," West deadpans.

I flip him off, and his laughter rings out around the car long after he's slammed the door.

Ella's eyes find mine in the rearview mirror and I glare back at her.

"Don't. Just don't," I warn, but predictably, she ignores me.

"Lunch went well then."

"This has nothing to do with him," I hiss, folding my arms over my chest like a petulant child and staring out the window, much to West's amusement when he joins us.

Ella and West chat away about classes and the upcoming year as he drives us back to the house and I happily lose myself in my own head.

"There you go, ladies. I take payment in the form of blow jobs and orgasms," he teases as he pulls the car to a stop in front of our new house.

"You'd better give Clara a call then, she's especially desperate today. She might even go for it with your tiny cock."

West scoffs. "She couldn't handle me, even with all her practice."

"Sure, you keep telling yourself that, big man," Ella quips before we climb out and let him head off to his afternoon training session with the team.

"Hey honey, we're home," I shout when we find evidence of Micah already being here the second we step into the house.

"Hey," Ella says happily when we find him sitting at the island in the kitchen with his computer and tablet set up in front of him. "Good day?"

Without sparing him a second glance, she marches toward the coffee machine and starts making herself a drink.

"I called the landlord about the electrics," Micah tells us.

My movements falter.

"Did they go out again?" Ella glances over her shoulder at me. Clearly, I did a shit job of hiding my panic again.

"Yeah, couple of times. Annoying as fuck. Can't see anything wrong, though."

"Didn't think you were an electrics nerd?" Ella jokes.

He rolls his eyes but ignores her. "There must be a bad connection somewhere or something. Anyway, he's going to get someone to come out and check it out."

"Great. Only been here a few weeks and we've broken the place already."

"How were your classes today?" I ask Micah, desperately needing to think about something other than how high the chances are that we're going to be plunged into darkness again tonight.

I think an early night is in the cards for me, so hopefully I can sleep through the blackout.

"Yeah, you know. Like we never stopped."

"You got that right," Ella agrees. "Although, you should have seen my new professor for creative writing. Holy hell, I think I might just need some extra one-on-one sessions for that this semester, if you know what I'm saying."

"El, the entire street knows what you're saying. You're about as subtle as a rhino."

She passes me over a coffee before pulling her laptop from her bag to join Micah.

"You gonna hang with us?" she asks when I linger like I don't belong.

"Um..."

"Just sit down, Vi. You can't tell me that you don't have work to do."

"Y-yeah," I stutter, finally pulling a stool out and making a start on that god-awful assignment I was set earlier.

By the time the guys reappear, the three of us are working in silence, and the scent of the dinner that Ella is in charge of tonight permeates the air.

# 4

## TRISTAN

"Yes. That's more like it," I bark at the guys before me running drills up and down the field.

My skin prickles with the attention of the head coach standing on the sidelines with his quarterback coach.

Most of their focus is on the players in front of us, but I know they're watching me closely.

When I announced that I was retiring from the NFL after two successful seasons, I don't think anyone really expected this to be my next move. But I already had my position here secured before I breathed a word of my career being over.

I thought it was a long shot, but Coach Butler was more than pleased when he answered the phone to find me at the other end all those months ago.

He was a fucking fantastic coach. I loved my time here as an MKU Panther, and the prospect of returning to help mold the players of the future stirred excitement within me that I hadn't felt in a while.

The second the idea hit me, I knew it was where I was meant to be, and not just because she's here.

No. It has nothing to do with Violet Brady.

Although, it did.

Since the day I promised Roman I'd take care of her, she's always been in the back of my mind.

I told myself when I left for Tennessee that I'd finally be able to put an end to my entirely inappropriate crush on his little sister. But that was far from reality.

As much as I wanted to cut ties to force myself to do the right thing, I couldn't. And nor could she.

I just hoped that she'd embark on college life and forget all about me.

She didn't.

Now we're in the same place again, and my obsession with the one girl I should stay far, far away from is only growing stronger once more.

Forcing myself to focus on the task at hand, I make a mental note of those who are struggling with this afternoon's session, ready to report back to Coach as he requested.

He's already got his first-string team for the season sorted. But that's not to say one of our new recruits isn't going to take the field by storm and fuck up all his plans. It certainly wouldn't be the first or the last time something like that happened.

Coach forces them to keep going until their legs must be like jelly. He always was a hard ass, but secretly I used to love it. I know all the guys before me do too.

Although there's a huge part of me that's relieved not to be worked as hard as they are, there's a part of me that craves it. Craves the exertion, the pain, the spasming muscles, the heaving chest, and the sweat.

A piercing whistle cuts through the air, and all the guys begin to slow before fighting to catch their breath.

"Carver is in charge," he barks before striding in the direction of the other members of his coaching staff, who are putting more players through their paces.

Forcing my previous thoughts of a certain off-limits brunette to the back of my mind, I focus on my job bringing the training session to a close and finally allowing the guys to head back to the locker rooms to clean up.

Letting them all go ahead of me, I swipe my clipboard and stopwatch from the sideline where I abandoned it and take off behind them.

"How's it feel being back here, then?" a familiar voice says from behind me, and when I look over, I find Luca Dunn, the Panthers' starting quarterback, slowing to a stop beside me.

"It's good, man. I feel at home here."'

"Not missing the bright lights of the NFL?"

I glance over, seeing the stars in his eyes as he talks about the NFL. It's no secret that both the Dunn twins are going to enter the draft next year, and if the rumors are true, then there could be a few teams with a fight on their hands to sign them. I have no idea where they've got their sights set, but I figure that I'll get their plans out of them in the coming weeks.

"Nah, I've always been a small town guy at heart."

"Well, it's good to have you back, man. I think you're gonna do well here."

He claps me on the shoulder before jogging toward where everyone else is disappearing to hit the showers, as if he hasn't just been put through a brutal three-hour session.

My knee aches at just the thought of putting myself through something like that—another reminder that I've done the right thing.

I couldn't be sitting in my apartment in Tennessee, or on the bench as the Titans trained, just waiting for the day I could rejoin them.

Stalking past the locker rooms and the booming laughter that filters through the crack in the door, I stuff down any resentment their banter and team spirit drags up.

Finding the office that I share with the other GA who's still out on the field, I fall down into my chair and rest my head back.

I've been at this four days, and I'm fucking exhausted.

I've barely stopped to take a breath since classes started on Monday morning. I can only imagine what life is going to be like when the first game of the season is upon us.

I didn't come here and apply for this position for an easy ride, though.

As if someone out there knows I need a distraction, or at least something that's going to stop me from passing out right here, my cell buzzes in my pocket.

Pulling it out, I can't help but smile when I find Violet's smiling face staring back at me.

I took the photo when she came to check on me earlier in the year. It's a candid shot that I'm not even sure she knows I took. But she was reading something on her own cell, a wide smile on her lips at whatever it was. The sight of her happiness, while I was drowning in some of the worst days of my life, was everything, and before I knew what I was doing, I'd taken a photograph to keep me company when she was ultimately going to leave me alone once more.

My parents had come out to help me, so had my sister, but they all had their own lives to get on with, and I really didn't want anyone fussing around me. Well, anyone apart from Violet it seemed, because I soon came to learn that I fucking loved having her looking after me.

**Pip: How's it going, big shot?**

**Tristan: It's… going. I think I might have underestimated the amount of work.**

**Pip: We're four days in, Tris.**

**Tristan: It's just a change of pace.**

**Pip: From sitting on your ass, I'll say.**

"Brat," I mutter as a shadow falls across the doorway.

Lowering my cell, I look up to find Coach studying me.

"All good, Carver?" he asks, his deep, rumbling voice bouncing off the walls around me.

"All good," I agree. "I'll have those stats over to you first thing in the morning."

"I know," he states confidently. "How's your recovery coming? I told Richards to expect a visit from you, but apparently, you're yet to head over," he says, mentioning the Panthers' head physio.

"Everything's great. Getting stronger every day," I assure him.

"Just as long as you don't go running back to the NFL on us."

"Would I?" I tease. "My blood runs purple, you know that."

He nods, accepting my words.

"I'll see Richards," I promise. "This first week has just been..." I trail off, not wanting him to know that I'm struggling before I've even started.

"It'll get better. You'll fall into a routine before you know it. Just ask Winters," he says, nodding to the empty desk at the other side of the room. "He was exactly where you were last year. I'm sure he'll have some stellar advice."

I smile, silently telling Coach that there's a very good chance that won't happen.

Winters, the other GA, well... let's just say that so far, he doesn't seem to be my kind of person.

I had hoped that we might get along, but it's not happening. I think he sees me as a threat. I get it, I got the NFL and he didn't. But that's hardly my fucking fault. Something tells me he's going to be holding it against me all year, though.

"I'll let you crack on. You've got a late-night class, right?"

I just about manage to hold in my exhausted groan.

"Sure do. I'll catch you in the morning, Coach."

He nods before ducking back out of the room and heading down the hallway.

Gathering up my stuff, I throw my bag over my shoulder with the intention of grabbing something to eat on the way to my sports management class.

The second I round the corner, I almost run head first into Winters.

His cold, permanently angry eyes lock on mine.

"Sorry," I mutter, sidestepping him and focusing on the exit.

Remembering that I ignored Violet's last message, I drag my cell back out to find she's messaged again.

**Pip: You need to have some fun.**

**Tristan: Who says I'm not?**

**Pip: Your schedule. Or did you manage to find a slot for those chasers?**

I shake my head at her comment as the reaction to those three desperate jersey chasers on Monday morning comes back to me.

**Tristan: I'm still working on finding enough time for them all.**

**Pip: I bet you are.**

I can't help but laugh as I picture her lips pursing and her eyes darkening as her anger and jealousy get the better of her.

I shouldn't have been so happy with the way she reacted to them, but I couldn't help it.

**Tristan: Doing anything fun tonight?**

**Pip: Nope. Just hanging out in my room, pretending that I'm working on an assignment.**

**Tristan: Pretending? What are you doing instead?**

**Pip: Talking to you, duh.**

**Pip: Actually, I just had a shower and thought I should check in.**

My brows lift at her comment, and my thumbs begin tapping out a reply before my brain can compute that it's a really fucking bad idea.

**Tristan: Fantasizing about me while you're showering. Not sure what to think about that, Pip.**

**Pip: Think whatever you want. I'm an immature undergrad, remember?**

"Fuck," I hiss to myself as I push out of the building and head toward my car.

I regretted those words the second they rolled off my tongue. I never said them to hurt Violet. They were meant to assure her that I didn't want the desperate chasers. Clearly, that's not how she heard them. In all honesty, I wasn't expecting to see her eyes darken quite like they did. I can't deny that it affected me, though.

She's flirty. She always had been. Well, for the past few years, anyway. I just put it down to her getting older and growing in confidence. I've never allowed myself to think it could mean more than that.

But for just a beat after those words passed my lips, she'd looked like I'd just stolen her puppy.

Pulling my car door open, I throw my bag inside before falling into the driver's seat as I think about what I can reply with that is going to keep this conversation on safe ground. It certainly can't be what I really want to send. The thought of her messaging me right now wrapped in just a towel with water droplets clinging to her skin... well, it makes things stir within me that really shouldn't.

**Tristan: The sooner the chasers realize they're barking up the wrong tree with me, the better.**

**Tristan: Did you have a good day?**

Her reply isn't as instant this time, and I have little choice but to start my car and make my way toward a parking lot at the other side of campus for my class.

I've barely been driving a minute when my phone buzzes, tempting me into being distracted by her once more.

"Fuck's sake, Pip," I mutter to myself, forcing my eyes to stay on the road.

Then, it becomes even harder when it goes off again.

Pressing my foot to the gas, I take the next corner a little faster than I should, and before long, the parking lot I'm aiming for appears before me. Seeing as it's late as fuck for most students to be on campus, it's practically empty.

The car lurches to a stop, a beat before I reach for my cell.

**Pip: It was fine.**

**Pip: Missed you though. It's a tease, knowing you're so close yet so unavailable.**

"Don't I fucking know it."

**Tristan: It's almost the weekend, I'm sure you've got wild party plans that will make you forget all about me.**

The suggestion hurts, but it needs to be said. It's the truth, after all. She'll go out this weekend, probably hook up—hopefully with someone decent—and that could be her set for the rest of her life. Forcing me to have a serious word with myself that will result in me being able to stop fucking thinking about her.

**Pip: Oh... there are plans. You should come.**

As if that suggestion doesn't have a big red warning sign written all over it.

**Tristan: I'd love to, but I've got so much work to do.**

**Pip: All work and no play makes Tristan a boring, boring boy.**

I can't help but groan. When the fuck did I become such a sensible, dull adult?

*About the time you ripped your anterior cruciate ligament, asshole.*

**Pip: Sorry, I forgot you're so old you're practically a dinosaur.**

**Tristan: You're funny. I've got to get to class.**

**Pip: Boo. And I'm here all alone with no one to play with.**

I can just picture her sulking face as she types that, and fuck if it doesn't make things stir beneath my waistband.

**Tristan: Were you always this much of a brat?**

**Pip: Probably. You were just too busy being a superstar to notice. *winky emoji***

**Tristan: Get some work done. Stay on top of things. It'll make the partying better.**

**Pip: I know what will make the partying better…**

**Tristan: I gotta go. Chat soon.**

"Fuck. Fuck," I bark, slamming my palm down on my wheel.

What the fuck is it about that girl? She fucking affects me even through innocent—okay, maybe not-so-innocent—messages.

Grabbing my shit, I throw the car door open and stomp toward the closest store to grab something to eat before making my way to class. All the while, thoughts of Violet in a fucking towel fill my mind.

She turns me into nothing more than a horny fucking school boy. It's embarrassing, but I don't know how to make it stop.

Well, I have one idea. But it's the fucking opposite of what I promised Roman I would do. And it needs to get out of my fucking head.

# 5

## VIOLET

"LETTY," I scream, launching myself from the kitchen counter where I was doing shots with Ella and a very reluctant-looking Micah.

"Oh shit," Letty grunts when I collide with her, wrapping my arms around her and swinging her around the room.

Peals of laughter sound from behind me, along with a low, male groan. I don't know why he complains. He must be more than used to us by now.

"Girl, I missed you," I slur, those shots already getting the better of me.

"I was in your class this morning, Vi," she points out.

I shrug. That is not the point.

While we might have hung out over the summer, we haven't partied. Not properly. And I miss it. I miss getting fucked up with my family.

Thoughts of a dark-haired, off-limits boy flicker through my mind briefly, but I force them down, hoping they'll drown under the cherry Sourz shots currently filling my stomach.

"Come on, you need shots." Taking her hand, I drag her toward where Ella and Micah are sitting watching us.

"Uh... I really don't think I do. I brought stuff for

margaritas though, as requested." She pins me with an amused look.

"When did I ask that?" My brow wrinkles as I stare at her, trying to dig up a memory.

"You need to lay off the shots, or you're not going to even make it to the party."

"That is not going to happen. Tonight ladies... and gents," I quickly add when Micah coughs, "is going to be one of the best nights of our lives." I raise my new shot in the air, the red liquid sloshing and running down my arm.

"Assuming you don't pass out before it actually starts," Micah points out.

"Ugh, you're just jealous."

"Of... what, exactly?"

"Everything," I announce happily. "It wouldn't be fair if everyone were just this cool," I say, gesturing to myself.

"I'm going to shower. Can you two manage her?"

"Manage? I don't need— WHOA." My hand misses the counter I was reaching for and I tumble to the floor.

Laughter rips from my throat as I roll around, much like a turtle who's got stuck on his back.

"We've got her, don't worry," Ella assures Micah, the three of them totally ignoring me.

"Here, I brought burritos." Letty hands Micah a foil-wrapped package and suddenly, the scent of it hits me and makes my stomach growl.

"You have burritos?"

I'm on my feet in a flash, holding my hand out, begging for the goods.

"Hand it over, Hunter. You won't want to see me get angry," I warn.

"Is it as entertaining as when you're drunk?"

I snarl at her, snatching my burrito and hopping up on one of the stools.

"I think you should probably have some water to go with

that," Ella says, pulling the fridge open and grabbing a couple of bottles.

"So what's with the plan to get wasted before even leaving the house?" Letty asks innocently, ignoring all the alcohol and biting into her food.

"Violet is on a mission. She won't tell me why, but I have a suspicion."

They share a secretive little look that pisses me the fuck off.

"What?" I bark.

"Nothing," Ella assures me, but unlucky for her, I'm not drunk enough to let it go.

"No, it's not. Tell me what that knowing little look was about."

Letty sighs. "You need to get laid, Vi. You get cranky when you haven't had enough D."

The sip of water I'd just taken damn near sprays both of them.

"What? I am not cranky. I just want to have a good time with my friends. I don't need no man."

"So you're saying if a cute guy happens to find you to dance with later, you wouldn't be up for it?"

I lean forward on my forearms. "How cute are we talking?"

"From how long it's been, I'd say he doesn't even need to be that cute," Ella deadpans.

"Oh because you're one to judge," I hiss. "Going to be hooking up with Colt again tonight?"

I expect her to rip me a new one for mentioning his name, but to my surprise, she just shrugs. "Who knows. I wouldn't say no. Sadly, no one else quite hits the spot like he does."

"Bullshit," I cough, earning myself a hard glare. "You haven't given anyone else a chance to find the spot in... a long fucking time."

"No one has interested me. That doesn't mean I wouldn't.

Colt and I... we're just having fun, making use of each other when the time feels right."

This time it's Letty and I who share a look, something that Ella doesn't miss.

"He's nothing more than a fuck boy. You know this, I know this. The entire fucking college knows this. I'm not getting my hopes up or expecting him to suddenly start making wild declarations. We're fucking. That is it."

"As long as you know that."

She wants to get angry with me, I can see it in her eyes. But she also knows that I care, that I'm just looking out for her.

"I do. Now, shall I make a start on the margaritas? Then we need to go and make ourselves look beautiful."

"You're already beautiful, El," I say softly.

"Nothing a push-up bra, some makeup and hair straightener can't improve on though," she says happily, emptying the contents of Letty's bag.

"A-fucking-men to that. Let's get this year started off in style, yeah?"

The second we have a pitcher of margaritas made, we grab our glasses—which just so happen to be made of plastic because we have experience with this—and head up to the top floor to get ready.

We open both the doors to our shared bathroom and crank the music up.

Micah probably fucking hates us, but hey, he's more than welcome to join.

"What are we wearing, bitches?" Ella shouts, racing back into my room with a whole host of outfit options hanging from her arm.

"Well, you wanna hook up, right? So smallest, sexiest dress you've got."

"You're right. These were a fucking stupid idea," she says, discarding a pair of shorts and pants from the pile.

"Careful, El. There's easy access and then there's just desperate," Letty mutters.

"Pfft, Clara and her band of merry hos will be there, so I don't think we need to worry. They'll out trump us on looking like whores any day."

Unable to argue with that fact, Letty takes a sip of her drink before pulling out her own tiny dress.

"And you were criticizing us?" I ask, popping my hip as I stare at the scrap of gold fabric.

"Ah, there is a difference. The only man I want to drive wild with this little baby is the one who put this on my finger," she says, happiness oozing from her as she wiggles her engagement ring for us, in case we forgot.

"You know, I think I preferred it when you two were hating on each other. You were more fun," I tease.

"Nah, I'm a better wing woman now and you know it," she shoots back.

"The guys are meeting us there, right?" Ella shouts, having disappeared back into her room.

A little disappointment drips through my veins, because the guy I want to turn up with the team won't fucking be there.

Why couldn't I have been a couple of years older? I could have done college with him. Been here as he took the field by storm and helped score the Panthers one of their most successful years.

"Yeah. They're going for team drinks first."

"Planning their strategies and game plans for the night," Ella quips.

"I can only imagine."

"Well, other than football, fucking is their favorite subject so..." I say, turning my back on Letty and pulling my closet open.

"What's up, Vi? Hoping to be the ball they're all discussing how to play?"

I frown, trying to make sense of her question. Is the analogy just fucking weird, or are the shots hitting me hard despite the food and two bottles of water I downed?

"Umm... I sure wouldn't say no," I mutter.

---

By the time we're all ready, the jug of margaritas is long empty and I've got one hell of a buzz going on. From the way that Letty and Ella are laughing at something that I'm not even sure was funny, I think they're on the road to wastedville right alongside me.

"Miiiiicah," I sing as I fall toward his bedroom door. I go over on my heel as the door swings open, revealing him sitting in the middle of his bed still on his computer. "Come on, bro. It's party time."

"You managed to sober her up then?" he deadpans as Ella and Letty come to a stop in the doorway behind me.

"Come on, Micah. It's time to hang up your computer and nerd glasses and come party."

Closing the lid of his laptop, he slides to the end of the bed, his eyes running over the three of us, but I don't miss the way he lingers a little longer on Ella.

"You're all on a mission tonight, huh?" he asks, lowering down to look in the mirror he has on his dresser and running his fingers through his hair, before grabbing his cell and wallet and dropping them into his pocket.

"That's it?" Ella blurts.

"Th-that's what?" he asks, his brows pinching.

"You're gonna run your hand through your hair and we just leave?"

"Uh... yeah. Is that an issue?" he asks, amusement beginning to dance in his eyes.

"You've been wearing that all day. At least make an effort.

Vi," she says, jerking her chin in the direction of Micah's closet.

She closes the space between them, her legs much steadier than mine as I search through his clothes for options.

"This one," I declare. "It makes your eyes pop."

"Girls love that," Ella agrees. "Arms up."

Completely baffled, Micah innocently does as he's told, and it's not until Ella has his shirt halfway up his body that he realizes what's going on.

"The fuck, El?" he barks, trying to wrestle his arms back down, but it's too late, and she tugs the fabric from his body, leaving him shirtless.

"Whoa, someone's been working out," Letty teases as the three of us focus on his abs that I'm sure never used to be there.

"Pants, Vi. We need pants. Those dark, tight ones he has."

I spin around, knowing exactly what I'm looking for, but Micah's panicked voice cuts through the air. When I glance back, he's got his hands around Ella's wrists, her fingers already tucked under the waistband of his jeans.

Micah stares down at her with dark, pained eyes.

"Ella," he snaps.

His chest heaves, and there's a very telling bulge in his current pair of pants that I'm assuming Ella hasn't noticed.

"Those are great, Ella. Just switch up the shirt," Letty says, clearly seeing what I can while Ella continues to be completely oblivious to how infatuated our roommate is with her.

"Fine. But if you don't get laid, just remember that I tried to help."

"Come on, El," Letty says, wrapping her arm around her shoulder. "I think the car is here."

Silence fills the room as the two of them walk away and descend the stairs.

"Here," I say, holding out the new shirt for Micah.

"Thanks," he mutters, looking all kinds of mortified.

Apparently, that's not enough to stop my drunk mouth running away with itself.

"You know, if you get her drunk enough and ask nicely, she might even suck it for you."

Micah's entire body jolts as if I've just shot him.

"It's cool, man. Your secret is safe with me. Although I must admit, it's a pretty bad secret. Think the only person who lives under this roof who is oblivious is the girl in question. So..." I slap him on the shoulder in support. "Well done, hotshot."

"You should go. I think I'm just gonna—"

"Oh, fuck no, Micah. It's the first weekend of junior year. And because I'm such a good friend, I'll even pretend to be hella into you and make all the other girls wish they were me."

"I really doubt—"

"Confidence, Micah. Confidence is fucking everything."

Taking his hand in mine, I drag him from his room and then the house.

Ella and Letty are waiting for us in the car, and I crawl into the back.

"Jesus, Vi," Micah grunts behind me when my skirt rides up and I give him a little show.

"That one was for free. You'll have to pay for the next," I quip over my shoulder, shifting around to give him space to join us.

"I feel fucking sorry for the guy you eventually nail down. You're hard work, Violet Brady."

"Aw, thanks. You say the sweetest things to me, Micah."

Thankfully, the journey to the venue of tonight's party is quick, and before I know it, I'm standing with another drink in my hand with the music vibrating through the building around me.

"Come on, let's dance," Ella cries, grabbing my arm to pull me toward the makeshift dance floor.

In a rush, I reach for Micah's hand, much to his horror, and tug him along with us.

In only seconds, the four of us are moving in the center of the crowd. Three of us are way more enthusiastic as we throw our heads back and lose ourselves in the music. One looks like he'll do anything possible to escape.

I don't let Micah leave, though. Instead, I pull him closer and dance with him like I'm imagining spending the night with him.

I'm not. And neither is he, but Ella does glance over every now and then, so I keep it up, feeling good that I might be helping my blue-balled friend.

Eventually, the team arrives and the missing two members of our family descend on the dance floor. Brax and West immediately close in on Ella, and the three of them dance together like they've done it a million times.

Letty melts into the crowd as she goes in search of her boy, and the girls around us disperse to find the rest of the team—well, those who don't try and steal West and Brax from Ella. They don't get very far, but we all know that their time will come.

It's always the same. We start parties together and one by one, we get distracted by a short skirt or the promise of a big dick and we peel away for a different kind of fun.

I look around to see if there's anyone here who stirs something inside me. But I quickly discover that I literally couldn't care less about any of the guys who are on the lookout for a girl to spend the night with.

There's only one person who's stuck inside my head.

And there is less than zero chance of him turning up here to party with the team.

I missed the boat on watching Tristan letting go at college parties.

"Are you okay?" Micah shouts in my ears when my dancing slows.

"I'm going to get a drink. You want one?"

"I'll come. I think I've maxed out on the dancing."

"You did good. You've certainly got the moves. Any girl would be lucky to be on the end of those thrusts."

"Seriously, Vi." He rolls his eyes at me but thankfully takes over drink-making, and a minute later I'm already halfway through drinking it.

The vodka burns all the way down my throat, but I don't let it stop me.

Although, as much as I might want to drown my thoughts of him out with alcohol, it never works.

# 6

## TRISTAN

"Come on, man. Just one drink. For old time's sake," Luca says after he's caught up with me as I make my way out of the training facility, ready to head home to spend a Friday night working.

Life really doesn't get much wilder than this.

I've only been here a few weeks, and I can barely remember what my life was like before I became an overworked recluse.

"You know I can't," I mutter.

Truth is, I could really go for a night out with the guys.

It's been too fucking long since it happened.

"Nah, fuck that GA shit, Carver. We were teammates, friends, long before that. Just one, then you can go running home."

"Who said I was going home?"

"You're funny. Were you planning on going out?" he asks, raising a brow at me.

"Well, no, but—"

"Come on. One beer at the Den. Then we're all heading out anyway."

"You're a bad influence, Dunn."

"You fucking coming or what?" Kane Legend calls from a Nissan Skyline as he rolls to a stop in front of us.

In his passenger seat, I spot Luca's twin brother, Leon.

"Yeah. Carver's coming too. Ain't that right, Tris?"

"You're gonna get me in trouble."

"Nah, Coach don't care. It's not like we're about to line up innocent freshmen to blow you or anything."

"Wait," Kane barks. "When did we decide against that?"

"Funny."

"Grab your car, Carver. You can't be a boring fucker all year."

"We're barely a week in," I point out.

"And you seem to be starting as you mean to go on."

"Fine. One drink, then I'm going home to work."

"Careful, you might tear another ligament with excitement like that," Legend deadpans.

"Keep it up, Legend. I can make your year even harder if you want."

"Pfft. I'm a better wide receiver than you ever were and you know it."

"You fucking wish," I mutter, taking off toward my car. Although, he's kinda got a point. He's pretty fucking killer on the field. All three of them are. It's why I already know that the Panthers are going to go all the way this year. With an offense like that, the championship is almost theirs already.

It's only a ten-minute drive off campus to the Den, the sports bar that the team has been welcomed into for generations. The owner, Arthur, is an old-school Panthers fanatic. The entire inside of the bar is done out in purple Panthers memorabilia. It's something of a shrine to his beloved players. And obviously, he likes to turn a blind eye to the fact most of the team is underage when they turn up here to make all Arthur's dreams come true.

Most of the guys are already there when I push through the doors. Most of them pay me little mind, too busy getting their Friday night started, but one pair of eyes locks on me almost immediately.

"Is that Tristan Carver, or are my old eyes deceivin' me?"

"Hey, Arth," I say with a wide, genuine smile as I make my way toward where he's standing behind the bar.

"It's good to see you, son. I was so fuckin' gutted when your season came to an early end."

"Nah, s'all good, Arth. It brought me home."

"Damn, I hope boys know how lucky they are to have you back."

"Those arrogant fucks?" I ask loudly, jerking my head in the Dunns' direction. "Doubtful."

"Love you too, Carv," Leon shoots back, blowing a kiss.

"It seems you might just have your hands full with this new career move."

"You're telling me. I wouldn't have it any other way."

"Grab a seat, son. We've got so much to talk about. Beer?"

"You got it, Arth."

Turning to look back at the booth the Dunns are sitting in, my eyes find Luca's, and he smiles and nods.

Yeah, he was right to drag me here.

"So, how are your parents and sister doing?" Arthur asks, sliding an opened bottle of beer my way.

"Yeah, yeah, they're all good. What about you? Found a lady yet?'

"Pfft, at my age? I'll be lucky."

I quickly lose myself in Arthur's stories, and before I know it, Luca steps up to my side to tell me that they're all heading out, much to Arthur's other customers' disappointment. They might leave the team to enjoy themselves for the most part, but they watch them with eagle eyes in the hopes of getting to know their beloved players better.

"Enjoy your night," I say, glancing behind him and nodding to Leon and a couple of the other guys.

"Too right. Partying with our girls. What could be better than that?"

My lips part, ready to say something stupid like, 'you're friends with Violet now, right?' but I manage to swallow the words at the last minute.

"No pulling any muscles. We need you in top form," I tease.

"You got it, Coach. Arth." He nods and quickly follows the others.

"Oh to be young again," Arth muses, watching them all go. "No parties for you then?"

"Nah, apparently I'm a grown-up now," I deadpan.

"Doesn't mean there isn't plenty of fun to be had."

"I'll see what I can find."

Pulling my wallet out, I throw a few bills down on the bar which quickly get shoved back toward me.

"On the house, man. It was so fuckin' good to see you."

"You're a good man, Arth. But I insist. Go buy yourself something pretty."

"Damn, I missed you."

"I'll see you soon, yeah?"

"Damn well better."

I barely make it two steps out of the bar when two little boys come running over to me, clutching Titans' jerseys to their chests.

"Please, sir. Could you sign our shirts?"

They stare up at me like I'm God, and I'm thrown for a moment. It feels like a lifetime since I've been stopped like this. But in reality, it's only been a few months.

A wide smile plays on my lips as I glance up at the woman standing a few feet away, watching her sons with a smile of her own.

I nod at her before taking the pen from the older of the two.

"What's your name?" I ask, dropping to my haunches and resting the jersey over my thigh so I can sign it.

"J-J-James," he stutters, making my heart melt.

"Well, James. It was wonderful to meet you. Are you going to be supporting the Titans again this year?"

He shakes his head. "No, not now you've left. I'll be focusing on the Panthers."

"That's good to hear. I'm sure they're going to have a fantastic year. And you are?" I ask, turning to his little brother.

"Richie."

"Hi, Richie. Do you two play?"

They both nod eagerly. "Yes, and we're going to play for the NFL so that we can buy Mom a big house so she doesn't have to work two jobs all the time."

Damn, these kids.

"Your mom must be a wonderful person. She's lucky to have you both."

James shrugs, as if wanting to look after his mom is a normal thing for a little boy to do.

"I hope you two have a good rest of the day. And enjoy the season."

"Thank you, sir."

"You're more than welcome. With a smile at both of them and then a nod at their mom, I head toward where I left my car while listening to the boys' excitement as they run back to her.

I'm still smiling at the boys' excitement when I pull up outside my apartment not long later. But even the memory of how their little eyes lit up isn't enough to lift my heavy heart.

The first Friday night on any college campus is the night all students dream of. And despite the fact I've done it all before, I can't help but yearn for those easy, fun days of my past.

Pushing through the front door, I jog up the stairs, or at least the best I can with my leg, until I'm on the top floor and pushing through to my place.

Ignoring the empty living room, I grab myself a beer from the fridge, eyeing the fresh ingredients in there for dinner options, but I quickly decide otherwise and pull my cell from my pocket instead, ordering takeout from my favorite Thai place.

With nothing better to do with my Friday night other than dwelling on the fun the rest of the world is having, I take my beer to my bedroom and drop into the chair at my desk, opening my laptop to continue writing up the stats that Coach has had me tracking all week.

Even after my food delivery, the minutes drag by, and after eventually emailing my spreadsheet over to Coach, I give up and fall into bed, drifting off to sleep with images of what Violet might be getting up to right now filling my mind.

My dreams are fitful and full of my worst fears, watching her dancing with almost the entire team, letting them touch her, use her, and take everything I want but can't have.

I know I'm dreaming, but that doesn't stop my body from burning up with jealousy.

When I suddenly come to, I'm covered in a sheen of sweat despite having kicked the covers off, and I'm hard as fucking nails.

"Goddamn, Violet Brady," I mutter, scrubbing my hand down my face as the images from my dream continue to linger.

A second later, a buzzing fills my room, and when I roll over, I find my nightstand empty, my cell now on the floor, vibrating with an incoming call.

I guess that explains why I woke so suddenly.

Reaching out for it, I wince as the brightness burns my retinas. But I forget all about that the second I see the photo of who's calling me.

"What's wrong?" I ask a beat after swiping to accept the call and pressing my cell to my ear.

"Triiiiistaaaan," Violet slurs down the line.

"Are you drunk, Pip?" I ask, rolling onto my back, my semi waking up again at the sound of her voice alone.

"Everyone left me," she whines. "Everyone has hooked up. Micah has gone home and I'm all alone."

Fuck. This has danger written all over it.

"Shall I order you an Uber? Where are you?"

"No, Tris. I don't want a ride home with some rando."

My free fist curls at my side.

"Where are you, Pip?"

"Uh..." She pauses as if she's thinking. Silence fills the line, making my brows pinch. Shouldn't there be music? People?

"Violet," I growl, my concern for her beginning to grow.

"Ooooh, I like it when you get all serious with me, Tris. Makes me feel all kinds of things."

She's drunk.

Off-her-fucking-face wasted.

*Do not read into her words.*

"I can't help you if you don't tell me where you are."

"Are you going to come rescue me again like a knight in shining armor, Tristan Carver?"

"Violet," I growl once more.

"Mmm... I want to hear that growled in my ear while you—"

"Where. The. Fuck. Are. You?" I spit, unconvinced I have the willpower to hear the end of that sentence falling from her lips.

A sigh echoes down the line.

"I don't know. I thought I could walk home but—" A sob rips up her throat. "I'm lost. I'm lost and I—"

"Can you send me your location?"

"Umm... I don't—" Hiccup.

"You're going to need to help me out here, Pip. Put me on speaker and open our messages," I demand, listening as she fumbles around to do as she's told.

I put my own phone onto speaker before swinging my legs

over the side of the bed and going in search of some clean boxers and clothes, seeing as it looks like I'm heading out to continue to fulfill my promise to Roman. Or at least, that's what I keep telling myself.

"O-okay."

"There's a little triangle symbol by where you write a message. Hit that."

"Uh-huh."

"Now share your live location."

"Yes," she hisses as a notification appears at the top of my screen.

"Okay, I'll be there in twenty minutes tops."

"Twenty minutes," she whines.

"Just stay where you are. Don't make this any harder than it needs to be, Pip."

"Okay," she agrees before dropping the tone of her voice. "I'll do whatever you say, Tristan Carver."

"Jesus Christ, you're trouble, Pip."

"Are you coming for me?" she asks suggestively, making my teeth grind.

*If fucking only.*

"I'm leaving my apartment now. You want me to stay on the line?" I ask, taking the stairs as fast as I can handle.

"I always want you on me, Tris."

I squeeze my eyes closed for a beat, trying to keep my head.

Thankfully, the roads are dead as I close in on her location.

"The sky is so pretty. Don't you think it's pretty, Tris?"

I glance up to see what she's seeing and find twinkling stars in the inky night sky.

"Yeah, Pip. It's pretty."

"Prettier than me?"

"Pip," I warn.

"Mmm... I like it when you tell me off. Give me all the flutters."

*Focus, Tristan. Fucking focus.*

"I'm coming up the street now," I tell her, my eyes scanning the space around me.

"My hero," she breathes. "I see the lights. You came for me."

"I'll always co—" I cut myself off before I dig myself into more trouble than I'm already in.

I slow down, scanning the street for her.

"Where the hell are you, Pip?"

"Staring at the stars, silly."

"Fucking hell," I mutter.

After a few more seconds, a dark figure on the grass outside one of the houses becomes clear.

"Why are you lying in someone's yard, Pip?"

"Why not? The grass is all spongy and shit. It's nice."

"Jesus Christ." Pulling the car to a stop at the curb, I throw my door open and climb out.

"Triiiiistaaaan," she sings as I make my way over to her. "I knew you'd come."

"How fucking drunk are you, Pip?"

It's a pointless question. I've known the answer since I first accepted the call, but still.

"Is that blood?" I ask, running my eyes over her to check for injuries, pointedly ignoring the little black dress that's doing little to cover her right now.

"This?" she asks, running her fingers over her chest. "Nah? It's just paint, big man."

"B-big—" Jesus. "Come on then, before someone calls the cops on your drunk and disorderly ass."

"Come lie with me and look at the stars."

"Maybe another time. You need a gallon of water and a bed."

"Mmm... a bed," she mumbles.

Reaching down, I grab her hand and haul her to her feet, for all the fucking good they do.

"Don't make me throw you over my shoulder," I warn when she wobbles around like a drunken idiot.

"Oh, yeah. I have absolutely zero issues with you throwing me around like a rag doll, big man."

Her words conjure up more images I really shouldn't be having right now, so instead of lifting her off her feet to make this easier for both of us, I keep her pinned to my side, badly guiding her back toward my car.

"My hero," she cries when I finally lower her into the passenger seat. "Whatever did I do while you were gone?"

Having zero interest in knowing about the guys she might have called on in her hour of drunken need while I was away, I strap her in and close the door.

"Get a fucking grip, Carver," I mutter to myself as I walk around the trunk. "Just take her home. Acting big brother, remember?"

Confident I've got it together, I pull the door open and drop down, only to be hit full force by Violet's sweet scent.

Refusing to look at her, I start the car and pull up the search screen on my GPS.

"Address?" I ask.

I know roughly where she lives, but not well enough to find it without any instructions.

When no response comes from the other side of the car, I glance over.

"Of course."

Her eyes are closed, her lips parted, and her breathing is heavy.

I sit for a beat, trying to talk myself out of what I'm about to do. But it's impossible.

Starting the car, I spin it around and head back in the direction I came from.

Other than her light snores, Violet doesn't so much as make a noise, and it's not until I'm trying to manhandle her out of the car to get her up to my apartment that she begins to stir.

"Mmm... I like your hands on me, big man," she murmurs.

"You could make this easier, you know," I mutter, doing exactly what I didn't want to and throwing her over my shoulder.

"You're trouble, Pip."

"And you've got the most incredible ass. Anyone ever told you that, Tris?"

"Stop staring at my ass, Violet," I warn.

"What else do you want me to look at? It's right in my face. Literally, it's the only thing I can see. Ooooh... I could touch it."

"Violet Bra— Fuck," I hiss as her small hands grab onto my ass cheeks, squeezing as I march into the elevator, not willing to carry her up multiple flights of stairs.

"Mmm... you like that, big man? There's plenty of other things I can do that I think you'll love too."

I place her down on her feet, desperate to get her hands off me.

"Yeah, like sleep off whatever you've been drinking tonight."

"Aw, come on. Don't be an old man about it."

I catch her wrists before her palms make contact with my chest.

"Violet, you're wasted."

"Makes it more fun, don't you think?"

"No," I hiss.

Her lips part to respond, but thankfully the elevator dings and the doors open.

With her hand locked in mine, I drag her toward my front door, more than ready to put her to bed. Alone.

I don't bother slowing down as we make our way through my apartment. Instead, I drag her straight into my bedroom.

"Ooooh... Tristan Carver's bedroom. Where all the magic happens." But as she says that, she looks around and her nose wrinkles.

Yeah, it's really not anything to show off. My apartment is beyond bare and basic. Tomorrow, when she's sober, I'll probably be embarrassed by the state of it, but right now... there's no way in hell she'll remember anything.

"No one else has even been inside this apartment, let alone the bedroom, Pip," I mutter, pulling open my closet door and grabbing her a shirt to wear.

"You've been here... a long time. I thought an NFL legend like you would have a different girl every week."

"It's not all fun and games like the media portray."

"Shame. Although, that suits me right now. You're all mine."

She closes the space between us and I manage to sidestep her before she reaches me.

"What's wrong, Tris? Been so long you forgot what to do?" she taunts.

"You need to sleep this off. Wear this," I say, throwing the shirt I grabbed onto the end of the bed. "You can sleep in—"

"I'm not a little girl anymore," she states, a deep V forming between her brows.

"I know, Pip. Just get—"

"So why do you still call me that?"

"U-uh..." I stutter.

"Don't you want me? Don't you think I'm hot?" she asks, dragging her hands up her sides.

"Violet, we're not doing this."

"But you brought me here. To your bedroom. And you've just confessed that—"

"I'm going to get you a glass of water," I say, backing up toward the door, for some stupid reason unable to take my eyes off her.

"Wait," she cries, and before I know what's happening, her dress is on the floor, leaving her in just her sexy lingerie. "I even grew boobs."

"Shit. Yeah. I know, Pip. Trust me, I know."

I fight to keep my eyes on her face.

"You want more, don't you, Tris?" She takes a step forward. "I can see it in your eyes."

"N-no. You need to put my shirt on and—" I swallow thickly when she reaches behind her back and unhooks her bra.

Refusing to look, I lunge for my shirt and drag it over her head.

"Get into bed, Violet. We are not doing this," I demand, my voice leaving little room for argument.

I march out of there with my cock straining against my sweats, fucking praying that she's too drunk to notice just how fucking tempted I am to do the wrong thing.

# 7

# VIOLET

I turn over, nuzzling the soft pillow beneath me, but something stops me from drifting back off into the darkness that wants to claim me, and it's not just the pounding of my head that seems to beat to the same tune as my heart.

It's the scent that's filling my nose.

It's...

I sit up in a rush, the world around me spins, and my stomach turns over. But it's the confusion and panic that races through me that's my focus.

My eyes lock on the Titans shirt that's framed and propped against the wall, and then they shift to a whole load of trophies to the side of it.

"Holy fuck," I gasp.

I'm in Tristan fucking Carver's bedroom.

No.

I'm in his freaking bed.

Looking down, I breathe a sigh of relief when I find that I'm wearing a Panthers shirt and... I lift the hem... my panties.

Fuck.

How the fuck did I end up here?

Pushing my fingers into my hair, I rack my brain for what happened last night. But the last thing I remember was dancing with... I don't even remember who.

"Shit."

I'm desperate to snuggle back under his sheets—it's what I'd do if I were home in the hope of sleeping off the hangover that's raging through my body. But I can't. He might not even want me here.

My eyes shoot to the other side of the bed.

The sheets are rumpled and the pillow is dented. But that could have just as easily been me as him. I'm not exactly a calm sleeper when I've been drinking.

Not wanting to dwell on the fact that I might have slept in the same bed as him and not even remembered it, I swing my legs off the edge, ready to hunt for a bathroom, when the sight of a glass of water and some pills on the nightstand catches my eye.

My heart melts at his thoughtful gesture and I quickly reach for both of them, throwing the pills back in the hope they get to work fast. I'm not sure I'm going to be able to face whatever I might have done last night to end up back here and dressed in Tristan's clothes while my head pounds quite so hard.

Finding a door on the other side of the bedroom, I shuffle over in the hope I might find a toilet and some toothpaste behind it.

Thankfully, I'm in luck. And not only do I find toothpaste but also a new toothbrush waiting for me.

I take my time cleaning my gross mouth and trying to rid myself of the stale taste of last night.

"Holy fuck," I gasp when I finally risk a look in the mirror.

My makeup is everywhere. My cheeks are covered in dark eye makeup and my lipstick is...

Oh God. Did I try to kiss him?

Unease knots my stomach as I attempt to do something about my face and the bird's nest that is my hair.

When I finally step out of the bathroom again, I once again cast my eye around Tristan's bedroom.

It's... not what I was expecting.

I'd been to his apartment in Tennessee a couple of times and it was modern and sleek. The ultimate bachelor pad. The complete opposite to this place. I mean, I've only got the bedroom to compare it to, but still.

In my quest for a very, very strong coffee, I venture out of the half-closed door and find a hallway with four others before it opens up to the living area beyond.

I pass three of the doors. They're all closed, and as much as I might want to peek inside, I keep my hands at my sides. It's probably already bad enough that I'm here.

I slow when I get to the final one, unable to ignore the fact it's open, and thank fuck I do, because what I find makes this whole situation more than worth it.

The room turns out to be a fully kitted-out gym, and right in the middle on a treadmill is a shirtless Tristan.

My gasp of shock rips through the air, and in a rush, I slap my hand over my mouth.

But when I lift my eyes from his glistening back, I find he's wearing headphones.

I stand there for way longer than appropriate as he pounds the treadmill like it's the easiest thing in the fucking world. I'd be a quivering heap on the floor after about thirty seconds, I'm so unfit. But he makes it look so easy that I almost start believing I could do it too.

His muscles in his back flex and ripple as he pumps his arms back and forth, and his legs are solid.

Before long, my thoughts of that powerful body turn less than innocent as I imagine how his thighs might look as he thrusts into me. I can only imagine how the front of him looks; it's been a long-ass time since he and my brother used to run around shirtless when I was a kid, and he's changed a hell of a lot since then. But I can only imagine his chest and stomach are as ripped as the rest of him.

My mouth waters and my pussy flutters as my imagination only gets more and more wicked.

Fuck. I bet he can deliver some powerful thrusts.

I can almost hear the banging of my headboard...

I startle when he suddenly slams his hand down on the controls, bringing the belt to a stop as he mutters his frustration under his breath.

Clearly, while I'm here thinking he looks like he's bossing his workout, he's not seeing it the same way.

I slink away so that I don't get caught perving while he's obviously frustrated and continue my exploration of his apartment.

Thankfully, exactly as I hoped, I emerge into a large, open-plan living-kitchen area and make a beeline for the fancy-ass coffee machine sitting on the counter.

It takes me a few seconds to figure it out, but before long the rich scent of my favorite drink fills the air around me. Keeping it black, knowing that I need the strong caffeine hit, I spin around to find somewhere to sit, only... there isn't anywhere.

I can only put it down to my desperate need for coffee which meant I missed the fact there is absolutely no furniture in here.

I hesitate, glancing back at the kitchen in the hope the island has a stool, but I come up short.

Not knowing what else to do, I make my way back to his bedroom, obviously stopping for another look at Tristan in the gym. He's moved to the weights bench, giving me a great shot of his arms as he lifts weights that I'm pretty sure should be utterly impossible.

With the image of those strong arms caging me in as he looms over me filling my head, I continue down the hallway.

Dragging his office chair in front of his French doors that lead to a balcony, I lower myself down and sip my coffee while staring at the view over the countryside that connects Maddison County to Rosewood in the distance.

His apartment might barely look lived in, but the size of it and the view really don't scream 'student accommodation' like our house does.

When he still hasn't emerged from his gym long after I've finished my coffee, I take a couple more liberties in my need to find myself something to do to keep me here and grab myself another of his shirts from his closet, shutting myself back into his bathroom.

Turning the shower on, I strip out of his shirt and my underwear and stand under the rainwater showerhead.

"Oh my God," I moan when the force of the spray hits me.

Tipping my face to the water, I let it rain down over me, washing the scent of last night and my mistakes down the drain.

When my skin starts to prune, I reach for Tristan's shower gel and shamelessly flip the lid and lift it to my nose.

A wanton moan rumbles deep in my throat and I rush to cover myself in his scent, trying to convince myself that it's almost as good as having him covering me.

I wash my hair, but it doesn't feel all that great, seeing as I'm forced to forgo my usual moisturizing conditioner to tame my locks.

Regretfully, I have to eventually turn the water off and get out.

I can only linger in here so long in the hope he might forget he's got a guest and step in here with me.

If he did... would he stay, or would he run?

Damn, I wish I could just wait and discover how that would play out.

I bet his body is banging while covered in fluffy white bubbles.

Snapping myself out of my thoughts, I reach for a towel and dry off before pulling Tristan's fresh tank over my head.

I stare at myself in the mirror, more than aware that I'm playing with fire with this choice when I could have chosen any other that was hanging in his closet that would have covered more skin.

But fuck it. I probably—no, definitely—did something mortifying last night to end up here, so I may as well continue.

His Titans tank has low-cut armholes, revealing probably more side boob than he's banking on for a Saturday morning, but I look hot, tempting even. And I fully intend to rock the look and prove to him that I'm not a little girl who needs looking after anymore, despite what I might have done last night.

I finger brush my hair before twisting it up into a knot on the top of my head and stealing a pen from Tristan's desk to secure it in place.

And after abandoning my underwear on his bed like a shameless whore, I walk out of the room with as much confidence as I can muster with the hangover from hell still lingering.

The apartment is as silent as it was earlier, so I can only assume that he's still working out. But when I poke my head around the doorframe, I find his gym deserted.

A bang comes from the kitchen, and I take off in that direction.

I come to a stop in the middle of the room, watching him as he preps a protein shake. He's got his back to me, and his headphones are still in so he's got no idea that I'm standing here.

Placing the lid back on his tub of powder, he screws the top of his shaker on and then spins around as he starts to shake it.

The second his eyes land on me, his movements falter and his eyes widen in shock before they drop down my body.

My skin tingles, my blood heating as he blatantly checks me out. My nipples harden beneath the thin fabric of his tank. I don't look down, but I'm confident that he won't be able to miss my potent reaction to him.

His inspection continues until he hits my toes and then he makes his way back up again, all the while I do exactly the same to him.

Just like I hoped, the front of his body looks like it's been sculpted from stone. His muscle definition is insane, and it makes me want to trace the lines with my tongue, especially those deep V lines that disappear beneath—

"Why haven't you got underwear on?" he asks, his voice deep and raspy, but his tone is short and it makes my heart sink.

"O-oh... um... It was just yesterday's, so... I-I'm sorry for whatever I may or may not have done last night. Do you know where my purse is? I'll just call an Uber and I'll be out of—"

He looks down at me, his expression softening from a few moments ago.

"I'm sorry," he breathes, placing his shake on the side and stepping closer. "You don't need to run away. You just took me by surprise, that's all."

"O-okay," I breathe, feeling all kinds of awkward as he stands there with sweat still glistening on his skin, calling out for me to taste.

All I'd have to do is lean forward and...

*Stop it, Violet.*

"I really need to go and shower, but you're more than welcome to make yourself breakfast or whatever."

I stand there, nodding like a fucking idiot.

"Then I can take you home when you're ready."

He continues to stare at me, probably wondering if all the alcohol last night has finally fried my brain, but eventually, I force my legs to move and head toward his kitchen.

I don't lose his attention.

Ignoring his burning stare, I pull the refrigerator open and peer inside.

I scan the contents, my frown deepening with every bit of meat and every vegetable I find.

"What are you, a caveman?" I mutter. "Where's all the good stuff?"

He chuckles, and it makes all the hairs on the back of my neck and down my arms stand on end.

"You want good stuff? I can give you the good stuff. Make us coffee. I'll be ten minutes, and I'll make all your dreams come true."

I spin around so fast I swear I give myself whiplash.

"Is that right? In only ten minutes?" I purr, unable to stop myself as I cross my arms under my breasts and lean forward on his island.

Tristan's eyes drop for a beat before he swallows harshly.

"J-just... make the coffee, yeah? I'll be right back."

He runs from the room as if the hounds of hell are snapping at his heels.

Glancing down, I find the reason for his quick exit.

The fabric of his tank is barely covering my nipples.

"You are nothing but a shameless whore, Violet," I chastise myself as the sound of a door slamming echoes through the apartment.

# 8

# TRISTAN

The second I step into my bedroom, the only thing I can see is her black lace panties on the end of my bed.

My fists curl, my need to storm over bubbling up until I can no longer contain it.

I swipe them up, balling the delicate fabric and lifting my fist to my nose. I suck in a deep breath that is filled with her sweet scent. My cock immediately tenting my shorts, an urgent ache in my balls for the woman who spent last night in my bed.

"Fuck. What the fuck are you doing, Carver?"

I stand there, my body aching with need. The desire to go out there and take what I so badly fucking crave is so strong I almost do it.

But then I look up, finding a row of photo frames on the shelf behind my bed, and my eyes lock with a young Roman. It's a photo of us that Violet's mom took one summer while we were running around the backyard having a water fight. Our smiles are wide, our joy palpable. I've got so many incredible memories of my childhood and early teen years with Roman by my side, but that day… it was the perfect summer's day, and I never wanted it to end.

Looking back, it feels like it was an omen, a final day of fun to enjoy my best friend before shit hit the fan.

I blow out a breath, letting my arm drop.

I'm more than aware that I should put her panties back where I found them. She's going to notice they're missing when she comes back in here, but still, I can't help myself. And instead of putting them back on the bed, I pull the top drawer of my nightstand open and drop them inside.

Striding into the bathroom, I drop my shorts and step into the already wet shower before turning it on and allowing myself to be blasted by cold water.

But it does nothing for the inferno that's raging inside me.

Images fill my head of storming back out there, lifting her onto the counter, wrapping her legs around my waist, and slamming my lips on hers. Taking her right there and then so she has no choice but to understand just how much I want her. How much I need her.

I've done everything I can over the years to stop her from seeing my desire for her. And apparently, it's worked.

I felt like the biggest cunt on the planet as she stood there in her underwear last night, trying to prove to me that she wasn't the child I keep convincing myself she is.

Truth is, she's a beautiful, sexy, strong, independent woman. A woman I can't get out of my fucking head.

Unable to deny myself, I wrap my hand around my aching length and slowly start working myself as images of what I could be doing to her in the kitchen right now play out in my mind.

I picture pressing my hand to her chest and forcing her to lay back. Dragging my tank up her body to reveal what she's hiding beneath. Spreading her thighs and finally getting a taste of her, discovering if she's as sweet as I've imagined she might be all these years.

"Fuck. Fuck," I grunt, my cock jerking violently in my hand as I come into the shower tray embarrassingly quick.

But as good as the rush of endorphins is, my release barely takes the edge off what I need.

Slamming my palm against the tiled wall before me, I groan out my frustrations as my semi continues to taunt me.

Aware that I promised her food, I ignore my dick, quickly clean up and get out.

Needing to be sensible, I pull on a pair of sweats and a t-shirt instead of staying shirtless like I usually would. And for good measure, I rummage at the back of my underwear drawer for a pair of boxers I accidentally shrunk a few weeks ago. They were already a little on the tighty-whitey side, but the extra hot wash they accidentally went through definitely didn't help matters.

With them in my hand, I take a deep, steadying breath and head back out to the kitchen.

The scent of coffee hits my nose and my mouth waters, although its temptation dies somewhat when my eyes land on something I want more.

Fuck, that tank is sinful on her.

My eyes remain on her as she scrolls through her phone where she's leaning against the counter with her hip popped.

She looks good. Too fucking good in my place.

"Here," I say, alerting her to my presence as I hold out the boxers. "They're way too small for me, so I thought..."

She stares at them for a beat and then down at herself.

"Uh... y-yeah. Okay. Thanks." She steps into them and I divert my eyes as I walk around her toward the kitchen. "Got too much for these to handle, huh?" she mutters.

I pause and look over my shoulder.

Our eyes collide and her cheeks flame red.

"Sorry. You totally don't have to answer that." An awkward silence falls between us, one I'm not used to or happy with when it comes to Violet.

"So... I promised you the breakfast of all breakfasts." I rub my hands together in the hope we can squash whatever it is that's happening between us and get back to normal.

"You really don't have to. I know you're crazy busy. I can just go."

"I'm never too busy to cook a beautiful, hungover girl breakfast," I tease.

"I bet you say that to all your conquests."

"Nope. Never. I can honestly say I've never made a girl breakfast before."

"Huh, so this is like losing your virginity all over again," she quips.

"Oh, hell no. I'm hoping it's going to be far less awkward and a whole heap more satisfying."

"Hmm... I sense a story there. Do tell," she begs, resting her chin on her fists, watching my every move as I pull things from the fridge.

"Not much to tell," I say, grabbing a chopping board and a mixing bowl, ready to get to work. "The summer before senior year, we went to that football camp."

"Ah yes, you went off for fun while I got left behind alone." Violet pouts.

"That's the one. Anyway. Some bright spark decided that it would be a good idea to run a girls' soccer camp at the same place during the same two weeks."

"Oh, that sounds all kinds of dangerous."

"Yeah, apart from we were all horny teenage boys who barely knew what to do with a girl, let alone a whole camp full of them."

"I bet Roman loved it. He was such a player."

"Oh hell, yeah. He had a plan to bag a different girl every night. It was bullshit. He just liked to rub my nose into the fact he'd lost his V card a couple months before to—"

"Missy," Violet sneers. "God, I hated that bitch."

"Oh really? You never mentioned," I deadpan. Violet

spent all our high school years trying to convince Roman that Missy was nothing but an epic bitch who was only interested in him because of his football player status.

It wasn't really necessary. Roman was no idiot. But as soon as he got old enough to realize that she would literally do anything to climb the social ladder, he saw past what an irritating cow she was and enjoyed the benefits.

"Anyway, after our coaches went to bed, a bunch of us jumped the fence they stupidly thought would keep us apart and went in search of some friends.

"Unsurprisingly, the girls had the same idea and the three of us bumped into three of them. And, well, the rest is history."

"Knox was there too?" she asks, her voice suddenly laced with venom that I'm more than used to being aimed toward her stepbrother.

"Of course. He wouldn't have taken to being left behind."

She scoffs at the mention of him.

"Anyway. One of the girls, Rachel, she latched onto me the second we all met up. We walked down to the lake together, started a fire and just hung out.

"One thing led to another and... well... you know. An awkward-as-fuck attempt at sex happened. I barely got the tip in before I exploded, and I'm pretty sure she wasn't even close to getting off," I confess. "Fucking fun though."

"Says you, who blew his load like a school boy," she teases.

"Hey, I take offense to that. I was a school boy."

"But still. Your rep was better than that. Or..." she taunts. "Was it all bullshit?"

"I soon honed my skills, don't worry."

"So you can do a full three minutes now, huh?"

"Oi, brat," I joke, throwing a mushroom at her.

"And I'm the brat," she asks, catching it as if she's on the team and immediately launching it back. I duck so it misses my head and instead bounces across the counter.

"So what about you?"

"What do you mean, what about me?"

"I gave you my story, let's hear yours," I say, taking a sip of my coffee.

"Oh… I'm still a virgin," she says, so fucking seriously that my mouthful of coffee sprays from my lips, covering the counter.

"Jesus, Tris. Don't ruin my breakfast before it's even ready."

"You're shitting me, right? There's no fucking way that—"

"What are you trying to say, Tris?" she purrs, walking around the island with her now empty mug, her hips swaying temptingly.

"I-I'm not saying anything, Pip. Just surprised, is all. After everything you tried to convince me of last night, I presumed…" My heart pounds so fucking hard in my chest as she gets closer that I can feel it in my damn toes.

"You presumed…" she prompts.

"That you had… that you had some experience."

Abandoning my knife, I twist around as she continues to draw closer. Stepping back, I bump up against the counter.

Her eyes leave me in favor of what I'm cooking before she reaches out for a slice of pepper and lifts it to her mouth, teasing her lips with the end.

Goddamn it. This woman is going to be the death of me.

"What did I say last night, Tris?"

"Umm…" I hesitate as her lips part and she pushes the pepper into her mouth, closing her lips around it in the most erotic way.

I swallow harshly, but it does little to squash my arousal.

This should not be so fucking sexy.

"Y-you… you… uh… just tried to prove to me that you're no longer Roman's little sister."

"Oh," she says after finally biting off the end of the stick. "And how did I do that?"

"By trying to show me all the things that make you a woman."

A smirk curls up at the corner of her lips.

"I bet you enjoyed that, huh?"

"I didn't look." But fuck if I didn't want to.

"You really expect me to believe that?"

Stepping closer still, her body heat seeps into me, sending all my blood south.

"I'd never take advantage of you, Pip. No matter how much you begged me to do so."

She leans in, her breasts brushing against my chest, making both of us gasp.

My brain misfires at her proximity, my cock straining for more contact, begging me to do something, to pin her back against the counter and do all the things I was imagining in the shower.

But then, before I even get to make a decision, she's gone, the air around me instantly plummeting.

"What's wrong, Tris?" Violet taunts with a coy smile playing on her lips. "I just wanted to put my mug in the sink." I stare at her for a beat before my surroundings come back to me, and when I look to my left, I find the sink there, with her empty mug inside. "Oh, and if you must know, I was sixteen. And I've regretted it ever since." Something dark flickers through her eyes, alerting me that there's so much more to that story than she's telling me, but I decide against pushing her for it.

"You deserve better than that."

"Too fucking right I do. Starting with breakfast. Although, I have no idea where the hell we're going to eat it," she says, glancing over her shoulder at my empty apartment.

"Shopping hasn't been all that high up on my to do list," I confess.

"You don't say."

"You know, as breakfasts go, this is pretty decent. Even with all the protein and veggies," Violet announces as we sit on my bed, having a breakfast picnic. It's dangerous territory, having her here, especially with the amount of side boob she's got on display in my tank.

Mostly, I can shove my desire down. It's what I'm used to. I've been doing it for... longer than I want to confess to, after all.

"Good, I'm glad you like it," I say, shoveling another mouthful of omelet into my mouth.

Things are still a little strained between us. The air is thick and crackling with something that's not usually there. It ensures my heart rate stays high and my blood runs thick through my veins.

I look up, staring at that photograph of Roman once more, and this time, Violet follows.

"That was a good summer," she whispers.

"It really was."

She sighs. It's heavy and full of pain and loss, the depth of it I can only attempt to understand.

"You still miss him?" she asks, her eyes still locked on the photograph of her laughing brother.

"Every day," I confess quietly. "But I like to think he's out there somewhere, watching my career."

"Maybe," she mumbles.

When I look back at her, her eyes are glassy with pain and grief.

I wish there was something I could do. But if I've learned anything over the past few years, it's that all I can do is be here. Stand by her side and support her like they would have done.

It's why I can't fuck this up. She needs me as a friend more than she needs me for everything else. I'd never forgive myself if something happened and I ruined this. If she ended up losing me as well.

"I-I'm sorry about last night," she says sadly. "Things have been… hard recently, and I needed to let go."

"It's okay, Pip," I say, reaching over and squeezing her hand in support. "I've got you. Whatever you need."

She lets out a long breath.

"Could you take me home? I've got tons of work to do, and I know you have too."

"I do, but you're welcome to—"

"Thank you, but I think I might have already overstayed my welcome."

"Never. You know that."

She smiles sweetly at me, and it makes my chest ache. There's too much sadness in it. Too much loss.

"Any plans for tonight?" I ask, needing to turn the mood around.

She chuckles. "I think it's probably for the best that I stay home and sleep last night off. Wouldn't want you having to come and rescue me twice in a weekend."

"I don't—"

"Tristan," she warns. "I'm sure you didn't come here expecting to pick up on the big brotherly duties again. Despite what last night might have indicated, I can actually look after myself."

"I know, Pip. I know you're not a kid anymore."

She stares at me for a beat, her eyes narrowing as if to ask, *do you? Do you really?* But her lips stay firmly closed.

"Finish up and grab your stuff then, and I'll take you home."

Swinging my legs off the bed, I take my plate and mug through to the kitchen and place them in the dishwasher. By the time I've cleaned up the kitchen, she appears behind me with her dress from last night bundled up in her arms and her shoes hanging from her fingers.

"Ready?" I ask, throwing the sponge into the sink.

"I really can call an Uber if you don't want—"

"I'm not letting you get in a fucking Uber looking like that," I growl.

She's still wearing my tank, and although she might have a pair of my boxers underneath, it's not exactly decent. And certainly not for anyone else's eyes.

Her lips form a perfect O at my words before she nods.

I grab my keys from the side as we head out, and I try really, really hard not to change my mind and drag her back to my bedroom.

# 9

# VIOLET

My emotions continue to fight for dominance as our house comes into view.

"Nice place," Tristan says.

"We were pretty lucky to find it this close to campus."

"You're telling me."

"So, this was..." Fun? Embarrassing? Fucking torture?

"Yeah. You know where I am if you need anything, yeah?"

"Thank you, Tris. I really appreciate—"

"It's nothing. You know that."

He reaches over and his large hand wraps around my bare thigh. He squeezes in what I'm sure is meant to be a supportive way, but the way his touch makes my skin burn and my core clench, I don't get all that many supportive vibes from it.

"I'll get your clothes washed and sent back to you."

"Don't worry about it. They look better on you than they do me anyway."

My lips part to respond, but no words leave my mouth.

Reaching for the handle, I push the door open, mumble another thank you, and bolt.

I want to say everything calms down the second I slam the

car door and walk away, but his burning stare means my skin continues to prickle with awareness as I step up to the front door.

Digging my key out, I shove it in the lock, give Tris a little wave and then slip inside. Falling back against the door, I suck in deep lungfuls of air that aren't laced with his scent in the hope it helps to calm me the fuck down.

It works. Kind of. But it's all shot to shit when I walk into our kitchen and find four sets of intrigued eyes staring back at me.

"Someone has been a naughty, naughty girl," West teases. "Was that Coach Carver we just saw dropping you off after the night before?"

"Fuck you all," I mutter under my breath, much to their amusement.

Dumping my stuff on the counter, I walk directly to the coffee machine, wishing there was a way to tap it straight into my bloodstream.

"She's even wearing his number," Brax points out when they get a shot at my back.

"Guys, leave her alone," Ella says, defending me and putting an end to their teasing.

I sense her approach me before she appears in my peripheral. "Is everything okay?" she whispers, studying me a little too closely.

Plastering a wide smile on my face, I lift my coffee from the stand.

"Of course. I'm going to go shower and get some work done."

I run out of the room before anyone can say anything, but I feel their concerned stares burning into my back.

"Fuck. FUCK," I bark loudly once I've slammed my bedroom door and fallen back against it.

Confusion, embarrassment, shame, and desire all rage within me.

On one hand, I want to say that I can't believe I offered myself up on a platter to Tristan last night. But really, I can. I've wanted a taste of him for almost as long as I can remember, and we've been dancing along this weird platonic yet flirting line for a while now. I guess it was only time before I did something to fuck things up. Hell knows he wasn't going to be the one to do it.

Until this morning, when I pressed my body up against his, I always thought I was getting my hopes up, thinking his flirting was anything beyond a little inappropriate, seeing as he'd decided years ago to be my replacement brother in any way he could. But there was no mistaking where his head was at this morning as his cock pressed against my hip.

Fuck.

Heat licks at my insides as I think back to how easy it would have been to do something, to see if I could have pushed him to let go of his rock-solid restraint.

Shaking those pointless thoughts out of my head, I dump my stuff onto my bed, push through to our bathroom, place my coffee on the side, and turn the shower on.

As much as I don't want to wash away his scent from my skin, I know it needs to happen or I'll spend the rest of the day dwelling on what could have been. I mean, I probably still will anyway, but this way, it might not be as bad.

To my surprise, it's hours later when a knock finally sounds out and Ella slips into my room.

"Hey. I brought you more coffee," she says, holding up her peace offering.

"Thanks."

"So, this looks fun," she says, glancing around my economics textbooks.

"The thing dreams are made of. You wanna hang out for a bit?" I ask, shoving my books and laptop away.

"Sure," she agrees, tucking her legs under her and getting comfortable.

"Go on, you can ask. I know it's killing you."

"You don't have to tell me anything if you don't want, Vi. You know that." She smiles at me, and her friendship wraps around me like a warm hug.

"I think... no, I know, I seriously embarrassed myself last night," I confess. But still, Ella doesn't ask questions. She just lets me talk.

"I don't remember it, but apparently I called Tristan drunk and asked him to come and get me."

"You just disappeared, Vi. We were looking everywhere for you. We only stopped when Micah tracked your cell and saw you were at Tristan's."

"Shit, I'm so sorry."

"It's okay," she says, leaning forward and squeezing my hand. "You were safe. Now, tell me what you did to embarrass yourself. I need some entertainment."

So I do. I relay what Tristan told me happened last night, along with what went down this morning.

"Vi, he wants you so bad it's not even funny."

"No, he doesn't. He's just upholding his promise to Roman."

She shakes her head. "Vi, open your eyes. That's what he thinks he should be doing, but deep down, it's more than that, and you know it. Can you imagine how hard that must have been for him last night when you stripped and offered yourself up on a platter?"

"Yeah," I whisper. "I felt it this morning."

She snorts a laugh.

"Was it big?"

"Ella," I gasp. "I didn't exactly reach out and cop a feel."

"You should have. I bet he'd have come in his pants."

I can't help but laugh, helped of course by his virginity story that he shared with me earlier.

"The great Tristan Carver loses his mind when his best

friend's little sister wraps her fingers around his mega cock," she teases. "I can see it plastered all over socials."

"Stop," I giggle, finally managing to swallow my coffee and not spray her with it.

"Seriously though, I think you should try again, when you're less wasted and know what you're doing. I bet you could shatter that resolve."

"Do I want to, though?" I ask out loud.

I mean, yeah, of course I fucking do. I've been fantasizing about Tristan since I discovered that boys weren't just gross, smelly human beings. But if I were to push this when he's made every effort not to blur the lines of our friendship over the years, then I could shatter everything we've built, and I'd never forgive myself. He's been my rock. I never would have been able to get through everything I have without him.

"Obviously, you do. I don't think that's in question. But I get it. You're scared. But," she starts making me cringe, because I just know that she's going to come at me with some sensible advice that'll send me into a tailspin. "What if it makes it better? What if you were never actually destined to be friends? What if he's the one, and you're both too busy fighting the inevitable?"

Damn Ella and her romantic heart.

"Is it worth the risk of finding out?"

"Only you know the answer to that."

I suck in a breath to answer her but quickly find that I don't have one.

"Just think about it." I nod, because what else is there to do? "So you're coming out with us again tonight, yeah? The Kappas are having their pool party."

I shake my head, making her smile drop.

"No, I think I'm just going to hang out here and get some work done."

"Vi," she complains.

"I think I partied hard enough last night. Next weekend though, yeah?"

"Sure," she says, thankfully conceding rather than arguing with me. "It won't be the same without you, you know."

Part of me craves another night of oblivion, but I know it's dangerous. I've fallen into the partying and drinking trap around this time of year before, and it's not a place I want to descend to again.

"You wanna help pick my outfit?"

"You know it," I agree with a smile.

Ella bounds toward the bathroom so she can slip into her room, and I climb from my bed to follow her.

The photographs on my nightstand catch my eye, and my movements falter as I stare at memories of my past. I focus on a photo of Roman and I when we were about ten. Mom took us for a short vacation hiking through the woods. It was fun. We spent our nights out on the deck, playing games and enjoying each other's company and our days discovering the woods.

"What do you think, Ro? Is your bro code still too strong?" Thoughts of my brother make my chest ache in a way I always hoped would ease over the years. But it never really has. I like to think it's because he's out there somewhere. That there is even just a small chance that one day we could reconnect. It's a hope that I can't help but hold on to.

Unsurprisingly, the photos don't give me any kind of answers, and with a heavy heart, I turn toward where Ella is probably rummaging through her closet like a woman possessed.

It's better to focus on the future, anyway. Living in the past only leads to more pain and heartache.

---

"You weren't feeling up to it either, then?" Relief floods me when I find Micah at the kitchen island a little while after Ella kissed me on the cheek and tried to convince me to drop in on Tristan again and try my luck, maybe under the ruse of returning his clothes. My concern over being here alone and the power of going out again was almost strong enough to force me to that party.

"Nah. I'm surprised you haven't gone, though."

"What are you trying to say, Micah?" I tease.

"It's just not like you to turn down a party. Is everything okay? Did something happen with Tristan?"

"What? No. Everything is fine. I'm just... I dunno, trying to be sensible or some shit. That hangover this morning was no joke."

"That's what happens when you get old."

"Dude, I'm like a month older than you."

"Did I say I wasn't having the same problem?"

"Fair enough. I was gonna order dinner. You down to order with me?"

"Sure. What are you in the mood for?"

"Umm... Thai?"

"You choose, I'm just going to take some of this upstairs." He gathers up most of his books before heading toward the stairs.

"Has the electrician been by yet?" I say quickly before he disappears.

"Nope. I haven't heard anything."

"Great," I mutter to myself before going back to ordering our dinner.

We have a chilled night with music playing in the background as we both work and chat about everything and nothing. It's nice. And after the dramatic night before, it's exactly what I needed.

It's only ten when my eyes refuse to work any longer, and after tidying up the kitchen, I head up to my room, more than ready to crawl into my bed.

Stripping out of my clothes, I throw them, Tristan's tank

and boxers and my dress from last night into my laundry basket. My bra drops to the floor, and the sight of it makes realization hit.

I left my panties on his bed...

A wicked smirk pulls at my lips as I think back. They definitely weren't there when we went back in to eat breakfast.

He stole my fucking panties.

I rush to pull on a tank and some booty shorts before washing my face, grabbing my cell and snuggling down, thoughts of what he's done with my underwear making me move faster than I usually would.

I ignore all the drunken pictures from Ella, West, and Brax when I sink into my bed with my cell in my hand in favor of pulling up my conversation with Tristan.

**Violet: Thank you for rescuing me last night. I really appreciate it.**

I figure I'll start off lightly instead of going straight in with panty-stealing accusations.

It's only thirty seconds before he begins typing, causing butterflies to erupt in my belly.

**Tristan: I told you. I'll always rescue you.**

I can't stop the wide smile that splits across my face.

**Violet: Are you out doing something wild tonight?**

**Tristan: Yeah, I've got a date...**

All the air rushes from my lungs and my stomach drops into my feet. The disappointment is so fucking real it's almost like a living, breathing, actual thing.

**Tristan: With my sports management textbook.**

"Asshole," I hiss.

**Violet: Oh yeah? Sounds wild. I hope she puts out. *winky emoji***

**Tristan: That sounds like it could end up all kinds of painful. I think I'll leave things at a simple kiss.**

**Violet: Kinky.**

**Violet: Speaking of...**

My heart pounds as I prepare to type out my next message. I could be way off the fucking mark with my assumptions and they could have just been kicked under his bed, but... fuck it. Here goes.

**Violet: Do you have any idea what happened to my panties?**

The message is read instantly, but he doesn't do anything for the longest fucking time.

White noise fills my ears as my heart pounds harder.

Fuck.

Did I just fuck that up?

Is he freaking out that I'm assuming things? Or...

Is he guilty?

I bite down on my bottom lip as thoughts of him wrapping them around his...

No, no. Do not go there, Violet.

My thighs clench as my head conjures up that image, regardless of telling myself not to.

Finally, though, he starts typing, and I swear to fuck, it takes so long for the message to come through that I start to wonder if I'm going to pass out from the anticipation.

I'm expecting an essay from how long the dots are bouncing, but when it finally pops up, I can't help but frown.

**Tristan: Panties? *smirky face***

Fire licks at my insides.

He knows exactly what I'm talking about.

**Violet: Yeah, small, black lace, smell... like me.**

My thumb hovers over the send button, second-guessing whether I should actually send that or not. But it seems fate has other ideas, because my nose tickles and a sneeze erupts. When I look back down again, I gasp when I realize I accidentally hit send.

"Fuck," I half gasp, half laugh.

I wish I could see his face right now.

**Tristan: These?**

A second later, a photo of my panties hanging from his finger appears on my screen.

I swallow thickly as it hits me that he did steal them.

But why? Why would he—

**Tristan: Not sure if they smell like you, though...**

"Oh shit."

Nervous and excited butterflies collide within me and make my head spin.

The next photo that comes through has me sitting bolt

upright in bed and my eyes practically popping out of their sockets.

**Violet: Tristan Carver, you did not just send me a photo of you sniffing my panties.**

**Tristan: Yeah, they're definitely yours. You know, you really shouldn't go around leaving your panties in random guys' bedrooms.**

**Violet: One. You're not a rando. You're one of my best friends. And Two. I didn't leave them. You stole them.**

**Tristan: Huh, well… when you put it like that…**

I squeeze my eyes closed as my hormones rage.

**Tristan: What are you doing?**

**Violet: Other than sitting here in shock over this conversation?**

**Tristan: Shocked or horny?**

**Violet: Is this really Tristan I'm talking to?**

Sure, we've done our fair share of flirting over the years, or at least, I have. But he's never been so… blatant before. I mean… He. Stole. My. Fucking. Panties.

**Tristan: The one and only. Wasn't my photo evidence enough?**

**Violet: Is everything okay?**

**Tristan: Tell me what you're doing...**

Despite him not being here, I hear that demand growled in my ear as if he's standing behind me, and it gets me all kinds of hot.

**Violet: Just got into bed.**

**Tristan: On a Saturday night? Are you losing your edge, Pip?**

**Violet: Why does everyone think I'm a party animal?**

**Tristan: Look at your Insta.**

**Violet: You look at my Insta?**

**Tristan: More than I should confess to.**

**Violet: Have you been drinking?**

**Tristan: Maybe. Is that an issue?**

**Violet: No, but it explains a lot. Are you about to prove to me that you're no longer a little boy anymore and return the favor?**

**Tristan: I think you already know I'm not. You felt the evidence this morning.**

Holy shit, this could be headed down dangerous territory. But am I strong enough to stop it?

**Violet: Not enough to come to a final conclusion…**

I'm not entirely sure what kind of response I'm expecting to that comment, but it sure as shit isn't the photo I get thirty seconds later.

"Fuck me, Tristan Carver." You are a fucking god.

My mouth waters as I stare down his tense abs above the waistband of his boxers and to the huge, unmistakable bulge straining against the fabric.

**Violet: Someone's feeling playful tonight.**

**Tristan: Maybe I'm just sitting here thinking about all the regrets I have.**

**Violet: Regrets?**

**Tristan: Always doing the right thing instead of what I want.**

**Violet: Life's too short not to take what we want.**

**Tristan: I'm starting to think you might be onto something. But what about the consequences?**

**Violet: That's the risk you've gotta take if you want something bad enough.**

He doesn't respond for the longest time, and I start to think he's not going to.

Sinking lower under my sheets, I keep my cell in my hand, waiting to continue our conversation. While I wait, I flick between those two photos, my body burning up the longer I stare.

Before I know what I'm doing, I've slipped my hand into my panties and I gasp when my fingers find my swollen clit.

"Fuck, Tristan," I moan as I play myself. I'm so worked up that my release builds in only seconds. The photo of his reaction from sniffing my panties in front of me sure helps.

I'm just about to fall when a new message pops up.

**Tristan: What are you doing now?**

**Violet: Still in bed.**

**Violet: Looking at your photo...**

**Tristan: And...**

My teeth sink into my bottom lip as I dip two fingers inside myself.

**Violet: Enjoying it.**

**Tristan: Fuck.**

**Violet: You're doing the same, aren't you?**

**Tristan: A gentleman never tells, but fuck, I wish...**

**Violet: You wish what?**

**Tristan: So many fucking things. So many.**

**Violet: Enlighten me.**

**Tristan: That I could see you.**

The temptation to open my camera up and make his wish come true is strong, especially as I edge my own release, my muscles quivering with the need to fall.

But I manage to fight it.

**Violet: One day. Night, Tris. Sleep well. x**

**Tristan: You're gonna leave me like this?**

**Violet: Dream of me.**

**Tristan: That won't help.**

**Violet: *explosion emoji***

**Tristan: Fuck, baby girl.**

"Oh shit." My release crashes into me, my hips jumping from the bed as I ride it out, his name a plea on my lips as I imagine him being right here, watching me like he wants to.

**Violet: Night, old man. x**

Before I can think better of it, I put my cell on silent so he can't tease me with messages and pad through to the bathroom to clean up.

When I slide back into bed, I drift off to sleep with images of Tristan getting himself off in his bedroom with my panties wrapped around his cock.

# 10

# VIOLET

The scent of burning, of death and destruction fills my nose, making me retch as the sight of the only home I've ever known gets engulfed in flames.

"NO," I scream, but no sound leaves my lips, or if it does, it's swallowed by the cracking and shattering of the building before me. "MOM. Mom, please. Please." My screams turn to sobs as I sink to the floor, watching as the orange flames lick higher into the sky.

Fear like I've never known wraps around me right before my eyes as the building, my life, my family all disappear.

"Violet." His voice drags me from the fear as his warm hand presses to my upper arm. "It's going to be okay, Pip. I promise you. "I'm not going to leave your side, okay?"

I nod absently, barely registering his words but accepting his support, his warmth.

"Violet. Violet. VIOLET." A sharp jolt forces my eyes open and I have to blink a couple of times to clear the images of the recurring nightmare from my brain. But before I manage to do that, the scent of burning hits my nose and the darkness surrounding me threatens to send me into the depths of fear that I do everything I can to stay out of.

My chest begins to heave as I lose control of my breathing and my hands start to shake.

"Violet, I need you to stay calm, okay?" That voice. It's not the one from my dream. It's not Tristan.

"It's—"

"Violet. We need to get out of this house right now, okay? Are you with me?"

Warm hands cup my cheeks and I fight to focus on the eyes staring into mine.

They're soft and full of concern but also fierce determination. It's not a look I've ever seen on him before.

I nod, but the movement is so slight that he never would have known if he wasn't holding my face.

As the seconds pass, the smell of burning that fills so many of my nightmares gets stronger.

"W-what's happening?"

"The basement is on fire. We need to get out. Can you walk?"

"Where is everyone? Is everyone safe? If they're in bed then—"

"Violet," Micah soothes. "I need you to stay calm. Everyone is fine. They haven't come home yet. It's just you and me, okay? And we're going to get out."

I nod with a little more conviction this time.

"Okay, come on. Firefighters are on their way. We need to get out before—"

"Get me out of here. Please. Please just—"

"I've got you, Vi. You can trust me, okay?"

I nod again, allowing him to pull the covers from me and drag me to my feet.

My legs barely hold me up as I fight to stay with him, to stay in the present and not sink into the dark depths of my past. Of my nightmare, which isn't so much a nightmare as a memory.

Micah wraps his arm around my waist and guides me from the room.

"Wait, no," I shriek, rushing back to my bed and grabbing the photo frame on my nightstand.

"Okay, now we're leaving," he says, sweeping me into his arms. I'm not sure if it's because he thinks I'm a flight risk or just unable to do this myself, but I appreciate it as he marches me from my room, the smoke immediately thickening around us.

"Tuck your face into my neck, okay? I'm not going to let anything happen to you, I promise."

I do as he suggests, squeezing my eyes tight as the smoke surrounds us, making each breath harder and harder.

We're on the middle floor when there's a loud crash somewhere below us that forces a scream from my throat.

Micah's arms tighten around me.

"I know, Violet. I know what you've been through, and I fucking promise you I won't let you go through that again. Trust me, okay?"

A million and one questions dance on the tip of my tongue. I've never told any of my new family the truth about my past and the loss I've suffered, but he knows.

There's no real reason other than not wanting to relive it that's stopped me from telling them. I have no issue with them knowing the truth. But hearing that Micah knows fills me with a strange sense of contentment.

"Oh my God," I whimper when I make the mistake of lifting my head from the crook of his neck as he hits the ground floor. The fire is already engulfing the back half of the living area and kitchen. Thankfully, though, there's a clear path to the front door. Not a second later, Micah rushes us through it, allowing us to suck in deep lungfuls of clear air.

We both cough and splutter, but at no point does he let go of me.

"I'm so sorry, Vi. I'm so fucking sorry."

I don't register my surroundings until he places me on my feet.

Red and blue flashing lights fill the dark sky around us, sirens cutting through the silence.

"Get in."

"W-where are we going? Where is everyone else?" I ask, clutching my photo frame to my chest like it's my lifeline.

"I'm getting you away from this. You don't need to see it. Everyone else is on their way, and I'll be coming right back to help once I've got you safe."

The shattering of glass makes me wince as the first fire truck appears at the end of the street.

Unable to watch our home go up in flames, I turn and drop into Micah's passenger seat.

"I've got you, Vi. Everything is going to be okay. Everyone is safe."

I nod, accepting his words, but I don't respond. I can't. Everything is just too raw, too real, too painful.

I'm utterly numb as Micah drives. I don't even question where we're going. I just let him take me away from my living nightmare.

Our surroundings are a blur. I don't even realize Micah has brought the car to a stop until the door is ripped open beside me and I'm hauled into another strong set of arms.

Tristan's scent fills my nose and I break down, huge, ugly sobs racking my body as I lose myself in my memories. Of the night that changed the course of my life. The night I lost everything. Everything but Tristan.

Knowing that I'm in his arms once more ensures that my tears don't stop, and I have no idea how much time has passed when I finally begin to calm down.

His large hand rubs up and down my back, the other still holding me tightly against his body.

Sensing that I'm coming back to him, he presses his lips to the top of my head and whispers, "I've got you, Pip."

His words wash through me, calming the panic that's gripping my entire body in a tight hold.

Sniffing one more time, I look up.

Tristan's eyes widen as he gets a look at my face.

"Violet," he breathes, lifting his hand to brush some strands of hair that are stuck to my damp cheek.

I shake my head. "I-I can't, Tris. I can't go back there. Make it stop."

His eyes flick between mine, indecision darkening them. "Fuck, Violet, I—"

"Please," I whisper.

Rejection begins to burn through me and I start to feel myself slipping back into a darkness that not even Tristan will be able to pull me out from.

I don't know whether he senses that, or his restraint just snaps, but before I fall into the dark pit of despair, I'm shifted on his lap so that I'm straddling him.

I quickly glance over his shoulder, shocked to find that I'm in his bedroom. Did he carry me up here?

His hands circle my waist as he stares me dead in my eyes.

"Anything, Pip. Fucking anything for you."

His lips slam down on mine, his hands shifting to my ass to drag me closer.

"Oh God," I whimper as his tongue brushes my lips, giving him the opening he needs to deepen his kiss.

His fingers twist in my hair, moving me exactly where he wants me, taking control like I imagined he would a million times over the years.

A low growl rumbles deep in his chest as I kiss him back with the same passion, the same life-altering need until I'm grinding my hips, rubbing myself against him to find some friction.

"Fuck, you're addictive," he murmurs, kissing along my jaw and then dropping down my neck.

"Tristan," I cry when he sucks on the sensitive skin beneath my ear.

"Fuck. Again," he demands.

"Tristan. I need you. I need you to—"

"Hush now, Pip. You're not the one in charge here."

My eyes pop open at his tone, and heat rushes between my thighs.

Threading my fingers into his short hair at the nape of his neck, I tug, forcing him to look at me.

"Then show me," I taunt.

I barely finish talking before my back hits the mattress beside us. When my eyes open, I find him looming down at me.

"I'm not fucking you, so you can get that idea out of your head right now, Violet," he growls, making disappointment sit heavy in my stomach. "I can't. If I do that, then..." He trails off, and I frown up at him. But my brain is too fried to force him to continue that train of thought, especially when he follows it up with, "But I'll give you what you need."

A second later, cool air surrounds my breasts as my tank is dragged down and his lips wrap around my nipples.

"Oh shit, yes."

"This what you wanted, baby girl?'

*Baby girl?*

Panties. Fucking. Ruined.

"Yes, yes," I cry, barely able to find the brain power to conjure up that word.

His eyes don't leave mine as he teases me, circling his tongue around my peak and grazing it with his teeth, giving me just a taste of what he's really capable of.

"More," I beg, arching my back and shoving my tits in his face.

He takes them in his hands, pinching my nipples between his fingers as his lips find mine once more.

"Even better than I imagined," he confesses into our kiss, which only serves to turn the heat up between us even more.

Hooking my leg around his waist, I drag his big body down so his weight is pressing me into the mattress.

He makes me feel tiny, delicate, special, and I fucking love it.

My hands explore the exposed skin of his back, loving the way his muscles bunch at my touch as our kiss turns from being soft and gentle to wet and dirty.

Our tongues duel and our teeth clash as we try to get more of each other, almost as if we've been waiting all our lives to finally find out what this might be like.

Oh wait, we have.

Needing to up the ante, I tuck my toes into the waistband of his sweats and try pushing them down over his ass.

Feeling him hard against me is no longer enough. I want to experience it with no fabric between us. I want to see him. All of him.

"Violet," he growls in warning. "I told you—"

"You're not fucking me," I finish for him. "Which is a fucking stupid thing to say, by the way," I point out. "But I get it. I think."

"Good. Then stop trying to take over."

He gives me one final, knee-weakening kiss before he descends my body. This time, he's not content with my tank tucked under my breasts. Instead, he wraps his fingers around the bottom and drags it up my body, leaving me bare for him.

"Fuck, you have the best tits, Vi." And just to prove that point, he lowers his head and sets about showing me just how much he loves them.

By the time his soft kisses and sharp nips from his teeth descend, I'm a writhing, panting mess just from what he's done to my breasts alone.

"Oh God," I whimper when he tucks his fingers into the waistband of my shorts and drags both them and my panties down my legs. The second they're free, he snatches up my panties and curls his fingers around them, bringing them to his face just like in that photo.

"Fuck, you're wet for me," he groans.

"Tristan," I beg impatiently. "Fuck my panties, you can have the real thing."

I spread my legs for him, exposing myself, and his eyes turn feral.

My panties fall from his fingers as he stares at me.

Heat burns my cheeks and all the way down my chest.

I'm pretty body confident most of the time, but fuck if his rapt attention doesn't make me start to question things.

"Do you have any idea how long I've fantasized about tasting you?" he asks, directing the question right at my pussy.

My heart races so hard it makes my head spin, my entire body pulsating to its erratic beat.

"Tris, please. I need—"

"Fuck, yeah you do."

In a flash, he's on his front with his giant hands wrapped around my thighs and dragging my cunt toward his face.

"This is mine, Violet. Mine. You got that?"

"Yes. YES," I scream when his tongue licks up the length of me. "OH MY GOD, TRISTAN."

My back arches, my feet dig into the mattress as he sets this insane pace, sucking, circling, and biting my clit.

"Holy fuck, how did you find that so fast?"

"As I said, I know everything about you, Pip. Now shut the fuck up, I'm busy."

"Tristan," I cry as he pushes two thick fingers inside me, curling them just so. "Fuck. Fuck. YES."

He works me right to the edge, I've got my toes over and I'm ready to fall, and then he pulls back and slows down.

He kisses and nips at the skin of my thighs, teasing me with the closeness of that talented tongue while my release fades. My clit pounds, my need for him to push me over the edge bordering on painful. My thighs attempt to close to find some friction but he quickly senses what I'm doing and stops me.

"Asshole," I hiss, rolling my hips as if doing so will tempt him back.

He chuckles against me.

"I think you love it." A growl rumbles deep in my chest, but I don't deny it. Right now, he's giving me everything I need and more. The only thing I can think about is him. "More?"

"Hell yes."

His brow quirks as if he wants more from me. "Be a good girl and you might get it."

I suck in a breath as I realize what he means.

"Please," I moan, my voice breathy and desperate.

He dives for me again, making my eyes roll back in my head.

Why has it never been this good before?

*It has*, a little voice says in my head, but I banish it before the thought has time to bloom.

I thought I'd had decent head in the past few years, but fuck. Tristan is making me think that I've only been with fumbling idiots. Because his tongue... fuck me. It should be illegal.

My toes curl and my fingers pull at his hair, trying to get him even closer, not that I think it's physically possible.

"Want to come this time?" he asks, his deep voice rumbling through me and pushing me closer to the release he's promising.

"God yes. Please, Tris. Please."

I get to that point where I think he's going to let me fall, and the motherfucker pulls back again. My entire body is locked up so tight with my need to let go that my fists curl, ready to fight for what I crave and a pained cry leaves my lips.

"I don't think so."

"Have I ever told you how fucking infuriating you are?" I snap, my blood boiling.

"Yes," he states as if this situation isn't even affecting him. But his eyes defy his blank expression and flat tone. That and the fact I've already felt how hard he was just from kissing me. There's no way in hell his cock isn't trying to punch its way out of his sweats.

My only regret right now is that I can't see the evidence of it.

"Never while you've been between my thighs, though. This trumps all those times."

Pushing himself up on one elbow, he studies me as he sweeps his fingers through my wetness, circling my entrance, making my body shudder and ache with need.

"Tell me how badly you want to come," he demands.

"Tristan," I warn. "Now isn't the time for talking."

"Huh," he mutters. "I disagree. I want to hear exactly what you want me to do to you. You were so quick to sell yourself to me last night. Well, here I am. Now tell me what you want next."

Pushing up onto my elbows, I stare down at him.

His eyes hold mine as he continues to tease me, keeping my release just in reach but impossible to latch onto as he dips his fingers inside me just slightly.

Sucking in a deep breath, I tell him confidently, "I want to come all over your face, Tristan. And then I— FUCK," I bark when he follows my orders, cutting off my attempt of explaining what I wanted to do to him after.

This time, when he drags me to the edge, he doesn't pull back.

And fuck me, the torture was worth it.

I collapse on my back as I ride out the strongest orgasm I've ever experienced.

It rocks through every inch of my body, pulling my muscles tight and flooding me with pleasure.

He doesn't stop working me until the release subsides, leaving my limbs twitching and endorphins rushing through my bloodstream.

"Oh shit, Tris," I say sleepily. "If I knew you were that good, I'd have set fire to something sooner." I don't even register my own words, I'm too blissed out.

Reality is so far away from my mind right now that my fear, my panic, and my concern for my friends are a distant memory.

I'm so out of it that I don't realize Tristan has gone until his warmth spreads down the length of my body. His arm slips under my back and turns me so that I have no choice but to curl into him.

Laying my head down on his chest, I listen to the steady beat of his heart as my arm drapes over his stomach and my legs twist with his.

"I've got you, Pipsqueak. Get some rest."

I want to argue, to demand he gets up so that I can return the favor and do all the things I've been imagining, but with his warmth and support surrounding me, and the bone-deep exhaustion from the orgasm he so skillfully delivered, sleep claims me all too quickly.

## 11

## TRISTAN

In only seconds, Violet's breathing gets shallower and a smirk twitches at my lips. I did that. I made her come so hard she basically passed out.

Should I have caved to her demand to make it all go away?

Who the fuck knows at this point.

It's all my fault.

No, it's the rum's fault.

Drinking was a bad idea, but fuck. I was alone in my apartment for the... fuck knows how many weekends in a row, and I missed her, damn it.

I regretted dropping her off at home the second she climbed out of my car, but I could hardly call out and demand she come back. Well, I mean, I could have, but I wouldn't.

Shifting a little, I push my hand into my pocket and pull out both of our cell phones. Micah passed hers to me before I walked away from him earlier.

I was fucking terrified when I got his call and heard him explain what was happening, but mostly, I was relieved when he told me that they were already on their way to me. That he was bringing Violet to me.

Checking her cell first, I find a whole stream of message notifications from her group chat with her roommates.

Not wanting to invade her privacy, I put it down and unlock mine, shooting Micah a message telling him to let the others know that she's okay, and that she can stay with me as long as they need to be out of their house. Dangerous move? Hell yes. But I'm past caring. There is no fucking way I'm letting her go anywhere else while she's dealing with everything that tonight will have dragged up.

I wait for him to read the message and confirm that he's let her friends know so they're not worrying and drop it to the bed with hers.

Snuggling closer, I breathe her in, hoping that she feels safe with my arms around her.

My cock is still rock hard, my balls aching for release. But just like earlier, I push my needs aside and focus on her.

It's how it should be. And she more than deserves it.

With her hot and naked body pressed up against mine, I find myself drifting off to sleep much faster than I was expecting.

Unfortunately though, it's not filled with sweet dreams of her…

"Tristan, the house is on fire. You need to come now." Knox's deep, panicked voice rocks through me, and I'm on my feet with my heart in my throat a moment later.

"What?" I boom. "What happened? Are they all inside?"

"I-I don't know, Tris. I don't fucking know."

"Where were you?" I ask. "Are you safe?"

"Yeah, I just came back from the Creek a-and—"

"Call for help. I'm coming. Fuck."

I can barely breathe as I run through the house, probably waking everyone as my feet pound on the floor and I fly out the front door, not stopping it from crashing back against the wall—something Mom chastises me far more often than she should.

The drive across town to the house I've spent almost as much time in as my own is a blur. I've never felt panic like it, or at least I haven't until I turn at the end of the street and the sight of my second home almost completely engulfed in flames comes into view.

"NO," I roar.

My eyes fly open in fright, my heart thrashing in my chest, and confusion reigns as my brain begins to wake up.

"No," a soft female voice cries from beside me before something collides with my shin, making me wince. "NOOO," she screams louder, her small body thrashing about harder.

"Violet," I breathe, hoping it's loud enough to wake her but not to startle her. But when she just continues, lost in the throes of her nightmare, I know I need to do more to break her from it. "Violet, wake up, baby girl."

Reaching for her, I gently shake her, and after a few seconds, her movements slow and her eyelids begin to flicker to life.

I didn't turn the light on my nightstand off after she fell asleep. If she woke first, the last thing I wanted was her freaking out because it was dark.

Finally, her lids lift and I find her stunning emerald eyes staring back at me. The pain and fear darkening them makes my chest ache.

I so fucking wish I could take it away for her.

"You were having a nightmare," I whisper, not that it's necessary. She knows full well, I can see it.

"Sorry." She rips her eyes from mine and looks down, ashamed.

"Hey, don't do that," I say, tucking my fingers under her chin and forcing her to look up at me. "I'm here, Vi. Whatever you need."

Leaning closer, I rest my brow against hers.

Our breath mingles as our eyes hold.

I've never felt closer to anyone than I do at that moment.

It's like she lets me see right down into her soul, and I'm floored with gratitude that she trusts me enough to allow me to.

Wrapping my arm around her waist, I tug her closer, needing the warmth of her body against mine.

"Tris—"

"Shh, baby. I'm right here. Everyone is okay. They know you're safe. You've got nothing to worry about."

She nods gently, her eyes filling with tears.

"C-can I shower?" she whispers. "Th-the smell of b-burning..." She trails off, pain making her voice crack.

"Of course, baby. I told you, whatever you need."

Her teeth sink into her bottom lip as she fights the need to say something.

"Anything," I assure her.

"W-will you come with me? I don't... I don't want to be alone."

I quirk a brow at her. "Will I come and stand with you while you're naked and wet in the shower?" I confirm. "I mean, I'm sure I can suffer through it."

Her lips twitch until she gifts me with one of her incredible smiles.

"There she is," I murmur, grazing my fingers up her spine, making her shudder with desire.

It would be so easy to just roll her over and take what I've been dreaming about all these years. Maybe one day soon I will. But it can't be now. Not while she's hurting like this. Lost in her memories.

I'm more than happy to let her use me to get her out of her own head. I'll make her come more times that she can count if it will help. But I am not claiming her.

Not like this.

"This shouldn't feel so... so right," she whispers, a small frown marring her brow as if the thought of us fitting perfectly together confuses her.

"You really thought it would be anything else?" I ask, edging closer until my lips are almost brushing hers, making my intentions more than clear.

"No, not really," she confesses. "I'm still a little shocked though, I guess."

"You think it'll still be as good the second time?"

"Are you asking permission to kiss me, Tristan?" Her eyes sparkle with mischief, and it makes my blood hit boiling point.

With a sigh and more self-control than I knew I possessed, I drop a chaste kiss on her lips and roll away from her, walking straight into the bathroom to start the shower for her.

I'm taking a piss—or at least trying to, but the only thing my dick is interested in right now is getting inside her—my back to the door, when I sense her join me.

My skin tingles and my dick gets harder once more.

"Fuck this shit," I mutter so that only I can hear before tucking myself away, for what good it does. The second I turn around, she's going to know exactly how affected I am by her, exactly how much I need her.

"Holy shit," I gasp when I spin around, finding her still standing in the doorway.

I run my eyes over her body, taking in her sinful curves as my mouth waters.

She's so fucking beautiful. So perfect.

"For me?" she asks, ripping her eyes from me and nodding toward the steaming shower stall.

"Y-yeah." She gives me one more look over, her eyes lingering on the tent of my sweats before she steps inside.

I move closer the second she disappears around the corner, my need for her reaching an all-time high.

"Jesus, Violet. You look like my every wet dream come to fruition," I confess, lifting my hands to rest one on the wall and the other the shower screen, caging her inside as the spray of water hits me.

I'm addicted, utterly fucking enthralled, watching the water run in rivulets down her body.

It's not until my frustrated groan rips through the air that I realize I'm squeezing my length through my sweats.

"Come on," Violet says, holding her hand out for me.

"Vi, I'm not sure—"

Her head tilts to the side, and she gives me this look. A look I've not been able to resist since we were teenagers. I've no idea if she knows she even does it, but it's like my fucking kryptonite.

"Fuck, yeah. Okay."

Shoving my damp sweats down my legs, I kick them out of the shower stall and then move closer, only Violet's raised hand stops me.

Her eyes drop to my boxers and she shakes her head.

"Pip, come on," I beg. "I'm not—"

"Going to fuck me. I know. I'm not asking for you to. I just... want to feel you against me, all of you."

"You're going to regret this," I warn her.

"I doubt it," she states confidently.

I look over my shoulder, and my eyes land straight on that photograph of me and Roman once again.

Obviously following my gaze, her voice cuts through my thoughts.

"It's a little late for that, don't you think? And, he's gone, Tris. His opinion stopped mattering a long time ago."

Turning back around, I stare into her green eyes. They're so much like his it makes my gut knot with uncertainty. I've spent so long convincing myself I can't have this, that I can't have her, that giving in is making my head spin.

"It's just you and me now, Tris. Fuck everyone else."

Knowing that she's right, I tuck my thumbs into my boxers and quickly kick them off, striding under the stream of water with her and pressing the length of my body right up against hers.

"Is this what you had in mind, baby girl?"

"Mm-hmm," she hums as she runs her hands up my chest and loops her arms over my shoulders. "Could be better." Reaching up on her tiptoes, she brushes her lips against mine in the sweetest kiss.

"I see your point."

Wrapping my arms around her waist, I pin her against me and plunge my tongue into her mouth. She hungrily accepts my kiss and we stand there making out like teenagers for the longest time with water raining down on us.

We're both desperate to take it further, but we both also seem to be on the same page, because neither of us pushes it.

And when we finally part, all I do is reach for the sponge and my shower gel and set to work washing the scent of that fire from her skin, before I encourage her to spin around and lather up her hair with my shampoo, massaging her scalp until little whimpers and moans of pleasure fall from her lips.

"Tristan," she breathes, leaning back against me.

"You good now, Pip?" I ask in her ear. Over her shoulder, I don't miss the way her nipples pucker as my deep voice rumbles through her and my breath tickles against her skin.

"Y-yeah. Now take me back to your bed."

"Goddamn, Violet. What are you doing to me?"

"Right now, nothing. But I'm hoping that might change sometime soon." She spins around, her eyes holding mine for a beat before she takes a step back and they drop down my body.

My cock jerks, knowing it's got her full attention.

Her tongue sneaks out, licking across her bottom lip, giving away where her thoughts have gone.

"Violet," I warn.

"Just wondering if you're as good with that as your fingers and tongue, because fuck, Tris. That was insane."

I can't help the cocky smirk that spreads across my face.

"I guess only time will tell."

"Just so you know, patience has never been one of my skills."

I can't help but laugh as I think back to her demanding something from Roman or her mom as a kid.

"Don't I know it."

Dropping a kiss on her lips, I reach out to turn the shower off and then step out to grab us both towels.

With one around my waist, I wrap the other around her and direct her back to my room.

I dry her off and then grab her one of my tanks—because she looked so fucking hot in the one yesterday and I can now shamelessly stare—and then encourage her to get back into bed.

"Where are you going?" she asks in a panic after I've pulled on a clean pair of boxers and move toward the door.

"Surprise. Just wait."

I take off before she can demand I get back into bed and set about making her favorite nighttime treat. Or at least, it used to be when we were kids, and something tells me that she needs a little bit of those good memories right now.

# 12

# VIOLET

I almost burst into tears once again when Tristan walked back into his bedroom with two mugs of hot chocolate and a packet of cookies. Clearly, I was wrong yesterday when I assumed he only had boring, healthy food here.

The sight was so incredibly welcome, the gesture so touching. It was everything.

My fear from waking up to that burning smell that at one point in my life I never thought I'd rid myself of, the sheer terror of those flames engulfing our house, was pushed a little bit further back as he got into bed with me. We enjoyed our early morning snack, and just like I assume he'd planned, with the warmth of the chocolate in my belly and being tucked into his side, I fell back to sleep fairly fast.

I have no idea what time it is when I finally wake, but the sun is streaming through the cracks in the curtains. I lie there for a few minutes, feeling surprisingly okay.

When I first got here last night, I didn't think I was ever going to be able to put myself back together again.

And if it weren't for Tristan, there's a chance I wouldn't have been able to. But just like every time life gets the better of me and my grief threatens to consume me, he was there being everything I need and helping me take the weight.

Only, he did it in a way we've never experienced before, and fuck… it was—

"I know you're awake, Pip," his deep voice rumbles from somewhere.

Reaching back, I find the bed empty and cold.

Pushing up onto my elbow, I scan the room for him.

I find him resting back in his chair, still wearing only a pair of boxers and with a mug in his hands.

"Hey," I breathe, unable to fight the smile that splits across my face at the sight of him.

Leaning forward, he rests his elbows on his knees and holds my stare for a beat.

His lack of words and the way his brow wrinkles makes my stomach sink.

If he's about to tell me that last night was a mistake and that he regrets it, I might just vomit right here in his bed.

"Hey, Pip."

"W-what's wrong?" I ask nervously, sitting up and pulling the sheets with me, already feeling too vulnerable.

"Are we…" Releasing his mug, he pushes his fingers through his hair nervously. "Are we okay?"

"What?" I ask, a bubble of laughter escaping me. "Of course we are. Why would you even think we wouldn't be?"

He shrugs.

"Things got intense last night. I wasn't sure if you'd wake this morning and—"

"You think I'd regret what we did?" I ask, reality slamming into me.

"I dunno, Vi. You were in a really bad place and I… I shouldn't have—"

"I asked you to. Hell, I begged you to. You did exactly what you should have," I assure him.

"So you don't regret it?"

Throwing the covers back, I swing my legs over the edge of the bed and pad toward him.

He tries to do the right thing and keep his eyes on my face, but he fails when I'm halfway across the room and they drop to my legs.

Plucking the mug from his hands, I lift it to my lips and take a sip.

"You make good coffee," I confess, quickly draining the contents and putting it on his desk before climbing onto his lap, not settling until I'm straddling him.

His hands find a home on my bare ass as I wrap my arms around his shoulders.

"Life's too short for regrets, Tris," I whisper before stealing a kiss.

His mouth parts the second I lick across the seam of his lips. A deep groan rumbles deep in his chest as his fingers grip me tighter, dragging me further on to his lap.

Pride swells within me.

Hell yes, I have the power to unravel this incredible man and turn him into nothing but a ball of need.

Heat floods my core at the thought alone before a loud gasp rips past my lips when he grinds me down on his hard length.

"Tristan," I cry when he thrusts, delivering the perfect pressure against my clit.

"Are you going to come for me, baby girl?"

"Fuck, I love it when you call me that."

"I know. It makes you gush. You like this too, don't you, baby girl?"

"Mmm?" I mumble, too lost in what he's doing to my body to register his words.

"You like it when I talk dirty to you," he breathes in my ear, his voice dripping with lust. "You're so fucking wet, baby girl. I can feel you soaking my boxers."

"Yes."

"You're gonna come all over me like a good little girl, aren't you?"

"Tris," I cry as he drags me down even harder against him.

"How long have you imagined this, Violet? How many years have you been fantasizing about fucking me?"

"Too many."

"Tell me. Tell me how badly you want me to push inside your tight cunt and fuck you until you can't remember your own name."

"Yes, Tris. P-please. All of it, I want it all."

He latches onto my neck, sucking so hard I start to wonder if he's actually broken the skin. The pain only adds to the pleasure building in my lower belly.

My pussy clenches, desperate to grip onto something. Something hard, and thick and—

"Come for me, baby girl. Show me how much you want me. Now," he demands, and I'm powerless but to do as he desires. I fall over the edge, screaming out my release into his silent apartment.

"Holy fuck, that's so beautiful," he says, complete awe in his voice as he watches me come back to Earth.

"You're telling me. Fuck. You're insanely good at that."

"You know just the thing to say to a guy, Pip." He smirks.

"My turn," I state, dropping my lips to his neck and grazing my teeth down his skin, making him shudder.

"Violet, I—"

"Have absolutely no argument because I've got you off twice now and I deserve it after being so sweet?"

"Not exactly where I was going," he mumbles.

"You don't want me to suck your cock, Carver?" I ask, pulling back and quirking a brow at him.

"Fuck, Pip. Of course I do. I just—"

His eyes flick once more to that photograph and then to the one I rescued from my house that's sitting on the nightstand on my side of the bed.

When the hell did I claim a side of his bed?

"Ah, I see."

He lets me go when I climb from his lap and cross the room.

Jumping onto the bed, I reach for the frame.

"Sorry, bro. Probably for the best you don't witness this."

I lay it down, hiding Roman's beady eyes from Tristan.

I do the same with mine before turning back to him.

He's sitting much like he was when I woke up, slouched back with his legs spread wide, looking utterly relaxed. Although this time, his lips are deliciously swollen from my kisses and his boxers are barely containing his erection.

My mouth waters as I stare at it, wishing I could banish the fabric covering him with just a look.

"Better?" I ask, stalking back toward him.

He spins his chair a little so he's facing me.

"I guess." His eyes drop to his tank I'm wearing, and I take the silent hint and peel it up my body, leaving me naked for him.

"Fuck." He lifts his hand, rubbing his thumb over his bottom lip.

He watches me, his dark chocolate eyes almost black as I sink to my knees before him.

"Violet—"

"There is no argument you could give me right now that will make me believe you don't want this, Tris. So don't even try."

"I-I wasn't going to argue," he says, swallowing nervously.

"Oh, well then, please continue."

I slide my hands up his thighs, smiling when his entire body jerks at my touch.

"I probably— shit," he hisses when I begin kissing the length of the scar on his knee.

I hold his eyes as I move higher.

I wouldn't have thought it possible, but they get even darker.

"Oh fuck," he groans when my lips find him over the fabric. "I'm not gonna last, Vi."

"So?"

Tucking my fingers under his waistband, I wait for him to lift his hips to help me out before dragging the fabric down his solid thighs.

His cock springs back against his stomach, precum covering the tip, making me lick my lips in my need to taste him.

It's only fair. He spent plenty of time down in Neverland last night.

Pushing up, I lower my head and lick up the length of him.

"FUCK," he barks, his hips jumping.

His fingers thread into my hair, but he doesn't try to take control. He just lets me do my thing.

Reaching out, I wrap my fingers around the base of him before licking around the head, letting his taste flood my mouth.

He stares down at me as if he can't actually believe what he's watching.

His lips are parted and his chest heaves as I sink down on him.

"Fuck. My imagination is shit, because this... fuck. This is... this is... fuck, Violet," he groans when I take him right to the back of my throat.

I give him the best of my skills, taking him deeper each time until I'm almost gagging around his length.

Tears stream from my eyes and the second he notices, he reaches out and wipes them away with his thumb before caressing my cheek like I'm the most precious thing in the world.

"Baby girl, you look so good sucking my dick."

I moan around him, making him grunt.

His fingers tighten in my hair, pushing me to take him a little deeper.

"Yes. Fuck. Yes."

His length swells, his grip on my hair almost unbearable before he lets out the filthiest growl I think I've ever heard and he spills his cum down my throat.

"Fuck. Fuck," he groans. "Violet, fuck."

I don't stop until he's finished, and then I pull off, licking at his tip, cleaning him up.

"Fuck me, you're something else, baby girl."

Before I get a chance to offer myself up, he's on his feet and his lips are on mine.

There's no way he can't taste himself on my tongue, but it doesn't seem to stop him. If anything, it only urges him on.

"Tristan," I squeal when he lifts me off my feet and throws me back on the bed, quickly following me and pinning me to the mattress with his big body.

"Might never let you out of this room," he murmurs, dipping his head low to kiss me.

---

Sadly, Tristan couldn't keep that promise, because not only did both our cells start ringing, but my stomach was growling for food so loudly it was embarrassing.

Didn't stop him from getting me off another three times though, and when we finally walk out of his bedroom, my legs don't work quite right and I go crashing into the opposite wall.

"Problem, Pip?"

"Yeah, you broke my legs with that stupidly talented tongue of yours. Where'd you learn to eat pussy like that, anyway?" I ask, immediately realizing my mistake. "No. Don't answer that... I don't need to know about all the chasers you've been practicing on."

He throws his arm around my shoulders and I glance over,

quickly getting distracted from our conversation by his bare chest and those V lines that disappear into his sweats that should be fucking illegal.

"Jealous, baby girl?"

"Hell no. I'm the one you can taste right now, not them. Should I be worried?"

"Fuck no."

All the air rushes out of my lungs when he slams me back against the wall and steals another kiss that does very little toward helping my shaking legs.

"Can't get enough of you," he growls into our kiss.

"Tristan," I moan, arching into his body, feeling entirely the same way.

It's like all the years of holding back have exploded into this epic, I-must-have-you-now desire that I can't get enough of.

If only he would give in to whatever is holding him back and fuck me.

When my cell starts ringing again in his pocket, he finally pulls back, but only enough to rest his brow against mine.

"The world stops for no one."

"I need to talk to them, find out what's going on."

He nods, taking my hand and leading me toward the kitchen. He hands me my cell before rounding the corner to make us breakfast.

"You really need to go shopping."

"Yeah," he agrees. "We do."

Butterflies erupt in my belly at his words, and I desperately try to stuff them down and to not get carried away, but it's really fucking hard when he's being nothing but perfect right now.

I hop up on the counter before focusing on my cell and hitting redial on Ella's bazillion missed calls.

"Violet Brady, where the hell have you been and what have you been doing?" she screeches down the line.

"Uh... sleeping?" I don't mean for it to come out as a question, but it does, and she definitely doesn't miss it.

"Oh yeah, sure. From what I've heard, the last time you were seen, you were wrapped up in a certain hot football player's arms."

*Thanks for that, Micah.*

"What's going on? How's the house?" I ask in a pathetic attempt to change the subject.

Tristan's chuckle from the other side of the kitchen tells me that I was about as subtle as a house brick to the face.

"Ugh, it's not good. The basement is totally fucked. Everything on the ground floor is ruined. Thankfully, they managed to stop the fire before it got to the boys' rooms."

"So all our stuff is okay?" I ask.

I've already had to completely replace everything from my life once; I really don't want to do it again.

"Hopefully. I'm not sure when we're going to be allowed back into the house to get it, though. I don't think it's safe. It's still taped off so they can investigate what started the fire."

*It was arson.* The words from the fire marshal all those years come back to me.

I squeeze my eyes closed as pain and grief rock through me.

Back then, I couldn't come up with a single name for who would want to do that to us.

Sadly, I was proved wrong only a few hours later when one of the last people I ever thought could be capable of something so awful was thrown behind bars, shattering the last few remaining pieces of my battered heart.

"Violet? Vi, are you still there?" Ella says, her words bringing me out of my nightmares.

"Y-yeah, sorry."

"He's walking around naked, isn't he?"

I can't help but smile. "Not entirely, no. But I'm not complaining," I confess, watching the muscles of Tristan's back pull and twist as he does whatever he's doing at the counter.

"Lucky bitch," Ella mutters.

"Where are you, El?"

"Umm..."

"Ella," I warn.

"Ugh, fine. I'm with the guys."

"As in, you're at the team's place?"

"Maybe."

"And you're jealous of me? You've got a whole fucking team to yourself right now."

"If only," she sighs.

"Whose bed did you sleep in?" I ask, although I'm pretty sure I already know the answer.

"Colt's."

"Ella, you're meant to be going cold turkey," I remind her, thinking back to the new school year resolutions we all made only a week ago.

"I know, I know. They were having a party when we got here and he was so sweet when he heard what happened and kicked everyone out, including the chaser he was dancing with and—"

"You took her place."

"I was upset and worried. I needed consoling."

"Of course you were," I deadpan. "He's not going to want you warming his bed until we can get back into our house," I warn her. Colt is a player of epic proportions. I'm pretty sure Ella is the only girl he's ever done repeat performances for. Something that I think she secretly believes means something. But I fear she's on a one-way road to ultimate heartache when he gets picked in the draft come spring and disappears to the other side of the country, where he'll find a whole new bunch of chasers to fuck his way through.

"It's cool. You don't need to worry about me. So, tell me more about your hot football god. Did he console you good?"

"Ella," I breathe, although my humor comes through, giving me away.

"Oh my God, he did. Are the rumors true?"

"Rumors?"

"Violet," she shrieks. "You have stalked that man the whole time I've known you. You can't tell me you haven't read what his... skills are."

"Yeah, throwing a ball. Kicking it too."

"Sure. Sure. Can I talk to him?"

"What? No. You cannot talk to hi— what the hell are you doing?" I squeal when Tristan plucks the cell from my hand.

"Ella," he growls down the line, setting off those butterflies and flutters again.

He listens for a few seconds, a wicked smirk curling at his lips as he stares at me.

"Uh-huh," he mumbles, his eyes dropping down my body as if I'm sitting here naked. "Yeah. Fully distracted. Yeah."

"Tristan," I hiss, knowing that he's feeding Ella with all the juicy gossip I was holding back.

He moves closer, nudging my knees apart with his free hand and stepping between my thighs.

He chuckles, and it hits me right in the clit.

"I'd say so, yeah. I mean, if you've read it then— Ah, ah, ah, be a good girl, Pip," he chastises when I try to reach for the phone.

"I can't answer that," he says after listening for a few more seconds.

"Oh yeah. Blew my fucking mind," he confesses, staring so deep into my eyes I swear he can see right down into my soul.

"Yeah, for as long as needed. Yep," he laughs. "Okay, bye."

He smirks at me before pressing my cell back to my ear.

"You lucky fucking bitch," Ella shouts. It's so loud that Tristan doesn't miss it, and it makes his smirk wider.

"Was that really necessary?" I ask, directing the question at both of them.

"Enjoy it, babe. You deserve it. Speak later. Have one for me, yeah?"

"No. No, I will absolutely not..." My words trail off when the dial tone rings down the line.

"Seriously?" I hiss when all he does is lower his head like he's going to kiss me, which of course I want him to do, but... I sigh. "Did you just confirm what Ella has read in the gossip column about your talented tongue?"

"You think I've got a talented tongue?" he asks, his voice all deep and sexy, and damn it... he's dragged me back under his spell again.

"No, Tristan. I don't think. I know. And now so does my best friend."

His eyes narrow and he pouts. It's so fucking cute it almost shatters my faux frustration over this. "I thought I was your best friend."

My lips part to say something, fuck knows what though, but he saves me from coming up with something by making use of my parted lips and pushing that talented tongue into my mouth.

"Mm-hmm, maybe I could be convinced to forgive you," I mutter into his kiss.

Despite already having had more than my fair share of orgasms this morning, heat unfurls in my lower belly as his kiss gets dirtier and his hands begin to roam.

The scent of his breakfast cooking fills the air around us but neither of us pays it any mind, too lost in each other.

Or at least, we are until the buzzer to his apartment cuts through the air.

"Shit," he hisses, pulling back to stare at me with hungry eyes.

"Who's that?" I ask, breathless.

"Fuck knows. No one knows my address."

"I really am special, huh?"

He takes a step back and attempts to do something with his hard cock that's trying to punch its way out of his sweats.

"You've no idea, Pip," he murmurs, giving me one last longing look before heading out to see who it is.

Jumping to my feet, I attempt to sort myself out in case whoever it is on the other side of that intercom is going to be expecting an invitation inside.

I finger brush my hair and smooth down Tristan's tank, but I figure there isn't much else I can do since I have literally nothing else to my name right now.

Tristan speaks, but his voice isn't loud enough for me to make out what he's actually saying. A few seconds later, buzzing fills the space and the door is opened.

I stay hidden where I am, not wanting one of his football buddies to see the state of me, or find out what he's been doing. I don't think him being with me is against the rules. Yeah, he's a GA, but it's not in a department I ever step foot in. It's not like he's supporting any of my classes or professors.

With a sigh, I rest back against the counter, nervous energy racing through me as I wait to find out who it is.

A minute later, another male voice fills the air. I push from the counter immediately and run through to the hallway.

"Micah," I cry, flying at him, making him drop whatever was in his arms in favor of catching me.

My memories from last night might be hazy, but with Tristan filling in the blanks since, I know I owe Micah everything. If he didn't wake me then... No. Don't go there, Violet.

"Hey, Vi," he says a little awkwardly, patting me on the back.

"S-sorry. I just... Thank you, Micah," I say, hoping he can hear the sincerity in my voice.

"Anytime, you know that, Vi." He smiles awkwardly before I realize I'm totally blocking him from entering.

"Sorry," I mumble, moving back into the apartment. It's

only then I notice the bags he dropped. "What's this, you moving in too?" I ask teasingly.

"It's not everything, just as much as I could grab. I hope I got all the important things."

I stare at him, my brows pinching.

"What are you..." He gestures toward the bags, and I drop to my knees and unzip one.

The putrid scent of burning hits my nose, threatening to bring those memories back to the surface once more. Thankfully, the sight of what's before me helps push them back into the box they belong in.

"Micah, how did you... Ella said the house is closed off."

He shrugs as if going inside a potentially still dangerous building to rescue my stuff is nothing.

"Thank you," I cry, emotion burning up my throat, tears filling my eyes.

"Like I said, I couldn't get everything but—"

"I can't believe you did this." I shake my head, having a quick rummage through the bag.

"It's nothing, Vi. I've got stuff for everyone."

"You're fucking crazy. You could have been hurt."

He holds his hands out from his sides.

"All in one piece."

"You want some breakfast?" I offer, hoping like hell that Tristan has cooked up enough for three.

"I don't want to intrude."

"Nah, come on, man. We owe you."

Tristan grabs the bags and takes them to the bedroom while I lead Micah through to the kitchen.

"Uh..." I stutter, realizing my mistake with Tristan's lack of furniture.

"I hear eating standing up is the new big thing," Micah jokes.

"Silver lining and all that," I mutter. "Coffee?"

"Please."

I make his drink while Tristan returns to the oven and then pulls some plates down. All the while, a million and one questions spin around my head.

Passing Micah's coffee over, I stare at him, seeing him differently to all the times I've looked at him since we started as freshmen.

"What?" he asks, watching me watch him.

"You're hiding things, aren't you?" My eyes bounce between his eyes as if I can read those secrets in them.

# 13

# TRISTAN

Intrigued by Violet's question, I pull my oven-baked frittata from the oven and place the hot pan on the stove, turning around to watch their encounter.

I probably should give them some privacy, but fuck that. I'm man enough to admit that I'm too selfish to walk away from Violet right now.

"Violet, don't do this," Micah begs. Clearly, he doesn't know my girl quite as well as I do, because there is no way she's going to let it go.

And only a second later, I'm proved right.

"You said you knew, about what happened to my—"

"You remember that, huh?"

"Micah, come on. It's me. You can tell me."

He scrubs his hand down his face, indecision flickering through his features.

"You're not just an IT nerd, are you?"

"Vi," he warns.

"Fuck," she gasps, pushing from the counter and lifting her hands to her hair.

My muscles twitch to go to her, but I don't want to interrupt.

"You're one of them, aren't you?" I ask, thinking of the Hawks, a dangerous gang who rule the nearby Harrow Creek. Although, their reach over the years has expanded and they're now living amongst us.

It's no secret that Micah is friends with Ellis Harris, one of the leader's brothers. The second Violet learned that little fact about one of her new housemates, she told me. But she's never had any reason to suspect they were anything more than friends who share a love of computers and being epic nerds.

"No, Violet. I'm not. I fucking promise you, I'm not."

Violet backs up until she collides with the fridge.

"You swear to me? You fucking swear?"

"I do. I'm not a Hawk, Vi."

Despite the distress written all over her face, she nods, accepting his words.

"So who are you?"

This time, he's not so forthcoming.

"That's not important. All you need to know is that I'm on your side."

"What the hell is that even meant to mean?"

"That I would never, ever do anything to put you, or anyone you care about, in danger."

"B-but—"

She bends over, covering her face with her hands, and I finally push from the counter and pull her into my arms.

"It's okay, Pip."

"You knew about this?" She looks up at me with wide, pleading eyes.

"Of course I didn't. I knew as much as you, that he was friends with Ellis and had connections to—"

"Don't," she begs, not wanting to even hear their names.

"Why is it that no matter what I do, I'm always surrounded by this bullshit? First Letty being a Creek kid, then Kane, and now you," she says, mentioning her old roommate and her now fiancé as she pins Micah with a look that makes him fold in on himself a little.

"I know, Vi. But I won't bring any of their shit to your door. I know just how much you need to be away from all that."

"Why didn't you tell me you knew?"

"Why didn't you tell me what you've been through?"

"Touché," she mutters.

"I'm sorry, Vi. I thought I was doing the right thing in allowing you to keep your secrets."

Violet sighs, relaxing in my arms as Micah takes a step closer.

"I'm sorry too. I trust you, Micah. It's just after everything..."

"I know. You're scared. I totally get that."

"I won't have them in my life again. Or be able to have any influence on anyone I love. I won't."

"They don't have any influence on me. I'm just friends with Ellis."

"You just happen to be connected?"

"Violet," he says, his voice suddenly colder and holding a warning I wasn't expecting. "I really, really need you to forget that little fact about me. Can you do that?"

A shudder rips through her at his question.

"Are you in trouble?" she asks, concern for her friend filling her voice.

"No. But if what I've told you were to get out and people started looking in places they shouldn't..."

"We won't say anything," I confirm.

He breathes a sigh of relief and pushes his glasses up his nose, but his frown doesn't soften.

"Right, breakfast," I say, hoping to shatter some of the tension that's fallen around us.

"E-excuse me, I just need a moment." Violet rushes from the room like she's got the devil snapping at her heels. I guess, in her head, she might have.

"Violet, wait," I call, but I'm too slow.

"I'm okay," she shouts from deeper in my apartment.

"Shit," I hiss, combing my fingers through my hair.

"You haven't told her, have you?"

I frown, staring at the guy who's drilling me with a look that I wouldn't have said he was capable of when I first answered the door.

"T-told her what?" I ask, confused as fuck as to what he's talking about.

Silence crackles between us as the seconds tick by.

One thought pops into my head, and it makes a cold shiver run down my spine.

Surely not. But...

If Micah is connected and knows about Hawk business, then it makes sense that he might—

"He's out."

"FUCK," I roar, the spatula in my hand flying across the room and colliding with the wall, grease from the frittata spraying the light paint.

"You didn't know," he states.

"Does it look like I fucking knew?"

He walks over and retrieves my spatula before Violet comes back in and sees it.

I use those few moments to attempt to school my features and smother my shock.

The last thing she needs right now is to walk back in on me panicking.

"Where is he?"

"No idea, man. If he's got any fucking sense, probably long gone."

"You met him?"

"Never. Only know what I've heard. But I'm assuming you don't think he's got all that much sense."

I shake my head.

I bite on the insides of my cheeks as I consider what he might do.

"He won't come here," I say with more confidence than I feel.

"You sure about that?"

"Yes." No. "He's got nothing left here to return to. The Hawks won't want him. He killed one of their men. He's lucky to be out." How the fuck did that even happen? I keep that thought to myself, because the longer we talk about this, the more chance we've got of Violet walking back in mid-conversation.

"If you say so."

"Fuck," I hiss, grabbing a plate and sliding it in front of him.

"Do you think she's okay?" he asks, looking toward where Violet disappeared.

"I'll go find out. Enjoy."

His lips part to say more, probably to tell me that I need to confess the fucking bomb he's just dropped on me, but he wisely thinks better of it and stuffs some frittata into his mouth instead.

Pushing the bedroom door open, I expect to find her inside, but the room is empty. The bathroom door is shut, though.

Padding over, I lightly knock on the door so I don't startle her.

"Pip, are you okay?"

Silence.

"Can I come in?"

When she still doesn't answer, I take matters into my own hand and swing the door open.

"Shit, Vi." I rush forward to where she's leaning over the sink with her head hanging between her shoulders.

The second I touch her back, she startles, clearly totally unaware of my arrival.

Her head snaps up and her eyes find mine in the mirror in front of them.

They're dark and tormented, and the sight makes my chest ache, my need to take her pain away stronger than ever.

"I'm okay," she says, rolling her shoulders and standing tall. "Let's go eat."

"U-uh," I stutter like an idiot, utterly bemused by her ability to bounce back.

"What's wrong? Aren't you hungry?"

"Starving," I confess before twisting my fingers with hers and leading her back to the kitchen for our impromptu breakfast.

Concern fills Micah's eyes when Violet steps back into the room, but that look soon hardens when he turns to me.

I shake my head, urging him to keep his mouth shut.

I'll tell Violet what's going on when the time is right.

Not that I ever really think there will be a right time.

"Here you go," I say, pushing her plate over.

"It's good," Micah announces, "although, not exactly Ella's pancakes."

Violet snorts a laugh at his comment. "Is that a euphemism?"

Micah's face immediately turns beet red, much to Violet's amusement.

"What? No. I just mean that she makes... ugh, whatever," he sighs when she continues to laugh.

"Sorry. I'm sorry. Yes, she does make very good pancakes."

"I should go," Micah says, taking a step back as he lifts his plate as if he's about to clean it up for me.

"Leave it," I say.

He backs away from the counter, looking at my girl with regret in his eyes.

I'm not sure if it's because of what he's had to confess or because of what he knows. It really could be either.

"Wait, I'll walk you out," Violet says, dropping her fork and following him.

I watch her go, hating that Micah has seen my girl looking freshly fucked and entirely edible in my tank, but equally confident that he's not interested in her in that way.

There's no heat in his eyes when he looks at her, and I couldn't be more grateful.

The temptation to follow them and listen to what they're saying is huge, but I manage to stay put and finish my breakfast.

After only a few minutes, I hear the front door open and close before my girl returns.

"Hey," I say when she pauses in the entrance to the room.

"Hey."

She looks totally unsure of herself, and it makes my heart jump into my throat.

"Is everything okay?" Her brow quirks, forcing me to hear those words. "Sorry. Stupid question."

She shakes her head. "I'm fine. I'm just..." she sighs and walks over, stepping right into my side when I lift my arm for her. "I always sensed there was more to Micah than met the eye. I guess I just pushed it aside for fear of him bringing *them* back into my life."

"He's not from around here though, is he?" I ask, remembering her telling me about her housemates over the past few years.

"No, he's from Seattle. Or at least, that's what he told us."

"You think he's made his backstory up?" I ask, my brows pinching.

She might be right, there does seem to be more to him than the IT nerd they have him pinned as, but I'd really like to think he's not been deceiving them quite that much.

"I guess only time will tell. But I swear to God, if I find out he's lying to me and he is one of them then I'll..." she trails off, not really having anything to follow that up with. "I won't have them in my life again, Tris. I can't."

"I know," I whisper, dropping my lips to her hair as guilt knots up inside me.

I need to tell her, I know that. But right now, with everything she's dealing with after last night?

I squeeze my eyes shut, trying to convince myself that it can wait a few days.

He won't come here. I'm confident of that.

I think.

"Did you want to finish your breakfast, or—"

"Or?" she asks, looking up at me with wide, hopeful eyes.

"I thought we could go shopping. I seem to be lacking a few things in my life right now, and I figure with you moving in that—"

"I'm moving in?" she asks, her brows shooting up.

"Well, yeah. Did you think I was going to kick you out?"

She shrugs. "This is your place, and you're so busy with—"

"I'm never too busy for you, Vi. I promise." Dipping my head, I capture her lips in a sweet kiss. Her mouth moves against mine as if we've been doing this our entire lives.

I pull back long before I'm ready to, but I know that if I let it go any further then the only place we're going is to my bedroom, and that is not how I want today to go.

Okay, so it is a little bit.

"Umm..." Vi hums, lifting her fingers to her lips. "About this..."

"Not now, Pip. You've got enough serious stuff going on without trying to put us in a box. Just... enjoy it, yeah?"

She nods, although I can see a million and one questions swirling around her eyes.

Silently, I beg her not to go there. Not yet.

I want her, I have for a long fucking time. That is not in question here. But putting a label on it, doing the exact thing

Roman always warned me against all these fucking years later… it still makes me feel weird.

It shouldn't. I know that. My connection with him should have been severed the day he left our lives and his sister became my number one Brady. But some of that loyalty, that bro code still lives on. I can't help it.

Eventually, she nods and takes a step back, her expression dropping.

Shit.

"I'm not saying I don't want this, Vi. I fucking promise you that."

She nods again. "Okay." She smiles at me, but she looks anything but convinced. "So, where are we going shopping?"

"Go find something to wear and you'll see."

She hesitates for a few seconds. I know why and I hate it, but other than suggesting she goes out wearing my clothes, she doesn't have many other options. I have every intention of fixing the issue as soon as possible.

I smile at her, and after a couple of seconds of lingering, she disappears down toward my room where I left her bags.

Once I've cleaned up, I join her, and much to my delight I find her standing in the middle of my room in just a black lingerie set.

"You know," I murmur, leaning against the doorframe, "I think I could get used to you being here."

She shivers as she rummages through one of the bags. I like to think it's my presence, but it could quite easily be the soft breeze that's blowing through the room from the window she's opened.

"Have you always been this much of a perv?" she asks, shooting me a look over her shoulder.

I can't help but chuckle. "Yes. I just used to be way more discreet about it."

"Good to know," she says, pulling a black dress from her bag. "It all smells like destruction." Her nose wrinkles in the cutest way, and if the scent she was talking about didn't cause her so much pain, I'd tease her for it.

"Repack everything you're not wearing and we'll fix it."

She nods and, after covering her sexy curves from me, does as she's told while I find some clothes of my own.

Once we're ready, I throw her bags over my shoulder, take her hand in mine and tug her toward the front door.

# 14

# VIOLET

Tristan and I have the best day. I can't remember the last time I laughed so hard my belly hurt and I had tears streaming freely from my eyes that weren't full of grief and pain.

After stopping at a launderette and handing my bags to an elderly woman who smiled up at him like he'd just hung the moon when she greeted him personally at the door, Tris took me to an out-of-town mall where he encouraged me to shop like it was going out of fashion and diligently followed me around all the clothes shops, holding my bags and giving his opinion on what I pointed out.

People watched us—well, him—everywhere we went. Guys pointed Tristan out to their friends, little boys stared at him as if God himself had just strolled past, and women ogled him and undressed him with their eyes until I started to feel a little murderous.

He was mine.

Well, technically he wasn't, because he didn't want to put a label on us. Something I've been trying to put to the back of my mind since he said it.

After I'd given my credit card a serious workout, he took me for sushi for lunch before we hit the furniture shops.

I was expecting him to take the lead and choose what he wanted for his apartment, but to my surprise, he wanted my opinion. We tested out almost every couch in the place before finding one we both agreed on before moving onto sideboards, artwork, a mirror for the hallway, and even a rug for the floor.

He allowed me to choose cushions for the couch and some décor that would make the place feel a little more like home. Girly things. Things I never would have thought he'd willingly want in his home, but he seemed more than happy every time I picked up something new and added it to the overflowing cart he was pushing around.

Despite Tristan's insistence that they'd be able to deliver everything the next day, his NFL godlike status apparently didn't stretch to special delivery times, so he'd have to wait just like a peasant. Something I teased him endlessly about.

He was never really one to use his celebrity status to get places—or things—and I knew he hated even trying it, but the second he told me that the only reason he did it was for me, well, yeah, I melted.

He backed me up against the wall in the shop as if we were alone inside his apartment, cupped my cheeks in his hands, and stared down into my eyes and told me that I deserved it. That I deserved to be able to live somewhere I was proud of, somewhere that I could be comfortable. Happy.

Damn, he knew exactly the right things to say. I could have climbed him like a tree right there and then in that store.

"Violet. Vi. Vi."

"Ow," I complain when something hits me around the back of my head.

"When I asked you to lunch, I wasn't expecting to sit here talking to myself while you check out in favor of living in your Tristan Carver fantasy."

My chin drops as I stare at Ella sitting opposite me in one of the campus coffee shops.

I'm done with classes for the day, but Ella still has another before she can escape back to the team house where she's still hanging out with Brax and West.

Micah is staying with some computer nerd friends—not Ellis Harris, which surprised me. But since his visit on Sunday morning, we've only talked in our group chat since then.

I'm still not really sure about everything he confessed to me. But as torn as I am about who the person really is that I've been living with for the past couple of years, I still haven't said a word to the others. And I won't.

I have to trust our judgment that despite everything he might or might not be involved in, he's a decent person.

He's been nothing but a good friend to all of us, so I can only hope we're right. After all, I've been fooled before. And know just how quickly things can change with very little influence from the wrong people.

I let out a pained sigh.

"He still withholding the D?" Ella asks with a smirk.

"Ugh, why did I tell you all this?" I mutter, slumping down in my chair and tipping my head back in frustration.

"Because you love me, and you know how addicted I am to a little sexy talk."

I glance over at her. Her golden hair is curled in soft waves, and her makeup is totally on point. She looks beautiful. Stunning. No one would ever have a clue that the woman before me ever suffered the kind of abuse she did as a kid for the way she looked. She oozes confidence and sex.

"Addicted to sexy talk or just sex with a certain football player?" I ask, a pathetic attempt to divert the question back at her.

She sees straight through me and quirks a brow.

"Ugh, fine. Yes, he's still withholding. Although, I've

barely seen him since Sunday night, so it's not all that much of a challenge."

I think back to the past three nights. By the time he got back from the training facility or classes, I was already fast asleep in his bed. He's told me that he's trying to front-load his week so that we can spend some time together this weekend, but all that does is make me feel guilty.

I didn't turn up at his house and fall into his bed under any illusion that I was about to become his priority. And neither should I be. He has classes, a job, a future to carve out just as much as I have, and I would never, ever get in the way of that.

"That sucks," Ella says, frowning.

"It is what it is."

"Tell me about his tongue again."

"Oh my God, you are insatiable."

"Me? I'm pretty sure your words to me on Monday morning were, *I could lie on my back with his face between my thighs for the rest of my life and I would die a happy woman.*"

"I'm not denying they're true," I mutter, thinking back to just how good he is.

Frankly, it should be illegal to be that good. And that hot, and that kind and sweet, and—

"Oh, there she goes again, off into Tristan Carver fantasy land."

"You're not funny," I say, pulling my cell from my bag and checking the time.

"But I really am, and you know it."

"Have you seen the time?" I ask my oblivious friend.

She pulls her own cell out, her eyes almost bugging out of her head when she realizes that she's about to be late.

"Shit, Richardson will slaughter me if I'm late to another class."

"Week two and already on your professors' radars as being the naughty kid," I tut.

"Shut your face, Brady. At least I'm not fucking a GA," she points out with a glare.

"Technically, I'm not."

She rolls her eyes. "Tonight," she says, gathering up all her bags and attempting to somehow also pick up her travel mug. "I have money on tonight. Christen your new couch. Laters, baby." She salutes me, covering herself in coffee before flying out of the coffee shop.

In a much slower and hopefully classier way, I finish my lunch, gather up my stuff and head out with hopes of Ella's parting words being true.

I've still got a couple of hours, but all the furniture we picked out is being delivered later.

Tristan promised me that he'd be back to help me, but I can't say I have high hopes as it's due during practice.

I'm sure I can cope with directing a couple of delivery drivers to the living room to drop it all off. It's not exactly rocket science.

I'm halfway across the quad, heading for my car, when that shiver of awareness runs down my spine again.

My heart rate picks up as I scan my surroundings to find out who might be watching me, but just like last time I don't find anyone paying me any attention.

But when the feeling doesn't dissipate, I spin around, convinced I'm under someone's scrutiny.

The second I spot a familiar face heading my way, I relax.

"Hey, how's it going?" Micah asks after jogging the final few steps toward me.

I narrow my eyes slightly at him.

"Were you just watching me?"

"Uh..." Lifting his hand, he rubs at the back of his neck awkwardly. "Y-yeah. Sorry. I just wasn't sure if you wanted to talk to me after..." he trails off, his expression darkening with sadness.

"Answer me one question. Honestly."

"Sure. Anything," he agrees, although I must admit he looks a little nervous doing so.

"Is the Micah I know the real version?"

His brow wrinkles at my question. Clearly, he wasn't expecting that. Which of course does make me want to ask more than my one question.

"Yes, I'm me. I promise you that."

His eyes beg me to believe him. My gut wants me to. But my head… the pain that is constantly at the back of my mind, the reminder of what gangs like the Hawks can do to people is never far from my thoughts.

"Okay. I'm sorry, I just—"

"I get it, Vi. I should have told you sooner. I just… well, I like being this version of me where no one knows who I'm connected to or what I'm capable of." My eyes narrow in suspicion. "N-nothing like that. I just mean with this." He indicates to his laptop bag.

"I get it, Micah. And I promise, whatever you tell me, it won't go any further."

"Thank you. Just forget it all, yeah?"

"I'll try. What did you tell the others about getting their stuff?"

"Just that I broke in after the authorities had left. They were less suspicious than you."

"Obviously. You didn't confess to knowing all their secrets while carrying them out of a burning building."

"Very true. Maybe it should have been Ella I had to rescue. Could have spilled a few more of my secrets, huh?"

"Mic—"

"Don't. Don't give me those puppy dog eyes. We're all friends. We all agreed on it. Plus, she's not interested, so it's a moot point."

"But you never—"

"Vi, seriously. I'm an IT nerd with glasses. I'm so far from her type it's not even funny."

"Her type keeps breaking her heart. Maybe a change is what she needs."

"Yeah, maybe. But she needs to figure that out in her own time, don't you think?"

"Being sensible is no fun." I pout.

"Speaking of fun, how's living with Tristan? You both seemed... cozy Sunday morning."

I can't help the wide smile that spreads across my face. "Thank you for taking me to him."

"You're welcome. I'm sorry you had to go through that again, but I'm glad you've got him to distract you."

His eyes sparkle with something and I groan. "Ella has told you all, hasn't she?"

"Nah, I just overheard her talking to Letty. Something about a magic tongue. Sounded interesting."

"And they say it's just the girls who are the gossips," I mutter lightly.

We chat for a few more minutes before we walk toward the parking lot together, ready to head home for the night.

"Any news on the house?" I ask before we part.

"Not yet. I'll let you know when I hear anything, but it could be a while."

"This was not how I expected us all to be starting junior year."

"It could be worse." I think about heading back to Tristan's place, about filling it with the furniture we chose together and finally being able to find homes for the cushions and trinkets I bought.

Contentment like I haven't felt for years washes through me as I think about that apartment being my home.

But I quickly realize it has little to do with the place and everything to do with the man who lives there.

He's always been my safe place. The one I always turned to when shit went wrong.

I told myself for years that he'd just replaced Roman. But it was a lie.

How I felt about Tristan has never been anything like what Roman and I shared. He was my big brother and I idolized him. Well, until the day I discovered the truth and he destroyed everything I ever thought I knew about him in the blink of an eye. But Tristan... I'm pretty sure I was falling for him before I even knew it was possible. And then once I knew it was, the knowledge that Roman would never accept it stopped me from even considering it being a possibility. Plus, a little distraction came along and made me look elsewhere for a while.

Now though, everything has changed once again. But he's still there. Still the center of my world. Exactly where he should be.

The drive back to Tristan's apartment is short, and despite the fact I know he's not going to be there, butterflies flutter in my belly. The second I pull up, I grab my cell and shoot him a message, hoping like hell he's going to be able to reply.

**Violet: I'm at home. Do you still think you'll be able to make it back?**

Hope surges through me at the prospect of spending the night hanging out with him. Hell, who am I kidding? I have much bigger plans than just hanging out, and it starts with his tongue and ends with his big, delicious—

**Tristan: Yes, I should be back before the delivery. Have you had a good day?**

**Violet: Yeah, it's been good. Will be better when I see you.**

**Tristan: What are you wearing?**

**Violet: What do you want me to be wearing...**

Heat floods my veins as I wait for him to reply. I really should go in, but I'm powerless to move until I find out.

**Tristan: That little red underwear set.**

"Good choice," I whisper to myself, picturing his face as we walked around the lingerie section of my favorite store. I knew it was his favorite the second he laid his eyes on it. There was no choice in whether I was going to buy it or not.

**Violet: Well, I guess you'll have to wait and see...**

**Tristan: Tease.**

**Violet: You know it. See you later, big man. *winky emoji***

I've still got a smile playing on my lips as I unlock Tristan's front door and let myself into his apartment. I dump my bag by the door and kick my shoes off.

I make my way through the empty apartment to grab myself a drink before heading toward his bedroom to get ready for tonight.

Pulling open the top drawer of the unit he's given me to keep my things in, I find the red lingerie set he was talking about staring right back at me.

"You'd better work some magic tonight," I tell it. "I need that man buried as deep inside me as he'll go."

Hearing my own words sends a shiver of need racing down my spine as desire sits heavy in my lower stomach.

Snatching up the almost-see-through lace, I take it through to the bathroom with me to freshen up. I have plans for tonight, and that involves every hair on my body being gone and my vag is ready for all the attention.

I run the shower, letting the water heat up as I take off today's makeup and strip out of my clothes. The steamed-up shower screen behind me catches my eye in the mirror.

Reaching for my cell, I open the camera and prop it up against a bottle of fancy soap on a shelf above the sink.

Hitting the countdown setting, I run behind the screen and press my naked body up against it.

I have no clue how it'll look, but in my head, it's hot as fuck and hopefully will encourage Tristan to put his foot down a little on his way home.

I wait until the picture is taken before rushing over to see the result.

I can't help but laugh at myself when the photo stares back at me, because it's perfect.

**Violet: I miss you...**

**Tristan: Damn, me too, baby girl. I won't be long. Promise.**

I don't bother messaging back, I just send off that photo. My heart jumps into my throat. Thoughts of him being with the other coaching staff, or the team, right now make me panic a little. Not so much over them seeing it, more so getting Tristan in trouble.

My temperature increases the second he starts typing and my hand trembles as I wait impatiently.

**Tristan: Fuck. Now I'm hard. Again.**

**Violet: *angel emoji***

Then I force myself to put my cell down and step under the water to clean up.

I wash and shave every inch of my body, scrubbing at my skin with my new raspberry shower gel and lathering up my hair.

With only my lingerie on, I dry and curl my hair before applying a light layer of makeup. I'm not trying to look anything but myself tonight. Just… a really hot and sexy version of myself, hopefully.

When I'm happy, I spray myself with perfume and tidy up.

I'm dumping my dirty clothes in the laundry when I hear a bang from the other end of the apartment.

Grabbing my black silk robe from the back of the door, I thread my arms in but leave it hanging open as I rush out of the room to find him.

My heart races at the thought of having his eyes on me, and it's safe to say that I'm already ruining my new panties with anticipation.

In seconds, I'm spilling into the empty living area, my eyes locked on where he's about to emerge from.

But the second a person appears, my world drops from beneath my feet.

I shake my head as our eyes hold for a beat.

He might look different from the last time I saw him, but there is no mistaking the identity of the man standing before me.

"No," I whisper, disbelief flooding me. "No, y-you can't be here. You aren't welcome here."

His eyes drop from mine, taking in what I'm wearing. Or not wearing.

"Oh? But you've dressed perfectly for the occasion."

# 15

## KNOX

Lifting Tristan's keys was probably the easiest thing I've done since walking out of those prison gates.

Well, that and dropping into Reid Harris's car and leaving that shithole behind me.

I've followed Tristan's career from behind bars, watching as he lived out the dream he was so obsessed with as a kid.

I'll admit, after spending almost all of my young life in the shithole that is Harrow Creek, I never truly believed he'd achieve it.

No kid I've ever met achieved anything other than losing their free will when they sold their soul to Victor Harris. Myself included.

It's just what happened.

But it seems things might just be changing, because Tristan hasn't been the only one I've been watching, but Kane Legend too.

I never in a million years thought he'd ever find his way out of the Creek, let alone sever ties with the Hawks. He was blooded in around the same time as me.

But he was so connected to the Harrises even before his

parents died that I was convinced he was on a one-way road to Hawks royalty.

Shows just how little I know.

I knew my time locked up was going to be shorter than it should have been. It helped to be connected to one of the most dangerous gangs in the state. But when I was told I had a visitor about a month ago and found Reid sitting at a table, ready to tell me that my freedom was coming, I must admit I was shocked.

I thought I was going to be doing at least ten years for the fallout of that fateful night.

Seems though, with Reid Harris's rise through the ranks, he managed to grease the right palms and make me a free man once more.

And let me tell you, that is a weird fucking feeling after five years of hell.

I'm sitting outside Tristan's new apartment building when her car pulls up. It's a little sporty blue Chevrolet. Totally her.

My hands grip the wheel of the car I've borrowed from Devin Harris as I wait for her to get out.

It's not the first time I've seen her.

The first thing I did after showering and dressing in some of the clothes the Harris brothers had left for me was to lift a set of their keys from the house and go out in search of my obsession.

Tristan and Kane weren't the only ones I tried to keep my eye on while I was incarcerated, but unlike my little Violet, they were easy to keep tabs on with their high-profile personas.

Most of the time, I only had her social media to feed my need to watch her grow up.

And fuck has she.

As a teenager she was breathtaking. But Violet the woman?

Fuck.

And I'm not just saying that because the only action I've

seen since I was seventeen has been my right hand, and the only woman I've laid eyes on in person was one of the guards, and I'm not convinced she was even female.

It wasn't hard to find her address thanks to the kit Reid had helpfully left for me in my new room, and I was soon sitting outside her house, waiting to lock eyes on her for the first time since that night.

I thought I was prepared. I'd stared at photos of her for long enough over the previous five years. But shit. Nothing could have prepared me for when she walked out of the front door, laughing with a pretty blonde at her side.

Everything was great until two guys followed them out. And it got even worse when one of them threw their arm around Violet's shoulders and pulled her into his side.

Jealousy like I'd never experienced before raged inside me. Before I knew what I was doing, I was standing beside the car, ready to storm down the street and rip her from his grip.

But then she looked up at him and smiled, and my entire body just froze.

I didn't move. I knew I should, but it was impossible as I watched him open a car door for her and allow her to drop inside like a fucking gentleman.

Watching her be treated the way she deserves was a bitter fucking pill to swallow, and I stood there trying to process all of it long after they drove away.

I knew there was a chance that I'd turn up and find her in a happy, committed relationship. Hell, it was more than fucking likely. Violet Brady was every guy's idea of the perfect girl. Smart, sassy, sexy. There's a fucking reason why I struggled to find anyone else to compare her to from the day we met.

And it's not like she'll have been thinking about me every waking second since I was dragged away that night, leaving her in Tristan's arms.

She hates me now. There is no chance of her feeling anything else toward me.

She did feel differently once, though.

I drag my teeth over my bottom lip as I think back to the months before we were ripped apart.

Oh yeah, she definitely felt something for me other than hate back then.

I tug at my pants when they start to get a bit tight from just my memories.

Fuck me, I'm pathetic.

She takes so long to get out of her car, I start to wonder if she's decided to move in there.

The morning I turned up to watch her emerge to go to class and found her house black with ash, the lower ground windows blown out and hazard tape across all the entrances, my heart dropped to my feet.

And it only got fucking worse when I discovered where she'd gone.

It hasn't escaped my attention how fast Tristan decided to return to Maddison County after his injury. I never expected him to retire so early into his coveted career, but to return here, to where Violet was... Well, even from behind bars, it told me a lot about his priorities.

I saw the way he looked at her when we were all kids. I recognized that look. That longing.

It was one I felt right alongside him.

Pussy never made a fucking move, though. He was too busy kissing Roman's ass. Not literally, pretty sure both were as straight as an arrow. But still. They both had high hopes of hitting the NFL together. They could have, too, if Roman didn't discover he had one major issue: his addictive personality.

Okay, yeah. Some of it might not have been helped by me. But fuck. I was just a kid. A kid who'd been ripped out of his hometown in favor of having to fit in with a whole other family because my father had finally found 'the one' or whatever.

I got it. Rose Brady was different from all his other conquests. I could understand the appeal when comparing her to the whores he used to bring home in the Creek. But no Hawk manages to balance gang life with being a normal fucking civilian. I don't know what my dad thought would happen—that Victor would give him a few free passes? Whatever it was was a fucking fantasy, because the only thing hooking up with Rose achieved was to rip apart the lives of three—not all so innocent—kids.

Violet lost everything.

I was thrown behind bars.

And Roman... Well, fuck knows.

That's one person neither me, Reid, or any of his contacts have managed to dig up any intel on.

It wasn't how it was meant to end, but I've come to terms with the fact that it was inevitable over the past five years. I have no idea what promises Dad made Rose, but whatever they were, I'm pretty sure they didn't include burning to death together in her own house.

Finally, Violet pushes her door open and steps out.

My mouth instantly dries out as I watch her walk across the street in her short denim skirt and slash-neck sweater that exposes the tanned, smooth skin of her shoulder.

Her hips sway as she walks, her hair flicking back and forth where she's tied it in a high ponytail.

My grip on the wheel tightens, and my stomach knots with my need to follow her.

Watching her for the past two weeks, waiting for my opportunity to fully get her alone has been painful. Torturous. But now my chance is here, there's a part of me that doesn't want to take it.

I should start the engine and drive off into the sunset, away from Maddison County and Harrow Creek. Away from the Hawks, Reid. Away from Violet.

But I've never claimed to be selfless, and with everything I've endured, I'm pretty sure I'm owed the chance to look into her eyes again.

But even with Tristan's key burning a hole in my pocket, I find myself sitting there, just staring up at the window like a grade A stalker.

It must be almost an hour later when I eventually find my balls and push the door open.

Thanks to Tristan's arrogance, I manage to let myself into the building with ease.

I know he might not have grown up in the Creek, but still. Who leaves their keys dangling out of their bag as they move across campus? Fucking morons, that's who.

Well, more fool him, because I'm about to take over his life, his apartment, and apparently, his new girlfriend for a few minutes.

While I might not have been surprised to find that he'd taken her in after their house fire, I sure was fucking shocked to see him backing her up around the corner of one of the buildings a couple of days ago while she was between classes like a couple of horny teenagers.

Maybe Tristan has grown a pair of balls since I last saw him and finally took what he always wanted.

I guess I should feel guilty for the fact I'm about to walk in and fuck it all up.

But I don't.

Because my need to get close to her again is too fucking strong.

I pause at the front door, just staring at it like a pussy as I wonder what she's doing inside.

"Get a fucking grip, Bowman," I hiss, getting pissed off with myself.

Anyone would think prison turned me into a fucking pussy, standing out here scared to face the girl I endured it for.

"Fuck," I mutter, pushing the key into the lock, twisting the handle and throwing the door open with such force there's no question that someone's arrived home.

Shock stops me from reaching back to close the thing as I step into the hallway and find it empty.

And as I round the corner, I find more of the same.

Is he living in a fucking squat?

But then movement in the doorway catches my eye, and the second I look over, I swear all my fucking Christmases have come at once.

"No," she breathes, her soft voice causing goose bumps to race over my body.

She stares at me with wide, terrified eyes as I make my way down her body.

There's a robe covering her arms, but beneath that, she's wearing sheer, red lingerie that leaves very, very little to the imagination.

I'm hard as fucking steel long before I've even got to her panties.

"No, y-you can't be here. You aren't welcome here."

Her words hit exactly where I think she intends, slamming into my chest with the force of a baseball bat, and my anger, the injustice over everything I've been through because of her —for her—surges through me so powerfully I have no chance of stopping it.

"Oh? But you've dressed perfectly for the occasion," I snarl, taking a step toward her.

A gasp of shock, or maybe even fear, rips through the air as I close the space between us.

But before I get to her, she manages to shove some steel into her spine and stands taller.

She doesn't even bother covering up.

And fuck if that doesn't make me want her more.

She always was a feisty little thing. Especially when cornered or challenged.

"You need to leave," she spits when there are only a few feet between us. "Tristan will be back soon and he'll—"

"He'll what, Firefly?"

Her entire body jolts at the use of my old nickname for her.

"We don't want you here, Knox. No one wants you here."

"Funny," I murmur, finally coming to a stop and lifting my hand. She leans away from my touch, but I'm not having any of it.

I've spent years wondering if her skin is as soft as it used to be. I'm not fucking denying myself the chance to find out the truth now she's right in front of me.

My knuckles brush down her cheek and she sucks in a sharp breath as we connect.

"I hate you," she seethes. "I never, ever wanted to see you again."

A smirk curls at my lips as I drop my eyes to her mouth, and then lower.

"Did you want to tell your body that, Firefly? Because it seems to me, your nipples are more than interested." I lean closer, caving to my need to breathe her in, stopping when my nose brushes her ear. "I bet your panties tell a similar story too. You can't lie to me, I know you missed me."

"Fuck you," she screams.

I see her arm coming a mile off, but I let it go, allowing her to take out her anger, her hatred on me.

Her palm slaps across my cheek, the skin immediately burning with the impact.

The fire in her eyes ignites something inside me and my smirk grows.

"Come on, Violet," I say, holding my hands out at my sides and stepping back. "You've got more than that, haven't you?" Her chest heaves as she stares at me. Her green eyes are cold and full of loathing. Her tiny fists curl at her sides with her need to cause me pain.

"You ruined my life, Knox. You ripped everything away from me."

I take a moment to consider her statement. "Some might say you ruined mine, but okay. I'm listening."

"What?" she asks, her voice full of disbelief. "How dare you? How dare you stand there and— argh," she screams, before flying at me arms flailing, teeth bared as she unleashes everything she's got on me. "I hate you. I hate you. I HATE YOU," she wails, small fists crashing against my chest, barely having an impact on me. I'm not going to admit it, but it's kinda like having a fight with a toddler. Or, so I would think. I've never actually spent any time with a toddler in my life.

I allow her to continue assaulting me, insulting me until she starts to run out of steam. I get it. I know why she thinks she hates me. But things aren't always what they seem, and there's no way in hell I'm going to let her continue with this charade while I turn around and start over elsewhere. This place is my home just as much as it is hers. Well, maybe not Maddison County so much. But fuck going elsewhere. Plus, after what Reid's done to help get me free, I doubt he'll take too kindly to me walking away.

But the second she starts to slow, I move, grabbing her wrists, forcing her to turn around and pressing her against the wall with her arms at her sides.

"Are you done?" I growl in her ear.

She bucks against me, but all it achieves is her grinding her ass into my more-than-obvious erection.

"I fucking hate you, Knox. I hate you more than I thought it was possible to hate another human being."

A snarl of injustice rumbles deep in my throat.

"Yeah? Well, there were days I hoped I'd never have to see you again too, Firefly. But here we fucking are."

# 16

# VIOLET

His words rattle around my angry, confused brain as my heart continues to beat to an erratic tune.

I know why. There's a horny sixteen-year-old girl who still lives inside me who remembers just how hard she was crushing on her stepbrother. And that stupid little hussy is just begging to be let free.

I mean, she's not entirely stupid.

Knox has grown up good.

Like, really fucking good.

I swear he must be almost two feet taller than when I last remember looking up at him, and in width. Damn those shoulders. There's a good chance he spent his entire time locked away in the prison gym or in with whichever cellmate had access to a tattoo machine—and, thankfully, some half-decent skills.

While Tristan was the hot playboy jock who made my girly heart beat out of rhythm, Knox was the rough-around-the-edges bad boy who would break your heart and refuse to give the shards back afterward.

They were polar opposites. They always were. And nothing has changed all these years.

Both are as tempting and forbidden as each other.

Knox even more so because of what he did.

Why am I even allowing him to touch me right now?

"Get the hell off me," I hiss, jolting against his weight once more and immediately noticing my mistake "Are you getting off on this, you sick fuck?"

His evil laugh hits my ears and my teeth grind.

"I said... Get. Off. Me."

This time when I try to free myself, he lets me go.

Cool air immediately washes down my back and makes my skin break out in goose bumps.

It's fucking ridiculous.

This monster he... he...

"You killed them," I blurt the second I spin around and find his heated stare.

Wrapping my robe around my body to stop him looking, I force all the hatred I've felt for him since the day I woke up in hospital with Tristan holding my hand to the surface.

"You killed them and I will never, ever forgive you."

"And you think I didn't lose everything that night as well?" he roars back, as if his pain could ever rival mine.

"Don't you dare stand there telling me about everything you've lost. You did it. If it weren't for you, we all still could have been happy."

He scoffs like it's the most insane thing he's ever heard.

"He never would have made it until now," he mutters under his breath.

"What?" I snap, really not in the mood for his bullshit.

"You and your mom weren't meant to be there," he explains like it should make any difference. "It was a hit on my dad. He'd pissed Victor off and—"

"Fucking hell, Knox. Why does it always have to lead back to that stupid fucking gang?"

His lips part to argue, but he must realize he doesn't have a leg to stand on—or at least, he does for a few seconds.

"That stupid fucking gang is my life, Violet. Before our parents met and Dad tried his hand at being a normal human being, they were all I had. Those boys, they were my brothers. If it weren't for them having my back then—"

"Maybe they shouldn't have. My mom didn't deserve your cunt of a father. She was better than that."

He doesn't so much as react, which surprises me. He and his dad always seemed close when we were teenagers.

"You think I don't know that? Moving out of the Creek, trying to build a normal life was a pipe dream that was only ever going to end in bloodshed."

"So why the hell are you here? Fuck off back to the pits of hell and rot away until you get scooped back up and dumped in prison where you belong, with the rest of the pointless cunts who live there."

His lips purse in anger as he glares at me before landing a blow I was not expecting.

"Is that what you say to Kane and Letty?"

All the air rushes out of my lungs at the mention of my friends.

"W-what?" I breathe.

A wickedly sinful smile curls at his lips. "Ah, Firefly, don't tell me you didn't know that they're Creek scum too."

"Of course I know that. That doesn't mean they're like you, though."

"Oh, so Kane doesn't talk about all the people he's killed? No?" he asks, his brows lifting as if he's actually expecting an answer from me. "What about Letty's father? Did you know how deep he is?"

"Shut up. Just shut the fuck up."

"You're a hypocrite, little Brady."

A red-hot wave of fury shoots through my veins. "They didn't kill my mom," I scream. "They didn't fuck up my brother so bad that I've no idea if he's dead or alive right now."

My chest heaves as the tears I've been fighting to contain

finally spill down my cheeks, a pained sob erupting from my throat.

But all he does is stand there and shake his head.

"I'm not responsible for the actions of others, Firefly."

"Fuck you, Knox," I snarl, hatred for this beautiful man dripping from my voice.

He takes a step toward me, and I immediately jump back as if I've been burned.

His eyes drop from mine in favor of my body. But he's disappointed this time, because I've covered myself up.

"You know," he growls, his voice so deep it takes me a hot second to force my body not to react, "that's not a bad suggestion, Firefly."

I might want to say that I hate this man with every fiber of my being, but it seems my damn vagina is on a different page. Fucking slut.

"I wouldn't go anywhere near your filthy, traitorous cock even if you—"

A roar rips through the air, and both of us look up just in time to find Tristan flying into the room with his eyes locked on Knox.

"Get the fuck away from her," he bellows a beat before they collide.

He catches Knox by surprise and the two of them crash to the floor, Knox taking the hit hard. Good. No less than he fucking deserves before Tristan's fists start flying.

Holy fuck.

I stand there watching as Tristan lays into him. His fists slam into Knox's face as he lies pinned beneath Tristan.

It takes me a few seconds to notice that he's not fighting back. And while that might confuse the fuck out of me, I can't help but be glad he's not returning the hits and hurting Tristan.

But only two more strikes later and all that changes. If I was thinking that Tristan had overpowered Knox, then I was clearly very, very naïve. One second they're on the floor, and the next, Knox has thrown Tristan off and is getting to his feet.

"You're not fucking welcome here," Tristan spits, echoing my words. "And you're certainly not welcome to let yourself into my fucking apartment." He shoves Knox hard in the chest, attempting to force him back toward the door.

Knox's fists curl dangerously at his sides, and after the show of power getting himself out from beneath Tristan, I really don't want to know just how brutal his blows could be.

"Tristan, stop," I beg. "Knox, just leave. Just walk away and forget we even exist."

They both stand glaring at each other, chests heaving, blood splattered over both of them.

But then, Knox risks looking over at me.

He studies me with tears still rolling down my cheeks and what I can only assume is the darkness of my pain and grief filling my eyes.

"You're so naïve, little Firefly. You think you know everything, don't you? But really, you're just a little girl who everyone kept in the dark."

"Says the man who's been locked away for five years. What the hell do you think you know any more?"

I glare at him, trying desperately hard not to be affected by the blood coating his face or the way his right eye is swelling. He deserves it. He deserves it and more.

"I know everything, Firefly. Every-fucking-thing."

Shoving his hand into his pocket, he pulls a set of keys free and throws them at Tristan.

"Thanks for the easy access, bro. You want to protect your girl? You might want to up your game. You wouldn't want someone stealing her from right under your feet."

A feral roar rips from Tristan's throat, but Knox is one step ahead and sidesteps his fist. Although, he can't leave it there and swings a hit of his own that sends Tristan stumbling back until he collides with the wall.

"Tris," I cry, rushing toward him, ignoring the wild beast that looms over us.

"I'm okay," he says when I cup his cheeks, inspecting his split brow.

"Leave, Knox. And if you're sensible, you won't come back."

His eyes drop down my body, but despite being covered by my robe, he doesn't seem disappointed.

"Yeah, we'll see. See you soon, Firefly. Maybe next time we can bare even more. After all, that little red lingerie you're wearing would look even better on the floor." His words hit me like a truck, and I physically jolt as Tristan vibrates with anger.

"Stay the fuck away from her. She's not interested in anything from you," Tristan growls, but Knox is anything but intimidated.

"Scared, Tris? Scared your girl is going to want a real man when she learns the truth?" Knox taunts.

"Just get the fuck out," I scream, unable to listen to any more of his bullshit.

The tension around us continues to get heavier for long seconds as I stare up at Tristan, taking strength from his unwavering eyes, but eventually, a door slams behind us and I collapse into him.

"It's okay, Pip, I've got you," Tristan says into my hair as his arms wrap around me, holding me against him.

No other words are said between us as we stand here, running over the last few minutes in our minds.

A million and one questions dance on the tip of my tongue.

When did he get out?

How did he find us?

Why does he even want to see me?

"How did he get in here?" That one doesn't stay inside.

"Motherfucker stole my keys. I had to get an Uber back here."

I pull back and look up at Tristan in shock.

My brows pinch, but I don't get a chance to reply because he twists his fingers in the back of my hair, tilts my face as he wants it, and slams his lips down on mine in a bruising and claiming kiss.

I want to tell him that it's not necessary. Not just for the fact Knox is gone, but also that he's no threat to what Tristan and I have, but I'm too consumed by the brush of his lips against mine to find the words.

His other hand slips down my body, his fingers tugging at the tie around my waist until the silk parts, exposing the lingerie I wore just for him.

My stomach knots as I remember the way Knox's eyes blazed when he found me wearing practically nothing.

I guess I shouldn't be surprised, he's been locked away with criminals for the past five years. But then, I'd be naïve to think he didn't come out and spend his first few days knee-deep in pussy to make up for lost time.

"Get out of your head, baby girl. It's just you and me," Tristan murmurs, his burning hands sliding over my waist, turning my blood to lava.

He moves them up, squeezing my breasts through the sheer fabric of my bra.

"Tristan," falls from my lips as he begins backing me up.

He pushes my robe from my shoulders and I allow it to flutter down my arms until it falls to the floor.

"Fuck, baby girl. This is—" He swallows thickly as he looks down at me in the tiny underwear. "Tell me he didn't see this," he demands.

"I-I thought he was you," I confess.

"Motherfucker," he grunts.

"Forget him, Tris," I say, as if doing so is that easy.

One visit from the boy from my past and he's already up inside my head way more than he should be.

I've spent the past five years coming up with all the things

I'd say to him if I ever saw him again. I thought I'd channeled so much hate toward him that nothing would crack the hard shell I'd constructed to stop him from getting close.

But then, there he was when I was least expecting him, and... and nothing was like I was expecting.

He was nothing like I was expecting.

Damn him for only getting hotter.

It shouldn't be enough to make my hate lessen. He ruined my life and killed my mother. But still, deep within me, I remember a different side to that boy. One he never showed anyone else, or at least, I hoped he didn't. And damn it if the little girl inside me is having a harder job than I expected separating that boy from the monster he turned out to be.

"You're the only thing I want to be focusing on right now," he confesses, continuing to back me up toward the bedroom.

The second my calves hit the edge of the bed, he presses his hand between my breasts and gently shoves me until I fall onto the mattress.

His eyes run over every inch of me, committing every one of my curves and freckles to memory.

Lifting his hand, he runs his fingers through his hair before reaching for his shirt and dragging it over his head, exposing inches upon inches of tanned and toned skin to me.

My mouth waters and my muscles clench with need.

"Tristan," I moan.

"Fuck, baby girl. You undo me," he murmurs before crawling onto the bed and sliding his palms down my thighs.

My hips buck, offering myself up to him, more than happy to give myself over if it means I don't need to think about what just happened, about why Tristan's got a trickle of blood running down his brow or the man who got this close to me.

I close my eyes for a bit, forcing all of that into the lockbox in my head that everything from that night belongs in.

"Just me and you, baby girl. Are you with me?" he asks,

hovering so close to my pussy the heat of his breath almost burns me through the lace.

"Yes. God, yes," I agree, reaching out to twist my fingers in his hair. "I need you, Tristan. I need—"

"Fuck," he grunts, dipping his head lower to lick me through my panties.

"Oh shit," I gasp, my back arching as pleasure shoots around my body.

That tongue. That fucking tongue.

"I've missed you," Tristan groans, and I can't help but laugh when I wonder if he actually means me, or just my pussy.

"Tris, please," I beg, needing more.

"Greedy girl," he breathes against my inner thigh, nipping at the soft skin before he hooks a finger under my panties and exposes me to him.

"Look how wet you are for me," he groans, his eyes darkening as he stares at my cunt.

I stare him dead in the eyes as he watches me over my body, but still an unwanted image of being pinned against the wall by someone else recently slams into me.

Fuck, I hate him.

I hate him.

I hate him.

But—

I slam those stupid, fickle feelings from all those years ago down and force myself to focus on the here and now.

I don't want that twisted murderer between my thighs. The girl who did was a stupid, naïve little lovesick fool. But I'm not that girl any more, and he's certainly not that boy.

He's a man. A man who—

"Yes," I cry when Tristan finally stops studying me and gets to work. "Fuck. I missed you too."

He chuckles against me, and it only adds to the sensations he's inflicting on my body.

Alternating between sweeping his tongue against my clit with the most incredible pressure and spearing it inside me, he builds up toward my release.

"More," I beg, feeling my orgasm in touching distance but not quite close enough.

I scream when he thrusts two fingers deep inside me, bending them to find my G-spot and allowing his tongue to focus on my clit.

"Come for me, baby girl."

His deep, rumbling voice is the final thing I need to tip me over the edge, and I cry out his name as I fall into an endless bliss where nothing but the two of us and this moment exists.

"Oh shit." I barely hear Tristan's grunt of frustration, but I sure as shit know the second he releases me and climbs off the bed.

"Hey, where are you—" Banging from the front door answers my own question for me. "The furniture."

"Yeah," Tristan agrees, attempting to do something with the boner that's trying to punch through his pants. "Fuck it," he says when the knocks pound once more.

He marches from the room without so much as putting a top on, and I shiver as my body cools and the high of my release begins to drift off.

Voices float down to me, but I don't pay them any attention as I roll off the bed and pad through to the bathroom, wincing at the state of my damp underwear.

I come to a stop in front of the sink and stare at myself in the mirror.

I hate the darkness in my eyes that stares back at me. I close them, refusing to see it, but the second I do, memories flood me.

*"Hey," Knox says, poking his head around my door. "You still awake?"*

*"I would be now, wouldn't I?" I sass back, making him roll his eyes at me.*

*Things were tense when he and his dad first appeared in our lives and moved into our house. But it wasn't long before Roman and Knox became friends, and add Tristan into the mix and they're like the three musketeers.*

*"Can't sleep," he confesses. "Mind if I come hang out?"*

*It's not unusual for us. Roman sleeps like the dead, whereas Knox and I seem to both be night owls. It's how we managed to first bond when he came here—we'd find ourselves in the kitchen for drinks and snacks while the rest of the house was in silence.*

*When he first moved in, I won't lie, I was kinda terrified of him.*

*He was thirteen, I was twelve, and he was this larger-than-life boy from the rough neighborhood. The kind I've always been told to stay as far away from as possible. But here I was, living with him and having secret late-night meetings in the kitchen. Three years on, we've mostly abandoned the kitchen in favor of hanging out in each other's rooms, watching movies until the early hours.*

*"Of course," I say, scooting over in bed to give him some space to join me.*

*Pulling his cell from his shorts pocket, he places it on my nightstand and slips under the covers with me.*

*"What are we watching?" he asks, staring at the TV.*

*"No idea, I was just flicking through."*

*"Stop," he says suddenly when I land on a random channel.*

*I watch for a few seconds, trying to figure out what it is.*

*The eerie music and the tension oozing from the screen really should give it away, but it's not until a clown suddenly appears on the screen and a scream rips from my lips that realization hits me.*

*"Shush," he half scolds, half laughs.*

*It's no secret to either of us that Roman would flip his lid if he were to find us in bed together like this. And I can't lie, knowing that only makes me want to do it more. I love my brother something fierce, but I also love driving him crazy until I'm sure actual steam is going to shoot from his ears, and this, well... something tells me his whole head might pop off.*

*I've never been a rebel, but Knox brings something out in me. Something that allows a hot-as-hell boy into my bed in the dead of night.*

*"We are not watching this," I state, reaching for the remote, but as always, he's faster than me.*

*"Don't be a pussy, Firefly."*

*Just like always, his use of that nickname for me makes butterflies erupt in my belly and my reactions slow. I love it, and every time it falls from his lips, I crave hearing it even more.*

*Maybe even whispered in my ear...*

*"You know I hate scary movies," I pout, reaching for the remote again.*

*"Nope. You're going to have to be brave."*

*I lunge forward again, but the asshole just smirks at me before lifting the covers and the waistband of his shorts and stuffs the remote down there.*

*"You did not just..." My words trail off, getting swallowed by his laughter. "I'm burning that."*

*"Get it if you want," he offers with a smirk, holding his waistband up from his cut torso.*

*My blood heats at the thought of shoving my hand into his shorts and...*

*"Don't be an asshole, Knox," I hiss, hoping like hell he can't see how hot my cheeks are blazing with only the low light of my bedside lamp and the TV flashing before us.*

*"Don't say I didn't offer." He shrugs, getting comfortable once more with my freaking TV remote in his shorts. "Now, enjoy the movie with me, Firefly."*

*He slides lower in my bed, and for some reason, I can't take my eyes off him.*

*His dirty blond hair is a little long, falling into his blue eyes, and his chin is rough with the stubble he's been growing over the past year or so.*

*The bad boy from the wrong side of the tracks is turning into more of a man every time I see him. And I'm not the only one who's noticed. All the girls at school seem to follow him around like lost puppies. It's mortifying—not that they seem to notice. But I get it.*

*"You're staring. Either tell me what you're thinking or watch TV."*

*My chin drops in shock, but no words come out. They can't. I can hardly tell him what I'm thinking about right now. So instead, I twist back around, tug the sheets up to cover my body and reluctantly stare at the TV.*

*I'm only wearing a tank and shorts. It's not an unusual outfit for when we hang out together, but I've never felt as naked as I do right now.*

*"Why are you hiding from me?" Knox asks without taking his eyes from the TV.*

*"J-just cold," I lie.*

*Without another word, he shifts closer, lifts his arm and tucks me into his side.*

*My entire body locks up as his warmth seeps into me.*

*"W-what are you doing?" I whisper as the music turns tense once more. But I'm pretty sure my racing heart has more to do with the boy pressed up against me than it does the impending fright that's about to come from the TV.*

*He shrugs. "You said you were cold. Just... helping out."*

*"U-uh... okay. Well, th-thank you."*

*He laughs at me. Actually fucking laughs.*

*I want the bed to swallow me whole and never let me back out again.*

*"You're cute, Firefly," he says, "Now relax, I've got you."*

*Relax, yeah. Like it's that easy.*

*The minutes feel like hours as the movie continues to scare the shit out of me every few seconds. I spend most of it staring at the corner of my room, hoping we might be about to have a power outage to end my misery. But it never comes.*

*At some point, I find my eyes shifting back to the TV as Knox remains at my side with his arm around my shoulder. His heat and scent ensure that I'm constantly aware of every small movement or noise he makes, and the soft tickle of his breath over my shoulder and down my arm means my skin is constantly covered in goose bumps. Something I hope he's putting down to fear from the movie if he's noticed.*

*The movie lulls me into a false sense of security, and while I'm distracted by the boy next to me, the damn clown takes me by surprise by popping up and filling the screen.*

*I scream and twist into Knox's body in my quest to escape from the terrifying thing.*

*Sucking in a breath filled with his scent, I open my eyes, and find my face buried in his chest.*

Shit.

*Warmth hits the back of my head before his fingers twist in my hair. Shock has me looking up.*

*My breath catches when I find his usually light blue eyes darker and hungrier than I've ever seen.*

*What the—*

*"I'm sorry," I blurt, attempting to pull myself free of his body, but his grip tightens, stopping me from retreating. "Knox?" I whisper, it's so quiet, I wonder if he even hears it over the sound of the TV. But then something rumbles in his chest and his eyes drop to my lips, and I know he did.*

*My heart pounds and blood whooshes past my ear, drowning out the eerie music, and the only thing I'm aware of is him. His scent, his warmth, his hard body pressed up against mine.*

*"Tell me to leave," Knox suddenly says, his tone almost pleading as his brow pinches.*

*"W-why would I do that?" I ask, genuinely confused.*

*"Firefly, if I stay then—"*

*"Don't leave," I blurt, not ready for our secret nighttime rendezvous to be over yet. Although thanks to that clown, I may never let him leave me alone in the dark ever again.*

*"Shit, Violet. I—"*

*"You what?" I ask.*

*When his eyes drop to my lips, everything becomes blindly clear to me.*

*Feeling brazen, I reach out, resting my hand on his abs. They bunch beneath my touch and that noise rumbles in his throat again.*

*I know he's been with girls before. I hear all the gossip at school, and I've also eavesdropped on him with my brother and Tristan before, talking about what happens in Harrow Creek, where he grew up.*

*"Have you been kissed before, Firefly?"*

*Shame burns through me before I shake my head.*

*"Damn, you're killing me." His eyes bounce between mine before dropping to my lips once more. "Fuck," he breathes before pushing forward and giving me little choice but to fall back against my pillows as he looms over me.*

*My chest heaves, my breathing beyond erratic as I'm engulfed by his big shadow.*

*"Last chance to tell me to leave," he warns.*

*"Never," I whisper before the entire length of his body presses against me and the warmth of his lips grazes mine.*

*He takes it slow, easing me into it, but as sweet as that is, I can't take it and I reach out, thread my fingers in his hair and drag him closer.*

*He groans, his tongue pushing past my lips, showing me exactly what to do, and I finally lose myself in him.*

*With his hand on my waist, he drags my body even closer, and I gasp when I feel something hard against my hip.*

*That's the remote, right?*

## 17

## TRISTAN

"You owe me one hundred bucks," a delivery guy says the second I open my front door.

My brows pinch as I try to get my head out of Violet's pussy—not literally—and focus on what I'm actually doing.

"Fuck me, it's really *the* Tristan Carver."

I'm not in any kind of mood for pleasantries, so I just back up, leaving the door wide open for them.

"Just dump it all in the living room, I'll sort it later," I demand. "Just make it quick, yeah?" I wince at my own entitlement.

I half expect them to call me out on it, but when they just walk into the apartment with a couch between them, all I get is knowing looks.

Glancing down, I remember that I'm half dressed with my aching cock tenting my pants, and I figure they understand my issue perfectly.

Looking back over my shoulder, I think about my girl laid out on my bed in that lingerie.

Lingerie that he's now tainted.

How dare he fucking break in here and get a look at my girl like that?

She's mine.

My fists curl, the splits in my knuckles from pounding them into that motherfucker's face opening up once more.

"You might want to clean your floor down here, man," one of the guys says, and when I walk over, I find blood splattered over my light wood floors.

Great.

"Yeah, I'll get right on that," I mutter, lifting my hand to inspect the damage.

I stand there with my mind running at a million miles a second as the guys come up and down, bringing in more of the furniture Violet chose on our shopping trip on the weekend, and despite their insistence, I send them away before they get a chance to open everything up and put it together.

What I need right now is them gone and my girl in my arms.

I should have fucking told her.

I knew that the second Micah told me, and every minute that passed since. But I could see those dark shadows of her past in her eyes since that fire, and every time I tried to tell her, the words just dissolved on my tongue.

I didn't want to cause her more pain by warning her about something that might never happen.

But it fucking did.

It happened.

That motherfucker was here, in my apartment, touching my girl.

Anger surges through me as I angrily sign the delivery note for the guys and send them on their way, swinging the door closed and flicking the deadlocks in case that cunt has made a copy of my key or something stupid.

I saw the fear, the pain, the grief in Violet's eyes when she looked at him, and like fuck am I going to let him that close to her again.

He should be locked up, or a million miles away. Not right here in Maddison County, reminding her of everything she lost that night.

I step into the bedroom right as she emerges from the bathroom with her fingers pressed against her lips, as if she's imagining kissing me not so long ago.

"Violet?" I don't mean for it to be a question, but that pain is still oozing from her and I hate it.

Her hand drops and she stares at me.

She's still wearing only that red underwear set, and as much as I love it, my fingers twitch in my need to rip it from her body.

"Do it," she encourages.

My brows pinch.

Did I just say that out loud?

"Tristan, please." She shakes her head as if she's trying to remove what's happened this evening from her mind.

Fuck, I wish she would.

She must have so many questions, so many that I have no desire to answer.

All I want is what we've found since she arrived in the middle of Saturday night. I want us. No bullshit. But I fear I'm on borrowed time with all that.

All I've ever done is to protect her. To try and help her live a life after losing everything. But I can't help feeling like it's about to bite me in the ass big time.

But right now, I refuse to dwell on that. Not while my girl is standing there, looking utterly lost.

I close the space between us in a heartbeat, take her face in my hands and brush my lips against hers.

She whimpers at my contact before her fingers start to work on my waistband, letting me know that she's not in the mood for sweet and caring.

"Whoa, Pip. There's not— fuck," I gasp when she pushes her hand into my boxers and grasps my cock.

"I need you, Tris. Please."

There is an awareness flicking in the back of my mind somewhere that she's using me. Using me to bury her pain. But I push all of that aside because I figure she could be asking anyone, but she's not. She's asking me, and I'm powerless but to give her what she needs.

"Shit, baby girl." With one hand twisted in her hair so I can hold her in place as I plunge my tongue into her mouth, I use the other to help her push my pants and boxers down my legs.

I kick them off before making a start on hers.

Reaching behind her, I find the clasp, and I'm about to open her bra when she stops me.

"I wasn't kidding. Ruin them. I'll never wear them again now that Kno—" She cuts herself off before his name rolls off her tongue.

"Violet."

"Do it."

Bringing my hand back to the delicate cup of her bra, I tuck my fingers under the lace and rip downwards.

It practically disintegrates at my touch, and she hisses in delight.

"Make me yours, Tristan," she begs before I repeat my previous action and rip the other cup, exposing her breasts to me. Dropping to my knees, I suck one of her nipples into my mouth, pinching the other between my thumb and forefinger.

"Yes, more. Everything, Tris. I need everything."

Her fingers grip my hair painfully as she holds me in place as I lave at her breasts, teasing and nipping her. But before long, she gets too impatient and tries pushing my head lower.

"Greedy," I mumble against her belly.

"For you, always."

Her confession turns my blood to lava and I reach out,

ripping her panties from her body, discarding the red lace on the floor as I wrap my arms around her legs and flip her onto the bed.

Somehow, she manages to lose her ruined bra, so when I run my eyes up her body, she's beautifully bare for me.

I study her as I wrap my hand around my cock, my need for her exploding beyond the point of restraint this time.

"Please," she begs, opening her legs for me, letting me see how much she needs this. "Tristan, I need you to fuck me."

"Jesus, how have I managed to hold off all these years?" I mutter absently to myself as I pull open my nightstand to grab a condom.

"Tris, I'm on birth control, we don't need—"

"I'm not risking fucking up your future, Pip. It's not happening."

Her lips pop open in shock, but she stops arguing. Instead, her eyes drop to my cock and she watches intently as I roll the rubber down my shaft.

Crawling between her legs, I stare down at her, sprawled out for the taking. But I don't take, not yet.

Cupping her jaw, I stare her straight into her eyes and suck in a deep breath.

"I need you to know," I say thickly, "that once I do this, I'm never going to let you go," I warn her.

She swallows nervously. "I'm yours, Tristan. Pretty sure I always have been. Oh God," she whimpers as I run the head of my cock through her wetness. "Please."

"Do you have any idea how long I've wanted you? I used to lie awake in Roman's room while he snored, wondering what you'd do if I invited myself into your room," I confess, remembering all too well how many nights I laid there rock hard with thoughts of her on the other side of the wall filling my head.

She sucks in a sharp breath.

"Every single one of my teenage fantasies involved you, Pip. Every. Single. One."

"Tristan," she begs as I push my tip just inside her.

"It's always been you, Violet. Always," I confess before thrusting my hips and filling her in one quick move.

"Yours," she cries, my hand on her hip the only thing that stops her from shooting up the bed as she adjusts to my size. "Shit, Tristan. Move," she demands. "I need—"

I roll my hips and her words die.

"Fuck, we should have been doing this years ago." She reaches up and twists her fingers in my hair, dragging my face down to hers for a wet and dirty kiss as we find our rhythm.

"Your pussy feels like heaven," I groan into her mouth. "So tight, so wet, so mine."

She gushes around me, her muscles rippling, forcing my own release to make itself known all too soon.

"Make me come, Tris. Stop holding back," she demands. Her heels slam into my ass, forcing me to up my pace.

"Filthy, filthy girl," I growl in her ear, making her entire body shudder with pleasure.

"And all yours."

A groan rumbles deep in my chest.

"I was a fucking dumbass as a teenager. Should have been doing this. I should have been your first, Pip."

Her nails rake across my back, the pain of it making my hips move faster.

"You'd have liked that, huh?" I continue, loving how my words are making her cunt contract. "If I snuck into your room. I could have been the first one to spread your thighs and taste your pussy. The first one to push inside you. The first name you screamed as I made you come so hard you knew your life would never be the same again."

"Tristan," she cries.

"Yeah, baby girl. Just like that."

"More. More. I need—" Her words cut off on a gasp when I find her clit. "Oh shit, yes."

I fuck her deeper, bottoming out with every thrust as my thumb rolls over her clit.

"Come for me, baby girl. Come for me, then I'll fill you with my cum." The second the words roll off my tongue, I regret the condom.

Fuck, I need to see my cum running out of her cunt like I've never needed anything else in my life.

"Oh Jesus. I love dirty Tristan."

Hooking my other hand under her ass, I lift her, fucking her at an angle I know will make her scream as I grit my teeth to hold on long enough to push her over the edge.

"Yes, yes. TRISTAN," she screams as her body finally quakes, her release rocking through her. Her cunt squeezes me so tightly that I have no choice but to follow her over the edge, my cock jerking deep inside her. But my regrets sit heavy in my stomach, knowing she can't feel my cum filling her up.

Goddamn it, that was not the time to be a gentleman.

I don't pull out until she's come down from her high, and when I do, I tug the rubber off, tie it and throw it toward the trash can by my desk. It misses, but I don't make a move to fix it.

Spent, with the rush of my orgasm racing through my veins, I fall down beside my girl and pull her into my arms.

"Thank you," she breathes, making me laugh.

"You're welcome, baby girl."

She wraps her arm around my waist and hooks her leg over mine, and we just lie there with each other for the longest time.

All the things I should be confessing to her run around my head, the secrets I'm keeping slowly poisoning me from the inside out.

"I'm sorry, Pip," I whisper.

She's so still, her breathing so even that I'm not even sure she's awake. And when she doesn't react to my words, I start to believe she is.

But then, she lifts her head from my chest, her eyes finding mine, and I realize my mistake.

Her brow wrinkles with a frown, and I can't help but reach out and try to smooth the lines from her skin.

"What have you got to be sorry about?" she whispers, her eyes searching mine.

My lips part, although I've no idea what I'm about to say when she gasps as realization strikes.

"You knew," she breathes.

In a rush, she scrambles from my body and off the bed.

"Baby girl, come back," I urge as she stands there, glaring at me with her hands on her hips.

My cock jerks at the sight of her. Her fire makes me burn red hot for her, even if I'm the one who's fucked up and should be on my hands and knees groveling for forgiveness.

"Don't baby girl me," she hisses. "Why, Tristan? Why didn't you tell me that he was out? That he could—" A sob rips up her throat, cutting off her words.

Pushing myself up, I rest back against the headboard and keep my eyes on her as my heart begins to beat out of control.

"I was going to but—"

"But what? I've been living here all week, sleeping in your bed. If I knew you were lying to me then I never would have—"

"NO," I boom, throwing the covers off and stalking toward her. "Do not say whatever was about to roll off your tongue."

Her face twists up in anger.

"I had every intention of telling you, Violet. I just... after the fire, I couldn't do it. You were hurting so much after being dragged right back to that time, and I didn't want to make it worse."

"That wasn't your call to make, Tristan."

Her chest heaves as she stares up at me, pain and betrayal darkening her eyes.

"I deserved to know. I had as much right if not more than you to know that he could ambush me like that. You should have told me."

"I didn't think he would come back here."

She throws her hands up in frustration.

"Oh yeah. How well did that work out for you?" she hisses, pulling her side of the closet open.

"Pip, what are you doing?" I ask as she reaches in and drags some clothes out before reaching for some underwear and pulling a pair of panties up her legs.

"I trusted you, Tristan. I—" She cuts herself off again, focusing on pulling her clothes on.

I stand there naked, practically bleeding out all over the floor as I watch her prepare to run from me.

"Pip," I breathe, reaching out and wrapping my fingers around her upper arm.

She stills with her back to me, but she doesn't look over.

"I trusted you, Tristan. I trusted you more than anyone else in my life. And you lied to me."

She shrugs her shoulder, effectively slipping from my grasp and then the room.

"Violet, don't run from me, please. Let me just—"

She spins around, finally looking at me when she's at the front door.

Her eyes hold mine before they defy her and drop down my naked body.

I'm not sure if she's aware she does it, but as her gaze holds my cock, her tongue sneaks out and licks across her bottom lip.

"Don't run, please," I beg.

My voice makes her eyes snap back up to mine, and she stares at me with hurt and confusion swirling in her emerald eyes.

"You don't get to keep secrets from me, Tristan. I'm not a

little girl anymore. And," she adds when I open my mouth to tell her that I'm more than aware that she's not, "you don't get to distract me with sex. That's an asshole move."

"I know," I confess, lifting my hand to the back of my neck as my skin prickles with regret.

"I want you, Tristan. I want this," she says, throwing her hand out, gesturing to the apartment and the newly delivered furniture that she raced past, "but I won't live with a liar or someone who doesn't think I can handle the truth. I'm not weak, Tristan. And frankly, it's insulting that you think I am."

"No," I argue. "I know more than anyone how strong you are, Violet. I didn't tell you because I didn't think you couldn't handle it. More like I couldn't handle watching you struggling with all of this."

"Then that is on you. My life has been one massive clusterfuck since I was sixteen. At this point, there is nothing I can't handle." She holds her hands out to her sides. "So go on, throw it at me. Anything you might be hiding."

I swallow nervously. I fucked up not telling her about Knox, there is so much more to that whole thing than she realizes. And while I might only be making this worse for myself by keeping my lips shut, it's not my story to tell.

"Right, well," she mutters, pulling the front door open.

"Wait." I dart forward, grabbing her arm again.

"No." She jumps out of my reach. "You don't get to pull the puppy dog face and wiggle your magical dick in front of me to make me forget about this, Tristan."

"I-I wasn't wiggling—" I shake my head. "I'm sorry, Violet. Please just come back in, we can talk and—"

"I'm leaving," she states.

"And what if he's out there?" I ask in a last-ditch attempt to convince her to stay.

"If you don't think I can handle Knox, then you really don't know me as well as I thought you do."

I think back to the scene I walked in on earlier and my fists curl once more. It certainly didn't look like she had anything handled.

"Are you coming back?" I call as she reaches to slam the door behind her.

"I don't know. I guess you'll just have to wait to find out."

The slam echoes through the silent space around us and I fall against the wall, regrets slamming into me.

"MOTHERFUCKER," I boom, bending over and dropping my head into my hands. "You stupid, stupid motherfucker."

I knew something was wrong the moment I discovered my keys were missing. But I never would have imagined my day would end up this fucked.

# 18

# VIOLET

I don't let myself break until I'm in my car and have turned the corner away from Tristan's apartment.

Part of me thought he'd chase me, but the second I heard his roar of anger from the other side of the front door, I knew I was safe.

Watching his face drop as I told him I couldn't trust him hurt as much as discovering the secret he's been keeping.

But fuck him. He never should have kept the fact Knox is free from me. He allowed me to be blindsided by his appearance earlier.

A violent shiver runs down my spine.

He could have been watching me for days, for weeks. I never would have known, or even thought to be suspicious.

I sit bolt upright, wiping my hands across my cheeks as reality hits me.

He could have started that fire in our house. He could have been the one to try and ruin my life a second time. Hell knows he's got form.

But why?

I slump back in my seat with a sigh.

Why does he hate me so much?

We were friends. No, more than friends.

In the dead of night when everyone else was sleeping, he was everything to me. He shed his bad boy gangster image at my door and was just Knox. The sweet boy who would listen to my teenage girl issues and kiss me until I forgot all about them in favor of him.

He was the one who—

I slam that line of thought down.

It was bad enough being assaulted by memories as he pressed me up against the wall earlier.

Only now, he's not the boy I remember. He's a man.

A man who's capable of a whole host of things that really should make me run in the opposite direction. But just like before, and despite everything, my first thought earlier wasn't running.

And I hate myself for it.

"I'm sorry, Mom," I whisper. "I'm fucking this all up."

My tears come harder with that realization, and I drive with my vision so blurred that I really should pull over and get a grip of myself. But I never do.

I continue down the familiar roads, leaving Tristan and his bullshit lies behind me, as I drive straight back into my past.

My tears are still clinging to my lashes as I pull through the gates and roll to a stop in front of the house.

I kill the engine and rest back, staring up at the building before me.

Just like every time I look at it, think of it, even pride washes through me. Pride and a whole shitload of grief.

Mom would have loved it. She's the reason I did it.

To start with, I was content to just walk away and forget about everything that ever happened here.

But in the weeks and months after her death, I knew I couldn't abandon her and the house she loved like that.

She'd already lost so much. Dad when we were just kids,

her parents way, way too young, and then her new love and her life all in the same night.

Before losing her, I never put any thought into the afterlife, but while I was trying to keep myself together with the help of Tristan and his parents after my world fell apart, I realized that if there is one, that if she is up there somewhere looking down on me, then she'd have hated that I left her home as a pile of ruins and ash.

Thanks to Mom's financial background, she ensured that both Roman and I would be looked after in case of her death, and with Knox joining our family, he was also included in that. With Knox in prison and Roman gone, it made things more complicated than necessary, but eventually, I turned eighteen, claimed what I'd been left and immediately set to work.

Only Tristan, his parents and sister, and the builders of course, knew what I was up to.

It was my project. Something I felt I needed to do for Mom.

And hell, am I so glad I did.

Pushing the door open, I climb out.

The clouds are heavy above me, the air crackling with an impending storm that I'm sure wasn't there when I ran from Tristan's apartment. Although I was so intent on getting away, I could have just missed it.

A little excitement flutters in my stomach, pushing some of the grief and anger aside.

One of my favorite things to do as a kid was to sit out on the deck with Mom and Roman, hot chocolates in our hands, some cookies between us as the rain lashed the yard and lightning streaked through the sky.

My only wish back then was for a bigger and better deck. One with a huge swing that we could cuddle up on under a blanket together.

That was also the first thing I drew and described to the builders I hired to bring this place back to life.

Longing for those easy days with my family, I climb the steps to my new deck, the one of my dreams. Unlocking the storage closet at the end of the decking, I pull out the cushions and place them on the swing before opening the house and slipping inside.

Disappointment hits me just like it does every time I come back here when the old scent of my home, my childhood, doesn't hit me, instead, a clean yet unlived-in aroma.

Forcing down my emotions, I set about making my hot chocolate just like Mom used to and grab the packet of cookies in the cupboard.

Despite the fact I don't spend much time here, almost everything I could need if I felt the urge to run away—much like now—is here. I could survive here alone, hiding from the world for a pretty long time. Not that I really think Tristan would allow that to happen.

He knows where I go when life gets too much. He's the only one, though. Every time I've come to hide out over the past few years, I've always had this unrealistic fantasy that he could turn up, sweep me off my feet and whisper all the things I've wanted him to say to me in my ear as he carried me up to my bed.

It was stupid. He was miles away, living his best life. He didn't even know that I'd checked out, let alone that I'd run here.

A girl can dream, though.

Sometimes, it wasn't even Tristan.

It was Knox.

And that fantasy fucked me up more than I wanted to admit.

I used to put it down to the fact I was here, the place the two of us got close. Where we confessed our secrets and our dreams.

I always had a hard time separating the Knox I knew and

the Knox that always ended back up in Harrow Creek with his Hawk friends.

I wanted to believe that the boy I got to know in the dead of night was the real person, that the brutal, violent gangster was just a front, a part he felt he needed to play because of where he comes from.

But it was all a lie. As I ignored the warning signs and allowed myself to get lost in him, he got swallowed up by Victor Harris and the Hawks, and he wasn't the only one he was dragging down with him.

Hating where my thoughts have gone, I abandon my drink and make my way toward the stairs.

As always, my door is the only one that's open.

I push it wider and just stand there on the threshold.

Instantly, memories slam into me and I have to reach out for the doorframe for support.

*"Hey, can I come in?" Knox asks, poking his head around my door.*

*"No," I sniffle.*

*Lifting my hand, I swipe the tears from my cheeks and try to put myself back together.*

*I shouldn't be crying. It was just a stupid fight. But Roman always knows exactly what buttons to press to kickstart the waterworks.*

*Asshole.*

*"Come on, Firefly," he whispers, inviting himself inside despite what I just said.*

*"Knox," I complain when he reaches for my hands, drags me to my feet and wraps his arms around me.*

*I suck in a shuddering breath as his scent and warmth surround me.*

*It's been a few months since that night we first kissed, and we've done it more than a couple of times since.*

*Every single night I go to bed, hoping that he's going to slip into my room unnoticed and climb in with me.*

*Part of me wants to escalate things, to take it to the next level. But I'm scared.*

*I know he's already been with girls. That he knows what he's doing. And I can't help feeling like a naïve little virgin.*

*Plus, there's that massive elephant in the room that I try not to think about: he's my stepbrother. I'm pretty sure both my mom and his dad will freak the hell out if—when—we get caught. And I don't even want to consider what Roman would do. Over the past few weeks, he's been getting angrier and angrier at the world. More than once he's turned up with a busted face and ruined knuckles. And I've heard him begging Knox to take him to the Creek with him so they can party. The exact reason for our argument just now.*

*I'm worried about him, but apparently, it's not my place and I need to butt out of his life.*

*I might be his little sister, but I'm not stupid. I can see him spiraling, and I think I have every right to say something, to be concerned.*

*As I think about the cutting words he spat at me, another sob breaks free.*

*"Please don't cry, Vi. I don't like seeing you sad."*

*He takes my face in his hands and stares down into my eyes.*

*My breath catches at the intensity within his gaze.*

*"I'm sorry, I—"*

*"I know a way to make you forget."*

*His eyes bounce between mine before dropping to my lips.*

*"Kiss me," I blurt before thinking better of it. "Make me forget."*

*He remains motionless in front of me for a few seconds, so long that I start to think I screwed up. He's never second-guessed kissing me since that first night. Did he hear something in that argument that's made him change his mind or—*

*"Where are you going?" I ask in a panic when he suddenly releases me and marches toward my closed door.*

*My brows pinch when he doesn't pull it open but instead*

*grabs the chair from behind my desk and wedges it under the door handle.*

*My heart jumps into my throat as my head spins with what his intentions could be.*

*"Knox?" I breathe, my pulse picking up speed as he double-checks it's in place properly and turns back toward me.*

*When his eyes find mine, they're darker and even more intense than they were earlier.*

*My stomach tumbles with nerves, and it only gets worse when he reaches behind his head and drags his shirt from his body.*

*Oh fuck.*

*I've seen him shirtless countless times. Although, less recently. And I realize why the second his skin is revealed to me.*

*"Knox, when did you..." My words trail off as my eyes take in the ink on his chest and stomach. They're not big or anything, but hell if they don't make him look even more dangerous than he usually does.*

*He really is the bad boy that every mother out there warns their daughters about.*

*"You want me to stop, all you've got to do is say the word. Okay?"*

*I nod, my mind spinning with possibilities about what's going to happen next.*

*"Talk to me, Firefly. I need your words."*

*"Y-yes. I'll tell you if—" I swallow nervously.*

*"If," he prompts, cupping my jaw and forcing me to look up at him.*

*"If I want you to stop, I just say the word."*

*"Good girl." Before I get a chance to react to that praise, his lips are on mine and his tongue is pushing inside to find mine.*

*A moan rumbles in the back of my throat as I wrap my arms around his neck and willingly press myself against him when his hands find my ass and drag me forward.*

*He devours me, utterly consumes me until the only things I can think about are him and the sensations shooting off around my body from his kiss and innocent-ish touch alone.*

*"Gonna make you feel so good, Firefly," he promises, kissing across my jaw and then down my neck.*

*"Knox," I moan when he sucks gently on the skin beneath my ear, making my blood boil.*

*"I'm addicted to you, Violet," he confesses, making my innocent heart soar.*

*"Oh God," I whimper when he drops lower, kissing down my exposed chest until he hits the hem of my tank.*

*"Arms up," he demands, and I immediately do as I'm told.*

*He moves his lips from me for just long enough for the fabric to pass his face, and then his burning kisses are back.*

*"Okay?" he asks, glancing up at me.*

*I nod, unable to find any words as he brazenly cups my lace-covered breasts in his hand.*

*My head falls back and a moan rips free when he flicks his thumbs over my nipples.*

*"Oh shit."*

*I look forward again, desperate to watch him, just as he drops to his knees before me.*

*Holding my hips in his hands, he leans forward and peppers kisses down my stomach.*

*Something erupts between my legs that I've never felt before. Flutters. That's the only thing I can describe it as as his lips draw lower, hitting my waistband.*

*"Remember, just say the word," he reminds me before he flicks my skirt open and lets it drop to the floor, leaving me standing there in my less-than-sexy white cotton underwear.*

*My eyes slam closed as mortification floods my veins.*

Jesus, Violet. That's a surefire way to turn off an experienced boy like Knox.

*"Violet," he growls. "Don't do that."*

*Before I know what's happening, he's on his feet again, his fingers are in my hair, and his lips are back on mine.*

*He walks me back toward my bed. The second my calves hit the mattress, I have no choice but to allow him to lay me down.*

*Without breaking our kiss, he crawls between my thighs and lifts me higher up the bed.*

*His hands roam around my body, his touch leaving tingles in its wake.*

*My loud gasp rips through the air when he presses himself against me... there.*

*He's hard. Really freaking hard. And it feels. God. It feels insane.*

*"You feel that?" he asks, although my reaction a second ago was evidence enough that I did.*

*"Y-yeah," I stutter, barely able to force my brain to function as he begins grinding against me. "Oh God."*

*"Good?"*

*I nod, my teeth sinking into my bottom lip as my body burns up.*

*"Has anyone ever made you come before, Firefly?" he asks, his voice deep and raspy. It sends a shiver down my spine and makes my skin erupt in goose bumps.*

*I shake my head, my cheeks burning with embarrassment. But my need to continue is stronger.*

*"Have you made yourself come before?" he asks, holding my eyes firm.*

*Again, I shake my head.*

*"Damn. You shouldn't be giving me this," he tells me with absolute certainty in his voice.*

*My lips part, ready to tell him that I want him to have it, but he beats me to it.*

*"I'm going to take it, though. I don't have all that much good in my life, Firefly. But you... fuck. You show me how things could be. What I could deserve if I were a different person."*

*"No, Knox," I attempt to argue, but he rolls his hips again*

*and it comes out as nothing more than a needy plea.*

*"You're close, baby," he tells me. "Want me to continue?"*

*I eagerly nod as my body tightens like a spring. I've no idea what's going to happen, but I do know that I want to know how it feels when I finally snap.*

*Tucking his hand under my ass, he tilts my hips a little and leans over me, claiming my lips in a bruising kiss as his hips pick up speed.*

*Only twenty seconds later, something explodes within me and I scream into his kiss as pleasure like I've never known takes over my entire body.*

*"Fucking hell," he groans as his movements continue while I writhe beneath him. "You're too fucking beautiful for me, Firefly."*

*"More," I beg without realizing.*

*"Thank fuck, because I need to see that again. Only this time, you're going to come on my tongue."*

*My eyes open impossibly wide at his words, but I'm powerless to say anything as he scoots down my body, wraps his fingers around the sides of my panties and drags them down my thighs.*

*I should be embarrassed being so exposed, but the second he spreads my thighs wide and stares down at me, this look of complete awe covers his face and I forget about everything apart from how his tongue might feel.*

*Apparently, it's meant to be— "KNOX," I cry when he licks me.*

*"Shh, Firefly. No one else in this house can know about this. I need you to be a good girl for me, okay?"*

*I nod, my eyes locked on his over my body as I clap my hand over my mouth and silently urge him to continue.*

"Fucking hell," I mutter to myself, my body burning up just from those memories alone. Anyone would think that Tristan hadn't got me off only a few hours ago.

Knox has taught me a lot of things over the years. But that

afternoon... That was by far one of my favorites. That along with—

I shake my head, forcing myself to step out of my memories of better times in favor of focusing on the shit show I'm living right now.

Ignoring the ache between my thighs, I look around my bedroom once more and walk away.

My heart is in my throat as I make my way back downstairs. The second I collect up my mug and cookies, a loud crack of thunder cuts through the air and I race out to the deck.

Curling my feet up beneath me, I stare out over the yard as the first fat raindrops begin to fall.

The deep growl of the impending storm continues to rumble above me as I wrap my hands around my mug and bring it to my lips, gently blowing over the surface to cool it.

I glance to my side, hating the space there. Hating that once again, I'm all alone in this world.

Without taking a sip, I lower my mug once more and let out a long sigh as the events of today spin around in my head.

I'm chewing on a cookie when the first bolt of lightning streaks through the dark night sky, lighting up everything around me for just a few seconds.

Something settles inside me, being out here in the middle of the turbulent weather. It was always our happy place, and even with them gone, it makes me feel closer to them. Even if it is wrapped in pain and sadness.

Throwing the rest of my cookie into my mouth, I drag the back of my hand across my cheek, wiping the wetness away.

I drink my hot chocolate and let its warmth comfort me along with the sugar hit from the cookie while the storm continues to rage only a few feet away. It's not until there's a succession of bolts of lightning that a loud gasp rips from my lips and I realize that I'm not here alone.

I'm being watched.

## 19

# KNOX

All eyes turn on me the second I step into the living room at the Harrises' house. It's only a few minutes from Tristan's place, something I've no idea if Reid knew or not when he put me up here. I can only assume he did, seeing as Reid fucking Harris seems to know everything there is to know about everything.

I'm hardly surprised. He was always like that as a kid—inquisitive as fuck and always getting into trouble with his need to know more.

His destiny might have always been to take over the Hawks from his dad, but I swear that shit was in his blood long before he knew what his life was going to be.

He's fucking good at it too.

I might have been lacking visitors during my time in prison—mostly my fault, after refusing to see anyone the first few times they asked. Okay, Tristan. I refused point blank to see Tristan. But Reid was always there for me, no matter what.

I was scared. Scared to hear that I'd made the wrong call with the fallout of that day. Terrified that by doing what I thought was right, I'd only fucked everything up more than it already was. And it was pretty damn fucked up. Even I could admit that.

Being locked up in that prison cell, it was easy to pretend that everything—aside from the obvious—was okay outside. That the girl who had become everything to me over the past couple of months was surrounded by people who loved her, who could get her through the coming days and months.

Pain lashed at my insides, knowing what she lost that night.

I probably should have been grieving too. But the only thing I lost was her. Her, Tristan, and Roman.

My dad... yeah, I didn't care all that much about him.

I'd been deep enough in with Reid and the Hawks to know that my father was on borrowed time. He was firmly on Victor Harris's shit list, and no one stays on there very long.

I can't lie, I was pissed when I first discovered we were moving out of Harrow Creek and straight into a ready-made family.

I should have seen it for what it was immediately. Dad was running. Although nowhere near far enough.

I want to believe he did actually love Rose. That there was something between them. The alternative is a little hard to swallow. The thought of him targeting them doesn't sit right with me. It's how I know that while I might be his son, I'm not like him.

They were innocent. Roman had a promising future and Rose wanted nothing more than to see her children live happy, successful lives. But he wiped it away from both of them and caused my firefly more pain and suffering than she ever deserved.

But he's not the one who ended up taking the blame for what happened that night.

That's me.

I'm the one she hates. I'm the one she probably regrets ever going near, ever kissing, ever...

"Fuck," I hiss, shoving my hair back from my brow as images from our past play out in my mind.

They've been on repeat for five years. I've dissected every single second of our time together and tortured myself with it.

But as much as taking myself back there hurts, it's what's got me through.

The promise of seeing her again, even if it has to be from a distance, it's what I've dreamed of.

And fuck if it wasn't better than I ever imagined.

Feeling her body against mine after so long, breathing in her familiar scent.

I knew my obsession with her when I was a kid was a little unhinged. I put it down to the lack of affection I'd grown up with. I might have been with girls before, but never in the way I was with Violet. None of them made my heart race and my hands tremble like when I was close to her.

She should have turned me away that first time I invited myself into her bed. She should have kept our late-night meetings to the safety of the kitchen. But fuck me, am I glad she didn't.

The only problem was, the more I got of her, the more pieces I wanted to keep.

And nothing had changed.

Hell, discovering that she's now Tristan's, only adds fuel to the already out-of-control inferno of jealousy that's raging inside me.

She remembered too.

She might have wished that I'd burned to nothing but ash in that fire with our parents, but in those emerald eyes, I saw a flash of recognition, of longing.

She hasn't forgotten a moment of what happened between us.

And despite the fact she may never forgive me for what I've done, seeing that... it was enough to remind me of why I did what I did that night.

If only it had gone to plan.

"What the fuck happened to you?" Devin barks, amusement dancing in his eyes, reminding me of the beating I took not so long ago.

"Fuck you," I grunt, marching through the living room toward the kitchen for a much-needed drink.

I drag the refrigerator open and pull out two beers, immediately twisting the cap off the first one and downing it.

"Living your best life now you're a free man, huh?" Devin says, having followed me. I'm not surprised—he's not one to be left out of the gossip. Thankfully though, the twins stay put in the living room.

"Something like that," I mutter, throwing the bottle in the trash before starting on the second one.

"You finally go to the Creek?"

I shake my head. I haven't returned yet. Well, that's a lie. I've been over the border, but only as far as Reid's place. He might be happy bringing me straight back into the fold as if I never left, but I'm not quite as willing to dive back in.

I'll take his jobs, pay off the debt I'm now in for my freedom, but I've no desire to go back there. Not until I have to, at least.

I'd be naïve to think it won't happen eventually. I'm a Hawk. I have been since the day I was born.

I sold my soul to the devil long before I had to get my hands dirty to ensure my future as a free man. The ink that I've been gifted with alongside my freedom is merely a rite of passage, something that all young boys in the Creek dream of, but the reality is so very different from what we're led to believe.

"So who've you been dancing with then? Violet finally figure out you've been stalking her and proved that prison turned you into a pussy?" Anger licks at my insides the second her name rolls off his lips.

"Don't fucking talk about her," I snarl.

"Bro, you are fucked, you know that, right?"

Prior to me being put away, Violet was my dirty little secret. It should have stayed that way. But my obsession has apparently been written all over my face since I got back here. That and he followed me one night to see where I was slinking off to.

"I'm not talking about this with you." I drain my second beer and push from the side.

"My advice not good enough for you?" he teases.

"What fucking advice, Dev? You can barely make a woman come let alone anything else."

His brow practically hits his hairline at my words.

"I'll have you know, Bowman, that I had some chick screaming my name seven times in one night recently," he states proudly.

"Sure you did," I drawl, heading for the door.

I have every intention of heading up to my room, but the second I reach for the door he closed so we could talk in private, his words stop me in my tracks.

"Just tell her the truth."

I suck in a deep breath as I consider the words I've imagined saying to her a million times over in the past five years.

"I can't," I breathe, pulling the door open and marching back out of the house.

Devin's keys are still in my pocket, so I jump back into his car and take off before I've even considered where I'm going.

The sky is dark, the clouds heavy with rain, and the air is electric with the impending storm.

It pretty much matches my mood as I drive away from the Harrises' part of town in favor of losing myself in the quiet country roads.

As a kid, Maddison County seemed like the most boring place on the planet. As far as we could tell from the depths of the Creek, it was filled with pretentious old people who drove Priuses around and worked dumb desk jobs.

The idea of living that kind of suburban bullshit life was abhorrent. Not when we could spend our days running around the shithole we lived in wielding guns, running drugs, fighting and killing our enemies. We literally thought we were living in our own computer game. I guess, in some ways we were. It was all fantasy. The reality was dark, brutal, painful, and full of nothing but regrets and secrets.

I guess nothing has really changed.

Huge raindrops begin splashing against the windshield as I turn into a familiar neighborhood. I pass the suburban houses I hated when Dad first moved us here, and I can't help a weirdly comforting nostalgia washing over me at the sight of them. I craved our old dirty trailer, the noise, the late-night parties, the gunshots, the chaos.

I thought he'd lost his mind, bringing us here.

He had, I just wasn't aware that this wasn't his worst idea. That came in the form of defying Victor Harris's orders.

I pass house after house, closing in on the place that I called home for a few years. A place I never wanted to be, a place I never thought I'd fit but ultimately, I did.

I found a little bit of solitude in that house. Or at least I did with the boys who lived there, and the tempting girl who stupidly opened her heart to me.

I have no idea what to expect as I close in on the driveway to that house. I haven't seen it since the night it was going up in flames, and quite frankly, I never planned to visit again. I guess it was naïve of me to think I wouldn't want to revisit the best times of my life. I'd be an idiot to even try to convince myself that those moments weren't in her bedroom while she was in my arms.

My breath catches when I turn the final corner of the street and discover a new set of gates. But it's not just the gates that surprise me, but the fact they're open.

I pull over and abandon Devin's car on the side of the quiet road and walk toward the gates. Thunder claps above me, the rain instantly soaking my shirt. But now I'm here, I need to see.

I know the property, or more so the land, has never been sold. It didn't take much research to find that out. But I've been assuming that it had been abandoned. That Violet would have walked away and left the horror of that night behind us.

"Oh shit," I gasp as I slip around the perimeter of the land and find the opposite of what I was expecting.

It might be dark, the sheeting rain making it hard to see much, but there is no mistaking the huge, familiar house that stands before me.

And it's not just the house that surprises me because there are lights on.

If it's possible, the rain gets harder as the first bolt of lightning streaks through the night, lighting up the house before me and giving me a glimpse of its beauty.

I shake my head in disbelief.

She rebuilt it.

Her family home that I watched burn and crumble almost around me stands before me, almost as if nothing happened. Only better. Bigger. More perfect.

It's a massive headfuck.

If it weren't for the vivid memories of that night that still haunt my dreams, then I might think it never really happened.

But it did. The regrets, the scars, and the pain of the last five years are a constant reminder that it was very real.

Another crack of lightning allows me to see why there are lights on.

There's someone sitting out on the deck.

No. Not someone.

Violet.

My little firefly.

*"Is anyone sitting here?" I ask, pointing to the small space*

*beside Violet that I have no chance of squeezing into.*

*The second it started raining, I pressed my foot to the gas to get back to the house faster.*

*Dad and Rose are out for their weekly date night, and I've just left a wasted and high Roman behind in Harrow Creek.*

*I should have thrown him in the car and forced him to come back. But when he threw a punch the second I so much as suggested it, so I thought 'fuck it' and headed home alone. The temptation of having Violet to myself until our parents returned was too much to ignore.*

*So I left the stupid fuck to drown in cheap vodka and even cheaper pussy and made my way back to his little sister.*

*I knew we were on borrowed time, sneaking around behind everyone's backs, but I couldn't stop.*

*I was addicted to my little firefly, and with every touch, every kiss, I was only falling deeper into her trap.*

*I was drawn into her light like a moth to a flame, and hell if I ever wanted that to change. I knew it was going to, though.*

*No one was going to approve of our relationship.*

*I was the bad boy gangster from the wrong side of the tracks. Rose might have fallen in love with my father and allowed us into her home, but I'm not naïve enough to think she'd want me for her daughter.*

*Why would any mother who doesn't live in the Creek want a Hawk for their daughter?*

*We're about as close as you can get to the devil.*

*But that doesn't mean I'm going to walk away from her. It's impossible, she's buried herself too deep inside me for that. Which is fucking ironic, seeing as I haven't even been inside her yet.*

*I might only be seventeen, but growing up in a place like the Creek, being a Hawk and friends with its future leader meant we grew up fast. Hanging out with a girl, getting to know her, and spending hours only making out in her bed is not my MO. But then, Violet isn't like my usual girls either.*

*She's sweet, caring—real. She's not just after a bit of Hawk dick, so strung out with her bullshit existence that she needs a little attention and pleasure to drown everything out.*

*Violet is the polar opposite of those girls.*

*She's...*

*She's everything.*

*"What the hell are you doing?" she gasps when she finally realizes that I'm walking toward her with the rain soaking through my clothes. It's been a scorching summer's day, and despite the sun sinking, it's still almost unbearably hot. I'll dry again in minutes, I'm sure. Although, that doesn't stop me from reaching behind my head and pulling my shirt from my body.*

*The move is almost entirely selfish, because I have an obsession—yeah, another one—with the way Violet stares at my body. I'm almost as addicted to that look of awe she gets in her eyes as I am with her own bare skin.*

*Fuck, just the thought of her insane tits makes my cock ache.*

*Over the past few weeks, I've dished out more orgasms than I thought I ever would without receiving one in return. But I quickly discovered that watching her come is better than any release I've ever had.*

*She's so fucking beautiful when she throws her head back and cries out my name.*

*I make my way toward her, not caring about the fact she'll easily be able to see the way my cock is tenting my jeans with the soft lights that line the deck.*

*She knows I want her. That is not a secret. But she's nervous to go there. And I get it, I understand. I actually fucking love the fact she's holding back, being the opposite of what I'm used to. It'll only make it so much sweeter when it does happen.*

*"Coming to watch the storm with you. What do you think?" I say, jogging up the steps to the deck and marching over to her.*

*Resting my hands on the back of her chair on either side of her head, I lean forward and steal a kiss.*

*"Hi," I say, staring down into her eyes.*

*"Hi," she squeaks, sounding way too innocent and looking entirely too tempting sitting out here in nothing but her tiny pajamas. The fabric of her tank is thin enough to clearly show how hard her nipples are from my kiss alone, and I don't need her to stand up to know that half her ass will be on display in her shorts. "I thought you were partying in the Creek," she says, staring up at me with large eyes that suck me right in.*

*"And I thought you were doing homework," I tease.*

*"I was until the storm started. I wanted to watch."*

*"So did I," I confess.*

*Her brow pinches as she hears my unspoken words.*

*"You came back to watch the storm with me?"*

*"It isn't as much fun alone, is it?" Her smile only gets wider. "Shift over."*

*"Your jeans are wet," she says, her eyes dropping to the sodden fabric.*

*"Okay."*

*Pushing from her chair, I rip the button open, kick off my sneakers, and shove the wet fabric down my legs.*

*Her gasp cuts through the air as thunder rumbles dangerously in the distance.*

*When I glance over, I find her eyes locked on where my cock is more than obviously hard beneath my boxers and her teeth sinking into her bottom lip.*

*"Better?" I ask, shamelessly holding my hands out to my sides so she can get a better look.*

*"U-uh... yeah."*

*Before she gets a chance to move, I wrap my hands around her waist and lift her from the seat, lower my ass to it and place her on my lap.*

*A contented moan rumbles in her chest as I wrap my arms around her waist and hold tight.*

*"I missed you," she whispers, tilting her face and kissing my neck.*

*My chest swells at her words. I'm pretty sure no one has ever missed me before.*

*Sure, my dad likes having me around to continue his Hawks legacy. My mother clearly didn't give a fuck because she left when I was a toddler and never looked back. And I'm not sure anyone in the Creek would really notice if I just fucked off. Reid might, but he's got plenty of future Hawks vying for his attention. I'd be stupid to think I was anything special to him.*

*Just another dumb wannabe that will ask how high the second he tells me to jump.*

*Bitterness swirls around in my gut at the thought. Reid's been there at my side all my life. He's my best friend. But I know that he'd sell me out in a heartbeat if he needed to. He's a Hawk through and through. It literally runs through his veins. And nothing is more important to any Harris than the Hawks.*

*"I missed you too, Firefly."*

*Sliding her hand up my chest, she wraps it around my neck and nudges my jaw with her thumb to make me look her way.*

*The second I turn, she captures my lips in a filthy kiss that does nothing for the boner that's happily pressing against her thigh.*

*The thunder claps and the lightning strikes around us, but we never part, too lost in each other, in the connection we've found between us to care about anything else.*

*Our tongues duel and our teeth clash. It doesn't matter that she's the good girl from Maddison County who's grown up with money and a loving mother and that I'm the bad boy from the Creek who has done things she couldn't even imagine. When we're together, we're just us. Just two kids lost in the moment, in each other. It's a heady feeling. One I never want to lose.*

*Shifting, I grab her ass and twist her around so she's straddling my waist.*

*She gasps as my hard length grazes her pussy.*

*"Knox," she moans into our kiss, her hips rolling against me.*

*"Fuck, Firefly. You undo me."*

*My fingers tighten on her ass, dragging her harder against me.*

*"Gonna make you come for me, baby."*

*"Yes," she breathes, her hot breath racing down my neck as the coolness from the rain pelts the ground around us.*

*I roll my hips as she does, grinding myself against her, desperate to remove the two thin layers of fabric and sink inside her.*

*"You make me so hard, Firefly. Can you feel it?"*

*"Knox," she moans, arching her back and pushing her tits closer.*

*Releasing her with one hand, I drag the straps of her tank down her shoulders and expose her breasts.*

*"Oh God."*

*"You're so beautiful, Violet," I tell her before leaning forward and sucking one of her nipples into my mouth.*

*She cries out as the heat of my lips surrounds her before I begin teasing her tight bud with the tip of my tongue.*

*My cock is so hard it's painful as she uses it to get herself off. Precum leaks from the tip, soaking my boxers and mixing with her wetness.*

*"I can feel how wet you are for me, baby. You gonna come all over my dick?"*

*She nods, unable to find any words as she races toward her release.*

*Pinching one of her nipples, I lick at the other one, her movements above me becoming jerky and erratic the closer she gets.*

*"Come for me, Firefly. I want to watch you fall over the edge and hear you scream my name."*

*I nip at her breast with my teeth, and the bite of pain is the final straw that makes her shatter.*

*"KNOX." My name echoes around us as a loud clap of thunder booms overhead.*

*Her body quakes, her muscles convulsing as she rides out her release before collapsing onto me in a breathless heap.*

*"Fucking love watching you come, Firefly."*

*My entire body shudders with need when she kisses down my neck.*

*"I want to watch you, too," she confesses quietly before sucking on my earlobe.*

*Fuck yes.*

*"You don't have to do anything, Violet. Watching you is enough." I never in my entire horny teenage life thought I'd ever say that and actually mean it, but then, I guess I'd never met anyone like Violet before.*

*My muscles bunch the second her hand lands on my stomach and descends south.*

*I swallow roughly, terrified that I'm gonna blow the second she touches me. I'm already riding on the edge from her dry humping me.*

*"Shit," I hiss as her fingers slip under the waistband of my boxers.*

*Misreading my issue, she sits up in a panic.*

*"Am I doing something wrong?" she asks, her eyes wide in fear.*

*"Baby, you've got your hand in my pants. Trust me, there's not much you can do wrong."*

*Twisting my fingers in her hair, I drag her forward and kiss her, hoping to give her the confidence she needs to continue.*

*After a few seconds of hesitation, she continues her exploration.*

*"Oh fuck," I grunt when her delicate fingers wrap around my length.*

*Lifting my hips, I shove my boxers down, freeing my cock for her.*

*"I-I don't kno—"*

*Hating hearing her sound so unsure of herself, I wrap my fingers around hers and encourage her to stroke me.*

*A growl of desire rips from my lips as she follows my instruction like a pro.*

*I release her after a few seconds, allowing her to continue without me.*

*Sitting back, her gaze drops to where she's holding me, her eyes widening at the sight.*

*I won't lie, my chest does puff out a little that she's in awe of my size. It seems the arrogant bad boy within me never really leaves.*

*"Fuck, baby," I groan, obsessed with the sight of her fingers wrapped around me.*

*"Okay?" she asks nervously.*

*"So fucking good. I'm close."*

*"Yeah?" she asks, unable to fight the proud smile that curls at her lips.*

*"A little tighter."*

*She instantly does as she's told, and not three seconds later, my balls draw up, pleasure flooding my veins a beat before my cock jerks in her hand and I come all over my stomach.*

*I groan as the orgasm claims me, but mostly, it's for the way she stares at me. Stares at her delicate fingers wrapped around my thick shaft and then up to the sticky evidence of what we just did.*

*Lightning cuts through the sky once more, illuminating both of us.*

*"Firefly," I say, reaching out and tucking my fingers under her chin so I can find her eyes.*

*My breath catches in my throat when I do, because her usually sparkling emerald eyes are dark with desire and her lips are swollen from our kisses.*

*"Fuck. You're everything," I confess, dragging her forward and pushing my tongue into her mouth once more.*

*She kisses me like she'd die without it, and in only a*

*minute, I'm hard for her again. Helped by the fact that she hasn't let me go.*

*Seems my innocent little firefly might just like my dick after all.*

*"Knox," she breathes when she realizes just how much she affects me.*

*"I told you, you undo me, baby."*

*Her hand starts stroking me again, and I somehow manage to find some self-restraint to put a stop to it. Not that I don't want to let her spend all night making me come to make up for lost time, but because I want more from her than just that.*

*"You wanna be crazy with me?"*

*Her eyes flick down to my cock once more. "I thought we already were. Anyone could see us out here, Knox."*

*It's not entirely true. The house sits quite a way back from the quiet road beyond the gates. No one, unless they were snooping right now, would see us. Or our parents, if they decided to come home early. I'm pretty sure their headlights would give them away long before they spotted us. Or at least, we can hope that would be the case.*

*"I'd never let anyone see you like this, Firefly. You're mine. All fucking mine."*

*She squeals as I stand with her in my arms.*

*"What are you doing?" she asks as I back her up against the railing, the spray from the rain hitting our skin.*

*Regretfully, I cover her tits back up before tugging my boxers over my aching dick.*

*"We're going to play a game," I tell her, my lips brushing hers.*

*"Oh yeah?"*

*"When I get to one, you've gotta run." Her brows rise in interest. "And you're going to have to guess what I'll do to you when I catch you."*

*"You sound confident that you will."*

*"Baby, I'll always catch you."*

# 20

# VIOLET

My heart jumps into my throat as the dark figure loitering by the bushes takes a step closer.

"No, no, no," I whisper to myself.

I came here for peace, for some space to think, not to be stalked and forced to face my past once again.

He moves closer still, the rain splashing from his huge body—a body I barely recognize from that of the boy I used to know—and I have to squeeze my eyes closed in an attempt to squash the memories that are threatening.

*"When I get to one, you've gotta run." Intrigue rips through me at his words.*

*Knox Bowman is an enigma that I'm still desperately trying to figure out. I overhear all these awful, brutal things when he's talking openly with his dad or Roman. But then he slips into my room and he's the sweetest, most patient guy. It's a headfuck. But one I'm completely addicted to. I love knowing that I get this secret side to him. It makes me feel special, like this thing we've found together could be something. Sadness knowing that we could never be anything serious washes over me, but it's wiped away when he speaks again. "And you're going to have to guess what I'll do to you when I catch you."*

*Forcing a smile on my lips, I taunt, "You sound confident that you will."*

*"Baby, I'll always catch you."*

*Without lingering to enjoy the butterflies and happiness his statement conjures up in my belly, I take off running across the deck and down the steps to the yard.*

*The rain hits my heated skin and I laugh as I imagine steam coming from my body. Having his hands on me, his lips, his words in my ear... it makes me burn for him in a way I never thought really existed. But it does, and it's a heady feeling knowing that he experiences it too.*

"You undo me, Firefly."

*My stomach twists, remembering his words.*

*Me.*

*Boring, average me. I do that to him. I make him hard constantly. I make him want me. It's... it's unbelievable. But it's true. I see it in his eyes, I feel it in his touch. I felt it beneath my fingers as I jerked him off.*

*Heat unfurls in my lower belly as I remember how he felt, the look of awe on his face as I followed his instructions, the way his dick jerked in my hand as he came, coating his stomach.*

*I look back over my shoulder just in time to see him wipe his cum from his stomach with his discarded shirt before he takes off running after me.*

*My movements falter as I watch his body move. He's a work of art, pure muscle, strength and power.*

*"You're not making it very hard, Firefly," he calls, closing the space between us with every step.*

*"Maybe I don't want to run," I confess, moving back slowly as rain runs down my body, soaking me to the bone. It's not cold, it's refreshing if anything. But with the way Knox is watching me, even if it were the middle of winter, I know that I wouldn't feel it with his burning stare.*

*"That's brave of you, baby," he says in a deadly tone that*

*gives me just a hint of the gangster he always leaves at the door when we're together.*

*"I'm not scared of you."*

*A dark chuckle leaves his lips. "You probably should be. Do you have any idea what I'm capable of?"*

*I nod. It might be a lie, I don't have any concrete evidence, but I have a very good idea.*

*"I've killed people, Violet." Despite assuming it might be the case, my shocked gasp still rips through the air. "With the same hands I touch you with."*

*I nod, keeping my eyes locked on his.*

*"I've done bad things with bad people. Things that would horrify you."*

*"I don't care, Knox."*

*"I'm a bad person, Violet. One who shouldn't be anywhere near someone as sweet and pure as you."*

*"That's my decision to make, not yours."*

*"I'll fuck this up. I'll do something to hurt you, or one day, I won't make it out of the Creek."*

*"Never. You're better than that," I tell him confidently.*

*"I will hurt you," he warns me, the words twisting me up inside, because as much as I don't want to believe them, there's a huge part of me that knows they're true. Even if he has no intention of hurting me, the way he lives his life makes it almost inevitable.*

*"You're worth it."*

*All the air rushes from his lungs at my confession.*

*I don't realize that I'm frozen in place until his warmth burns down the front of my body and his brow presses to mine.*

*"Fuck, Firefly. I don't deserve you," he says roughly, his dark blue eyes boring down into mine as the rain continues to pound around us.*

*"Knox, don't—" My words are cut off when he lifts me into his arms, sweeping my feet from the ground and backing me up*

*against a tree that stands tall in our yard. "Oh God," I gasp, feeling him hard against my core once more.*

*"Can't get enough of you, baby. Addicted," he confesses before pushing his tongue past my lips.*

*The storm continues around us as he utterly consumes me. Every kiss, every touch makes me burn for him, the pounding rain barely cooling the inferno that's erupting between us.*

*My body aches for the pleasure he can give me. It begs me for more, to take it further, to let him give me everything. To give him everything.*

*He shifts us from the tree in favor of laying me down in the grass. He drops between my thighs, continuing to grind into me in the most delicious way.*

*His lips move from mine, kissing and sucking down my throat, whispering confessions of how he feels about me, words that make my heart soar and happiness consume every inch of my body.*

*"I need you, Violet. I need you so fucking bad," he groans against my collarbone.*

*"So take me." The words fall out without instruction from my brain, but that doesn't mean they're any less genuine.*

*He stills above me, and I panic that I might have just said the wrong thing. My heart pounds even more erratically as I wait for him to do something.*

*After a few seconds, he looks up. The intensity in his eyes is something I'll never forget, and it sends a violent shiver through my body.*

*"Shit," he hisses as goose bumps erupt across my skin.*

*The storm has mostly passed now, the thunder only rumbling in the distance and the rain beginning to slow.*

*He scrubs his hand down his face, rubbing at his rough jaw. "You deserve more than this, Violet. More than me." His voice is rough and full of emotion.*

*"No, don't do that. I want this. You."*

*"You'll regret it."*

*"Then they're my regrets to live with. But right now, I don't want to be with anyone else, I want you, Knox. All of you."*

*"Goddamn, Firefly. You wreck me."*

*But despite my words and the desire in his eyes, he never gives me all of him. Instead, he lifts me into his arms and carries me all the way up to my bathroom. He starts the shower, waits for it to warm, and then steps under the spray with me still in his arms.*

*He strips and washes me like I'm the most precious thing in the world before wrapping me in a fluffy towel and laying me out on my bed.*

*Nothing else happens between us, instead, I drift off to sleep locked in his embrace and never feeling more contented in my entire life.*

*He might not believe he's good enough. But I know for a fact he is. He needs to have more faith in himself...*

A heavy sigh passes my lips. I truly believed he was worthy that night. That together, we could conquer anything thrown our way.

If only I knew that we were on a one-way road to our lives being thrown into complete chaos. And all at his hands.

Despite wishing that his presence was a sick and twisted part of my imagination, a vision from all the daydreams about how good things used to be, when I resurface from that most recent memory, I find him almost at the railings.

"You're not welcome here," I shout over the sound of the rain that pounds around him.

Ignoring me, he drags me right back into the past.

"Do you remember what I said to you the last time we were here?" He holds his arms out to his sides, water running from his fingers.

My heart jumps into my throat.

Was he reminiscing too?

"You've said a lot of things to me, Knox. Most of which were laced with lies and bullshit. Did you want to be more specific?" I quip, anger raging almost as strongly as the storm around me.

"Firefly, I—"

"NO," I bark, hopping up and spilling hot chocolate all over my white t-shirt.

I wipe my hand over the fabric as if by some miracle it'll make the brown stain disappear in an attempt to keep face.

"You do not get to turn up here unannounced and act like nothing has happened. Didn't you get the fucking hint earlier? I don't want to so much as look at your face ever again, you—"

"It wasn't me, Violet," he blurts, successfully cutting off the abuse I was about to spit at him.

Disbelief washes through me and I throw my head back and laugh.

But while I'm doing that, I don't notice him move closer.

"It's not fucking funny, Violet," he growls, coming to stop at the bottom of the four steps I'm standing at the top of.

His deep voice makes goose bumps erupt over my skin as my body remembers all the things my brain is trying desperately to forget.

I knew when I was sixteen that I never should have gone anywhere near him. Hell, he told me himself that I'd regret it.

I was so fucking naïve and in love with him, I couldn't see what was right in front of my face.

So what, he gave me a handful of my first orgasms and opened my eyes to a whole world of pleasure I didn't know existed up until that point?

So what, I willingly gave my heart away despite him warning me that he'd shred it sooner or later?

"You're fucking unbelievable. You have no right to be here. No right to be telling me all this shit. You're meant to be gone. You pleaded fucking guilty, Knox. You killed them. You burned this entire place to the ground. How can you stand there and pretend that that didn't happen, try to make me think that we're kids again with no concerns about the future?"

"I told you I'd fuck up," he says like it'll make all this better.

"You ruined my entire fucking life, Knox. You didn't just cheat on me with some Creek whore, you ruined... My. Entire. Fucking. Life," I scream, my emotions, anger, and grief colliding.

He doesn't say anything as I stand there with my chest heaving, my fists balled at my sides and the sheeting rain soaking the front of my body now I'm exposed.

"You know me better than that, Firefly," he eventually says, his voice firm, sure, and just with a hint of his own lingering anger.

"No. All I know for certain is that I never knew you. That boy who used to sneak into my room was a lie, wasn't he? He was acting, pretending to be nice, sweet, and caring just to get his kicks with his forbidden stepsister. All of it was a joke. I see that now."

"Bullshit."

A loud, heart-stopping clap of thunder shakes the ground beneath us not a second after he spits that word before a bolt of lightning streaks through the sky, striking the tree only feet from us.

"Oh shit," I gasp as my feet leave the floor and I'm hauled into a solid chest. "What the hell are you doing?" I screech as his arms lock around me, moving us farther away from the tree as the rain soaks through my hair and clothes.

I kick my legs and tug at his arms to force him to release me, but I achieve nothing.

His heated stare makes my skin burn and my blood boil.

"Put me down. I don't need protecting from lightning, you dick."

"No? So what do you need protecting from?" he asks, a smirk pulling at his lips as if this is actually amusing him.

I gasp as my back slams against the side of the house.

Knox's hands drop to my ass, and the unmistakable hardness of his cock presses against my pussy.

"You," I hiss, fighting against my need to roll my hips.

I will not be that wanton, desperate girl for him.

Not again.

We are long past the time where I beg this boy—this man—for anything other than for him to walk out of my life and never return.

When his eyes widen and his nostrils flare, I realize that I just fucked up.

"You think I'm going to hurt you, Firefly?" he asks, his brows dipping as if even suggesting it is the most insane thing he's ever heard.

"Too late for that. You've already ripped me to pieces. I have nothing left for you to ruin."

Fire fills his eyes as he stares back at me. It's the reminder I need that this man before me is no longer the boy I thought I knew.

That boy was so sweet. This man though, he's... angry. Pissed off at... me?

It was hard to tie teenage Knox with the gangster from the Creek I knew that he was. But now, I see it.

Danger and hatred at the world ooze from him.

I might not be scared. I might believe him when he says he'll never hurt me physically. But my words are also true. He hurt me worse than I ever thought he could, and I'm not sure it's something I'll ever be able to forgive. Even if he is telling the truth and he pleaded guilty for something he didn't do.

I shake my head, trying to clear that doubt away.

He pleaded guilty. He was locked up for arson and murder. No one in their right mind would have put him away if someone else were guilty... would they?

Anxiety over the whole thing knots at my stomach.

Knox is a Hawk. Sending someone down for something they didn't do is the least of what they're capable of.

"I never wanted to hurt you, Violet. I fucking swear that to you." There's such sincerity in his voice that it makes my heart ache.

The little girl who was so in love with the forbidden boy surges to the surface without permission.

Straightening my spine, I stuff her back down where she belongs and remind myself that I'm now a strong, independent woman who doesn't take any shit from anyone. Even the boy who stole my heart all those years ago.

"I don't believe you."

Hurt flickers across his face, although he's quick to cover it up.

"Fine. I have ways to prove myself."

Before I know what's happening, his grip on my ass tightens, his fingertips biting into my skin as his lips slam down on mine.

My brain backfires and that little hopelessly-in-love girl I've been trying so hard to control jumps to the surface and does a little celebratory dance as Knox's tongue pushes past my lips.

His taste fills my mouth, and memories of our time together as kids come rushing back.

I arch into him, grinding against his length as my body burns hotter.

He kisses me with a roughness, a passion, a hunger that I don't remember him having.

His weight presses me back against the wall as the storm continues to rage around us.

His desperation is palpable, his need for me to believe him right there on his tongue.

But as much as I might want to take the easy route here and allow myself to be swallowed up by him, I can't.

I owe it to Mom to keep my head.

Because if he's lying to me...

If it was him and he had any kind of hand in ending her life long before she deserved to go then—

"Stop." Pressing my hands against his solid chest, I push with everything I have to make him back up.

But he doesn't. He just keeps kissing me despite the fact I'm no longer returning it.

"Knox. Stop," I demand much more forcefully this time.

My harsh words cut through whatever daze he was in and he pulls back.

Confusion wars in his dark, hungry eyes, and a deep V forms between his brows.

I hate the lost look on his face. I fucking hate it. But I swallow down my emotions and drag up some strength.

"Put me down. We are not doing this."

Without any hesitation, he does. Not a second later, my feet hit the ground and he takes a step back.

A violent shiver instantly rips through my body as he takes his warmth with him.

Rain lashes at my dry front where he's protected me from the worst of it, plastering my shirt to my body.

"Firefly," he breathes, looking utterly defeated.

The sight of his slumped shoulders, his lack of fire threatens to smash through the wall I've put up, but I refuse to let it happen.

Not until he's told me everything.

And maybe not even then.

"Tell me the truth, Knox," I demand.

The sensible thing to do would probably be to go inside so we could talk like adults. But then, we never did things the right way, so why bother now?

Indecision flashes in his eyes.

"Tell me the truth or walk away and never step foot anywhere near me again. I don't need you in my life, Knox. I've managed to cope for the past five years without you just fine." Lies. I've not been fine. I've been surviving with a broken and battered heart and more loss and grief than any young adult should ever have to deal with. But unless he can stand before me and change the past, there's not much either of us can do about that.

Silence falls as the magnetic pull I've always felt between us only gets stronger.

It should have been severed the day he pleaded guilty.

I thought it had.

But apparently, not all the threads were cut loose, because that tether is pulling as tight as it ever did back then.

Lifting his hand, he pushes his sopping wet hair from his brow, his eyes not leaving mine for a second.

"I didn't start the fire, Violet."

His words slam into me like a truck and my breath catches as I attempt to unravel the truth.

I want to tell him I don't believe him, to send him away and continue as if he never returned to my life. But if he's telling the truth, then...

"Who did?"

He shakes his head, droplets flying from the length of his hair as he does so.

"It was gang bullshit, Violet. My dad was meant to be the only one here that night. You and your mom were never meant to get caught up in it."

# 21

# KNOX

My entire body sags in relief as that truth peels from my lips. But as good as it might feel, I'm not about to get the reaction I've dreamed of when it comes to clearing my name.

She doesn't believe me.

I can see it in her eyes.

Taking a step closer once more, I lift my hand and cup her jaw, letting the warmth of her skin race down my arm.

Fuck, I've missed her.

Missed this electric connection between us.

She might be trying to convince herself that she hates me now, but it's still there, making my blood boil and my cock hard. Just like she did back then.

"It doesn't matter what wasn't meant to happen," she hisses. "All of it did happen. I lost my mom, my brother, my home, my..." Her eyes dip for a beat before finding mine again. "You."

"You never lost me, Firefly. I was just... misplaced for a few years."

A sad laugh bubbles up from her.

"You believe that, don't you? You really think that you could break into Tristan's apartment, ruin my peace here, and I'd bend to your will and we could return to being those reckless kids we used to be?"

"I've had to have some kind of hope over the past five years," I confess.

"Jesus," she mutters, slipping from between me and the wall at her back, forcing me to drop my hand and lose my connection with her.

"I think prison fucked with your head, Knox." My body jolts as she hits a little too close to the truth.

She stands there in the rain, her clothes soaked through and stuck to her body, teasing me with her insane curves that are even more mouthwatering than they used to be, and all I can do is long for easier times with her.

"I was fucked in the head long before prison, baby, and you know it. But sneaking into your room night after night and making you mine was probably the single most sensible thing I did."

"I should have taken your warning more seriously, huh? You told me that I'd regret it, and just look at me now."

She throws her hands out from her sides before turning her back on me.

The move is something akin to how I'd imagine it feels to have a knife pushed straight through your heart.

"Leave, Knox. You're no longer welcome here, or in my life. Take your gang bullshit and force it on someone else."

She's gone before I have a chance to recover from that dismissal. The door slams and cuts through the sound of the rumbling thunder and pounding rain, announcing her painful departure.

I expected it. Her cold shoulder, her hate. But fuck, expecting it and experiencing it are two very different things, and it cuts deeper than I thought it would.

I take a step forward, ready to chase her, but my cell phone starts vibrating in my pocket, making my movements falter.

"Fuck," I hiss, stuffing my hand into my pocket and pulling out my damp cell.

Five years ago, it would have been fucked. But it seems that life really has moved on since I've been locked up, because these things are fucking waterproof now.

Unsurprisingly, it's Reid's name that stares back at me.

He's the one who gave me the cell when I found him waiting outside the day I was released, and I haven't given the number to anyone else.

It rings off in my hand, something that's sure to piss off the beast. But fuck it.

My eyes dart between the windows before me, but the lights are now out, stopping me from seeing inside. Or more importantly, stopping me from seeing her.

She's there, though. Somewhere. I can feel her eyes on me.

My skin burns with her stare and my need to force my way inside the house and make her listen to me.

Make her believe me.

But then my cell starts up again, and I regretfully swipe the screen and lift it to my ear before shooting a hard stare at each window, silently promising her that this isn't over before turning my back on her and heading toward the open gates.

"Yes," I bark down the line as an ominous clap of thunder rocks the ground beneath my feet.

"You're in a good mood," Reid quips, sounding entirely too happy with himself.

"You just got laid, didn't you?" I mutter, frustration and bitterness threatening to swallow me whole.

It's my fault. I'm more than aware of that.

"And I'm assuming you didn't. Where the fuck are you, anyway?"

My lack of response is apparently all he needs to know the truth.

"You actually spoken to her yet, or are you still going class A stalker on her ass?"

"Fuck off," I grunt, pulling Devin's door open and dropping into the driver's seat with a squelch.

Reid chuckles darkly down the line, making anger stir in my gut.

I'm happy for him, I am. He's managed to get everything he wanted, and a few things he never expected along the way. But I'm also jealous as fuck.

He's got his life together, and here I am, falling apart all over the place.

And all because of the girl I gave my heart to when I was just a kid.

"I'll take that as the latter, then. Prison turned you into a pussy, you know that?" he teases, trying to force me into action.

"I've spoken to her."

"And yet you sound like a miserable fuck, so I'm assuming she didn't immediately forgive you and drop to her knees."

"Sadly not. She hates me."

"Only one way to fix that, man."

Voices sound out in the background before Reid chuckles at something one of them says. Resting my head back, I blow out a pained breath, imagining him hanging out at home. Happy.

"I'm not ripping her heart into more pieces than I already have."

"On some level, she has to know. It's just easier to pin it on you."

Silence falls between us as I briefly consider his words.

He's right. I know he is. But there's a reason we did what we did. And if we just rip it all up, then it was all for nothing. And those years I spent locked in hell cannot be for nothing.

"Did you actually want something?" I finally grunt.

"Can't I just want to shoot the shit with my oldest friend?"

"Sure you can. But that's not why you're calling and we both know it." I slump lower in the seat, my wet clothes quickly turning cold around me.

"Fine. I've got a location for you."

"What?" I bark, sitting bolt upright. "Where?"

My body aches as painful memories slam into me from my time away. The need for vengeance burns through my veins.

"Hazard Grove."

"What the fuck is he doing there?"

"Hiding. Hence why it took us so long to find the motherfucker."

"Since when do the Devils side with the fucking Ravens?"

"Since now, apparently," he mutters.

"What about the rest of them?"

"Either dead or back inside. Seems we're not the only ones hunting for them."

Can't say I'm fucking surprised.

"So, give me the fucking location," I demand, my need to watch the life drain out of the motherfucker who made my time away so fucking unbearable getting the better of me.

Reid laughs, but it's anything but amused.

"Yeah, no. That's not fucking happening."

"Why the fuck are you telling me this shit then? I need the cunt bleeding out and dying at my feet."

"And you'll get it. But not by storming in without a plan. You'll be the one who ends up fucking dead that way and—"

He cuts himself off, piquing my interest.

"And?" I prompt.

He sighs, and I imagine him pushing his finger through his hair, a pained expression on his face just like when we were kids and his old man used to demand he did something Reid didn't agree with.

"And I just fucking got you back, all right?"

"Aw, bro. You going all soft?"

There's a rustle of movement down the line before a soft

female voice purrs. "There's nothing soft about Reid Harris. Ain't that right, big boy?"

The sound of a zipper being pulled down fills the line before Reid groans.

"Jesus fucking Christ."

"Fuck," he barks.

"Goodbye, Knox. I'll let him back out to play again soon," she teases.

"Call me later, asshole," I grunt before pulling my cell from my ear, discovering that the call has already been cut.

"Motherfucker," I hiss, jamming my finger into the start button and heading back toward the house I'm currently calling home.

---

Avoiding the déjà vu of all the younger Harris brothers turning their intrigued gazes on me as I walk through the living room with sopping wet clothes, I head for the stairs and straight up to my room with the bottle of vodka I stopped off for on the way home.

I've already drunk a quarter of the bottle, the alcohol hitting me harder than I've ever known. After five years of being dry, it's like being a kid again.

It's fucking mind-blowing. And I can only hope that other pleasures will be as intense after so long of going without.

I fight the burn as the vodka flows down my throat, my eyes closing as I remember what it was like being on the receiving end of Violet's touch. I had a taste of her desire, her passion, her hunger tonight, but it was nowhere near enough.

I knew the first time I kissed her, the first time she made me blow in my pants without even knowing, that she'd ruined me for anyone else. And all these years on, even with the distance between us, it seems nothing has changed.

Not for me, at least.

Stripping out of my clothes is harder than I expected, and when I finally manage to drag my pants from my feet, I throw them toward the laundry basket in the corner as if they personally offended me.

My skin burns with the heat of the shower raining down on me, my head spins from the vodka, and my cock continues to ache, standing proud and hard from my body.

Resting my forearms on the tiles of the small stall, I hang my head, running the events of the evening through my mind.

She's been the only thing that's got me through the past five years. Through the gang rivalry that's rife inside Iron Marsh Prison. It might be located on neutral ground, but that seems to be forgotten the second any member of the surrounding gangs step through the front door. And those unlucky few who get thrown in there without a connection or affiliation to one are soon swallowed up and spat out if they're not strong enough.

Banishing those thoughts from my head, I focus on her.

My firefly.

My little bit of light in all the darkness.

My breath catches as I wrap my fingers around my length, forcing my brain to think it's her, that she never sent me away, that she allowed what was burning between us to explode like it used to.

Before long, I'm coming into the shower tray at my feet, but it's far from fulfilling.

My imagination might be good, it's had to be over the last few years, but it's not that fucking good.

I fall into bed naked with water droplets still clinging to my body and what remains of the vodka in my hand.

It's not until I've finished all of it and am staring up at the ceiling with my mind spinning, thoughts of my girl filling my head, that I finally pass out. Unlike in the past, my slumber is no longer a safe haven full of dirty dreams of my green-eyed goddess, but instead a place of horror and full of vivid memories of my time in Iron Marsh.

# 22

# VIOLET

I know what I'm doing the second I hit the light switches and plunge myself into darkness as I take off running blindly up the stairs.

But I don't know any other way to sever this... this connection between us.

The second our eyes lock, the moment he touches me, everything falls away, just like it used to.

And that's dangerous.

Even more so now than before.

I've worked hard over the past five years to carve out any part of my heart that once belonged to Knox Bowman, but it seems that all I really did was put it on ice.

Because one look at him and...

"Fuck," I hiss, stumbling through my bedroom door and toward the window. The soft lights from the deck outside help to illuminate the way, but they're not enough to fend off the panic that's bubbling up within me the longer I'm surrounded by darkness. And it's happening in this house, where all my fears stem from.

Fuck.

This was a really fucking bad idea.

My hands tremble violently and my breathing gets choppy as I stand just to the side of the window and peer out.

He's still there. Just like I knew he would be. Standing in the middle of the yard, looking lost with his shoulders slumped in defeat as he stares at the house.

His eyes move between each window. Realization hits me like a truck.

He's looking for me. Searching for any clues that his presence affects me. That the hatred I spat at him might not be entirely the truth. That I can still feel what he obviously can.

But I can't let him see it. I have to keep my walls up.

I barely survived Knox Bowman back then. I sure as shit won't survive him a second time around, no matter how much I've tried to harden the fortress around my heart since the last time I saw him.

*"It wasn't me, Violet."* His confession rocks through me once more.

He said those words with such sincerity as his eyes begged me to believe him.

But I can't, can I?

He stood and pleaded fucking guilty to all charges during the trial following our parents' deaths.

Why would he do that if he wasn't the one who struck the match?

And if what he's saying is true and it was a gang attack, a hit on his father, who did do it? Why didn't they come forward and take the punishment? Why did Knox have to go down for it?

My life following that fire would have been so much easier if I'd had him beside me, holding my hand along with Tristan as I tried to come to terms with everything.

Hell, I'd have had one less person to mourn if he was still there. And maybe, just maybe, I wouldn't be scared of the dark now if I had him holding me at night.

When he tips his head back and looks directly at my

window, my body jolts, my panic momentarily forgotten as the connection between us crackles and sizzles like I'm sure that tree out in the yard is.

Silent pleas of his innocence fill the space between us, making that knot of confusion that's taken up residence in my stomach twist tighter.

I'm so confused. Exhausted. Fed the fuck up of all the drama and the pain that comes hand in hand with it.

I don't look away from him—I can't as my body aches, begs for me to run back out there and jump into his arms.

But I won't. I found the strength to walk away earlier, and I need to stand by that.

Even if he is telling the truth. He's still lied to me for five years. It's not like he hasn't had a chance to reach out and try to fix this before now. I can't imagine he was all that busy locked up in a shitty cell.

Finally, something forces him to move and I soon realize it's his cell that's distracting him from me. But he doesn't answer it. Instead, he just stares down at it like he doesn't know how it works.

Stepping closer to the window, my fingers curl around the ledge as I try to see more, to discover who's trying to contact him, to understand all his secrets and why he's done the things he has—why he's doing the things he is.

But I never get them. And I won't, not if I'm going to continue to hide in the dark, refusing to face my demons and the truth of my past.

Grief rips through me when he finally swipes the screen, lifts the cell to his ear and turns his back on me.

It shouldn't matter that he's giving up, that he's walking away.

He's already told me that this isn't over between us, but his dismissal, his lack of fight makes me feel like it might be, and I hate myself more than ever for being hurt by that.

It's what I want. What I demanded of him.

*"Leave, Knox. You're no longer welcome here, or in my life. Take your gang bullshit and force it on someone else."*

A loud sob erupts from my throat as my eyes track him through the yard before he's swallowed up by the darkness.

I stumble back, colliding with the wall as my body trembles with a mixture of grief, loss, and panic.

I fight to keep control of my breathing as I look around the haunting shadows of my room, but it's not a fight I stand any chance of winning. Before long, I give up and let my memories, my fears, my nightmares consume me.

---

I didn't bother even attempting to go back downstairs. I convinced myself that I was safe, that I did lock the door when I ran from Knox and I stripped out of my still-damp clothes and crawled into bed.

I pulled the sheets up over my head, hiding from reality as I prayed that sleep would claim me and take me to a world full of laughter and smiles instead of my reality that is full of pain, lies, and grief.

*"What do you think he'd do if I kissed you right now?" Knox asks, his deep voice washing through me as he lowers his ass to my lounger, making my nipples harden behind my bikini top and my lower belly clench.*

*Ripping my eyes from his shirtless, glistening torso, I glance over his shoulder to where Roman and Tristan are playing basketball.*

*"He'd kill you. Tristan too," I say confidently.*

*My brother and his best friend might not be Knox. They haven't grown up surrounded by blood, destruction, and violence like he has, but I have no doubt that they'd turn to it if necessary. Especially when it comes to me. They're both possessive, unbearably so. And I have no reason to believe that either would accept my relationship with Knox. Not in a million years.*

*My skin burns with his attention, forcing me to look back at him.*

*His eyes track down my body, taking in the small triangles of fabric that are covering my breasts, down my bare stomach to my indecent shorts that I've left undone to expose my bikini bottoms beneath, purely with the wicked intention of driving him wild.*

*It was a risky move, coming out under the guise of sunbathing and studying. But really, I was coming out to perv because hot damn, Knox and Tristan shirtless and bouncing a ball around the yard… the thing all teenage girls' dreams are made of.*

*The look on Knox's face the second he saw me sauntering out wearing my hot pink bikini and denim shorts made the risk more than worth it.*

*The pain on his face as he tried not to react was amusing as hell. I almost felt bad for him. But then, I guess that's what you get for messing around with one of your best friend's little sisters—who just so happens to be your stepsister—behind closed doors.*

*"Vi, what the fuck?" Roman had barked when he'd noticed his teammates had paused in favor of checking me out. Yeah, even Tristan had taken notice, which shocked the fuck out of me. But I put it down to him being startled by the amount of skin I was exposing more than anything else, and that was only proved to be true when he opened his mouth.*

*"You need to put some more clothes on, Pip," he'd growled, backing up my brother. Idiot.*

*"Pretty sure it would be worth it," Knox says, dragging me from reliving their reactions only a couple of hours ago.*

*"I'd rather you hung around a little longer. I'm not done with you yet."*

*A wicked smirk kicks up the corner of his lips, his eyes dropping to my body once more.*

*"Oh yeah. What do you have in mind for me, Firefly?"*

*"A girl doesn't tell all her secrets, especially not to the bad boy who wants to corrupt her."*

*His brow quirks, his smirk growing.*

*"Wants to corrupt her. Correct me if I'm wrong, but I fell asleep last night with your taste on my tongue and your cum coating my fingers."*

*My body burns red hot as he whispers those words. I swear, my cheeks are about a second from going up in flames.*

*"Knox," I breathe, my voice all deep and raspy with need.*

*"Fuck, you're making me hard, Firefly." Shifting his hand, he squeezes himself through his shorts.*

*Pride swells in my chest, just like it does every time he tells me or shows me how much I affect him.*

*"I thought you were going for a piss, Bowman," Roman barks over.*

*He chuckles before glancing over his shoulder.*

*"Trying to convince little sister to make herself useful and prepare us all sandwiches."*

*"Fuck off," I bark. "I'm not doing anything for you idiots."*

*"Aw, please, Vi. You make the best subs."*

*I glare at my brother as he dribbles circles around Tristan.*

*"He's not wrong," Tris agrees. "How about you sort us lunch and we'll order takeout tonight? Might even let you have a beer or two. Ow, what?" Tristan offers before getting hit upside the head by my annoyingly overbearing brother.*

*"Don't offer my sister alcohol. She's sixteen."*

*"Yeah exactly. Sixteen, not six," I call.*

*"Sounds like a sweet deal to me," Knox murmurs before pushing to his feet and heading toward the house without looking back at the guys.*

*I realize why when the sound of the ball bouncing hits my*

*ears again and Knox pauses in the doorway, giving me a shot of his very tented shorts.*

*Heat floods me, the desire to follow him almost too much to deny.*

*But I force myself to stay exactly where I am, lifting my cell from beside me in the hope I appear completely unaffected by Knox's little visit.*

*I'm busy scrolling through Insta when a message comes through.*

***Knox: Can you help me out with something?***

*Excitement unfurls in my belly as my thighs clench with need.*

*Images of him up there with his hand wrapped around his hard cock fill my mind and my mouth waters as an idea hits me.*

*He's tasted me time and time again now. I haven't been brave enough to return the favor, but maybe...*

***Violet: I'm sure you've got it handled.***

***Knox: I really don't. It's too big a job for me.***

***Knox: I'm going to make a mess.***

***Knox: A BIG mess.***

*"Oh my God," I mutter, squeezing my eyes closed and remembering what kind of mess he made over my tits the other night when he snuck in and woke me up with his kisses and roaming hands.*

***Violet: You're wicked.***

***Knox: I'm worse than that and you know it.***

*I glance over at Roman and Tristan, but they're well distracted with their one-on-one game. Neither of them so much as looks up as I push to stand and move toward the house.*

*My heart pounds so hard I can feel it in every inch of my body as I climb the stairs.*

*My bedroom door is open, which is not how I left it, and I take that as my clue as to where he is.*

*Pushing it open, I expect to find him on my bed, but I quickly discover it's disappointingly empty.*

*But then my eyes catch on my bathroom door and my blood continues to heat.*

*Closing the door behind me, I take off across the room and swing the bathroom door open with a flourish.*

*My breath catches and my chin drops when I find him resting back against the counter, gloriously naked and slowly working his hand up and down his thick shaft.*

*"I see your problem. It is big," I quip, kicking the door closed and flipping the lock.*

*Moving closer, I let my eyes roam over every inch of his mouthwatering body before fixating on his cock, on the glistening moisture at the tip.*

*"That bikini is sinful, Firefly. But you know that, don't you? It's why you wore it. You wanted to get a rise out of me."*

*I shrug, my face nothing but innocent.*

*"It's just my swimsuit. No different from what I wore when we were on holiday last year."*

*He lifts his free hand, wiping his thumb over his bottom lip.*

*"Yeah, and don't I fucking know it. Hardest week of my life."*

*I can't help but smile at his words as I continue to close the space between us.*

*His cock bumps into my stomach as I step right up to him and tilt my face toward him, letting my lips tease his, but I don't kiss him.*

*"Firefly," he groans, but to my surprise, he doesn't take control.*

*"You're playing with fire right now, Knox," I tell him, brushing my lips down his neck. "If they notice we're both gone then—"*

*"You'd better work your magic fast then. Because nothing short of you getting me off will stop me walking back out there with a boner for my stepsister."*

*"Wicked," I murmur, kissing over his chest.*

*He chuckles, but it's quickly cut off when I suddenly sink to my knees before him and lean forward, licking the indent of his V line.*

*"Holy fuck," he barks, his hips thrusting forward.*

*My eyes hold his as I kiss down his thigh, summoning up all my courage to give him what I know he wants.*

*He's never pushed me for anything more than I'm comfortable with, and he always asks my permission like a gentleman when he does something new, but I can see his need for more from me burning in the depths of his blue eyes.*

*Sitting back on my haunches, I knock his hand away and wrap my own fingers around him.*

*"Yes," he hisses, his cock getting even harder in my grasp.*

*He's so thick, my fingers aren't even close to meeting. I can't imagine what it might possibly feel like pushing inside me. Heat floods my core as I think about it. Think about finally going all the way with him.*

*"What are you thinking about?" he asks, reaching out and combing his fingers through my hair.*

*"You," I confess. "And how you'll feel when you..." I trail off. We haven't talked about it, and I can only assume that's because he doesn't want me to feel pressured into anything.*

*"Better than anything you can imagine," he tells me.*

*"It'll hurt. How could it not?" I whisper, letting my anxiety show.*

*"Yeah," he says, not trying to sugarcoat it for me. "But then*

*after that, it'll be the best thing you've ever felt. I fucking swear to you. I'll make it so fucking good."*

"I know," I breathe before finding a little confidence from his words and the heat in his eyes. I stick my tongue out and lick his tip.

"Oh, fuck, baby." His fingers tighten in my hair, the other hand gripping the counter, turning his knuckles white. "Do it again."

So I do.

Only this time, I don't pull back immediately and instead start licking him like he's my favorite flavor popsicle. Although to be fair, I soon find out that he might be.

"So fucking good," he groans, giving me the confidence to continue.

Opening wider, I take him in my mouth.

The groan of approval I get is everything.

"Fuck. Look at you taking my cock like a good girl."

A groan rumbles in my chest at his praise.

"You like sucking my cock, don't you, baby? I bet you're dripping for me."

Pulling back off his dick, I stare up at him. His eyes are blown with lust and every muscle in his body is pulled tight.

"I really don't wanna fucking rush this, but we haven't got all day, Firefly. They're gonna notice eve—"

Not allowing him to finish that sentence, I take him back into my mouth, sucking him in a way that makes his fingers tighten in my hair and a sinful groan fall from his lips.

"Fuck, baby. I'm gonna blow. If you don't want to swallow then—"

I don't let myself second-guess what happens next. Instead, I take him as far back as I dare and suck.

The most erotic groan I've ever heard rips from his lips before his cock jerks in my mouth and his hot cum hits the back of my throat.

*I swallow him down as he stares at me on my knees with his cock in my mouth in complete awe.*

*"You're perfect," he whispers between heaving breaths. "And I'm really glad I had the forethought to clean up before you got here, just in case it was my lucky day."*

*I release him with a laugh, although it's mostly shock at myself for not even considering the fact he's been running around out in the scorching sun for God knows how long and I just blindly dropped to my knees and sucked him off.*

*Christ. Is that what dick drunk means?*

*More like dick freaking blind.*

*"I... uh... I appreciate that. But does that mean it doesn't always smell this fresh?"*

*Tucking his hands under my arms, he lifts me to my feet.*

*"I always smell like roses, Firefly. Now kiss me."*

*"Really?" I ask, wrinkling my nose. "I just had your dick in my mouth."*

*He chuckles, looking at me with so much emotion glittering in his eyes it makes my chest ache.*

*Times like this, I can almost convince myself that we could have something serious. Something that could last. But then I'm always dragged back to Earth and reminded of who he is, of who I am, and all the reasons why this is never going to be anything more than sneaking around and stealing as much pleasure together as we can.*

*"If you think the taste of my own cock will put me off, you really need to think again. I'm not sure there's anything you could do that would put me off kissing you. Ever.*

*"Sucking someone else's cock?" I blurt like a moron, immediately kicking myself.*

*A low growl rumbles in his chest.*

*"It was a joke. I was joking. I'm not suck—"*

*"I know, Vi. You're all mine. And I fucking love it."*

*Wrapping his hand around the back of my neck, he slams*

*his lips down on mine and flips our position, pinning me back against the counter as his cock hardens once more.*

*"Knox," I whimper, my body burning up for him.*

*"What is it, baby? You need something?"*

*Embarrassment floods me, but I don't allow it to put an end to this.*

*"Make me come," I demand, trying to own my sexuality.*

*"Fuck, yeah," he grunts before plunging his tongue into my mouth once more, hooking my leg around his waist and grinding against me.*

*Just as I'm starting to drown in him, he suddenly releases me and takes a huge step back, leaving me bereft of his touch.*

*"But not now."*

*"W-what?" I stutter, barely able to believe that he's going to leave me like this.*

*"I think we should go back outside, and you can continue watching me play, let that dirty imagination of yours run wild. And then later, when you can barely contain yourself, I'm going to make you come so hard you'll forget your own name."*

*My mouth opens and closes like a freaking goldfish as I glare at him across my bathroom.*

*"Are you going to be able to wait that long?" I ask, regaining some composure and remembering that he's hard again.*

*"Don't you worry about me, Firefly. I'm not likely to forget how insane your lips felt wrapped around my cock anytime soon."*

*Bending down, he swipes his shorts from the floor and tugs them on before blowing me a kiss and disappearing from the room.*

*"Asshole," I call after him, and I'm gifted with the sound of his laughter as he slips out of my bedroom.*

*Lifting my fingers to my swollen lips, I start plotting how I can get rid of Roman and Tristan so that we can continue where we left off sooner rather than later.*

## 23

## TRISTAN

I stand in the middle of my living room with my chest heaving and sweat glistening on my skin as I look around at everything Violet chose to fill my apartment with.

It looks... emptier than it ever has without her presence.

I let out a sigh and rub at the tension pulling at the back of my neck.

I fucked up.

I fucked up bad, and now I'm paying the price.

But I know she is too. She's hurting, she's scared, and she's alone.

I know exactly where she is. Whenever she runs, she always goes to the same place.

I want to give her the space, the peace to figure things out, to try to get her head on straight and process the fact that Knox is free and apparently here in Maddison County.

But I also really don't fucking want to.

I want to hold her in my arms and tell her that everything is going to be okay. That I've got her back, no matter what.

But I fear I might just have ruined my chance at all of that.

I should have just bitten the bullet and found a way to tell her the second Micah told me.

Why was I such a pussy about it?

*Because you know the truth. And not only that, you know how he used to look at her and you're scared you might just lose her.*

"Motherfucker," I bellow, my booming voice echoing off the walls around me.

Without another look at my new furniture, I storm through to the bedroom and throw myself in the shower.

Her scent still clings to my skin from earlier. I couldn't bear to lose it when she first stormed out. But now, now I need to pull my head out of my ass and do what I should have done when she first tried to run.

I should have chased her.

It's long dark by the time I get outside, the storm over, leaving behind fresh night air and the scent of rain on the warm ground.

If I didn't already know where she was going, then I would have the second the thunder and lightning started.

There's only one place she ever wants to watch a storm.

The drive to the outskirts of Maddison County is shorter than usual, seeing as the roads are deadly quiet at this time of night. But it's still long after midnight when I finally pull through the open gates that usually close off Violet and Roman's new family home from the suburban street beyond.

I used to love this place as a kid. It was like the ultimate playground with the woodland at the back. We had multiple tree swings, dens, and campfires over the years. It was our happy place.

Or at least, it was until we discovered other pleasures in life, like girls and alcohol.

Damn, growing up sucks ass sometimes.

I long for those lazy days with my best friend and his annoying little sister.

I should have appreciated them more. I should have told

Roman how awesome he was more, made fun of Violet's jokes less.

My breath catches as I pull up to the house and find it in total darkness.

She's here. I know she is. I've just pulled up beside her car.

But she never ever sleeps in the dark.

Stupid, irrational fears slam into me out of nowhere.

What if he followed her here?

What if he's in there with her?

What if he's taken her? Stolen her away from me?

They're ridiculous, all of them.

I saw the way she looked at him earlier with nothing but pure unfiltered hatred in her eyes, but I can't help it.

He always wanted her just as much as I did, I'd put everything I own on that fact.

It's something I haven't thought about since the day he was put in cuffs and dragged into the back of a cop car. But with him back and Roman gone, they're all coming back.

No matter how I might have felt about Violet back then, my loyalties were solidly with Roman, and I never would have done anything to sabotage our friendship.

But Knox... I didn't trust him as far as I could throw him. Something told me that if he wanted something, he'd go after it no matter who he had to mow down and whose feelings he hurt in the process.

It's something that I can't imagine has changed all that much while he's been locked away.

I know for a fact that leaving town, joining the Titans and embarking on a whole new life didn't help to get her out of my head. But then, maybe he was never as serious as I was about her.

He was all about pushing boundaries and doing everything he shouldn't.

I have no doubt he'd have gone after her just because she was forbidden.

My concern for my girl makes me move faster than I usually would, and it's not helped at all when I get to the front door and twist the handle, finding it unlocked.

My heart jumps into my throat.

I swear to God, if I rush in here and find her in his arms, I'm going to fucking kill him.

I move through the house in silence, grabbing a vase from the side before I begin climbing the stairs. If he's here, then having a weapon isn't going to hurt.

He's already proved to me that he can overpower me without much effort once today. I really don't need that happening again.

I shouldn't be surprised. He was taught to fight in the Creek. And those motherfuckers are nothing but dirty. In every sense of the word. Their work, their money, their women.

Her bedroom door is ajar when I get there, and I come to a stop, suddenly feeling like a teenage boy doing the one thing I always dreamed of: slipping into her room in the middle of the night and letting her know exactly how I felt about her.

My heart pounds and my fist clenches at my side.

If he's already in there then—

I throw the door open, not willing to even think about the end of that sentence, and step into the room.

It's dark, but I already know that it looks almost identical to how it did when we were kids. She recreated everything she could in this house. It's as comforting as it is disconcerting.

I tried to convince her to style it differently, to make it hers when she decided to rebuild the house, but she point-blank refused. And what the fuck was I going to do? Argue with a broken, grieving woman?

I scan the room quickly, my eyes finally landing on the bed.

The bed with only one person in it.

"Fuck," I breathe, abandoning the vase on the dresser as I walk deeper into the room.

Kicking my sneakers off, I drag my shirt over my head and drop my sweats before stepping up to the bed.

"Yes," Violet cries. "Yes, please." Her back arches off the bed as she flips the covers free. A wide smirk curls at my lips as I imagine her dreaming about me, and I can't help but wonder if it's my tongue or my cock she's begging for.

The moonlight peeking through the remaining clouds outside allows me to see enough to know she's only in her underwear. The sight makes my cock ache for her as I slip into bed beside her.

The second I'm close, she shuffles closer to my warmth.

"I need you," she whimpers, and being the whipped, obsessed motherfucker that I am, I give it to her, slipping my fingers into her panties, finding her dripping wet.

"You dreaming of me, baby girl?"

"At last," she cries, bucking her hips from the bed. "Make me come. Make me— yes," she moans as I sink two fingers deep inside her.

Her muscles clamp down on me, trying to drag me deeper as I circle her clit with my thumb.

She moans and mewls as I play her, and in only seconds her entire body locks up as her release slams into her.

She cries out, but her words are too muffled to make out what she's saying as she rides out her orgasm.

"Been waiting for you to come back," she mumbles as she rolls over and curls up, allowing me to wrap my body around her and hold her tight.

"Didn't know if you'd want me to follow you," I confess quietly. "But you should know that I always will. You're mine, baby girl."

I pause as her breathing gets shallower and she drifts off into a deeper sleep.

"I'm sorry, Violet."

---

Despite wanting to stay exactly where I was, ignoring that it was a Friday and that I should be at training and in classes, I knew I couldn't.

And as much as I know Violet needs me right now, she wouldn't want that either.

So long before the sun rises, I drag my eyes open and rip myself from my girl so that I can head back to MKU.

By the time I walk through the main entrance to the training facility, I'm exhausted and frustrated, and the last person I need to walk straight into—literally—is fucking Winters looking fresh as fuck and ready to slay the day.

"What the fuck, Carver? Don't your eyes fucking work?" he barks the second we collide.

Lifting my tired gaze from the floor and forcing myself back to reality, I meet his angry stare.

His brows immediately shoot up as amusement twinkles in his eyes. I haven't looked in a mirror yet this morning, but I can only imagine how I look after having Knox's fists collide with my face recently.

"Glad to see you're taking your new position seriously," he deadpans.

"Get out of my way," I bark, twisting to move around him, shoulder checking him in the process.

"Coach is going to have your ass for this," he warns like the fucking teacher's pet that he is.

I just about refrain myself from flipping him the bird as I stalk toward our office to dump my stuff and get changed.

I didn't have time to stop off at my apartment, but thankfully, I've got a locker here with a few sets of clothes in.

Tossing my bag on the chair behind my desk, I key in the code on the lock and grab a shirt and pair of sweats before hauling my ass toward a shower. I'm still covered in stale sweat and Violet's perfume, and as comforting as that might be, I need it to be gone so I can focus on my day.

Thankfully, Winters was wrong about Coach, and aside from looking at me with narrowed, concerned eyes, he never said a word about the darkening bruise that seemed to cover more of my temple and right eye every time I caught a reflection of myself.

Anger over the stunt Knox pulled yesterday continues to pull my muscles tight, and concern for my girl and how she's coping right now ensures my stomach is knotted up all day.

I manage to slip out of the training facility without being stopped by anyone so I can attend a full day of classes, and despite sending Violet more than a handful of messages to check in with her, they all go unresponded to. Although she reads them all.

We've got a week until our first game, and despite the fact I won't have the pressure of playing them anymore, I still need to be focused.

Coach is watching my performance just as much as he is our first-string team, and I need to up my game.

My future here isn't set in stone just because I fell out of a first-division NFL team. My name gets me nothing with Coach. He doesn't care about the past. Only the future. Things that we can have an influence on. I may as well be that douchebag Winters.

By the time our afternoon training session comes to an end, it seems that Coach has had enough of my ugly face, because the second he catches up with me, he directs me toward his office and closes the door.

"What's going on, Carver?" he demands, his deep, booming voice and intimidating presence making me feel like a kid again.

"It's nothing, Coach. Just someone from my past rearing his ugly head."

"You're not a fighter, son. Never have been," he points out, lowering his ass to his chair. "I'm assuming it involved a girl?"

Motherfucking Winters.

"It's nothing I can't handle, sir. You don't need to worry about me."

"Tristan," he sighs.

"My focus is on my job, Coach. That is not going to change anytime soon. Things in my private life are just a little..."

"Painful?" he suggests.

"I was going to say messy, but yeah, I'll take that."

He nods as silence falls between us.

I nod and push from the chair, assuming that I've been dismissed, but he speaks again when my fingers wrap around the door handle.

"If you need anything, son, all you need to do is ask. Don't tell the team this, but I'm not a complete cunt all the time."

I can't help but laugh at his self-assessment.

"Thanks, Coach. I appreciate it."

Without another word, I stalk back to my office, grab my stuff and head out.

I'm too busy checking Violet's socials to see if she's posted anything to pay too much attention to what's going on around me.

I dump my bags in the trunk, glad I seem to have missed the team who'd no doubt try to convince me to head to the Den again.

Damn, having a beer and shooting the shit with Arth right now seems like a fucking good idea.

I can't, though. I need to go and find Violet, convince her somehow to forgive me for being a stupid prick and spend the night proving myself.

But that all vanishes the second before my ass hits the seat and shock rocks through me as I realize that I'm not alone.

"What the fuck are you doing?" I bark. "Get the fuck out."

I shove Knox in the arm, but the solid motherfucker doesn't so much as shift an inch.

"Pass," he growls.

"How did you even get in here?" My hand drops to my pocket where I know my keys are because I just fucking used them.

"I've been boosting cars since before I could walk, Tris. Don't insult me."

His voice is so serious it renders me speechless for a second.

"Whatever. You need to get your ass out of my car, Bowman."

"Make me," he taunts.

Releasing an exasperated breath, I take a couple of seconds to get my tired brain to figure this out.

"What do you want?" I snap.

"What do I want?" he echoes.

"Yes, asshole. What the fuck do you want? Why are you here, fucking everything up all over again?"

When I risk a glance over at him, his brows are high, but it's the bruising that covers his face that really gets my attention.

I did that.

It might have only been for a few seconds, and he might not have even attempted to fight back to start with, but I still had him for a few seconds. I'll take it.

His amused chuckle throws me for a loop and my brows pinch in confusion.

"I came back to reclaim what's mine. But it seems someone is borrowing it."

"What's your—" Realization hits, sucking all the air from the car. "No. Hell fucking no."

"It's cute you think I'm asking for permission, Tris."

"Get out of my fucking car," I demand, refusing to even listen to this bullshit.

"Why the fuck would you want me to do that? Not when I've got something you want."

"You've got fuck all I want. Everything was perfect until you decided to show your fucking face. Why are you even out?"

"We both know why I'm out. Don't try to take the high and mighty road here, Tris. You don't think I'm more than aware that you're lying to her? That you have been since the day you both watched me get thrown in the back of that car?"

"Not my story to tell," I grunt.

"Aw, is that what you tell yourself to help you sleep at night? You're lying to her, Tris. And something tells me that when she discovers that, your perfect little world will crumble at your feet."

He must read something in my eyes because his grin turns feral, his eyes alighting with excitement.

"Oh shit, it's already falling isn't it? Aw, was it my fault? Shit." He shrugs, but his shit-eating grin ensures I'm more than aware that it's anything but sincere.

"Fuck off, Knox. No one wants you here."

"But that's where you're wrong, old friend," he taunts. "We all made a decision after the fallout of that fire. We all agreed."

"Yeah, and where the fuck is Roman?" I bark, my irritation levels hitting an all-time high.

"I don't know," he confesses, irritation flickering across his face for the first time since I found him sitting here in my goddamn car like he owns it.

"Oh, big bad Knox Bowman doesn't have an answer for everything. I'm shocked."

"Fuck you. I've got people looking for him."

"Hawks," I hiss. "Good to know you've severed your connection to that bullshit gang."

He shakes his head, lifting his hand to drag his hair back from his brow, but he doesn't say anything. He doesn't need to.

I know the reason he's sitting here right now is because they got him out. It doesn't take a fucking genius to work that out.

"He's a fucking pussy, running from all of this."

I grunt in agreement. I might love—have loved—Roman like the brother I never had, but he fucked up. He fucked up bad and left us to pick up the mess he left behind when he bailed on our agreement.

"He's probably dead," I finally say.

"Nah, that would be too easy. I'm gonna find him, and I'm going to bring him back here kicking and fucking screaming so he can confess all his sins to Violet."

"And you think that will force her to change her mind about you?"

"Hell no. I've got other ways to ensure that happens. Started on that little mission last night," he casually throws in.

My fists curl on my lap at the memory of finding the two of them in my apartment with her only wearing that sexy lingerie set that was meant for my eyes only.

"Breaking into my home isn't going to get you anywhere," I mutter.

"No," he agrees, surprising me. "But following her back home and watching the storm together like we used to sure went a long way."

"You're lying," I spit.

"Am I?"

"I know she didn't sleep at your place last night, Tris. I know she wasn't in your bed, bouncing on your cock."

One side of my lips curls up in a smirk.

"You're right," I agree. "She wasn't in my bed. I was in hers."

Fury tightens his features.

"You might claim to have watched the storm with her, but it was my name she was screaming after you left, it was my body she fell asleep curled around, and it was me she was dreaming about."

He shakes his hand, fighting to keep his expression neutral.

"I can't believe how long it took you to grow a pair of balls and take her, bro. I can only assume it was worth it though, right?" he taunts. "Memories of her tight cunt sure helped get me through my lonely, endless days in—"

I swing for him, but he sees it coming and blocks my attempt to shut him the fuck up.

"You're lying," I hiss.

He wanted her, I saw that in his eyes.

But he has to be lying.

There's no way. No fucking way that—

"She hasn't told you, has she?" His amusement over this whole exchange only grows. "You know, I'm actually starting to feel sorry for you. I do have to thank you, though."

My chest heaves as I glare at him, praying that he's bullshitting me, saying anything he can to get a rise out of me.

"It seems you've kept her nice and warm while I've been gone. But you can go back to attempting to rebuild your fucked-up life now. I'm back, and we both know which one of us she really wants. She made her decision the first night she let me slip into her bed when we were kids."

"Get the fuck out," I hiss, doing everything I can to keep my shit together.

He's trying to get a rise out of me, and fuck, I've been reeled right in. But no more. I will not react in the way he wants me to.

"But I didn't even get to tell you what you want to know."

"I don't give a fuck. Get the fuck out of my car and leave Violet the hell alone."

Thankfully, he reaches for the handle and pushes the door open.

"I'll go, but only because I've got better things to do than reminisce with you. But there's no chance in hell of me walking away from her. She was mine long before she was yours, and I've given five years of my life for her. She'll be back where she belongs before you know it. Maybe go and buy yourself some lube and tissues, ready for the lonely, sad nights you've got looming."

I jab the start button so hard it hurts before slamming the car into drive and shooting off without letting him even shut the door.

"MOTHERFUCKER," I boom as I speed out of the parking lot, watching him with his head thrown back in amusement in my rearview mirror.

# 24

# VIOLET

I press my finger to the buzzer for a third time, but I know it's wishful thinking at this point.

They're not here.

Hell, I don't even know why I'm here, but it seemed right. They are the only people who will understand what I'm going through right now. The only people I trust to talk through everything that's happened recently and give me their non-judgmental opinion.

Only, they are not fucking here, and I need—

The rumble of a car makes me spin around, and I breathe a sigh of relief when a familiar gray Skyline slips into a parking space.

Thank fuck, because despite not knowing where I'm going after this visit, I already know I'm not ready.

I should go home... to Tristan's...

He came for me last night.

I might not have realized it when he first arrived and slipped into bed, but when I woke sometime before sunrise, the brightness of the soft night-light on my nightstand confused me. I know I went to sleep in the dark, in the throes of a panic attack. I did not turn it on.

But then, there was a soft snore from behind me and I twisted around.

And there he was

Like my white knight always coming to protect me.

It was probably lucky that he turned up when I was asleep, because there's a very good chance I would have sent him away again otherwise. It would have been the last thing I wanted and needed, but I'd have stood strong and done what needed to be done, ripping a few more pieces of my heart out in the process.

My chest aches just thinking about him.

About Knox.

About how my life has turned into an even bigger disaster than normal in the past twenty-four hours.

"Hey, to what do we owe this pleasure?" Kane says as he comes closer.

His hair is still wet from the shower after training, but when I glance down at his exposed calves, I smirk when I spot a smear of mud.

*Good work, Legend.*

"I was hoping to see Letty," I confess.

"Ouch," he jokes, lifting his hand to cover his wounded heart.

"But actually, you might be the better option."

"Oh?" he asks, his key halfway to the lock. "Now I'm interested."

He pushes the door open and gestures for me to enter first.

"She'll be back in about twenty minutes. She picked up an extra shift at the coffee shop."

"I can come back," I offer.

"Don't be stupid. You've got something to say, I'm all ears."

I smile up at him as we reach their apartment door, never more grateful for the friends I've found myself surrounded by.

I kept my reaction to Kane's sudden appearance in my life via Letty as neutral as possible. I've tried not to tar him with the same brush as Knox, even when I know they've lived very similar lives and have the same friends.

I owed it to Letty to give him the benefit of the doubt, especially when he did the impossible and actually got out of the Hawks to pursue his football career. That was unheard of —from what I gather—but he managed it. So he had to be at least partly a decent human being, right?

"You want a coffee?" he asks, throwing his bags in the direction of their bedroom and then following me to the kitchen.

"Yeah, sure. Thank you."

Pulling out one of their kitchen stools, I watch him work in silence, anxiety knotting tighter in my stomach as I think about what I want to say to him.

"What's up then? Why would I ever be the better option to turn to for advice than Letty?"

I stare at him as he rests back against the counter with his hands wrapped around his own mug, while mine sits before me, the tempting scent of the rich coffee making my mouth water.

"You know Knox Bowman, right?" I blurt.

Kane's eyes go wide and his head rears back in shock.

"Uh... y-yeah, why?"

I blow out a long breath, my hands trembling in my hands.

"He's out of prison."

Kane's chin drops, his lips attempting to form words, but none come out.

"You know what he went down for?"

"Yeah, arson and killing his old man," he says as if it's the most normal thing in the world to be discussing. I guess when you've grown up in a place like Harrow Creek, it is. "Why?" His eyes narrow on me, as if he's seeing me for the first time, and my mouth runs dry at the confession that's about to fall from my lips.

"He didn't just kill his dad. He killed my mom, too."

"Oh shit," Kane gasps, his fingers raking through his damp hair. "I had no idea."

"Why would you? It's not like I go around advertising it. And I have like, zero desire to affiliate myself with that gang. Ever."

"Shit," he repeats, placing his mug down and pulling out another stool to sit on. "That was only like... four—"

"Five," I correct.

"Shit, five years ago." He nods, his eyes glazing over as he remembers. "Reid was pissed when he pleaded guilty. Really fucking pissed."

My heart begins to race as he reminisces.

"W-why?" I stutter, afraid of what the answer might be.

If Kane confirms what Knox has been saying then—

"Because he didn't do it."

Motherfucker.

I stare at him, but I don't really see him as my breathing becomes erratic and the world around me blurs.

He was telling the truth.

He didn't do it.

He didn't kill my mom and ruin my life.

He—

"Breathe, Violet. Focus on your breathing."

Warmth covers my cheeks as Kane starts demanding I breathe in and out slowly, my mind continuing to race and my body trembling.

"In. Out. In. Out. That's it," he praises when I finally manage to focus on his instructions and get a handle on myself.

"I'm sorry, Violet," he whispers, his eyes soft as he stares down into mine with concern.

I don't hear the front door or anyone join us until Letty barks, "What the hell is going on? Kane, what have you done to her?"

On any other day, I'd be amused by her knee-jerk reaction.

But then, I guess her fiancé does currently have his hands on another woman. Even if it is just my cheeks.

"I'm okay," I whisper, but I have no idea if it's loud enough for her to hear.

"You sure?" Kane asks.

All I can do is shrug.

"I'm sorry, Violet. I'm sorry your life got tainted by all of that. But I can assure you, it wasn't him. He took the fall," Kane explains as he backs up and allows Letty to inspect me for damage.

"I'm okay," I breathe.

"I'm gonna leave you to it," Kane says from somewhere. "If you need anything else, just shout."

"Wait," I cry before he has a chance to disappear.

Letty moves aside and I find him in the doorway.

"If it wasn't him. Who was it?"

He shakes his head, and my heart sinks. "I'm sorry, Violet. I have no idea. Victor, he... he marched to the beat of his own drum. No one ever knew what was really going on in his fucked-up head. Even Reid. But I can ask, see if I can find anything out for you."

"No," I say in a rush. "You're out. I wouldn't want—"

"He's my friend, Violet. I won't be risking anything by asking."

"Thank you," I breathe, my voice shaky as hell as he disappears from view.

Letty lowers herself down in front of me once more, her eyes bouncing between mine.

"What's going on, Vi? You're scaring me."

I glance at my still full coffee mug. "Do you have anything stronger than that?"

"Sure."

"Give me alcohol and I'll tell you everything. With any luck, you'll have some sound advice for me."

---

Thirty minutes and three strong cocktails later, I've bled out my pain, grief, and suffering all over her living room.

Concern covers Letty's face as she holds my hand and just listens. There's no judgment, no questions, no trying to dig deeper. Just unwavering support and encouragement.

"Shit, Vi. I wish you'd told me before."

One of my shoulders lifts in a shrug.

"I was hoping that I'd never have to revisit it. And with Tristan coming back, I hoped..." I blow out a long breath. "I've got no idea what I hoped, really. But he's been there through all of it. My rock. And with him back in my life, I thought maybe it was our chance."

"It is. Just look what's happened. He wants you, Vi."

"He lied to me. I don't—"

"I know. But don't you think that maybe he's scared too? You said that he's confessed to wanting you for a long time. Knox coming back is a threat."

"He never knew there was anything between Knox and me."

"Maybe on some subconscious level, he does."

"He's a guy, Let. Do they have a subconscious level?"

"True," she chuckles.

"Ugh," I groan, throwing myself back on her couch. "I'm so fucking confused."

"You need to talk to them. Both of them. Give yourself some time to figure all this out."

"While living with Tris?" I ask.

"You can crash here," she offers. "Get some space."

I shake my head. "I can't do that. You two need—"

"Stop worrying about everyone else. What do you need?"

I need to go back to when I was sixteen before all this happened.

"I'll get us a refill," Letty says, leaving me with my thoughts.

The sound of her and Kane chatting in the kitchen filters down to me, but it's not loud enough to hear what they're actually saying.

When she finally returns with two new drinks, she's got a wide smile on her face.

"Kane's headed to the guys' place for the party. You up for it?"

"Umm..."

"More alcohol and dancing. Seems like the exact thing you need right now."

"How do you do it, Let?" She frowns, not following my train of thought. "How can you push past the Hawks shit and everything you know Kane has done?"

"Actions don't define a person, Vi. You know that. Yeah, Kane has made some very, very questionable decisions in the past, but mostly it was because he had to. Life in the Creek." She shakes her head as she thinks back. "I don't think anyone can truly understand it unless they've lived there. But you just get swallowed up in that life. A few get out, but not many. Knox... he... he was a good kid. He was tight with Reid, and despite Reid's misgivings with his surname and DNA, he's also a decent human being. Loyal, trustworthy. Would do anything for those he deems worthy. Just because they're connected, it doesn't make them bad people."

"Your dad," I whisper.

"Exactly. He's one of the best people I know, but he still got sucked in. But that was Victor. He was like a leech. Once he got his teeth in, he was never letting go."

"And now?" I ask.

"Things are different. Reid is different."

"He's still a Hawk," I sigh.

"And he's still the boy you gave everything to all those years ago."

Silence falls around us and both our cells buzz.

"That will be Ella. Again. Shall I tell her that we're coming, or do you just want to hang out here?"

Another message comes through.

"We should go. She won't stop otherwise." Letty smiles in agreement. "Can I borrow a dress?"

She thinks for a moment.

"I've got just the thing."

---

Almost two hours later and Letty has worked her magic, and the girl staring back at me in the mirror doesn't look like she's on the verge of falling apart but instead appears confident and like she has her shit together.

What a fucking lie.

"Ready?" Letty asks, slipping her feet into her shoes.

"As I'll ever be."

I take one last look at myself in the fire engine red dress she's loaned me and nod.

Yeah, I look hot. I'm a little curvier than Letty, so it clings to me in all the right places and exposes more than a hint of what I'm rocking up top.

Desire sits heavy in my stomach as I think about what Tristan's reaction would be. It's the exact same shade as the lingerie he fell in love with. Before Knox ruined it, that is.

"Let's go have fun and forget about the world. It'll still be here tomorrow."

"Amen to that."

Letty has an Uber waiting for us outside, and in no time at all, we're being swallowed up by the huge crowd of mostly wasted students that have descended on the team's place.

"Violet. Letty," a familiar voice screams before an over-excited Ella emerges through the crowd and launches herself at us.

"What the hell have you been drinking?" I ask when she falls about laughing.

"I have no idea. Tastes fucking amazing though."

Letty and I share a look over her head.

"Lead the way, I need some of this magic juice," I say, giving as few fucks as Ella as to what the potion might be.

"Hell yes, my girls are ready to party."

The second we make it to the kitchen, I realize we're safe drinking whatever has Ella flying high because West seems to be the bartender, handing out multicolored drinks to his eager, barely dressed customers.

"Ladies, ladies, one at a time please," he teases.

"Come on, big man. I'm sure you can handle more than that," one of the chasers slurs.

"Jesus," I mutter, "they're out in full force tonight."

"When aren't they?" Ella quips, watching as Colt walks into the room with a little female fan club behind him.

He shoots her a look that is nothing but pure sex before turning to the fridge and pulling out a couple of bottles of beer.

"Where are the freshman? I thought they were the team's little bitches at parties?"

"Oh, they are. But the guys decided this year's group needed a more challenging initiation than that," Ella explains. "They've sent them out on a little mission."

My brows lift in amusement.

"Don't ask me what, though. I'm not privy to such things."

"You should suck Colt's dick harder, all his secrets might just spill right out of him."

"Un-fucking-likely. That dick is as locked up as they come."

"Come on, let's go dance. The guys can deliver our drinks when they've stopped entertaining the whores." Letty takes both our hands and drags us out of the kitchen and toward the crowd of gyrating bodies in the living room.

---

"Vi, you need to slow down," Ella says as I throw back my third... fourth... maybe even fifth shot in a row.

"I'm fine," I state confidently, although from the way her brow wrinkles, I have to wonder if those words sounded as sober as they did in my head.

"You're really not. Here," she says, sliding a bottle of water toward me. "You can crash here with me tonight."

"I'm not top and tailing with you and Colton fucking Rogers," I complain.

"And you think I'd share him with you? Don't move. I'm going to tell Letty you're staying."

I watch as she sashays through the room before twisting around with the boring bottle of water in my hand.

"Braxton," I sing when a familiar face saunters into the room.

He ignores the chasers who reach for him, instead beelining straight toward me.

"Make me one of those drinks you and West were handing out."

"No chance. Ella's cut you off."

"Braaax," I complain. "You're meant to be the fun one."

"You'll thank me tomorrow."

"Doubt it," I sulk, pushing from the counter and stumbling toward the backdoor. My sudden need for fresh air is too much to deny.

Swinging the door open, I step out, sucking in deep lungfuls of the fresh night air.

Despite the party spilling onto the front yard, it seems that no one has made it around here yet and I revel in the peace and quiet.

Movement in the trees to the side of me catches my eye, but as I squint, trying to see if it was more than my imagination, I don't see it again.

"Humph," I breathe.

Standing there in the middle of the backyard, I tip my head up and stare at the stars.

The sky is as dark and clear as the night I drunk-dialed Tristan and gave him little choice but to rescue me.

But he won't be doing that tonight, because I'm not calling him.

*He lied to me. Lied. He knew that asshole was free and he didn't tell me.*

*Why would he do that to me? I thought he...* hiccup... *I thought he liked me.*

*I thought he...* hiccup.

I move forward, my heels failing to cope with the grass beneath my feet, and I lose my footing, stumbling forward.

My heart plummets into my stomach as I prepare for the landing which is imminent.

It's going to hurt. But at least the alcohol will numb it. For now.

But the hit never comes. Instead, a strong pair of arms catches me and I'm hauled against a solid chest as a very familiar scent fills my nose.

# 25

# VIOLET

*"How drunk are you?" Knox asks after going through his usual routine of propping my chair under the door handle and stripping out of his clothes.*

*He slips under the covers, still wearing his boxers and hiding his body from me with the sheets. I love that he doesn't pressure me into anything, but equally, I kinda want to see all of him. He's a work of art, and it's addicting, watching his muscles flex and pull.*

*I chuckle at his question. "I've had two beers," I point out. "I'm not drunk at all." Unlike my brother, who stole a bottle of our parents' vodka and started doing shots with Tristan well over an hour ago like they were about to go out of fashion.*

*"That's good," he murmurs, sliding closer and snaking his arm around my body.*

*"Oh yeah, I thought you'd want me tipsy so you can take advantage," I tease.*

*He stills above me, staring down into my eyes with a serious expression on his face. "Never, Violet. I never want to take advantage of you," he says with such sincerity it makes my chest ache.*

*"Knox," I breathe, reaching up and twisting my fingers in his hair at the back of his head.*

*I tug him closer, and thankfully, he lowers down, the heat of his skin burning mine as his lips brush over the corner of my mouth in the most teasing of kisses.*

*"I need you," I beg. "Please."*

*"You're still thinking about earlier, aren't you, Firefly?"*

*"About how you got me close to exploding and then walking away? Yeah, I haven't forgotten that. I should send you back to your own bed for that stunt."*

*"Yeah, you probably should," he admits, although he makes no move to actually do so. "But you need me, don't you, baby?"*

*A moan of approval rumbles low in my throat as my body begins to burn up for his touch, for his kisses.*

*"Kiss me," I demand.*

*"My pleasure."*

*This time, he doesn't just tease me with what I need. He gives me everything.*

*My lips part to allow his tongue to slip inside and tangle with mine. He crawls over me, settling between my thighs and slipping one hand down my body, tracing my curves with his palm before dropping to squeeze my ass, making me moan.*

*"Addicted," he groans into my kiss. "And I can't stop thinking about how you looked sucking my cock earlier."*

*Just to prove that point, he moves closer, rolling his hips against me.*

*"Shit, Knox."*

*I've been so worked up all day that one brush against my clit and I'm almost falling.*

*"Fucking love watching you fall," he admits, pushing up so he can watch my face as he dry humps me.*

*"More," I beg. "I need—"*

*"I've got you, baby."*

*Wrapping his fingers around the hem of my tank, he drags it up my body, exposing my breasts. Immediately, he dips his head, sucking, licking and nipping at my sensitive flash, making me climb ever closer to that edge that holds so much promise.*

*He moves lower, his lips brushing over my stomach until he hits my panties.*

*"Sexy," he murmurs, tracing the lace edging.*

*Since we started hooking up, it's definitely had an impact on my underwear drawer. All my boring old cotton panties are now stuffed at the back, and in their place are much sexier, tinier lace options.*

*"Take them off," I breathe, desperate to feel him against me without a barrier between us.*

*"Love it when you're desperate for me. You want my tongue on you, baby?"*

*"Yes," I cry, hoping that both Roman and Tristan are drunk enough not to hear anything.*

*In seconds, my panties are on the floor and his large hands are spreading my legs wide and blowing a stream of air across my heated, sensitive pussy.*

*"Knox." One of my hands twists in his hair, trying to drag him closer. The other fists the sheets as anticipation floods my veins.*

*"Anything," he says before leaning forward and sucking on my clit.*

*Slamming my lips closed, I scream out behind them as his tongue gets to work, laving at my clit with the perfect pressure.*

*I climb high and fast, and the second he pushes two fingers inside me, I shatter.*

*I swear lights flash behind my eyes, my release is so strong.*

*"Worth the wait, huh?" Knox says smugly, and when I look up, I find that he's still sitting between my legs, but he's shoved his boxers down and he's fisting his hard length.*

*My mouth waters as I stare at him, remembering exactly how he tasted earlier, and my tongue darts out, sweeping across my bottom lip.*

*Every muscle in his body is pulled as tight as a bow as he watches me watch him. Precum glistens at the tip of his cock, and as much as I might want to taste him again, there's something else I want more.*

*I want to feel him inside me.*

*I want to know what all the fuss is about. And if it can possibly feel any better than his tongue.*

*"Do it," I whisper.*

*"H-huh?" he stutters, not following my train of thought.*

*"I want you to... I want you to have all my firsts."*

*His breathing falters as his brain catches up with him.*

*"I'm not worthy of them all, Firefly," he says sadly.*

*"You are," I argue. "I certainly don't want anyone else to have them."*

*His eyes flash with uncertainty despite the fact he clearly wants to.*

*"Violet, I—"*

*"Show me how good it feels. I want you."*

*"Goddamn, Firefly. How am I meant to refuse that?"*

*"You're not." My eyes drop from his to where his cock is so close to my entrance. "I'm on birth control," I tell him, despite him already knowing. "And I trust you."*

*"Big, big mistake, Firefly."*

*"Let me be the judge of that," I argue.*

*"I've never gone bare."*

*"Then we can both have a first together. I don't get many of yours."*

*Anger and disappointment flicker through his eyes, but I refuse to let him talk himself out of this because he thinks I'm worth more or some shit.*

*"Knox, I need you to fuck me. Please. I want to feel you deep insi—" My words are cut off when he presses against my entrance, pushing just the tip inside.*

I awake with a start, my heart pounding and my body burning up.

There's a fucking marching band in my head, and the longer I lie here, the worse it seems to get. Almost as if it's punishing me for being awake.

Needing it to go away, I attempt to turn over and snuggle deeper into the sheets, but the second I do, it becomes very apparent that I'm not alone.

My eyes fly open. The room isn't all that light, but the bright sunlight that does creep around the curtains is enough to burn the backs of my eyes.

But that isn't the most pressing issue.

That's where the hell I am.

I scan my surroundings, not recognizing a single thing, other than the fact it's quite clearly a hotel room.

What the fuck did I do last night?

Memories begin hitting me.

The cocktails.

Shots.

Dancing.

Talking to Kane.

Letty's advice.

I look down at the arm that's pinning me to the bed, and a loud gasp rips through the silent room when I find a whole host of tattoos staring back up at me.

No.

I scramble, my hangover momentarily forgotten, as I fight to get away.

"Stop it," a deep, sleepy voice demands, his grip on my body only tightening. "Go back to sleep, it's early."

My heart pounds and white noise fills my ears.

This can't actually be happening.

"No, I need to go." I continue trying to fight, but it's futile.

Even if I was firing on all cylinders, I'd never overpower him. Ever.

I'm dragged back, the entire length of his hot and hard

body pressing against mine, and damn it if my blood temperature doesn't spike just that little bit.

"Knox, you can't do this. You can't hold me here against my will," I argue, forcing as much anger and hatred into my voice as possible. But after my conversation with Kane last night, it's harder than before.

"You fit against me just as well as you always did, Firefly," he growls, his hot breath ghosting over my ear and racing down my neck.

A violent shudder rips through my body, and there's no way he doesn't feel it.

"You need to let me go," I continue.

"Listen to your body, baby. It realizes that it's exactly where it should be."

"Why am I here? Where even is here?"

He nuzzles my neck. Fucking nuzzles my neck, like we're long lost lovers finally reunited.

"Go back to sleep. You can't tell me that you don't have a hangover."

I silently fume.

"I know you do. I saw how much you drank. Sleep it off, we've got all day."

"No," I spit. "Absolutely not."

This time when I fight, I put every bit of my energy into it, and when I arch my back, forcing my foot out blindly behind me in the hope of catching him in the dick, he thankfully darts back to escape and lets his grip loosen.

I'm out of bed and backing far enough away from his reach before he's even realized what's happened. Or at least, that's what my hazy, alcohol-filled brain tells me, anyway.

"Violet," he groans, his eyes dropping down the length of my body. But as much as I might want to do the same and discover what state I'm in, I don't, and not just because he pushes himself up to rest against the headboard and lets the sheets pool at his waist, exposing his insane body.

Holy fuck, he's cut.

After a very brief trek around his torso, I find his amused eyes once more.

Goddamn him. He knows exactly how to get my attention, and he's not afraid to play dirty.

"Where are we, Knox?" I demand.

"In a hotel."

"Where?"

"Maddison County."

I suck in a deep breath in the hope it calms the inferno of confusion that's raging inside me.

"Why am I here?" I ask, changing tact.

"Because you were off-your-ass drunk and I didn't want to deliver you back to Tristan, but I also knew I couldn't take you back to where I'm staying, and your house was too far away."

I nod, understanding all those points.

"Where's my purse? My cell?"

"You can have them back after we've talked."

"You're a cunt," I spit.

"I'm more than aware of that fact, Firefly. Now," he says, throwing the sheets from the rest of his body and climbing to his feet, giving me an unobstructed view of the rest of him. Well, everything bar what's straining against the fabric of his boxers.

Seventeen-year-old Knox was a piece of art to look at. His handful of tattoos, his muscles, those V lines.

But adult Knox? He's a god.

It is not fair.

But then, nothing about my life is fucking fair, so I don't even know why I'm surprised.

"The main door is locked. I have the key. So don't even try to escape while I take a piss. We're having this out here. And if it ends in me finally having an orgasm without the use of my own hand, then even better."

My chin drops as shock rocks through me, but he's long gone by the time I even attempt to come up with any kind of comeback for that.

"There's water and pills on the side. Figure you'd need them."

I glance around the room, my eyes quickly finding what I so desperately need and I rush over, throwing a couple of pills back and downing the water.

And it isn't until I've done that that I finally stand in front of the mirror and take in the state of me.

"Fucking hell," I groan.

My hair is a matted mess, my makeup is everywhere it's not meant to be, and I'm wearing... I sigh heavily... Knox's tank.

The arm holes are fucking massive, resulting in me showing off a more than generous amount of side boob. I mean, he's seen it all before. But still, I'd rather not know that he undressed me last night and got an eyeful of my tits.

Lifting the hem, I breathe a sigh of relief when I find that I'm still wearing panties.

The sound of the toilet flushing fills the room—thanks to the fact he didn't shut the door—before he begins brushing his teeth.

Before I can stop myself, I storm across the room, kick the door wider and join him at the sink, plucking the other toothbrush from the cup, squirting toothpaste onto it and shoving it in my mouth.

He watches me intently, and I know that if I were to look over, or even up at the mirror in front of us, then I would see them dancing with mirth.

We stand side by side in one of the most surreal moments of my life before he finally spits, rinses and walks out.

I watch him go, surprised that he's willingly giving me space. But then, I guess there's only so far he can go. And I have no doubt that he's telling the truth about not being able to escape. He's not likely to lie about something like that.

By the time I've finished in the bathroom, I find him once again lounging back on the bed, this time totally out of the sheets, making it a fucking effort to look anywhere else but him.

He's playing dirty, and I hate that it's working.

*"He didn't do it."* Kane's words come back to me as I stare at Knox as he studies the room service menu.

"You hungry?" he asks innocently, as if I chose to be here and spend the night with him.

"Um..."

"I know you are. Pancakes?"

My mouth waters and my stomach growls, desperate for something other than liquid.

"As long as it comes with some very strong coffee."

Holding my head up high, I march around the bed, aiming for the chair in the corner that's angled to look out the window.

His attention burns into me as I pull the curtains back, flooding the room with the high morning sun before curling up in the chair, keeping my back to him.

The view isn't really much to look at, and it helps me figure out where we are as I clock the stores and restaurants that line the street beneath us.

We're only a couple of minutes from the team's house. It's probably the first hotel he found after abducting me.

I sit there silently, fuming, my head spinning with this whole disaster while the marching band continues—although, thankfully, the pills have started to kick in and it's beginning to get quieter.

I listen to Knox's deep voice as he places our order before silence falls between us once more.

But unlike all those times in my old bedroom, it's anything but comfortable.

The air between us crackles with unspoken words. The

chemistry that apparently hasn't so much as lessened in the past five years.

"Does anyone know I'm here? My friends will be—"

"Your little blonde friend knows. She caught me walking away with you."

"Great," I mutter, aware that I've probably got a cell phone with a bazillion messages on it asking who I've been rescued by this week.

I really need to stop partying and drinking. It does nothing but get me in trouble.

"Ashamed to be seen with me?" he quips.

"No one in my life now knows anything about my past."

"Apart from Tristan."

"Obviously." I can't help but roll my eyes. "But even he doesn't know the whole truth."

"So I figured."

"What does that mean?" I bark, stupidly twisting around and giving him my attention once more.

"We talked yesterday."

"Y-you did?" I question like a moron.

"Thought it was about time we cleared a few things up."

"Did you tell him more truth than you did me?"

"I only told him what was important," he says casually, dragging his eyes from mine and looking down at his hand.

"Which was?"

"That you're mine."

All the air rushes out of my lungs at his statement. He says it as seriously as if he was telling me that the sky was blue.

"I-I'm not yours, Knox. I haven't been for a long time. If I ever even was," I add bitterly.

"You were mine," he confirms, scooting across the bed and sitting on the edge.

I panic that he's going to come closer, but either he never intended to or my reaction to his proximity was enough to stop him, because he simply plants his elbows on his knees and stares at me just like he used to. As if he can see right down to my soul.

"Tristan..." I shake my head. "I haven't told him about us. I never told anyone about us."

"Was I your dirty little secret, Firefly?"

"That or my biggest regret."

"Ouch." He lifts his hand and covers his heart.

"What do you actually want from me, Knox? Five years ago, you were everything to me," I confess, deciding to do with some truth, even if it is going to hurt. "I couldn't see anything but you. And then you shredded my already broken heart when you pleaded guilty. Can you even begin to imagine how that felt?"

He shakes his head, regret filling his blue eyes. "I'm sorry, Violet. Truly fucking sorry. The last thing I wanted to do was hurt you. You were my girl."

His words are like a punch to my gut.

"You should have talked to me. You should have—"

"You were drowning, Violet. I couldn't tell you what was going on. It was a mess. It still is a fucking mess."

"Tell me," I beg. "Tell me all of it. I want to understand. I need to understand."

He scrubs his hand down his face, his eyes dropping from mine for a beat.

The loss of his attention is akin to someone throwing a bucket of cold water over me, and I hop up.

"You're still going to lie, aren't you?"

"N-no, I—"

"You don't get to lock me up in here, tell me that I can only be free when we've talked yet refuse to talk. You're the one who holds all the cards here, Knox. I did nothing wrong. Remember? All I did that night was go to sleep in my bed, like I did every night. Then the next thing I knew, I was in Tristan's arms, the house alight, my life going up in flames."

"In Tristan's arms?" he asks, a frown pulling at his lips. "Why?"

I hiss, crossing my arms over my chest and glaring at him.

He looks up at me through his lashes, and I have to really fight with myself not to react.

With Kane confirming what Knox was already telling me, it's softened my anger toward him, and bricks are falling from the walls I've built faster than I can control. Especially when he looks at me like that with the vulnerability he allowed me to see when we were kids.

It fucking wrecks me.

"Tristan wasn't the one to get you out of your house that night, Firefly. I found out what was happening. I raced to the house as fast as I could.

"You were still sleeping in your bed none the wiser when I found you. Your room was thick with smoke. How it hadn't woken you, fuck only knows.

"I didn't think we were going to make it back out. The fire was well out of control."

"But you did it. You did. You got us out," I say, without even questioning that he's telling the truth. I know it is. I can see it in every inch of his face.

"I did. I tried to go back for your mom too, but the flames were too hot and the stairs were consumed by it. If I could have done anything, I would have. I need you to know that, Violet."

"B-but, when I woke up, I was in Tristan's arms. H-how—"

"I called him and Roman the second I heard that there had been a hit on my dad. I got there before both of them."

I shake my head. "I don't remember you being there."

"Trust me, baby. I was. An ambulance came for you. Tris went with you. Roman and I stayed while the firefighters tried to contain the fire, and Victor came to ensure his dirty work had been carried out."

"It really wasn't you?" I ask, a deep frown pulling at my brows.

"No, Firefly. It really wasn't me. I'd have given my own life before ever hurting you."

A sob rips up my throat, and before I know what's happening, strong arms wrap around me and I'm surrounded by the person who was my everything so long ago.

## 26

## KNOX

The second she's in my arms, everything that's been wrong with my life for the past five years instantly rights itself.

This is all I needed.

Her.

My little firefly.

"Violet," I breathe, pressing my lips to her hair before sucking in a deep breath of her scent.

*I'm home.*

I thought I felt relief the day Reid told me he had a way for me to get out, and then again when I walked out of those gates and dropped into his car, but neither of them has anything on this moment.

Neither of us speaks. We just stand there, soaking up everything that we've been missing. Or at least, I hope that's what she's been doing too. Her tears soak my chest, but she doesn't make a sound as she drowns in the pain of everything she lost. I hate that I haven't been here to keep her together. I had to trust Roman and Tristan to do that in my absence. And at least one of them pulled through for her. It's the reason why

I'm finding it hard to hate him, knowing that he's been with her.

But eventually, a knock sounds out, notifying us that our breakfast is here, and she pulls her head from my chest.

"You should get that," she says, staring up at me with her huge, tear-filled emerald eyes.

Regretfully, I release her body, but only in favor of cupping her cheeks.

Another knock comes.

"Just leave it by the door," I shout.

Violet startles at the volume of my voice, but she doesn't move. Instead, she stays exactly where she is, staring right back at me as another tear falls.

I catch it with my thumb.

"Baby, please don't cry."

I press my brow to hers and she closes her eyes, absorbing my presence, and I can't help but do the same.

"Go and get the food, Knox," she finally says, taking a step back and severing our connection.

I stand there staring at her for long seconds after she's pulled away from me.

She wraps her arms around herself and keeps her eyes on the floor.

It fucking pains me to see her suffering, and I can't help but wonder just how bad it's been over the past five years.

And while I might want to hate him, I'm also incredibly grateful for Tristan. His family too, because I know they were the ones to help keep Violet together after everything blew up in her face.

*You did the wrong thing*, a little voice says in my head.

But it's too late now. I made a decision, and I trusted the wrong person.

And until I manage to find him and tell him what a fucking weak coward I really think he is, there's not much I can do about it.

Other than forcing my way back into her life and proving to her that the boy she knew all those years ago is still here.

I might be a little older, a little more jaded by life and carrying a whole heap of scars. Scars that include a heart that was shredded the moment I was forced to walk away from her, but deep down, I'm still me. The boy from the wrong part of town that she took a chance on.

"Firefly?" I reach for her, but she startles as if she was just in a trance.

"Just get the food, Knox," she whispers before walking back toward the chair by the window.

I desperately want to demand she crawls onto the bed and we have breakfast there like we have done so many times in the past, but I bite my lip as she curls back into it.

With a sigh, I stalk toward the hotel room door and retrieve our breakfast.

The second the scent of sweet pancakes and salty bacon hits my nose, my mouth waters and my stomach growls.

Placing it on the small table by the chair Violet is sitting on, I hand her the coffee first and then pull the other chair closer—although, with the small table between us, it's nowhere near as close to her as I'd like.

She sips her coffee in silence, and I watch her as she gets lost in her own head, giving her the time she needs to process everything that's happened since I crashed back into her life two days ago.

I drain my coffee before reaching for my plate. It's gone all too quickly and I'm left, still feeling hungry, while Violet's pancakes sits temptingly between us.

My eyes move from them to her, and I watch as she worries her lip, a deep frown creasing her brow.

"Violet, I—"

"I believe you. I believe you didn't start it, Knox."

All the air rushes from my lungs at her statement, and I slide forward in my seat.

"W-what made you come to that conclusion?" I whisper, pushing my hair back while something inside me dances in triumph. If she believes that then maybe, just maybe...

"I spoke to Kane. Confessed who I was, and asked about what he knew."

I want to be angry that she'd believe the word of a guy who's been in her life for barely a year when I've never been anything but truthful with her.

*Aside from the day you pleaded guilty, asshole.*

"What did he say?" I ask.

She shakes her head. "Not much. Just that he knew you were innocent. He was about as useless as you in telling me who did do it, though."

I want to smile, but I force it down. If I never needed evidence for how loyal Reid is, then there it is.

He managed to wrap the details of that night up so tight that not even his most loyal soldiers, or ex-soldier, where Legend is concerned, know the truth.

I fucking owe him everything. I'm going to be indebted to him for life, but something tells me he won't hold that over my head. Well, not too much.

"Violet, I—"

"I just wish I could understand why. It was gang shit, yeah. I get that, kind of. But why would you willingly rip my heart out like that?"

I dip my head, not proud of this answer. "I told you, Violet. I'd have ruined what we had at some point. It just happened sooner rather than later."

"That's bullshit," she hisses. "You made a choice."

"At the time, it felt like the right one."

Pushing to my feet, I slide her plate of pancakes back and lower my ass to the table.

She startles when I place my hands on her thighs, but her eyes don't shift from mine.

"Why?" she breathes, her voice rough with emotion.

My heart pounds as my need to tell her everything burns through me.

I should. My loyalty needs to be with her now but even still, when my lips part, it's not what comes out.

"I'll always protect you, Violet. Always. Since the day I walked into your house in Maddison County, you became the single most important person in my life. I tried to stay away. But even in those early days, you called to me like no one else ever had. The connection I felt with you... I couldn't deny it, or ignore it despite knowing I was all kinds of wrong for you.

"I hated my dad for moving us out of the Creek, and I hated him even more for inserting us into the middle of your family.

"None of you deserve to be tainted by our past, but I knew it would happen. I was just too gone for you to do anything about it by the time I realized how bad it was.

"If I could, I'd have taken you to the other side of the world to protect you. But I had nothing, Violet. No means to protect you. But I swore that night I first slipped into your bed that I'd always do right by you, and that was all I could try and do."

"You left me," she whispers. "When I needed you most, you left me."

I hang my head as the weight of my mistakes press down on me.

"I thought I was leaving you with Roman and Tristan. I knew they'd look after you while I was gone."

The bitter laugh that falls from her lips is all kinds of painful.

"Roman. You left me with Roman. He barely lasted a week after that fire before he checked out, leaving Tristan and his family to pick up the pieces.

"I had no one, Knox. No one. I thought you'd k-killed—" She hiccups, cutting off her words and I reach for her with zero consideration. It's like it's ingrained in me to console her, to protect her, to do anything for her.

She clings to me like a monkey, with both her arms and legs wrapped around my body tightly.

"I'll forever regret allowing you to think that of me, Firefly. But I would never have—"

"I know."

The shock her words causes makes my movements falter, and when she pulls her head from my chest and looks up at me with her huge green eyes that literally changed my life all those years ago, I forget about everything but us.

We crash to the bed and I just about manage not to crush her under my weight. But she never lets me go.

Her tongue sneaks out, swiping across her bottom lip, tempting me like a little kid in a candy shop.

One second, I imagine what it might be like to kiss her again, and the next, my lips are on hers and my tongue is pushing inside her mouth to find out.

In one sense, kissing her is like going back in time. It's easy to pretend we're just reckless kids sneaking around in our parents' house. But the pain that I can taste in her kiss is a harsh reminder of everything we've been through in our time apart.

I want to take it all away from her. Allow her to be that carefree teenager she used to be before her world imploded.

She hesitates to return my kiss to begin with, her mouth still against mine. Fear like I've never known washes through me that she's going to force me to stop. And all because of that fucking pussy, Tristan.

But with another sweep of my tongue, her resolve finally snaps.

Her grip on my shoulders and waist tightens as her lips move with mine, and despite my best intentions, my arms give out and I drop my weight onto her, the hardness of my cock impossible to miss as it presses against her heated core.

She kisses me like a savage, like she's trying to make up for the past five years of lost kisses. And I'm here for it.

Our tongues duel, our teeth clash, and our bodies writhe as we try to take what we've so desperately been missing from each other.

Time ceases to exist. The world outside this room might as well stop, all the people in our lives gone as we focus on us once more. On what we found in our late-night rendezvous all those years ago.

"Knox," she moans as I kiss down her jaw, nipping at her skin with my teeth in a way I remember she used to love.

"Missed you so fucking much, Firefly," I confess, finding her lips once again.

My addiction to her morphed into an obsession while I was locked away, and I fear both may have only just gotten worse again.

Flipping us, I grab handfuls of her ass and drag her down onto me.

She cries out as she rolls her hips, making use of my hard dick like she used to.

Fuck, I was way too fucking happy just watching her get off when we were kids.

My balls were constantly aching, my cock painful as I did the right thing and waited for her to get her hands or her mouth on me.

I should have been given an award for how fucking patient I was back then. Either that or a few extra tubs of Vaseline for when I finally got some alone time and was able to attempt to relieve the need she caused within me.

"Fuck, baby. Are you going to come all over my dick like the old days?" I groan into her kiss, hoping like fuck she's going to.

Despite my best efforts, some of my memories of those days have already begun to fade. That or I've used them up, because fuck, I spend hours obsessing over each and every one on my long, cold, and lonely nights.

Suddenly, she stills, rips her lips from mine, and sits up.

But despite the panic filtering through her features, all I can see is how goddamn beautiful she looks.

Her cheeks are red, her lips swollen, her chest heaving, and her nipples hard beneath the fabric of my tank.

"You own me," I breathe, unable to keep the words in.

Greedily sucking down lungfuls of air, she stares down at me with wide eyes, and although she stopped this, she doesn't seem to mind when I continue to rock her hips over my length.

"W-we can't, Knox," she stutters, her eyes dark with desire as her nails drag against my abs. Fuck if that doesn't make my cock weep for her.

"Because of him?"

"Yes," she gasps as I thrust my hips. "Tristan and a whole host of other reasons. I should be as far away from you as physically possible right now. You lied to me. He lied to me. Everything is so fucked-u— Knox," she cries when I thrust again, hitting her clit exactly right.

"Get yourself off on me, Firefly. Use me. Take what you need. I won't ask for a thing in return."

She stares at me with her swollen lips parted in shock.

To prove my point, I take the massive fucking risk of releasing her ass and laying my arms out at my sides.

"Use me," I growl, hoping she's as powerless to follow my demands as she used to be.

The second her hips roll, I know I've got her.

"I shouldn't be doing this," she whispers, almost as if she's talking to herself more than she is to me.

"You should. You deserve all the pleasure in the world."

Her movements quickly increase in speed, her little moans and mewls of pleasure getting louder, and somehow, I get even harder.

"I fell asleep every night thinking of you, baby," I confess, holding her eyes steady.

"Knox," she breathes. Disbelief fills her voice, as if she's not even sure this is even real.

As she begins to lose herself to her impending release, her hands move from my abs and she begins tracing the ink that now litters my body.

For a long time in prison, pain was the only way I could deal with the situation I landed myself in. Thankfully, there were plenty of rival gang members inside those concrete walls to deliver as much as I could handle. And if I needed more, then one of my cellmates over the years was pretty handy with a tattoo machine.

I know the second she finds the one that sits over my heart before her fingers get there.

A loud gasp rips through the air, but before she can do or say anything, she falls. And it's the most fucking beautiful thing I've ever seen.

# 27

# VIOLET

My release rips through me, but even with the mind-numbing pleasure, I'm unable to take my eyes away from that tattoo.

How did I miss it earlier?

"K-Knox, is this—"

"A firefly," he answers for me. Not that it's necessary. I can see exactly what it is.

Wrapping his fingers around my wrists, he tugs me forward and rolls us onto our sides.

Our bodies might not be touching any longer, but the heat from his body burns my skin as the aftershocks from my release continue to make my muscles twitch.

"There wasn't one second of my time away that I forgot about you, Violet. Every word I ever said to you was true. I just never got a chance to say the most important ones."

Reaching out, I press my fingers to his lips, too terrified to hear those words he's talking about. If he says them, it'll change everything.

And I can't cope with more of that.

Everything in my life is upside down.

"I have a question," I blurt.

He nods, encouraging me to ask.

"Did you have anything to do with the fire at our student house?"

He doesn't react for a few seconds, and I panic that I've just fucked everything up. But then, the corners of his mouth twitch up into a smile and he laughs.

"No, baby. I had nothing to do with it," he says before he suddenly turns serious, his brows pinching in concern. "You think it was arson?"

I shake my head. "No. We had electrical issues, it was more than likely that. We're waiting for the report. But then you turned up and..."

"I might tell you that I'll do anything to have you back, but I promise, I won't burn down your house. I'd never put you through something like that ever again. But if you really think it could have been suspicious, I can ask Reid if—"

"No," I bark. "I want nothing to do with him and that gang."

"Yet you're lying here in bed with me, Firefly."

"You always were the exception to my rules."

Silence falls between us, and my hand drops back to the pillow.

"You should get some more sleep," he whispers, but it's pointless, because with my hangover still raging and the high from my release fading, my eyelids are already falling closed, my exhaustion claiming me. And I only fall deeper into it when he scoots over and wraps me up in his arms and kisses my brow sweetly.

---

When I come to again, I'm alone in bed, but the second I breathe in, his familiar and comforting scent washes through me and I can't help but smile into the pillow. Of course, it's helped by the fact my hangover seems to have mostly gone.

Opening my eyes, I find the room empty. The only difference from earlier is that my purse is sitting on the table where I left my untouched breakfast.

I push up, ready to walk over and discover what kind of chaos my life has descended into while I've been locked away here with Knox.

Swinging my legs over the edge of the bed, my feet hit the thick carpet as thoughts of Tristan hit me.

He has to be freaking out.

What if he drove back to my house, thinking I was still there?

What if he's out there looking for me?

"Shit," I hiss, all my mistakes piling up on top of me like bricks.

Rushing over, I pull my cell free and stare down at the screen.

I've got a whole stream of messages in our housemate group chat, and another load from Ella individually, but it's Tristan's single message that makes my breath catch.

**Tristan: I hope he treats you right.**

My hand trembles as I stare down at those words.

What the hell do I reply to that?

The sound of the shower running eventually drags me from my daze, and I quickly figure that really, there is nothing I could say to Tristan that will make any of this any better.

I need to get Knox to take me home, and we need to talk.

Locking my cell, I push it back into my purse and walk toward the bathroom.

Steam billows from the open door and I can't help myself.

I slip inside and rest my ass back on the sink, my eyes locked on the man standing behind the glass screen.

It's a little fogged up, but nowhere near enough to hide anything from me.

His muscular back ripples, the ink almost coming to life as he moves his hands around his body, scrubbing himself with the soap the hotel has provided. The huge Hawk tattoo on his back makes my heart sink. That never used to be there, and I was ever hopeful it was because he'd get out. Clearly, that was wishful thinking.

"I know you're watching me, Firefly. I can feel your eyes on my body."

"Oh yeah?" I whisper, my cheeks heating from being caught despite knowing I would be.

He stands directly under the torrent of water, letting the bubbles rush down his body.

My teeth sink into my bottom lip as I watch them descend over his insane ass.

It's wrong.

Oh so fucking wrong.

But I can't help feeling that everything is also right.

Being with Knox, it's always been so easy. Like it was meant to be. Like we were two pieces of the same puzzle.

And while I might have crushed hard on Tristan during that hormone-fueled time of my life, he hadn't wriggled his way under my skin like he has now.

His support over the years, his friendship... it's been everything. Our relationship has strengthened to the point that I can't imagine my life without him.

And the past week with him... it's been no different .

I can't give that up to return to how things used to be with Knox.

I know that with absolute certainty.

But equally, walking away from this broken, yet beautiful man, or at least the boy I used to know that he's given me glimpses of since he stormed back into my life. I'm not sure I'm going to be able to turn him away either.

So, where the hell does that leave me?

But then, Knox turns around, and all those thoughts about

what happens next just fall from my mind as if they never existed.

Water rivulets run over his inked chest and abs before racing down his V line and over his—

My mouth goes dry.

"Y—" I have to clear my throat when I try to speak, but no words come out.

He chuckles, but I can't look up to see that smile because my eyes are locked on his dick.

"You and your tattoo artist were real close, huh?"

"There are some real long and boring days inside, Firefly. Gotta find the excitement wherever you can." His unspoken words in that statement intrigue me enough to finally lift my gaze.

"Should I be worried?"

Reaching out, he wraps his fingers around his shaft and strokes slowly.

"I'm aching for you, Violet. I have been for five years. My dick only gets hard for you."

I scoff. "I find that hard to believe."

"It's the truth. From the moment I first kissed you, there has been no other girl for me. I haven't so much as looked at anyone else. And that goes for the men I shared cells with. I promise you, this is as close as any got. And there was no pleasure involved."

"Strangely enough, I can believe that. Didn't it hurt?"

He shrugs as if it was nothing. "It was worth it."

My eyes widen at his comment.

"Whatever you say."

"Come closer," he demands, his hungry eyes trying to lure me in.

"Knox," I warn.

"Just to check out my ink. No funny business."

I quirk a brow at him. "Sure, I— Knox," I squeal when he

steps out of the shower stall, twists his finger in the front of his tank and drags me back under the water with him.

I'm soaked in a flash, the fabric immediately sticking to my body.

"Was that necessary?" I hiss, staring up at him through narrowed eyes in an attempt to look pissed off.

In reality, my heart is racing and my blood is verging on boiling point, being this close to his hard, godlike, naked body.

"Just look. Then you can clean up and—" He swallows, refusing to finish that sentence.

"And?"

"And then I'll take you home."

I can't help but sigh.

"I don't have a home here right now."

"Yeah, you do. It's with Tristan. And I know for a fact that he's going out of his mind right now."

His words shock me, but then after what he confessed earlier about taunting Tristan with what happened between us all those years ago, I guess I shouldn't be.

"You've spoken to him?"

"I've assured him that you're safe."

"He's going to hate you," I warn.

"I can more than handle that," he confesses. "As long as I get this."

I'm too lost in his eyes, his words, the sparks that are shooting between the two of us to notice he's reached out and begun pulling the sodden tank from my body until it's too late.

"Knox, I—"

"Fucking hell, Firefly," he groans as if he's in pain as the tank lands in the shower tray at our feet with a wet slap. "You're fucking breathtaking."

His eyes take in every inch of my body as my nipples harden to the point of pain and every muscle south of my waist contracts.

"I never deserved you," he mutters quietly.

"No. You didn't. But look where we are."

Forcing my eyes from him, I let them roll down his body, lingering a little longer on the firefly tattoo that sits right above his heart than I do on the others.

He has me inked onto his skin.

That's...

I let out a sigh as I continue staring at it, trying to get my head around its meaning.

I startle when his fingers thread through my wet hair and twist until I have no choice but to look up at him.

"It was always you, Firefly. Never, ever forget that."

My heart tumbles as I remember just how hard and fast I fell for him five years ago, but before I'm able to think about how quickly he's managed to turn it around, I'm forced to my knees.

"Knox," I gasp. "I thought you said— oh fuck," I mutter when my eyes find the side of his cock, or more specifically, the ink.

"More fireflies," I whisper, unable to believe what I'm seeing. "And... and violets."

"I'd have branded your name all over my skin if I didn't think you'd hate it, Violet."

"I-I don't... I can't..." I'm at a total loss for words as I regretfully move my eyes from his cock and find his as he stares down at me.

The blue of his irises has vanished, swallowed whole by his blown, desire-filled pupils. His chest heaves and his cock bobs in my peripheral.

"Fuck, I missed you. I—"

His words dry up as I lean forward and lick the ink on the side of his dick.

"Violet," he groans. "I meant what I said. I'm not expecting anything in return and I—"

His words falter as I wrap my lips around his tip and suck, teasing his slit with my tongue.

"Fuck. Fuck, Firefly." His hips jerk, desperate to sink deeper.

I do as he wishes, lowering down on him until he hits the back of my throat, and then a little farther still. Just a little reminder that I'm no longer that naïve and innocent little sixteen-year-old who didn't know what she was doing. These days, I pride myself on being able to make a man blow his mind in only a few short minutes.

"Oh motherfucking fuck shit," he barks incoherently. "Been five years, baby. I'm not gonna—"

Shockingly fast, his cock swells a beat before it jerks violently, coming down my throat.

His grip on my hair tightens as he rides out the longest release I've ever known, shooting ribbons of cum into my mouth, so much so I can't actually swallow it.

Pulling off him, I allow him to coat my tongue, reveling in his familiar taste.

"Show me," he demands, and like the good little girl I am with Knox, I shamelessly open my mouth and let him see what he's done.

"Fuck."

His finger trails across my top lip before he swipes up his cum and begins writing something on my neck with it.

*Knox.*

I barely get a chance to swallow what's left before he's tucked his hands under my arms and hauled me to my feet.

My back slams against the tiled wall, my panties are ripped clean off my body before my legs are wrapped around his waist, and... "Already?" I gasp when the hard tip of his cock nudges my entrance.

"Been like a lifetime without you. Gotta make up for it."

"Jesus."

He thrusts inside me, stretching me open for him and making me cry out his name.

"Knox, yes. Fuck."

My nails rake across his shoulders as he takes me hard and fast against the wall.

It's frenzied, frantic, and everything.

It's all the need and passion we've always felt for each other exploding all at once.

I paw at his body, desperately trying to get closer despite the fact it's not physically possible.

"I want to feel you choking my cock, Firefly. Then I'm going to fill you up so good, you'll forget anyone else was ever here."

"Yes, yes," I cry as he bites down on my earlobe, making me race toward that release he wants from me.

His fingers dig into my ass as he holds me up.

"Clit, Violet. I need to feel you coming."

Slipping my hand between us, I do as I'm told and in only seconds, with his thick cock hitting that magical spot inside me, I go off like a rocket.

An animalistic growl fills the bathroom before he unloads in my pussy.

"Motherfucker," Knox grunts. "Was it always this good?"

By the time he puts my feet back to the floor, my legs are weak and my knees barely hold me up.

My stomach growls loudly over the pounding of the water and our heaving breaths.

"Clean up, then I'll take you for food. I'll see if Tristan's home. We can take him something in way of a peace offering."

He kisses me, making my legs want to give in again before walking out of the shower, although he doesn't get very far because I reach out and catch his wrist.

"You do know I'm fucking him, right?" I state.

"You know I'm not giving him up, right?"

He looks back at me over his shoulder, his expression closed off once again, his eyes unreadable. There's pain in his eyes that shouldn't affect me, not after everything. But it does. And it cuts me deeper than I was expecting.

"He... he means a lot to me and—"

"I know, Firefly."

"Just because you came back, it doesn't mean I'll just put the brakes on my life, my relationships. What I've got with Tris, it's... I'm not willing to walk away from what we've found. I need you to know that."

"Yeah, baby, I know. I just figure that right now, I should pick my battles wisely. And trying to convince you to leave him wouldn't work in my favor."

"Wise, Knox. Very wise."

"Plus, it's only a matter of time."

"What is?"

"Until you realize I deliver far superior orgasms than that pussy could even dream of."

I bite down on my bottom lip to stop me from blurting something stupid out, like how talented Tristan is with his tongue.

## 28

## TRISTAN

I didn't get a wink of sleep last night.

It didn't matter that I knew where she was. That she was safe. The fact she wasn't with me, in my bed, in my arms meant I was never going to get any rest. Add in the knowledge that she was with him—the man she's hated for five years—and I was a fucking wreck, my stomach knotted with dread, the fear of losing her so soon pumping through my veins.

I fucking knew he wanted her back then. But I thought that was all it was. And that even if he did make the stupid decision to come back into our lives, then she'd never even look at him twice.

But if what he said to me in my car last night is true then...

Then there's a hell of a lot more history between them than I ever even considered. And that means—

My stomach bottoms out once more.

I'm not the only one who's been keeping secrets.

"Fuck."

I sit forward on my new couch, resting my elbows on my knees as I hang my head.

If it was true, then I should have seen it. Shouldn't I?

I'd spent enough damn time watching her when she was distracted, feeding my forbidden obsession. Surely, I'd have witnessed something that—

I cut my thoughts off with a shake of my head.

I don't need to be sitting here, second-guessing myself.

I know the truth.

I saw it between them in the seconds between me storming into the apartment and slamming my fist into Knox's face.

It's why he's here.

It's why he came back.

And ultimately, it's why he did what he did.

I fucking bought it too. His loyalty to the Hawks, being a good little soldier and doing as he was told. Taking the fall, the punishment for his father's betrayal, how he'd paid the ultimate price.

I fucking fell for it hook, line and sinker.

I knew it was bullshit. I knew he was innocent. He might have been the one to find the house first that night, he might have been the one to call me. But I knew it wasn't him the second I saw him fighting through the flames carrying my—his—girl in his arms.

Everything he's done... it was to protect her.

And I feel like a fucking fool for not realizing why all this time.

I throw myself back on the couch with a groan. Fire burns through my veins. My need to smash the place to pieces in the hope of expelling some of the anger that's raging inside me is almost too much to bear.

I push to my feet, needing to move, to do something, to cause some pain unignorable, but I only take one step toward my gym when my cell dings in my pocket.

I drag it out in the hope it's her. But the second the screen lights up, my heart drops and my anger surges once more as I stare at the contact I had no choice but to save when he started messaging me last night.

**Knox: You want a burger, bro? Our girl's hungry.**

**Tristan: Fuck you.**

But as I hit send, my stomach growls, reminding me that I haven't eaten in... a really long fucking time.

**Tristan: Burger, fries, onion rings, soda.**

**Tristan: And some kind of ice cream.**

**Tristan: *smiley face emoji***

I certainly don't feel that fucking smiley face, and I hope he reads it for what it is: *I want to punch you in your smug fucking face the second you get here, asshole.*

**Knox: Someone's hungry. Can't imagine why when you spent the night alone...**

The growl that rips from my throat doesn't sound anything like me as jealousy like I've never experienced before threatens to swallow me whole.

The second I'm in the hallway, my fist swings toward the wall. Pain shoots up my arm, but it's not enough and I repeat the action again and again until blood covers my light cream paint and my already busted knuckles are ruined.

"I fucking hate you, Knox Bowman," I bellow, my deep voice echoing through the silence of my apartment.

With her gone, even after only living here for a few days, I realize how fucking lonely I was. Having her here made it feel like a home instead of just a place to sleep, even when it didn't have any furniture.

I stop, leaning forward on my forearm as blood runs from

my knuckles. My chest heaves as I suck in the air I need while blood races past my ears.

I have no idea how long they're going to be. I mean, I'm only assuming from his messages that they're on their way and stopping for food. For all I know, Knox could just be taunting me and has no intentions of bringing Violet home.

He could take her to the Creek, make her his prisoner, and I'd never see her again.

Okay, so that might be a little bit dramatic. But this is Knox we're talking about. He just did five fucking years behind bars for no fucking reason. The man is fucking certifiable.

*You'd have done it in a heartbeat if you were in the same position*, a little voice says. Anything for Violet.

"Motherfucker," I hiss, pushing from the wall and stalking toward my bedroom, and then to the bathroom to clean up.

I throw myself in the shower, embracing the sting of my knuckles as my shower gel gets into the cuts.

I flick a towel over my body, rub it over my head and then pull on a pair of sweats. Only a pair of sweats.

If Knox wants to play, then he needs to understand that he's not the only one who can get down and dirty in order to get what he wants.

It's only a couple of minutes later when the buzzer rings around my apartment and my stomach knots. Anger and anticipation for what might have happened between them since I had little choice but to allow Knox to rescue her last night burns through me.

I want to look at ease, like I'm barely bothered by what's happened, but I know I fail the second I pull the door open and my eyes lock on Knox's amused ones over Violet's head.

Silence falls around the three of us as reality presses down on my shoulders.

I'm about to lose her to him.

I never even stood a fucking chance.

Ripping my eyes from his smug fucking face, I look down at Violet.

"Hey, Pip," I say like an imbecile.

She smiles at me, but it's forced.

"Can we come in?" she asks, looking around me.

"Oh shit, yeah." I step aside, unblocking the door.

The second I shut it behind them, the atmosphere only gets worse. The air is so thick it's hard to suck in a damn breath.

I don't realize that I'm still standing out in the hallway until the scent of fried food hits my nose and I stalk back toward the living room.

Violet and Knox are sitting on my couch, digging into paper bags of food.

Violet is wearing a dress that I assume she wore to the party last night. Her legs are curled up beneath her, the hem of said dress temptingly high on her thighs.

I swallow thickly, stupidly wondering if Knox knows what she's hiding beneath. My fist curls.

Of course he fucking knows. That's why he's so smug.

Dragging my eyes up, I take in her messy hair and her makeup-clear face. Her skin is pale and the shadows under her eyes are dark, pointing toward a hangover. Not that I can say that's unexpected. I already know, thanks to the man at her side, that she was so wasted last night that she passed out in his arms. Something I really, really didn't need to know. But there we go.

Feeling my stare, Violet lifts her head after throwing a couple of fries into her mouth.

Her eyes hold mine for a beat before they drop down to my half-naked body.

I can't help the smirk that twitches at my lips. That is, until Knox scoffs.

My amusement vanishes as I look over at him with a mouthful of burger.

"You're so transparent, bro," he mutters despite the food. "Violet wants more than a pretty body, don't you, Firefly?"

"Can we please not do this? I just want to eat in peace and without drowning in all this testosterone. Tris, come eat," she demands, pointing at the bag on the coffee table.

Unable to refuse, I grab the bag and drop into the chair opposite them, hating the fact Knox is within touching distance of my girl.

We eat in silence. I barely taste my food, each mouthful like swallowing rocks with the level of tension hanging over us.

My eyes continue to bounce between them, but neither says anything or does anything other than eat.

"What happened last night?" I finally ask, my curiosity getting the better of me.

"Oh man, you probably don't want those details," Knox quips like the fucking asshole that he is.

"Really?" Violet mumbles.

"He's just jealous, baby," Knox breathes, reaching over and squeezing her thigh. Right. In. Front. Of. Me.

I try to fume silently, but I realize how badly I fail when a loud growl hits my ears that I quickly discover rumbled from the depths of my throat.

"Knox," Violet hisses, shooting him a deadly look that only seems to amuse him.

"You can leave, you know," I mutter, my appetite long gone. "I never actually invited you in."

"But I brought you food, man," Knox teases.

"Fucking hell," Violet mutters, shoving what's left of her food aside and pushing to her feet. She pauses at the end of the coffee table and glares between both of us. "You two used to be friends, do you remember that?"

"Different lifetime, Pip. I think we can all agree that none of us are the same people we were back then."

"I'm not so sure about that. My girl's as sexy as ever, don't you think?" Knox quips.

"Shut the fuck up, Knox. Tristan is right, if you can't play nice then you need to leave," she warns fiercely. "Either remember those kids or just... go."

With that threat lingering in the air, she turns and walks away from both of us.

We both stare at her in that tiny dress until she disappears around the corner and into my bedroom. And damn if the sight of that doesn't make my cock swell.

"What the fuck happened last night?" I growl before I turn around and get a look at Knox's smug fucking face.

"You really want to know?" he asks, his smirk growing.

"Don't be a dick, Knox."

"I already told you. She was at a party at the football team's house. She was wasted. That little blonde friend of hers was trying to make her calm down. I watched her force a bottle of water on her through the kitchen window."

"Stalker," I mutter.

"Anyway," he continues, "she stumbled outside and I caught her before she face-planted the grass."

My fists curl at my sides, my nails digging into my palms as I think about her passed out in his arms.

"Why didn't you just bring her back home?" I ask. Stupid question. I'm aware of that, but it still rolls off my tongue.

"Do you have any fucking idea how lonely the last five years have been, Tris?" he asks, leaning forward. He ducks his head for a beat before looking back up at me. "How much I fucking missed her?"

I swallow thickly.

"I fucking love her, man. I have since I was sixteen. She was the only fucking good thing in my life. Well, that and the two of you. My life in the Creek was shit. And despite hating Maddison County at first, that house, the people in it soon became my solace.

"I never told either of you just how much you fucking changed my life.

"I was condemned from the moment my father shot his load in some whore. I was a Creek kid. Destined to a life of hell as one of Victor fucking Harris's soldiers.

"You all showed me a different life. Another way. Happiness that didn't involve drugs, alcohol, and violence."

"Shit, man," I say, scrubbing my hand down my face.

Disbelief floods me as I think about what he's really been through for the first time.

In the fallout of that fire, I thought about him being inside. But I was too focused on Violet, on Roman, for the few days he hung around at least.

I figured that Knox had made his choice, and that was for him to deal with. I had enough shit going on.

I was a senior. I had the pressure of my final season of high school football. I needed to get into MKU to ensure my future. And I had the girl I'd been craving for as long as I could remember breaking right in front of me.

Life was hard. But yeah, I'm man enough to admit that it was still a shitload better than it was for Knox as he was thrown in juvie for a crime he didn't commit.

"I don't want your fucking sympathy. I did what I did for reasons we now both know. And I'd do it again to protect her in a fucking heartbeat."

Glancing over my shoulder, I look toward where I know she is.

"I'm not letting you take her from me," I state.

"And I'm not handing her over."

When I look back, he's resting against my couch, his arms crossed over his chest and his ankle resting on the opposite knee.

He might appear relaxed, but there's a fire in his eyes that shows me that he's ready for this fight. And there's a fucking arrogance there which also tells me he truly believes he's going to win.

"Excuse me," I mutter, pushing to my feet and stalking toward my bedroom.

"Good luck," he calls from behind me, a lightness in his tone. If I were to look back, I'd find him laughing.

I half expect him to stop me, but to my surprise, I make it to my room and slip inside without another sound from him.

The bedroom is empty, but my bathroom door has been pushed shut.

Not willing to keep this distance between us, I stride across the room and quickly knock, but I fail to wait for a response, instead just throwing the door open.

My breath catches when I find Violet standing in a tank and a tiny pair of booty shorts.

If she was hoping to put an end to us fighting like a couple of horny teenagers, then she really missed the mark with the outfit choice.

Or maybe she had other intentions...

I slam that line of thought down before it has a chance to grow.

I close the space between us in only a few steps and she lowers the face wipe she was using to rid the lingering makeup from the night before.

"Tristan," she whispers, holding my eyes in the mirror.

"It's okay," I breathe.

"I'm sorry for—"

"Me too." Her head drops, severing our connection, and I panic.

Reaching for her arm, I spin her around, backing her up against the wall.

Tucking my fingers under her chin, I force her to look up.

"I'm sorry you never felt like you could tell me."

She shakes her head, tears filling her eyes. "It was never that, Tris. I just... I hated him. Or, at least, I thought I did. I tried to. He..." She sighs, her eyes glazing over as she thinks back. "He was my everything back then. He... he gave me..."

"I can imagine," I deadpan, stepping closer, desperately needing to feel her against me.

She rolls her eyes. "It was more than that. I didn't want to accept it after all that, but he was the one who started building the confidence I've needed to get through it all. That and your support," she adds, reaching up to wrap her hand around the back of my neck.

"I don't want to lose you, Pip."

"Tris," she breathes. "I might have secretly been with him, but that didn't stop me from wanting you as well."

"That's fucked up, baby girl," I tell her, my voice low and raspy.

She shrugs. "It's the truth."

"I appreciate it."

"You're not turned off, kn-knowing that I—"

I press harder against her, letting her feel just how not turned off I am right now.

She gasps. "Tristan."

"I want you, Violet. I've always wanted you. And it's going to take a lot to change my mind about that. I've tried, trust me I have. I wanted to do the right thing, to come good on the promise I made to Roman before I was even old enough to really understand what I was agreeing to."

"Roman's gone, Tris. Any promise you made him was severed the second he turned his back on us."

"I know. I guess I just really wanted to believe he might just come back once he sorted himself out."

"Yeah," she agrees. "I did too. But then I figured that it would have happened by now. Sometimes, I like to think he might still be out there. But really, it's more likely that he overdosed long ago and left us behind for good."

A lone tear finally falls, and I reach out to catch it with the pad of my thumb.

"Please don't cry, baby girl. I hate seeing you hurting."

Leaning forward, I rest my brow against hers.

"I missed you," I confess, staring right into her emerald eyes.

Looping her arms around my shoulders, she threads her fingers into the hair at the nape of my neck.

"Thank you for coming for me Thursday night."

"I wasn't sure you were aware."

"I knew."

"I'm sorry all this is being dragged back up again. That you've got to relive it."

She nods, her lips coming dangerously close as she moves.

"It was inevitable. It was naïve of me to think Knox would let the past lie."

"It's funny. I never thought he truly cared about anything. But I see it now."

"Stop," she begs, her grip on me tightening.

"Anything," I breathe against her lips.

It might have been what I wished for when I stormed in here, but really, it wasn't what I was expecting as she presses her lips to mine hesitantly. But if she thinks that motherfucker sitting out in my living room is going to put me off her, then she really needs to think again.

I might have fucked up in the past and allowed him to slip into the place I desperately wanted to be. But it's not going to happen again.

Violet is mine, and I'll die before I willingly hand her over to him.

# 29

# VIOLET

Tristan's lips press against mine and on instinct, mine part to allow him entry.

He consumes me. Utterly consumes me. And as his tongue slides against mine, his body pinning me harder against the wall, the thick length of his dick crushed against my stomach, all thoughts, fears, and regrets fall from my head.

He's my happy place, my solace, my savior.

"Violet," he growls into our kiss, his deep, raspy voice sending shivers skating down my spine.

I drown in him, and when his hand skims down my stomach between us, I refuse to let reality slip in.

"Oh God," I whimper when his fingers dip under the waistband of my booty shorts.

"Addicted to this pussy, baby girl."

"Tris," I moan, shifting my hips forward in an attempt to force his fingers exactly where I need them.

I cry out, sounding like nothing but a shameless whore when he circles my clit.

I was only with Knox an hour ago.

But it doesn't seem to matter.

My body wants Tristan too. No. It doesn't just want him. It craves him.

"Yes," I cry when he pushes two thick fingers inside me.

"So wet for me, baby girl," he groans before latching on to the soft skin of my throat, sucking hard enough to leave his mark.

It should put me off, knowing that he's only doing it to piss Knox off and mark his territory. But that's not the reaction it has. He knows it too, because he groans when I gush over his fingers.

My eyes are almost shut as I focus on the sensations rushing through my body, but that doesn't mean I miss the movement by the door.

My gasp rips through the air as a dark shadow spreads across the bathroom floor and Knox appears in the doorway.

He wraps his fingers around the frame, his dark, hungry eyes eating up the sight of me falling under Tristan's spell.

His attention locks on where Tristan's hand disappears into my shorts and he swallows thickly, his Adam's apple bobbing.

"Did you want something, bro?" Tristan barks and I startle, not aware that he knew about our audience. "I'm busy."

"Tris—" My warning for him to stop taunting Knox is cut off with a moan when he presses harder against my G-spot.

Silence falls around us as the air turns thick with sexual tension and desire. The only thing that can be heard is our increased breaths.

My body burns under the attention of the two men who are both so far under my skin I'm not sure a lifetime would be enough to get them out.

I tried. I really fucking tried to forget about Knox. I thought I had, to a point.

But one look at him and I know that I've been lying to myself for years. He might have been gone. But he never left me.

"Make her come, Carver," Knox demands, releasing his grip on the doorframe and rubbing his hard cock that's fighting to get out of his pants.

"Oh God."

"I want to watch you make her fall. See if you're any good."

"Fuck you, Bowman. Violet has been well looked after in your absence."

It's lies. He's only been 'looking after' me in this way for a week, but I don't have any words to argue as Tristan keeps finger fucking me like a savage.

Adding a third digit inside me, he presses his thumb to my clit.

"Shouldn't like watching this," Knox mutters to himself, his eyes blazing with heat, the sight pushing me that bit closer to the edge.

"She loves it," Tristan points out. "She's so fucking wet."

I look up at him, shocked that he's letting this fly right now.

I've learned a lot of things about my best friend in the past week, but I never ever would have thought that he'd be okay with this.

I guess it might be an entirely different story if he was the one watching.

"You sure that's her? I unloaded five years' worth of cum right inside her barely an hour ago."

Tristan stills, and I cry out in frustration.

I'm so close. So fucking close. And I really don't need them to embark on a cock-measuring contest right this second. Unless...

No. Shut it down, Violet.

Shut. It. Down.

"Tristan," I beg. "Please."

"Need me to take over, bro? If you're not man eno—"

"Shut the fuck up, Bowman."

Tristan picks up exactly where he left off, fucking me even harder. It's good, but damn, I wish it were his cock.

His or—

Fuck. I'm in serious fucking trouble here.

"Yes. Yes. Tristan," I cry as pleasure begins to saturate through my body, that explosion right there, almost in touching distance.

"Come for me, baby girl."

"And me, Firefly. I want to hear you screaming my name too."

I swear I hear Tristan grunt, "Fuck my life," but I'm too far gone to really register it.

"Tristan," I scream as my body quakes and lights flash behind my eyes. "Knox."

I feel the rumble of whatever Tristan says against my neck as I add Knox's name to my pleas, but I don't hear the words. And I think that's probably for the best.

"Fucking beautiful, baby. Only thing that would make it better would be if I could feel your juices running down my hand instead of his."

My eyes find Knox as I come back to myself. He's still palming himself through his pants, and I must confess, I'm disappointed. I want to see him come undone as well.

"As fun as this was," he says, shattering the tension around us. "And as much as I might want to find out what comes next, I gotta head out."

"What a fucking shame," Tristan mutters. "Don't let my front door hit your ass on the way out."

"Tristan," I warn.

Pulling his fingers from inside me, he takes a step back before lifting them to his lips and making a show of licking them clean.

"How do I taste, bro?" Knox asks, amusement filling his voice.

"She tastes fucking delicious. Shame you're too busy to find out for yourself."

My chin drops at his words.

Would he... would he allow that to happen?

"Maybe you shouldn't leave." The words are out of my mouth before I can stop them.

Tristan's grip on my waist tightens as he hears the unspoken suggestion in my statement.

"Maybe next time, Firefly. No one keeps Reid Harris waiting. Not even me."

The mention of the Hawks leader is like a bucket of ice water poured over my raging libido.

"Fuck off, then. We've got plans anyway."

But before Tristan has even finished talking, Knox surges into the room and shoves him aside. Shock sends Tristan stumbling toward the wall as Knox cups my face in his big hands and brings his lips down on mine in a wet and filthy kiss that I never want to end.

I arch into him, my hand skating down his body until I'm cupping his aching dick through his pants.

"Firefly," he groans, pulling back from my lips and resting his brow against mine.

"Go and do what you need to do." I hate saying the words, I hate that I'm sending him back to that life. A world and a gang that I hate. But what else can I do? It's his life. His past, and I have no doubt his future. I just need to figure out if that is something I can come to terms with. "I'll call you later."

"You will, huh?" he asks with a smirk.

"Yeah, I will. Be safe."

"Always, baby. Now I've got you back, I'm not letting you go again." He says that final bit a little louder so Tristan has no choice but to hear every word.

"We'll see," he mutters.

"Violet was mine long before she was yours, Carver."

"Yeah, because I had morals, asshole."

"I'm standing right here," I point out. "Next time we all find ourselves in a room together, you can both get your dicks out and measure them, yeah?"

"Now that sounds like a date I can't refuse, Firefly."

Knox leans in to steal another kiss before stepping back and allowing Tristan to swallow me up.

"I never said I'd touch either of them," I mutter when they both look at me with heated eyes.

"I'm sure we could convince you," Knox quips. "You seemed quite fond of my dick earlier, after all."

"Don't you have somewhere to be?" Tristan grunts.

"Sadly, yeah." Reaching up, he combs his fingers through his hair, his eyes taking one more leisurely trip around my body. "Talk to you later, Firefly. Make sure he treats you right."

Tristan scoffs but doesn't say any more. Instead, he holds me tighter, as if he's scared I'm about to race after Knox as he backs toward the door.

"I will," I whisper, but he's already ducked around the corner.

Tristan and I stand there in silence until the front door slams, and then it's like all bets are off.

His lips slam down on mine and he kisses me almost violently. Our tongues duel, our teeth clashing as he sweeps me off my feet, forcing my legs to wrap around his waist as he carries me out of the bathroom.

In seconds, my back lands on the bed and he crawls over me, never breaking our kiss.

"Need you, baby girl."

His tongue delves deeper once more as his fingers hook around the sides of my shorts. They're dragged down my legs and I help kick them off before he shuffles, I assume shoving his sweats lower.

In only a heartbeat, his cock is at my entrance and he's pushing inside.

"Gonna make you forget your own name, baby girl," he promises before thrusting forward and filling me in one quick move.

I want to chastise him for that previous comment, because we both know it's not my own name he wants me to forget, but I ignore everything as my body adjusts to his invasion and his kisses heat up once more.

He fucks me hard and fast. It's so different from the last time. That was a little frantic, full of anger and disbelief after what we'd both just experienced, but this time, it's pure desperation that comes off Tristan in waves.

I hate it. But equally, I love it that he's willing to fight for me. That he's not going to be the good boy he was before.

He knows what he wants now, and he's going to do everything he can to make it happen.

But to what end?

Where the hell is this going to go?

Individually, they're both possessive alphas who want their own way. Is there even a chance in hell that they'll be able to get their heads around sharing me? Because that is how this is going.

All or nothing.

I have both, or I have to walk away. And I'm not sure the latter is an option, because it would fucking break me.

"Fuck, Pip. Your pussy is… fuck."

Tristan looms over me, his dark eyes eating me up, and he thrusts into me hard enough to send me shooting up the bed.

"So fucking good."

"Yes," I cry, my back arching, forcing him to hit me just at the right angle.

Noticing my move, he tucks one hand under my ass, helping me out.

"Tristan," I scream when he slams against my G-spot over and over.

"Fuck, yeah. Milk my cock, baby girl. That's it. I'm gonna come so fucking hard."

"Oh God. Oh God."

"You want that, baby? To be so full of my cum you won't be able to forget that I was here."

"Yes. Yes. Please. Want it all," I chant between his thrusts.

My nails rake down his back as I edge closer to another release.

"Fuck, baby girl. Come for me. Now," he demands. At the sound of his dominant tone, I crash over the edge, free-falling, full of confidence that he'll catch me wherever I end up.

---

Tristan didn't let me go anywhere after he did exactly as he promised and filled me with cum.

I know the first time we were together that he was trying to be a sensible adult by using a condom, but hell if I hated the idea of there being a barrier between us. But feeling him against me, damn. It was everything.

Just like it was with Knox.

My entire body tenses as I think about him.

I've been with both of them within a matter of hours.

What the fuck is wrong with me?

"Stop," Tristan demands.

"I'm not doing anything," I argue.

"You are, you're thinking. Freaking out. I can sense it."

"Yeah, well. I think I have every right to be freaking out. What the hell is even going on right now?"

"Right now, I'm holding you as tight as I can in the hope it's not the last time I get the chance," he confesses, letting all his vulnerability bleed out of him.

Hearing it is akin to having a knife sliding right through my heart.

"You should have told me, Tristan," I say, back peddling a

little to the beginning of this whole situation. It might not have been so messy if I were expecting Knox to show his face.

"I know. I'm sorry. I was trying to protect you. To let you deal with one problem at a time and—" He sighs. "I fucked up."

"Yeah. You did."

"In my defense. I truly believed that he wouldn't show his face again. I had no idea how important you were to him."

Twisting around in his arms, I look up into his dark eyes. The pain within them makes my chest ache in a way I really don't like.

"I'm sorry I never told you."

"It was him, wasn't it? The first time that you regretted?"

I nod, my thoughts shooting back to those kids rolling around in my bed back at my mom's house.

"Yeah. I never regretted it until the moment that guilty plea fell from his lips. Then, I wanted to wipe him and everything we'd ever shared from my memory."

"And now?"

"He didn't do it," I state, half expecting Tristan to be shocked but equally unsurprised when he doesn't so much as react. "You knew that too, didn't you?"

"He was the one who called me that night. He carried you out of that burning house and placed you in my arms. Looking back now, it was obvious how he felt about you. It was right there in his eyes as he stared down at you, but I was panicking too much to see it. I was terrified that he didn't get to you in time. You were limp in my arms, and for a few minutes, I thought you were dead."

"Does that mean you know who did start that fire?"

"Violet," he warns.

"Fuck," I hiss. "You do. All this time, you knew."

"Don't be mad at me, please."

"Why?"

When he doesn't answer right away, it makes my heart rate spike.

"Tris?"

"Because knowing wouldn't have helped you recover or move on with your life. Because there were more important things for you to focus on. Knox did what he did for reasons I didn't even understand back then. But I respected him for it regardless, and I was willing to follow his lead. Plus, it was Hawks business, and there was no fucking way I was getting involved with any of that.

"I wanted football, MKU, a career. Getting tangled up with the Hawks in the fallout from that fire was a sure-as-shit way to fuck it all up."

I can't help but agree, but I still hate that he's known all this and kept it from me for so long.

But then, I was keeping secrets too. Pretty huge ones.

"When did you and Knox first... you know."

"Fuck?" I ask, weirdly liking the fire that alights in his eyes as jealousy swamps him.

"I was going to say start hanging out. But thanks for that."

I smile softly at him as I think back to our late-night chats in the kitchen not long after he first moved in.

"It started out totally innocently. We were both night owls, and more often than not, we'd meet in the kitchen in the dead of night. We'd chat. It was... nice.

"I was terrified of him when he first moved in. He was so different from any of the boys I'd ever met before, a world apart from you and Roman. But when all the lights were out and we were drinking hot chocolate and eating cookies around the island, he was just a normal kid.

"Eventually, we moved our midnight hangouts to my bedroom one winter when the house was cold and we just kinda never stopped.

"We watched movies, did school work, talked about all kinds of shit.

"Things just... evolved. And then one day, I realized that he had firmly planted himself in my head right alongside my biggest crush. Only, he seemed to want me back, or at least I figured he did the first time we kissed."

"So you're telling me that if I'd pulled my head out of my ass before him and kissed you, I could have been the one spending my nights secretly in your room?" he asks, regret dripping from each word.

"Maybe."

"So all those nights I was imagining sneaking out when Roman had fallen asleep, I would have found him in your bed, kissing you, touching you..."

"Possibly. I still wanted you, though. I always have. And I'm not sure that's ever going to go away."

He studies me, his eyes searching mine for the answers he's so desperate for, but he can't find them, because he's forced to ask the most pressing question out loud.

"Where do we go from here?"

"I-I... I don't know, Tristan. Despite everything, I'm not letting you go. But I'm not turning my back on him either.

"Both of you have owned pieces of my heart for years. There's no way I can choose between you."

"So you're saying you want us both?"

I bite down on my bottom lip, feeling like the greediest girl in the world.

I can't honestly be asking for them to share me, am I?

It's insane. It's absurd. Unconventional. And yet, all it feels is right in a way that it probably shouldn't. And surely, they're not going to go for it.

"Yeah, I guess I am."

"And how exactly is that supposed to work? Are we going to have to make a schedule?"

# 30

# KNOX

I drive out of Maddison County with a heavy heart and dread churning away in my gut.

She might have let me kiss her before I left, might have allowed me to push Tristan aside so I could have a minute, but there is no denying that she's his.

I saw how they were together with my own two eyes.

The passion.

The fire.

The... love?

He has everything I've wanted with her for as long as I can remember, and even more fiercely in the last few years where I've been locked up with nothing but thoughts of her to keep me company.

*Maybe you shouldn't have come back here.*

I hate the doubt. I hate that I'm questioning myself.

I should have seen it coming. I should have known that she wouldn't be single and be willing to jump back into my arms.

But Tristan...

Yeah, I never saw that curveball coming.

I would probably stand a chance if I were up against some pussy college kid.

But Tristan...

I shake my head.

It'll take more than a few mind-blowing orgasms to make her think twice about him.

They're living together, for fuck's sake. I know through convenience, but still.

They're together, doing whatever they want to do, whenever they like, and I'm here.

The outsider.

Just like always.

The only place I've ever truly fit in is Harrow Creek.

I pass the battered, old 'Welcome to Harrow Creek' sign just as that thought hits. But knowing it and accepting that this shithole could be where I belong are two very different things.

Ignoring the turning that would take me down into the pits of hell where all my childhood nightmares were born, I head up the hill, toward the house Reid Harris told everyone who listened when we were kids that he'd one day buy and do it up.

I always thought it was a stupid pipe dream. The place was a mess.

But really, I shouldn't have doubted him.

He's Reid Harris.

Motherfucker has always got what he wanted, whether by luck, the DNA that runs through his veins, or by sheer blood and determination—and there has been a lot of blood. Even before I went down, he was racking up the body count at double, if not triple the speed of the rest of us. I guess he was trying to prove a point.

One day, he would take over the Hawks. His corrupt daddy would finally meet his maker—possibly no thanks to his eldest son—and that would be that. A new king would be born.

I can't help but laugh to myself as I pull up to his almost-invisible gates. I pause the car, waiting for a member of his security team to allow me entry, and after looking into the small camera for longer than I think is probably necessary, the gates finally open, causing a break in what appears to be a long hedge to reveal the landscaped grounds of the devil's mansion before me.

The huge double doors open the second I roll Devin's car to a stop out the front of the building.

It's only the second time I've been here since being released, and I can easily say that I'm still as gobsmacked by the dark and sinister mansion.

But despite the doors opening, no fucker steps out to greet me.

"Egomaniacal motherfucker," I mutter, picturing him sitting inside on a golden throne, looking down over his minions in the valley below him.

But the second I step inside, I find that there is someone waiting in the wings to greet me. Or maybe scare the shit out of me.

"Who the fuck let Knox Bowman free?" a deep voice booms before a dead weight lands on my back, a pair of arms and legs wrapping around me like a monkey would who's got free at the zoo.

"JD!" I exclaim, throwing him off me so I can spin around.

He barely gives me a second to take a breath before he drags me in for a man hug, slamming his dangerous fists against my back.

"It's so good to see you, man."

While Reid might have been my best friend growing up, JD was right there in our little trio of epicness.

"Dude, there were visiting hours, you know?" I quip, pulling back and getting a look at him.

"Fuck me, look at the state of you." My eyes track the copious amounts of ink covering every inch of skin that's exposed by his loose-fitting tank.

"Nah, you're all good, bro. I've got my girl for that."

My lips part to ask one of the million burning questions I

have about that setup, but another deep voice booms through the colossal building and distracts me from JD's sexploits.

"Get your asses in here."

"Look out, the boss is calling," JD quips.

"I'm glad it didn't go to his head," I mutter, following him deeper into the house to find Reid.

I have to smother a laugh when JD leads me into what is obviously Reid's office and I find him sitting behind his desk in a chair that rivals the throne I'd pictured.

Oh yeah, this motherfucker really does think he's the king of the world these days.

But when he lifts his head from what he's studying, his expression softens at the sight of me.

"You've... looked better," he mutters, taking in each bruise Tristan left behind Thursday night along with the bright hickey Violet gave me this morning.

"Just having fun, man," I say, pushing my hair back from my brow and falling down into one of the chairs on this side of his desk.

"Anything we need to know about?"

"Nah, just trying to reclaim my girl," I tell them honestly.

"Ah, still not over that little crush on your stepsister?" JD teases.

"Little crush?" Reid adds. "He handed his balls over to her long before he was locked up."

"Okay, did you call me here to rip me about Violet, or was there another reason?"

"As fun as that would be, no. There is another reason."

I glance down the huge map that's laid out before him.

"Go on."

"We've got an opening to hit Shadow." I sit forward the second that motherfucker's name rolls off Reid's tongue.

"Go on," I encourage.

That fuck made my life a living hell inside. He was put

away by us—or Victor, more specifically—and he was hell bent on wiping out any Hawk that entered Iron Marsh.

He succeeded with most of them, helped by the fact he somehow had the guards on side.

They were meant to be neutral, but it soon became apparent that more than a few of them were on the Ravens' payroll, allowing Shadow to move around in the darkness of the prison by night, putting an end to whomever he wanted and covering it up by sunrise.

But it wasn't just the Hawks on his radar. It was anyone connected with them, too.

Hence why I found my cell mate, my personal tattoo artist, with his throat cut one morning when the sun rose on our little slice of hell.

Despite my best efforts, Shadow was untouchable. How the hell I made it out alive still shocks me. I'm pretty sure I lucked out the day he was granted his freedom long before his time was up.

But that doesn't mean I've forgotten.

Most of the scars he left on my body are now hidden beneath ink, but not all, and certainly not the marks he left on the inside. Those motherfuckers will last a lifetime. And until he's faced the same wrath as all those Hawks did, then I won't ever get the chance to lay it all to rest.

"The Devils have an important shipment, so they're going to be at the docks, leaving him less protected. We'll go in, get the job done, and be long gone before they get back and find their new little friend has been compromised."

"They're not going to just leave him alone. They're obviously protecting him for something."

"I'm not expecting him to be alone. We'll take enough men with us to wipe out anyone they've left behind. But they'll be Devils. And we're fucking better than them any day of the week."

"This is going to bring war to your doorstep. Are you sure that—"

"Yes," he confirms. "You might have walked out of that place a free man, but most of our men didn't have the same luck."

"Or skill," I add, remembering the number of times Shadow tried to take a hit on me.

"Or that," Reid agrees while JD chuckles.

"Say what you like about Victor fucking Harris, he trains good soldiers."

"Trained," Reid spits, his hatred of his father still as strong as ever despite the old man now being worm food.

"As long as you're prepared for the fallout of this."

"I'm more than aware. Things have been boring around here long enough. The Ravens want this motherfucker gone just as much as we do. If the Devils just so happen to be collateral, then so fucking be it."

"Fair enough," I mutter, sitting forward in my seat to get a better look at his map. "So, what's the plan?"

JD moves closer, rubbing his hands together, eager to get to the good stuff.

---

By the time I walk back out of Reid's haunted house, I'm fully prepped for Monday night. He's had soldiers watching the compound where the Devils are holding that cunt. We know their positions, what time they switch, even what time they go to take a piss. And I can't fucking lie, I'm gagging to head out on a job. I've been locked up and kept away from the fun side of gang life for way too long. It'll be just like old times: Reid, JD, and me going up against our enemies.

Gotta love those childhood memories.

I leave with the promise of meeting here again Monday afternoon before we head out, and the second I fall down in the driver's seat of Devin's car, I instantly long for another part of my past.

My firefly.

Pulling my cell from my pocket, I wake up in the hope she's already called.

My heart sinks when I find no notifications from anyone.

"Fuck," I hiss, dropping it into one of the cup holders. "She's turned you into a fucking pussy, Bowman," I mutter to myself before throwing the car into reverse and speeding out of Reid's estate.

Without anywhere else to go, I head back toward Maddison Country and the rest of the Harrises.

But this time, instead of avoiding them and hiding in my bedroom like a little bitch, I swing the living room door open and drop onto the couch.

"Ah, how nice of you to join us," Devin quips.

Ignoring him, Ellis turns to me. "You get the lowdown for Monday from Reid?"

"Sure did," I say, rubbing my palms down my thighs as excitement shoots through my veins once more.

"You remember how to shoot a gun, Knox?" Ezra asks, looking a little too smug.

"As well as I remember to ride a bike and fuck, yeah."

"Was wondering about the vampire who's been sucking on your neck. Wanna spill?"

Kicking my foot up on the coffee table, I glare at Devin as I reach out for the beer Ellis just ran off to get for me.

"Not really, no."

"So are we to assume you've given up on your little quest to get back into Violet's good books, or have you finally cracked her?"

"Dev," Ellis complains.

"What? Just because you're friends with her, it don't mean we can't get the dirty details."

"Wait. What?" I bark, turning to look at Ellis with wide eyes. "You're friends with Violet?"

"Yes and no," he confesses, shooting his brother a death glare. "I'm friends with her roommate, so I'm friends by association. Total coincidence."

"Right."

"Why are you freaking out? We didn't know there was any connection there until you turned up, jerking off over her every twenty-five seconds."

My chin drops. "I was not," I argue.

"Only because you had to have a rest to stop your dick getting all chafed up."

"You're a cunt," I hiss, throwing my bottle cap at Devin's head, which, amusingly, hits him right between the brows.

"So you're telling me you had no idea Violet Brady was Roman Brady's little sister? My stepsister?"

"No," Ellis says honestly. "I don't go around doing background searches on everyone I come across just in case they somehow happen to be connected to dear old daddy."

"Maybe you should. Might stop you suddenly finding out a girl you're banging is actually your sister."

The second I say the words, all the blood drains from Devin's face.

"Fuck. Can you imagine?"

"Another reason to make sure you always wrap it. Think of the poor kid you might make," Ellis quips.

"Do you really think he could have more kids out there?" Ezra asks, deep in thought.

"He cheated on Mom more than once. It's probably realistic to think that there is a whole town full of illegitimate Harris kids out there," Ellis muses.

"Fuck," Devin barks scrubbing his hand down his face. "Can you get us a load of DNA testing kits, E?" he asks, looking at Ellis.

"Fuck off," Ezra laughs. "You have a hard enough job

getting girls to suck your cock as it is, you can't add the hurdle of a DNA test. You'd never get laid again."

"Fuck you, little brother. When was the last time you got your dick wet, huh?"

Ezra shrugs, refusing to take the bait.

"I had a girl calling my name sev—"

"Seven times in one night," both Ellis and I finish, clearly both having heard the story.

"Oh fuck off. I'm not bragging or anything." Devin sulks.

"Sure you're not. If you need to, you can try to convince us you've got the biggest dick too," Ezra quips, making both me and Ellis snort.

"Okay, enough of this shit. We've got two hours before we gotta party, let's take Knox out to the range and see how on point his aim is after a five-year rest," Ezra suggests.

"Rest or no rest, you know I'll wipe the floor with your asses."

"Oh yeah?" Devin asks, pushing to his feet. "Let's go see. Then if you're lucky, we'll let you come party with the big boys. We've got some serious gear to shift tonight."

"Nah, man. I've got plans tonight."

The three of them pause, waiting for me to elaborate. But like fuck am I going to confess to wanting to be somewhere quiet for when Violet calls like she told me she would.

*Pussy.*

## 31

## VIOLET

Just like I promised, I called Knox on Saturday night while Tristan was working.

He'd told me that he wanted to take the rest of the weekend off so that we could hang out, but when Coach called him for the fourth time with some emergency tactics he wanted to discuss or something, I insisted he answer it and excused myself to the balcony that leads from the living room.

I rested back on the lounger I chose for this specific sun trap and prepared to have Knox's deep, rumbling voice in my ear, but to my disappointment, he never answered.

I told myself that it was Saturday night and he was probably partying, Harrow Creek style, like in the old days.

I really tried not to be disappointed that he wasn't waiting for my call. But I was.

Tristan made up for it when he finally got rid of Coach. He placed my feet on the cold tiled floor of the balcony on either side of the lounger and ate me until I was screaming his name into the night and forgetting all about the other man in my life. For a little while, anyway. Knox has this magic ability to always freaking be there, no matter how hard I try to get rid of him.

"I can't do any more," I cry, my body trembling, sweat rolling off me in waves as Tristan looms over me.

"Ah, come on, baby girl. One more," he says with a smirk.

Fucker hasn't even broken a sweat.

My fists curl at my sides as I fight to drag in the air my lungs are screaming for.

"I hate you," I hiss.

"No you don't," he argues smugly. "One more, then I'll run us a bath."

"Us?" I ask, my curiosity more than piqued.

"Sure. Unless you want to bathe alone."

"I think I'd prefer the company."

"I can even give you a massage. I did sports therapy classes, after all."

"Hmmm... now you're talking."

"So one more?"

"Tyrant," I hiss, pursing my lips in irritation.

"You'll thank me later."

"Will I?"

"Yeah, I'm going to let you order takeout."

I gasp, lifting my hand to my chest in faux horror. "Tristan Carver is going to eat takeout three days in a row. Who even are you?"

He chuckles. "I figure we've had enough exercise this weekend to make up for it."

"Speak for yourself. You look like you've barely lifted a finger."

His brow quirks. "I ran ten miles before you even stepped foot in here fifteen minutes ago."

"Ugh, whatever."

I blow out a long breath and prepare to give him one more sit-up.

The second I attempt to lift my back from the mat beneath me, my stomach muscles scream in horror.

"Come on, baby girl. Get up and you can kiss me."

He hovers just out of reach, and each time I get anywhere close he moves farther back.

"Asshole."

He chuckles but finally helps me out by wrapping his hand around the back of my neck, dragging me forward until my lips crash against his.

"Bath time," he announces long before I'm ready, pushing to stand and walking out of his home gym, his muscles on full display in just a small pair of shorts that hug his ass in the most insane way.

I watch him go, feeling like a complete failure.

If Tristan had any ideas about having a girlfriend he could work out with, then he seriously fucked up when he decided he wanted me. Not that I'm officially his girlfriend or anything. He still seems to be avoiding the whole label thing, which I guess is sensible, now Knox has crashed his way into our lives once more.

With a sigh, I try to get up. Everything hurts—even muscles I didn't know existed.

"Jesus," I grunt, finally getting my body to comply.

Maybe I do need more exercise than just sex.

Although, if that sex were to involve two—

Nope. Don't go there.

By the time I drag my exhausted ass to the master bathroom, there's a soft floral scent filling the air.

Pushing the door open, I find the tub filling with white fluffy bubbles and flickering candles everywhere I look.

"Whoa, anyone would think you planned this."

Tristan shrugs. "A guy can only hope, right?"

"So you're telling me that you didn't already have..." I reach out for the bottle of bubble bath and read the label.

"Rose and ylang-ylang scented bubble bath before I moved in?"

He laughs but fails to give me an answer, which only leads me to believe one thing.

Pro footballer and star wide receiver Tristan Carver loves a good old-fashioned girly bubble bath.

"Arms up, Pip," he says, gripping the bottom of the sports bra he ever-so-helpfully—and hopefully—bought for me.

"Trying to distract me from the bubble bath situation, big man?" I tease.

"Maybe. I don't need you questioning my masculinity."

Reaching out, I grab his semi through his shorts, making him suck a sharp breath through his teeth.

"I don't think we have an issue there."

"Minx," he growls, dipping his head to kiss and suck my neck.

"Tris, I'm all sweaty."

"You think I care?" he mutters against my skin. "Nothing will stop me from having you. Ever."

"Oh fuck." If that isn't one of the hottest things I've ever heard, I don't know what is.

He continues kissing down my body. Sucking and biting my nipples before he drops to his knees, dips his tongue into my belly button and then drags my shorts and panties down my legs.

"You're a goddess, Violet. I hope you know that."

I smile down at him, his muscles pumped from his workout and his shorts pulled tightly across his epic thighs, just about covering his impressive bulge.

"Hmm... I'm not sure. Maybe you should show me again."

He chuckles before surging to his feet and sweeping me off mine.

"In you go. Get nice and wet for me, yeah?"

"You don't need to put me in a bath to get that result, and

you know it," I say as the heat of the water surrounds my feet and lower legs.

Biting down on my bottom lip, I run my eyes down Tristan's body.

"Off," I instruct when they lock on his shorts.

"Anything."

Tucking his thumbs into the fabric, he shoves them down to his ankles, letting his dick spring free.

"Well, you know what they say. Every goddess needs a god, after all."

"Sit down," he commands before stepping in behind me.

His legs slide on either side of me before he pulls me back against his chest.

"I could get used to this," I whisper as the heat of the water soothes my aching muscles while his gentle touch and the feeling of his hardness against my back keeps my blood at boiling point.

"Never shared a bath with anyone before."

I still at his confession.

"Right," he murmurs, understanding my reaction.

I release a breath that's full of regrets and the weight of my lies.

"It's okay. We all have a past and previous partners, Vi."

"He's not exactly an ex though, is he? It's different to some chaser you might have fucked in the past," I say, desperately trying to keep any bitterness and jealousy from my tone.

It would be hypocritical of me to have an issue with his past conquests while mine is currently a huge part of our present.

"You still haven't heard from him?" he asks, sounding more concerned than I'm sure he probably should.

"Nope. But I haven't tried since last night. He sure hasn't returned my call, though."

"Maybe he's been busy?" I don't think it's meant to come out like a question, but it does.

"It doesn't really matter, does it? It just proves that he was all talk yesterday morning."

"Vi," Tristan breathes as if he wants to comfort me over this. Which is just... a massive headfuck.

"You should be happy," I mutter.

"While you're hurting? Never."

Water sloshes everywhere as I twist around, awkwardly putting myself on his lap.

"Hey," he breathes, reaching up to tuck a lock of my hair behind his ear.

"Hey." I smile shyly, feeling like a teenage girl who dreamed of getting the chance to get close to her brother's best friend. "How come you're so perfect?" I ask quietly.

He laughs, but there isn't much humor in it.

"I'm far from perfect, Vi. You just gotta look at the scar on my knee to see that."

"Scars don't show weakness, Tris. They show strength."

He stares up at me with so much emotion filling his eyes, it makes it hard to breathe.

"I've wanted you for so long, Pip. Longer than I think I even remember at this point. I should have been the one to show my cards sooner. I should have been the one watching late-night movies with you, keeping you company on nights you couldn't sleep."

Lifting my hand, I press my fingers against his lips to stop him. But he's not having any of it and pulls them away again.

"But I wasn't, and I'm man enough to accept that I'm not enough. As much as it fucking pains me to say."

A sob bubbles up my throat. "Tristan, no. That's not what this is about. You are good enough, you are everything. And if he never came back, then I never would have been missing out on anything, being with you."

"But he did," Tristan states coldly.

"He did, and—"

"There is no and, Pip. I get it, okay? I know this is complicated and unusual. But I refuse to put you into a cage, tell you what you can and can't do. I see it—I saw it. When I first saw you with him last week.

"There was something between you, something I never appreciated before. Something that I can't stop you from exploring. Even if it means that I lose in the end."

"No," I argue. "That's not happening. I'm not going to choose. I can't," I confirm strongly.

"But—"

"Remember last week, when you said you didn't want to put a label on things?"

He nods.

"It pissed me off, I won't lie. But now, it kinda feels like you knew something big was coming, and that by refusing to put that label on it, it would allow whatever this is to play out."

"Not wanting that label doesn't mean I want you any less," he says, his grip on my hips tightening.

"I know. I see it now. And it doesn't mean I want you any less either. I just... I want him as well."

"As long as you don't want me to want him," he growls, a smirk twitching at his lips.

"As hot as that would be, you're safe."

His fingers twist in my hair and he drags me down, slamming my lips against his and pushing his tongue into my mouth.

I lose myself in his kiss, letting thoughts of Knox and his sudden disappearance fall from my head.

In only a few minutes, I reach between our bodies, line Tristan's cock up with my entrance and sink down onto him.

"Holy fuck, Violet. Your pussy is heaven."

I moan loudly as I roll my hips, forcing him to hit that spot inside me that makes my eyes cross again and again.

"Oh shit," he breathes, his eyes locked on me as I take as

much pleasure from him as possible. "Use me, baby girl. Make yourself come all over my dick. Let me watch you fall."

"Yes," I cry, letting my head fall back as my fingers wrap around the edges of the tub, holding me up.

Embarrassingly quickly, I fall, screaming out Tristan's name as my pussy contracts around him.

"Fucking beautiful," he mutters, his voice deep and raspy with his own need for release.

"Next time, we go together."

"You think you have more orgasms in you than you managed sit-ups?"

"I fucking guarantee it."

"Let's see, shall we?" He thrusts up into me long before he's finished talking, sloshing water all over the side.

"Tristan," I cry, glancing over the edge.

"Cleaner comes tomorrow," he says carelessly.

"In case I needed a reminder that you're not one of us."

"Perks of fucking an NFL legend, baby girl. That and the stamina."

"Amen to that, Tristan Carver."

---

Something tickling my cheek rouses me from sleep, and a groan of annoyance rumbles in the back of my throat.

After Tristan and I eventually got out of a very cold bathtub last night, he followed through on his promise of letting me order another takeout, and I happily ordered more Mexican than two people would ever be able to eat in one night, along with making us a pitcher of virgin margaritas. But seeing as it was a school night, and Tristan starts at the ass crack of dawn, we fell into bed at a reasonable hour. I still ached from my attempt at exercising, and I can't say that my not-so-relaxing bath afterward really helped. But being wrapped up in his arms, I forgot about it all and drifted off.

Although I can't lie, it was with thoughts of another filling my head.

The tickle comes again, and this time I make a pathetic attempt at swatting the fly, or whatever it is, away.

But it doesn't work.

"Argh," I groan as I attempt to make my body comply enough to turn over, but the second I lift my head off the pillow, I still as a voice hits me.

"Firefly, it's just me."

My eyes pop open.

And sure as shit, crouched beside my side of Tristan's bed is the dark angel himself.

"W-what the hell are you doing?" I hiss, my voice is barely awake enough to work.

"Come to apologize."

I sit up, careful not to wake Tristan.

"What time is it? How did you get in here?" I ask, blinking against the soft light of the lamp on my nightstand.

"Almost sunrise. Come on, I want to show you something."

"Are you insane? We should be sleeping."

"I know. Trust me?" he asks, holding his hand out for me.

"Um..." I look back at Tristan.

"We'll leave a note, stop the old man from worrying."

"He's two years older than you," I point out.

"Come on." He takes my hand when I fail to offer it up and tugs me out of bed. "Put these on." He thrusts a pair of sweats and a hoodie at me, and I blindly comply like the easily led idiot that I am.

Damn it, Knox Bowman has always been my kryptonite.

Knox scribbles out a note at Tristan's desk while I pull a pair of sneakers on before leaving it on my pillow for him to find when he wakes.

"Come on, we don't have long."

Before I know what's happening, we're out of the building and climbing into a... "What the hell?" I ask. "Where the hell did you find a VW camper in the early hours of Monday morning?"

"That's for me to know and you not to ask about."

I'm still standing there, staring at the cute baby blue, very un-Knox-like vehicle when he pulls the passenger door open and gestures for me to get in.

"You're insane," I mutter, allowing him to help with totally unnecessary hands on my ass.

"You make me crazy, baby. You always have."

Gripping my chin, he leans in, brushing his lips against mine.

"I didn't brush my—"

"Shut the fuck up, Firefly," he grunts before crashing his lips to mine and kissing me breathless.

# 32

# KNOX

"Are you going to tell me where we're going?" Violet sulks from the passenger seat.

The camper runs incredibly smoothly considering its age and handles way better than I was expecting.

"Nope," I say with a smug grin.

"You're an asshole. Tristan is going to freak when he wakes up and finds me gone."

"I left a note," I argue, my smirk only getting wider as I think about him waking up and seeing what I left for him.

Yeah, there's a pretty strong chance he's going to want to punch me again.

But fuck it.

I've got the girl right now, and I couldn't be happier.

I take a sharp bend as we head toward the outskirts of town before reaching over and wrapping my hand around her thigh.

"I'm still pissed at you," she blurts.

"I know, Firefly. And I'm sorry. I told the guys I wasn't going to party with them but..." I sigh, remembering how they locked me in the back of Devin's car, pinned between the twins. "They didn't really give me a choice."

"And here I was thinking that big bad Knox Bowman doesn't do anything he doesn't want to do."

"Sorry to ruin the illusion, baby. But it was nice, partying with the guys again. Like old times."

She glances over at me, her expression softening.

"I should have messaged you, but things got wild fast."

"Oh?" she asks, glancing at my swollen fists as I grip the wheel. "They took you there to work," she surmises.

"No. I just... helped when things got out of hand with a couple of drunk assholes who thought they'd try their luck."

"Did they have a death wish? No one goes up against the Harrises."

"I don't think anyone had given them the memo. What's wrong, Firefly?" I ask when she lets out a heavy sigh.

"I just... I hate the thought of you working for them."

"I'm not involved in what the Harris brothers do, Violet. I was just there."

"Guilty by association," she points out.

"That's been true since the day I was born, baby. It's a bit late to be worrying about it now."

She sighs again, but thankfully, I take another turn and the landscape before us opens up, the first glow of the rising sun beginning to light up the sky.

"Oh wow," Violet breathes, staring out at the horizon.

"Wanna watch the sunrise with me, baby?" I ask, glancing over at her.

"Th-the sunrise?" she stutters in disbelief.

"Yep. I've come prepared and everything," I confess.

"Who even are you right now?" she whispers.

"Just a boy who's missed his girl."

"Knox."

The ground beneath us gets rough and we bounce along in the camper before I stop on a patch of grass where we can set up camp.

"Are we meant to be here?" Violet asks, looking around.

"Do you see anyone who's about to stop us?"

"Uh..."

"Come on. Be wild with me."

"Be wild watching the sunrise. Do those two things really go together?" she teases.

"I guess you're about to find out."

Killing the engine, I climb out of the camper and open up the back, grabbing the hamper of food and a basket full of everything we're going to need to make a fire.

"Here, lay this out," I say, handing Violet a blanket. "There are pillows inside too."

She doesn't move for a beat. Instead, she just stands and stares at me as if this isn't real.

Ten minutes later, we've got a fire crackling beside us with an old-school coffee pot on the top, and we're laid out on the blanket in each other's arms as we watch the sunrise.

It's up there with the most incredible moments of my life.

There were plenty of times in prison when, thanks to Shadow, I wasn't sure if I'd ever get to see another sunrise again. But here we are.

Things might not be exactly as I dreamed of when I was inside—I never once imagined having to wake her and drag her out of another man's bed to spend time with her. But I guess I can't really complain right now, either. She could still be hating me, after all.

The sun is the most incredible shade of orange as the coffee pot lets us know it's ready, and unsurprisingly, Violet lets me go in favor of a caffeine hit.

"Here you go, baby," I say after adding some cream to hers and passing the metal camping mug with the steaming coffee over.

"Fuck, that's hot," she gasps after taking a sip.

"It was literally on a fire, baby. What did you expect?"

She glares at me as I pull a bag of pasties from the hamper

and rip it open, letting the buttery sweet scent fill the air around us.

"All of this is incredible, Knox. Thank you," she says so sincerely it makes my chest ache.

"You're worth it."

Stealing a pain au raisin from the bag, she rips into it like a savage, making my cock jerk in excitement.

She falls silent as she continues to watch the sun and the morphing colors of the sky.

It's a comfortable silence that I remember all too well from our time before. And when she does finally speak again, she startles me.

"So what now?" she asks.

I study her profile, loving her messy hair, the pillow crease that still hasn't vanished in her cheek, and her makeup-free face. She looks beautiful. Mouthwateringly so.

"Well, I was kinda hoping to start your day right with a handful of orgasms before taking you back to head to class."

"A handful, huh?"

"At least," I admit.

"As fun as that sounds," she says, rolling onto her side to look at me. "That wasn't what I meant. I mean, what's next for you? You can't crash at the Harrises' for the rest of your days. What's your plan?"

I shrug. "I don't have one," I confess. "I wasn't expecting to get out yet."

"Why are you? Shit, sorry, that's—"

"It's okay. I've no intention of hiding anything from you." She glares at me and lifts a brow, silently pointing out there are things I'm actively hiding from her. "Apart from that," I breathe.

"Okay, so go on."

"Reid came to me with a job. If I could get the intel he needed, then he might just be able to organize getting my sentence overthrown."

"I'm assuming I don't want to know what the intel was?" she correctly guesses.

"Probably for the best you don't. Although, to be honest, even I don't know the whole story other than it involved a whole heap of blackmail and corruption. But that was none of my business. I just needed to get the job done in the hope of getting back to you."

"Are you in danger now because of it?"

"Not as far as I'm aware." Reaching out, I tuck a lock of her hair behind her ear. "The only person capable of hurting me now is you."

"Knox," she breathes, leaning into my hand when I cup her cheek. "So that's all over. You completed your secret mission and Reid granted you your freedom?"

"Well, the judge granted my freedom, Firefly. Reid just set it all up."

"So we're safe to assume the Maddison County judge is corrupt then," she mutters.

"Isn't it safe to assume that most of the legal system in this country is?"

She makes some kind of grunt of agreement that makes me laugh. "Thank fuck my major isn't law. What a waste of my time that would be."

"Aw, you can fight for my innocence any day," I say, rolling her onto her back.

"Innocent. Puh-lease, Knox. You haven't been innocent a day in your life."

"True that. I was born a Hawk, baby. And there is every chance I'll die as one too."

She sucks in a sharp breath. "I guess that tells me all I need to know about your intentions with them."

"It's my life, Firefly. They're all I've never known."

"Yeah," she breathes. "I know. I guess I just stupidly hoped that—"

"I've already told Reid my stipulations for coming back."

Her brows shoot up. "Something tells me that not many people live to do that. I can't imagine he takes well to being told what you will or won't do for him."

I chuckle. "Most men, no. They'd already have a bullet between their brows. I'm different."

"Thank fuck for that."

"I won't leave you again, I fucking promise you that, Violet."

She shakes her head, refusing to believe my words. I guess it would be naïve of her to.

I stare down at her, brushing my nose against hers, my mouth watering with my need to kiss her, but she still has questions, concerns. It wrecks me that she's doubting me, but it's right. I'd be more worried if she wasn't.

"Are you going to get your own place?" she finally asks. "Move back to the Creek?"

"No," I say, a little harsher than both of us were expecting if her wide eyes tell me anything. "I'm not living there. If I had a choice, I'd never go back there."

"But the Hawks are—"

"The Harrises are doing okay here. Reid is barely in the Creek in his mansion of death." Violet's brow quirks in interest. "I'll take you there one day. You can see for yourself."

"Uh... no, thank you."

"He's a good person, Firefly. Hell, he's done me enough favors over the years to prove it."

"He allowed you to be taken from me when I needed you."

"That wasn't Reid, baby. That was Victor. They're worlds apart. I trust Reid with my life. I wouldn't have trusted Victor with anything. He was bloodthirsty, power hungry and—"

"Reid isn't?" she teases.

"Oh, totally, but he's not only out for himself like his sperm donor. He believes in the Hawks, in his soldiers. He wants a future for all of us, for Harrow Creek. He doesn't want to burn it all to the ground in favor of lining his own pockets."

She nods. "If you say so."

"But to answer your question. Yeah, I'll get a place. I just want to figure this out first." Dipping lower, I brush my lips over hers. "Because more than anything else, I just want you. My home is wherever you are."

"Knox." I make the most of her parted lips and plunge my tongue inside, searching for hers.

"Fucking missed you, Firefly," I groan into our kiss, my grip on her hip tightening, dragging her against me so she can feel just how much she affects me.

"Knox," says again, but it's no longer a whisper but a plea for more.

"You want me to fuck you as the sun rises, Firefly?"

"New beginnings?"

"Fuck, yeah. I'm down for that, baby."

Without breaking our kiss, I hook her sweats over her ass and drag them down her legs.

"Oh God," she whimpers as the cool morning air washes over her sensitive skin.

Dipping my hand between her legs, I circle her clit, groaning as her wetness coats my fingers.

"Please," she begs, lifting her hips from the blanket and offering herself up.

"Greedy girl. You want my cock, don't you?"

"Knox," she moans, raking her nails down my back before grabbing my ass in an attempt to force me inside her.

"You want me to send you back to Tristan with my cum dripping out of you?"

Her desperate whimpers fill the air, giving me the answer I already knew.

"You want him to add his to it as well, don't you?"

"Knox, please. I need—"

"I know what you need, Firefly."

Lining myself up, I thrust forward, filling her to the hilt in one quick move.

"Yes," she cries, her back arching to try and take me even deeper.

Dropping lower, I brush my lips over her ear, sending a shiver through her body. Her pussy clamps down on me, squeezing so tightly I have to grit my teeth and force my release down.

Five years is way, way too long to go without sex. I'm like a fucking prepubescent boy shooting my load far too soon.

Focusing, I remember what it was I was going to say to her.

"I know something else you need," I growl in her ear.

"To come all over your massive dick?" she suggests, making me laugh.

"Well, yes. But you want us both, don't you, Violet?"

A groan rumbles deep in her chest at my question.

"You want to be pinned between both of us, so full of our dicks you can barely remember your own name."

"Shit, Knox," she gasps, but any argument she might attempt would be futile because she gushed all over my dick the second I painted that filthy little picture for her.

"We would fill you up so good, Firefly. Make you come so fucking hard. Then leave you weak, covered in our scents, kisses, marks, and full of our cum. We'd fucking own you, baby. Is that what you want?"

"Yes, yes," she cries, her body trembling beneath mine, her pussy squeezing me tight. But I'm not letting go yet, not until she's had another.

"Fuck, I love you," I blurt, slamming my lips down on hers not a second later to save her from having to come up with any kind of response.

Slipping my hand beneath her ass, I tilt her hips, ensuring I hit that spot that makes her scream with every single thrust.

My tongue caresses hers as I piston my hips. Hooking her leg over my shoulder, I take her deeper, forcing her to break our kiss.

"Fuck. That's—"

"I know, baby. Best fucking morning ever."

Sweat covers every inch of my skin as I continue with my punishing pace, but I still the second both our cells ding beside us.

"Looks like the old man is awake," I quip. "You think he wants a nice wake-up call too?" I ask, reaching for my cell.

"You wouldn't," Violet gasps, barely able to talk through her heaving breaths.

"I made him a promise this morning, and I never break my promises, Firefly."

Ignoring his message, I open my camera up and aim it down at Violet.

"How hard do you think he'll get, knowing you're getting fucked right now?"

Her cheeks burn brighter than the sunrise.

"He'll kill you," she breathes.

"It would be worth it," I admit, getting the camera angle just so and hitting record for a few seconds.

"Knox. Knox," Violet chants loudly when I hit her G-spot over and over and a smile curls up at my lips.

"Mine, Firefly. Fucking mine."

"Yes," she cries as she falls over the edge, her pussy tightening down on my cock and sending me crashing over the edge with her. I drop my cell, the video long forgotten as I collapse over Violet and claim her lips while I fill her up, branding myself inside her so she never forgets who owns her.

Even if I do have to share her.

# 33

# TRISTAN

*I've taken my girl.*
*Don't worry, I'll bring her back safe... and dripping with my cum.*
*You're welcome.*

"Motherfucker," I grunt, screwing up that asshole's note in my fist.

A shitty bit of paper was the last thing I wanted to find when my alarm blared and I rolled over in the hope of stealing a few minutes with Violet.

I throw it across the room, but it falls short of being anything dramatic when it just drops to the floor halfway between the bed and the trash can in the corner.

Falling onto my back, I stare up at the ceiling, willing the rest of my boner to sink. Knox sure made a good attempt with that note, but thoughts of my girl still keep it up.

Reaching for my cell on the nightstand, I wake it up and shut my alarm off. Before I know what I'm doing, I've got my conversation with Knox open in front of me.

Deciding against just messaging him, instead, I start a group chat with the three of us.

**Tristan: I sincerely hope the two of you are having fun.**

**Tristan: @Knox, you're a cunt.**

I sit and stare as the messages are delivered. Long seconds pass before the ticks change color, showing as read, and my heart leaps into my chest as they do.

At least that means they're not up to anything too distracting if they're reading messages from me.

Or at least, that's what I hoped. But when no response follows, I begin to think otherwise.

"Fuck's sake, Bowman."

Throwing the sheets off, I drop my cell to the middle of the bed and head for the shower. A cold shower. I've got a training session with a bunch of sweaty football players. The evidence that I woke up hoping to find my girl but discovering I was alone instead needs to fuck off. Fast.

I throw myself in the shower, brush my teeth and rub some wax into my hair before marching back into my room naked to find one of my coaching uniforms.

I have one leg in my pants when my cell dings in the sheets.

Reaching over, I find a response from Knox and open it without any thought.

I damn near drop the fucking thing when a video appears and starts playing, and my girl's moans rip through the air.

"Knox. Knox," she cries, sending anger surging through me almost as fast as it makes my dick stir back to life.

"You fucking asshole," I hiss, unable to rip my eyes away from my cell as he rails her. I'm so fucking enthralled in watching, I don't even think to look where they are. For all I know, they could be out in my living room waiting for me to join.

Whoa... where did that thought come from?

"Mine, Firefly. Fucking mine." Knox's declaration of ownership drags me back from my fucking weird imagination.

"I don't fucking think so, Bowman."

My thumbs fly across the screen, hitting the glass like a madman.

**Tristan: Make those claims all you want. You know she wants me just as much as you.**

My heart pounds as I consider whether those words are entirely true.

And I hate it.

I fucking hate that every time she's with him, I question everything she said to me after he left this weekend.

I've never been self-conscious or anything less than sure of myself and my surroundings. But there's something about Violet that makes me all kinds of vulnerable. And I love it as much as I hate it.

Putting my heart on the line is fucking terrifying. But it's also exhilarating. And I wouldn't give it up for the world.

His next reply takes longer, and I can only imagine why.

I stand there with my muscles locked tight and my fingers cramping as I hold my cell a little too tight, waiting, refusing to move from this spot until I get a response.

When it comes, though, I fucking wish I didn't bother.

The photo of Violet with the evidence of what they've just done running out of her fuels my anger as much as it does my desire, because fuck if I don't want to replace that with my own.

I don't reply. There are literally no words in the world that I could type back that wouldn't make me sound like a deranged, jealous, and possessive prick. So I just decide against it.

Putting my cell on silent to stop me from being tempted by anything else he sends to try and rile me up, I drag on the rest of my clothes and march through the apartment, quickly discovering my previous thought about them being here was just wishful thinking. There is no sign of anyone.

I make myself a protein shake and then head out, ready to rid myself of this anger and frustration by training with the guys.

When I pull up at the training facility, I cave and pull my cell from my pocket.

There are two messages waiting for me.

One from each of them.

**Pip: I'm sorry. I'll make it up to you later. Promise. x**

**Knox: We'll see about that. You might be too busy still...**

"Fuck's sake."

Shoving it into my bag this time, I push the door open and march toward the entrance, ready to put everything that's happened this morning out of my head.

How can you be in love with a woman who possibly loves you and someone else?

---

Today has been full on. Training overran, making me late for my first class, and it's been a shit show ever since.

"Excuse me," I say when I find Winters blocking the doorway leading back toward the offices within the training facility. I've still got a shit ton of work to do, but all I can think about is going home to my girl.

Knox, the asshole, has been texting me all day, ensuring I'm fully aware of what I missed out on this morning. The only good thing in all of this is that I know he dropped her off for class and hasn't spent the entire day with her. I just need to hope that he hasn't swept her up the second she finished for the day and I'll walk back into my apartment later to find him railing her over my new couch.

My dick stirs despite Winter's cold stare as he watches me like a creep.

"What?" I bark, my tolerance levels non-existent.

"You know," he says smugly, smoothing back his obnoxiously styled hair. "You really shouldn't be sneaking around with an undergrad."

"Right. And what I do in my spare time is any of your business because..."

He shakes his head and smiles fakely. "Coach told me to look out for you."

"Well, lucky for you, I don't need anyone watching my back. Especially not someone who's likely to stab me in it."

I take off, shoulder checking him as I pass. His tut of disapproval makes my teeth grind.

"And just so you know, she's not just an undergrad. She's been in my life almost since the day she was born. And she's fucking everything. Something, I suspect, you've no experience of. Now butt the fuck out of my life, and maybe spend a little more time worrying about your own miserable existence."

I'm feeling all kinds of smug about getting the last word in until I take three steps and look up to find our audience. Coach is at the back of the crowd with a smirk playing on his face. In front of him are Violet's housemates, West and Brax, with Luca, Leon, and Kane right alongside them.

"Uh..."

With a nod of approval and understanding, Coach disappears, leaving West and Brax to step forward.

"We're glad she's in good hands, Carver," West says, clamping his hand down on my shoulder.

"Always. You don't have to worry about her with me."

"And what about Bowman?" Kane asks, making me give him a double take before I narrow my eyes. "She came to me Friday night, wanting some answers about him."

"Right?"

"Just told her what I knew, man. Knox was innocent."

The others look between the two of us like we've suddenly sprouted an extra head each.

"Yeah, he is. I'm assuming you didn't tell her who it was."

He shrugs.

"I don't know who it was."

I narrow my eyes, studying him, trying to work out if that is the truth or not.

He used to be in just as deep as Knox, so something tells me that he's more than aware.

So why didn't he tell her?

"Right. Okay." I stare at him a little longer, but he gives nothing away. "Knox won't be an issue for Violet."

"She sent him away?" Kane asks, his brows shooting up in shock.

"No. Not exactly."

West steps up again.

"Wait. Our girl is living with you but failed to send this other dude away? What the hell is going on here?"

"Pretty sure she's fucking both of them, little bro," a deep voice booms from somewhere, and when I look over, I find West's older brother, Colt, has joined the party.

"Fucking hell."

"That right, Carver?" Luca asks, but it doesn't come out in the teasing way I'd have expected, given the situation.

"Honestly, I don't really know what's going on. We're just... taking it one day at a time."

"Sounds like... fun," Brax adds, finally breaking his silence.

"Okay well, if you're done grilling me, I've got shit to be doing."

"Trying to figure out a way to steal your girl back from the big bad gangster?" Colt offers.

Flipping him off—totally unprofessional—I march through them and toward my office, grateful that it's empty and Winters decided against riling me up some more.

I fall into my chair with a groan of exhaustion. But no matter how long this fucking Monday has been, I can't stop yet.

Waking up my computer, I get to work, praying that Winters has fucked off and that no one else is going to want me. Until I get home, of course. Then, I want someone's full attention to make up for this morning.

---

The sun has long set when I finally emerge from the building, and the parking lot is almost empty.

I messaged Violet about ten minutes ago to let her know I was about to leave and she replied instantly, telling me that she was waiting.

That thought was enough to get my body moving faster as I march around the corner toward my parking space, but my steps falter when I find a figure sitting on the hood of my car.

"Violet?" I breathe, tugging my bag up high on my shoulder and picking up speed.

"Told you I'd be waiting," she teases.

"Yeah, I know. I just didn't think—" My bags fall to the ground with a thud. I wrap one arm around her back while the other lifts to cup her jaw so I can move her exactly where I want her and slam my lips down on hers.

"Tristan," she moans into my kiss before sucking on my tongue in a way that makes my cock ache with need.

"Fuck, baby girl," I groan when she finally releases me, slipping her hands beneath my t-shirt and raking her nails down my back.

"Missed you all day," I whisper, refusing to take my lips from her as I drag her lower down the hood, giving her little choice but to wrap her legs around my waist.

She gasps the second the length of my cock presses against her.

Her hands change direction, quickly descending toward my ass before she squeezes, forcing us closer.

"Shit, baby. I need to get inside you."

"What are you waiting for?" she asks, her voice sounding way more innocent than it should.

"I'm not fucking you here, Pip. There are cameras and anyone could see you." I hate to be the sensible one, but the last thing we need right now is a fucking sex tape hitting the internet.

"Let me take you home. I'll be able to take my time with you."

"What if I want it hard and fast?" she counters.

"Then I'll give you that. But not here. I won't put you at risk like that."

The thought flickers in the back of my mind that Knox wouldn't give a fuck and would take her right here.

But even competing with that motherfucker isn't enough to force my hand.

Steeling my spine, I rip my lips away from hers.

"Come on. The sooner we get home, the sooner I can be inside you."

Lifting her from the hood, I carry her around to the passenger side of my car and lower her into the seat.

"Where's your car?" I ask, although I don't really give a fuck if we leave it behind, and I'm sure as shit not letting her drive it back alone.

"Letty dropped me off."

"Good."

Swinging the door closed, I jog around the other side, rearranging myself as I go.

The second the engine rumbles to life, Violet shifts a little closer and drags her hand up my thigh.

"You're trouble."

"Just drive, Tristan," she instructs, her voice rough with desire.

"Fuck. Yeah."

Throwing the car in drive, I press my foot to the gas and shoot off like a rocket.

I'm not even out of the parking lot when her hand moves higher, her little finger brushing the head of my cock.

"Shit, Pip. You want me to come in my pants?" I groan.

"I'd prefer it if it was in my mouth," she deadpans.

"Holy shit. Violet," I warn when she tugs at the little ties around my Panthers sweats I wore for our training session this afternoon.

"What? I'm just making the drive more... enjoyable."

"Fuck," I gasp when she pushes her hand beneath my waistband and her fingers wrap around my dick. "Or trying to get us killed," I mutter, desperately trying to focus on what I should be doing.

"I trust you," she says firmly. "Now lift up, I need a little more space for what I have in mind.

I glance over at her, losing myself in the wicked intent sparkling in her eyes a little too long before looking back at the road.

"Jesus Christ, Pip. I thought you were so sweet and innocent, you know."

"No, you didn't. And now you're aware that I was corrupted by a Hawk, you really should reconsider."

"Motherfucker. You're too good for him."

"So he keeps saying. But it didn't stop me then, and it won't stop me now, so..." She shrugs before squeezing my length hard enough to make me grunt. "Now lift up and I'll fix this for you."

"If we die, it's your fault. I just want you to know that."

"I can deal. Hold tight."

Before I get a chance to even try and stop her, she hops up on her knees, leans over the center console and licks the head of my cock like it's fucking ice cream.

"Fucking hell, Violet," I grunt, my hips lifting from the seat as my cock demands more of what she's offering up.

"Five minutes until we get home, right?" she confirms.

"A-about th-that, yeah."

"Easy," she says, sinking down on my length and taking me right to the back of her throat.

My grip on the wheel tightens, my knuckles turning white as I fight to keep my focus and my eyes open.

"Goddamn, you're good at that, baby." I'm desperate to twist my fingers in her hair and hold her down a little longer, but I don't trust myself to get us home safe with two hands on the wheel right now, let alone one.

"You can thank Knox later. He showed me the dark side and taught me all I know."

"I fucking hate that cunt," I mutter.

"No, you don't," she says confidently. "If you did, you wouldn't even be entertaining what we're embarking on right now."

"Who says I'm entertaining it?"

She chuckles but doesn't respond. Instead, she puts all her effort into her quest of making me come before I pull up at our house.

Something I have every confidence that she's going to achieve.

Dirty, dirty girl.

# 34

## VIOLET

I sit up, swallowing down Tristan's cum and wiping the back of my hand across my mouth.

"Perfect timing," I murmur, as he pulls into his parking space.

"Do you have any idea how close I just came to killing us both?"

"But did we die?" I ask with a laugh as I sit back and watch him try and put himself back together.

"You're trouble."

"Fun, isn't it? Don't you just wish you'd figured it out sooner?"

"You know I do, Pip."

He reaches his arm out, twists his fingers in my hair and drags me back over the console, slamming his lips down on mine and plunging his tongue into my mouth. There's no way he can't taste himself, but his kiss doesn't falter.

By the time he pulls back, my breathing is even more erratic and my blood is boiling.

"Let's go inside," he says, his dark eyes boring into mine.

"Ready to go again?" I tease.

"You didn't have anything planned for tonight, did you?"

"You know, anyone would think you were jealous, Tris."

"Of Knox stealing you from right under my nose and sending me fucking sex tapes of what I was hoping to wake up to? Whatever would give you that idea?"

"So? Let's go and make him pay."

I'm out of the car before he has a chance to respond. "Come on, old man," I call, already heading for the building when I hear his door shut. His footsteps pound behind me as I rush to pull my keys out and unlock the door.

"You're out of practice. Good job you're no longer on the field," I shout over my shoulder as I run full speed toward the stairs.

"Violet," he warns, his deep, rumbling voice making me push harder.

But inevitably, he catches me before I manage to get the door to his apartment open. He pins me against the solid wood, letting me feel every hard inch of him.

"Tristan," I moan, sounding like a desperate whore.

"How badly do you want my cock, baby girl?" he groans in my ear before biting me.

"S-so bad. Please," I beg, shoving my ass against him, making a growl rumble low in his throat.

"You'd let me fuck you right here, wouldn't you?"

"Yes," I confess. Although to be fair, it's pretty safe. He's the only one who lives on this floor. It's far less exposed than I could have been with Knox this morning.

"Dirty, dirty girl."

Before I know what's happening, he twists the key I'd abandoned in the lock, and the door swings open.

I gasp as the world falls away from me, but I don't plummet toward the floor like I first fear because Tristan is right there, wrapping his arm around my waist.

My feet leave the floor as he carries me inside the apartment, the door slamming shut a beat later before he spins me and presses me back against the wall.

He hooks my legs around his waist, allowing him to grind against me with precision. He grips both of my wrists in one of his huge hands, pinning them to the wall above my head and squeezing my breast with the other.

"Need inside you, baby girl," he groans.

"What are you waiting for?" I gasp, rolling my hips in time with his, the movement of our bodies even with the fabric between us building me higher and higher.

But I don't want to come with him dry humping me. I want to come with him buried deep inside me.

"Fucking hell. You wreck me, Violet."

Dropping his hand, he awkwardly hooks my skirt up around my waist and drags my panties to the side.

He dips his fingers between my folds, spreading my juices around.

"So wet for me. Did sucking my cock do this?"

"Yes," I cry when he sucks on the skin of my neck while pumping two thick fingers inside. "Cock, Tristan. I want your cock."

"Fuck, you're perfect," he groans, his voice full of awe as he works his pants down with one hand, but before he manages to free his dick, the buzzer sounds out around us. "Fuck," he barks.

"Ignore it."

His eyes blaze with heat as he follows my orders.

But before he manages to move, it goes off again. For longer this time.

"FUCK OFF," he bellows as if whoever it is will be able to hear him.

And maybe they can, because the buzzer starts going off intermittently.

"If that's fucking Knox trying to cockblock me, then I swear I'll—"

The second he releases my wrists, I reach over and press

the button down to find out. If it is, then I have every intention of letting him up to join the party.

"Who is it?" I ask, my raspy voice definitely giving away what we're in the middle of.

"Your favorite bitch. Now get off your sexy footballer and let me in. I have cocktails."

"Goddamn it, Ella," I groan.

"Be a good girl and hop off Carver's dick and let me in, yeah?"

"I would never force you to abandon good dick," I mutter indignantly.

"What? Yes, you would, and I'm pretty sure you have, multiple times. So suck it up bitch, and let me in. I have something I need to discuss with you. And I'm sure Tristan would rather I don't do that while standing out here for the entire world to hear."

"I'm going to make sure you fail all your classes this semester," Tristan warns as he finally admits defeat and places my feet back on the floor.

"Let her in, I'll go start dinner."

"But—"

"Do your thing, and the second she leaves, we'll pick this back up where we left off."

"Exactly where we left off?" I ask, longing for the feeling of him fucking me against the wall.

"Maybe, maybe not. You'll have to wait and see," he teases before pressing the button to allow Ella into the building as he steals one more kiss then stalks toward the kitchen, rearranging himself as he goes.

"This had better be good," I mutter to myself, smoothing my hair down and wiping at what is probably my very ruined lipstick.

I pull the door open just in time to see my best friend climb the final two stairs.

"You've got some really shitty timing, you know that, right?"

"I know," she agrees with a wide smile. "I watched you both arrive." She's got a knowing twinkle in her eye.

"I hate you."

"No you don't," she says happily, inviting herself into Tristan's apartment and dumping her bag in my hands. "Everything we need for some sex on the beach to get our week started the right way."

"I'm not getting drunk," I state, remembering the hangovers I've suffered recently.

"I'll make them weak," she promises with a wicked glint in her eyes.

"Sure."

She takes off deeper into the flat as if she knows where she's going, giving me little choice but to follow.

"Oooh, this is fancy," she says, looking around Tristan's living room.

"Violet chose it all," a deep voice rumbles from the kitchen.

Ella spins on me, her eyes wide with excitement.

"You've really got quite the setup here, huh?"

"I just helped," I argue, although it's not true. Tristan did let me choose everything. But I think she's reading way too much into that fact.

"You're living with him," she whispers. "Like, ball and chain, husband and wife, living with him."

I shake my head. "It's just temporary," I argue, not liking the way my stomach knots as the words pass my lips.

"Sure. Anyway," she says, walking toward where Tristan's voice came from to find the kitchen.

Her eyes quickly scan the room before they land on Tristan.

"Hey, Coach Carver. Nice place you got here."

"I'm glad you agree. Can I assume you're going to want

food to go with those cocktails?" he asks, shooting her a flirty look I'd want to kill him for it was given to any other girl.

"Oh, and he can cook. Sounds wonderful, Coach," she teases.

"It's Tristan," he grumbles.

"Suuuure." She grins.

"So, to what do we owe this pleasure?" he asks, taking the bag from me and studying the contents.

"Well," she says, looking between the two of us and then back to the empty living room. "I heard a little rumor about my dirty best friend earlier, and I need to know if it's true or not."

"You already know I blew him on the way home," I quip as a loud crash sounds from the kitchen, drawing both our attention.

"Sorry," Tristan mutters. "But how exactly did you know that?" he asks Ella.

"She was waiting for us," I say while she follows up with, "And I didn't assume Violet was bent over helping tie your shoes."

"Jesus fucking Christ." He rakes his fingers through his hair before downing the shot of vodka he just poured into a glass.

"Anyway, as fun as that must have been. This is better..."

She wiggles her brows before blurting, "Rumor has it, Tristan Carver isn't the only one stuffing your—"

"Motherfuckers," Tristan barks, slamming his palms down on the solid counters with a loud slap.

"It's okay," Ella surmises. "We don't have secrets in our house." Her confidence makes me wince noticeably. "What?"

"Fucking hell. Can you make those drinks faster, Tris?" I ask. No, beg.

I might be all in when it comes to what's happening with both him and Knox right now, but trying to explain it to my hopelessly romantic and quite traditional best friend, not so much.

"Drink," I say the second Tristan slides two glasses of the pink cocktail toward us.

She narrows her eyes but does as she's told before studying me closely.

"Violet, are you or are you not fucking two guys at once, openly?"

I swallow nervously.

"Why don't you two go and sit down to have this conversation?" Tris suggests. "I'll just focus on this." He gestures to all the ingredients lining the counter.

"Good idea. Come on, El."

"I know I always used to joke about Letty getting in the middle of a twin sandwich, but shit, Vi. Are you actually doing it?"

"They're not twins."

"And so not the fucking point. Who the hell is Knox, and is he as hot as Tristan? Because if he is, fucking hell, girl." She fans herself with her free hand as she lowers her ass to the couch.

"He's as hot," I confirm with a smirk, "but in a totally different way."

"Oh my God," she exclaims, sounding freakily like everyone's least favorite *Friends* character. "Tell me you have photographs," she begs.

"Um... I don't actually. Well, I do, but they're five years old."

"They're five— I think I need the whole story here, Violet."

With a sigh, I fall back on the couch beside her.

"Knox was... is, I guess, my stepbrother."

Ella's chin drops.

"And Tristan is your brother's best friend. That's some forbidden, kinky shit right there, girl."

I can't help but chuckle.

"But five years ago? Where's he been? Why is he back? Wait... have you been together all this time?"

"What? No. He... um... he went to prison for..." I suck in a breath, ready to tell my whole truth. "Killing our parents."

"Oh shit," Ella gasps when her grip on her glass loosens and she tips half her cocktail straight into her lap.

"H-he killed... Fuck, Violet. You need to keep talking."

So I do.

I tell her everything I should have told her when we first met. All my truths, my pain, my grief.

She sits there with tears in her eyes as she listens to every word I say. At some point, she reached over and took my hand in hers, offering me her support as I talked through the hardest parts.

"He really didn't do it?" she asks when I finally run out of steam.

"No. I really believe that he didn't. Knox doesn't shy away from the hard stuff, and if he were guilty, he'd tell me to my face, I have no doubt."

"He's innocent," Tristan agrees from the doorway. I've no idea if he's been standing there listening, but I appreciate his presence all the same.

"Shit," Ella breathes. "And now you're sharing her." It's not a question—she already knows the answer, even if she's struggling to get her head around it.

Tristan doesn't reply, but I don't miss the way his jaw tics.

He might be okay with this current setup for now, but I also know for a fact that he'd be happier keeping me all to himself. Sadly, that isn't how this is going. Because giving myself wholly to him would mean turning my back on Knox, and that is not happening.

"So where is the bad boy, then?" Ella asks, looking between the two of us.

"No idea," I say, anxiety and concern for what he's doing these days knotting up my stomach.

He told me only this morning that he was fully committed to the Hawks. It's something I'm going to have to try and come to terms with and work on the fear that overtakes me when I consider what his life in that gang involves.

"I'm sure he'll be in touch. He might storm through that door any moment and sweep you off your feet."

"I fucking hope not. He's already stolen her once today. Violet is mine tonight."

"Holy hell, girl." She fans herself once more. "You know, I've always had a fantasy about being the filling in a male sandwich—"

"You don't say," I deadpan, knowing just how much she teased Letty about the Dunn twins.

"I—" she starts but quickly figures out that she doesn't have any words to follow it up with.

"I get it, El," I say as Tristan turns away once more to dish up with a smirk on his face. "I really fucking get it."

She turns to me with an excited smile. "When it happens—"

"If," I interrupt.

"When." She rolls her eyes. "When it happens, I want all the details."

I glance to where Tristan is moving around the dining table and think of Knox, wondering just how it'll feel with both of them touching me, kissing me, fucking me.

My body heats, my thighs clenching as desire pools low in my belly.

"Oh my God, you're imagining it, aren't you?"

"If it happens," I say, dragging myself from my lust-filled thoughts. "I'll tell you some of it. The rest is purely for us."

Her eyes soften as she hears my unspoken words. What's happening here between us is more than a hookup that I'll tell her all about the next day.

It's... okay, so I still don't know exactly what it is, but it is definitely more than that.

Knox told me he loved me this morning, and I'm pretty

sure I see the exact same thing in Tristan's eyes every time he looks at me.

The only question really is... am I capable of loving two men as wholly as they deserve? Or is this whole thing just a fantasy that's going to leave us all a little bit more broken than we already were?

"Dinner's ready," Tristan calls, dragging me from my thoughts.

"Yes. It smells insane. Come on, Vi. Something tells me you're going to need some stamina the second I walk out the front door," Ella teases.

"Here's hoping. Cockblocker," I mutter.

She throws her head back and barks out a laugh.

"Delayed gratification. Just think how much better it'll be later."

"It's a good job I love you," I scoff, following her through to the kitchen.

"Ohh, looks amazing, Coach. What is it?"

"My homemade pad thai. Loaded with protein and veggies."

"Ooh, Tristan Carver knows the way to a woman's heart."

I just about manage to bite down on the inside of my lips to stop me from blurting something about his tongue skills having a more direct line than his kitchen ones. As if he can read my less-than-pure thoughts, Tristan's eyes lock with mine over Ella's head and he mimics eating me out, turning me into a puddle of need as I fall into the chair.

Ella is utterly oblivious as she grabs her fork and digs right in.

"Oh my God," she mumbles around a mouthful. "This is so fucking good." Or at least, that's what I think she says.

---

Anticipation zaps through my veins the second I close the front door behind Ella.

I feel lighter, freer, now I've told my best friend everything about my life. I knew she would never judge me for any of it. It was my own fear of talking about the past that stopped me before, something I think she understands. She keeps her own past struggles close to her chest, after all.

The second I walk back into the living room, his eyes burn a trail across my skin, goose bumps rising in its wake.

"Naked. Now," he demands, sitting on the edge of the couch and resting his elbows on his knees. "Right now. I want to see every inch of you, baby girl."

A shudder of desire rips through me. How is it that with only his eyes and words he can turn me into a melting ball of need?

Not wanting to waste a second, I pop the button on my skirt and let it fall to my ankles before dragging my tank over my head, leaving me standing in just my pink underwear.

"Fuck, Violet," he groans, falling back on the couch, his eyes eating me up as his cock begins to tent his pants.

My mouth waters for another taste of him.

"More?" I ask, my voice raspy.

"Always more. Show me your tits, Pip."

Reaching behind me, I unhook my bra, but I don't let it fall, much to his annoyance. Instead, I spin around, giving him my back and thong-clad ass before the lace hits the floor.

"Tease," he groans.

"Ah, Tristan," I moan loudly, making a show of cupping my breasts.

"Baby girl, stop hiding from me," he warns, the deepness of his tone making my stomach erupt with butterflies.

"What are you going to do about it, big man?"

I tuck my thumbs into the sides of my panties, but I don't get a chance to shove them down because there's a thud behind me before pain radiates from my ass cheek.

I try to hop forward, but large hands around my hips hold me in place as a burning hot tongue laves at the bite mark he just left on my ass.

"You bit me," I breathe, my panties fucking ruined with the possessive move.

"Yeah, I did," he states, taking over from me and dragging my panties down my legs. "You're mine to do what I want with, right?" he asks, his hot breath against my heated skin.

"Yes."

"Good. Now open your legs."

I do as I'm told.

"Wider. Let me see that beautiful cunt, baby girl."

I spread them as much as I can and he groans behind me.

"Look how wet you are for me."

My entire body jolts when he runs his finger up my inner thigh, collecting my juices.

"Need you, Tris."

There's rustling fabric behind me, but I don't look back. I trust him.

A second later, he appears, lying on his back between my legs, staring up at me with nothing but pure need and awe written all over his face.

He's taken his shirt off, leaving inches upon inches of toned, hard muscle for me to feast on, but before I really get a chance, he dishes out his next order.

"Sit on my face, baby girl. I want to eat you until you're screaming."

I drop to my knees faster than I thought possible, and the second I'm close, he wraps his hands around my thighs and yanks me down onto him.

"Fuck yes," I cry as he licks up the length of me, reawakening the release that was stolen from me when we were messing around earlier.

Lifting my hands, I cup my breasts once, pinching my own

nipples and adding to the sensations he's unleashing on my body.

My release surges forward head-spinningly fast. In only minutes, he's got me balanced right on the edge, driving me crazy and refusing to let me fall despite how much I beg and plead.

I'm right there once again when there's a loud crash in the apartment, followed immediately by another slam.

If Tristan hears it with my thighs pinned to his ears then he doesn't show it, he just continues eating me like a starved man.

I want to jump up and see what it was, but also, I really fucking don't. Not when I'm so—

"Oh fuck," I bark when the reason for the noise makes himself known. "Knox," I cry, my concern for him almost enough to dampen down my impending orgasm, but then Tristan does this thing and I finally fall. "TRISTAN," I scream while my eyes remain locked on Knox and the copious amounts of blood covering him as he leans against the wall to hold himself up.

# 35

## KNOX

"Are you sure you're ready for this?" JD taunts from the other side of Reid's car.

I glance over, the moon lighting him up enough to notice the smirk playing on his lips.

"Fuck you, man. That cunt is mine. I want him bleeding out at my fucking feet, staring me dead in the eyes so he knows exactly which Hawk sent him straight to hell."

"That's more like it." He reaches over and punches me in the shoulder harder than necessary.

"What the fuck, asshole?"

"Will you two quit it?" Reid barks from the driver's seat.

"Sorry, boss," JD teases.

Mav sits up front beside Reid, but he barely says a word.

It seems that hell really must have frozen over since I've been gone, because I never expected to come out and find myself in a what... a throuple with my firefly and Tristan, but also Reid and Mav are... friends? Hell, they're more than that now.

Back when we were kids, they were mortal fucking enemies. Mav was older, but his dad being Victor's second meant he always came behind Reid in the ranks, something he fucking hated and ensured everyone was aware of from a very young age.

Now though, despite all odds, Mav is Reid's second in command. And from what I can tell, the two of them are doing a kick-ass job.

"Anything?" Mav asks when Reid's cell lights up the darkness around us.

"Not yet," he says, putting it back to sleep again.

We're stationed about half a mile out from where we know Shadow to be hiding, just waiting for the signal to let us know that they've all left.

They were meant to have been gone an hour ago, according to his intel, but they're still fucking there.

It's making me antsy.

I'm putting on a brave face, because I want this. I fucking need this. But the reality is, I haven't run a job with the boys in over five years. And we never embarked on anything of this level back then.

We might have been out for target practice. I might still feel at home shooting a gun. And thanks to Shadow, hell knows I can fight for my life if needed. But I'm still more nervous than is probably helpful right now.

I need to be focused, not questioning my ability to get the job done like we used to.

Hoping that it's dark enough, I allow my fingers to drum against my thigh in the hope of expelling some of my pent-up energy.

Silence fills the car, the only thing I can focus on is the rapid beat of my heart as we wait.

And wait.

And wait.

Eventually, the buzz of Reid's phone is loud enough that all of us hear it, and JD and I sit forward.

"Is that it?" he asks, sounding as impatient as I am.

"Yes." Without another word, Reid brings the car to life and shoots off out of our hiding place.

"Nervous?" JD asks.

"No," I spit, hating that he's clearly sensing more than I'm willing to admit.

The drive toward the location pinpointed as Shadow's hideout is fast.

Just like our hiding spot, the entire place is in darkness, and as we get closer, Reid kills the headlights.

There is nothing around us but darkness, and it's even worse now there are clouds covering the moon that previously gave us a little light.

"Coms," Mav instructs. "Then, the second we get the signal, we're going in. Okay?"

"Okay," JD and I agree.

The earpiece feels weird. It's way more techie than we ever had in the past, but I guess that's just something else that's changed in my time away.

"Remember the plan?"

"Yes, boss," JD drawls. "The others take out any Devils who've been left behind, and we go for Shadow, who's being kept safe in the middle of the building. The only blood we spill is his," he mocks, I think attempting to mimic Reid's voice, which I'm sure only pisses him off.

"Great," Reid hisses, confirming my previous suspicion.

"Should have gotten laid before this job," JD helpfully suggests. "Would have helped chill you the fuck out a bit."

"Just focus, yeah? We need this to be clean."

"Trust us, boss. We've got this nailed."

Silence falls, but it barely lasts long enough for me to think about what we're about to do before a voice crackles through the small speaker in my ear.

"All set. Moving in... Three. Two. One."

"Let's go," Reid adds, throwing his car door open, the

interior light waking up and bathing us in light for the first time in long minutes.

Double-checking my weapons and ammo, I follow Reid and Mav's footsteps toward the building with JD right at my side.

"We got this, man," he says encouragingly.

"I know. I've got no doubt."

By the time we get to our entry point, the lock has already been smashed off, allowing us to slip inside without any drama.

The bright lights make me wince after being in the dark for so long, and my vision is blurred for longer than I need it to be. The scent of cleaning fluid is so strong, it burns my nose, making me wonder what the fuck this place is actually used for, other than to hide scumbags like Shadow.

Grunts and groans sound out around us, and I just have to fucking pray the pain is being inflicted on Devils and not the other way around.

Voices sound out in my ears, but I barely register any of the words that are said. Instead, I just focus on Reid leading the way.

If there were an issue, he'd have bailed.

I trust him.

I trust him with my fucking life.

He comes to a stop at a doorway, then turns and looks directly at me.

Squaring my shoulders, I tighten my grip on the gun in my hand.

"Ready?" he asks quietly.

I nod once, and it's the only confirmation he needs to reach out and throw the door open.

He goes first, ever the leader, and I follow, Mav and JD taking up the rear. It's not until the four of us are inside the pitch black room that the lights flicker to life and our mistake unravels before us.

The intel was correct. Shadow is here. But he's not fucking alone. And they're ready for us.

"Fuck," Mav grunts behind me before JD lets out a roar.

I'm the only one with a gun ready, and I quickly aim as a Devil lunges toward me.

But I hesitate. I fucking hesitate to pull the trigger, remembering Reid's warning back in the car.

*The only blood we spill is his.*

I glance in his direction, and my eyes lock with his cold, evil ones. I just catch the triumphant smirk that twitches at his lips before something collides with my outstretched arm and the gun that I was holding goes skittering across the concrete floor.

"Motherfucker," I roar, my flight or fight instinct kicking in, and I drive my fist into the cunt's face. The punch lands with a sickening crunch.

Sadly, it's nowhere near enough to put him down, and as the sound of the others fighting their battles rings out around me.

I quickly discover that the motherfucker has a mean left hook when he manages to land a punch that I swear makes my brain rattle around in my head.

My vision blurs as blood runs from my brow, the taste of it filling my mouth as he manages to knock me off my feet.

His fists slam into my ribs, sending pain searing around my body as he takes the upper hand for a few minutes.

The mocking tone of Shadow's voice fills my ears as he taunts me.

"You thought I forgot about you, didn't you, kid? You thought you were better than me. That you managed to escape my wrath when I was set free. You got in my way time and time again, making my job harder than necessary."

"Fuck you," I spit, when my attacker makes a fatal fucking error, allowing me to take control.

Flipping us, I rain hell down on the cunt's face, hitting him over and over until he has no chance of retaliating.

"Knox," Reid bellows, making me look up just as Shadow pulls his own gun.

"NO," JD roars, launching himself at Shadow as a loud shot pierces through the room.

My ears ring as I frantically scramble to my feet, hoping like fuck the guy beneath me is out of it enough not to follow me and that that bullet didn't find a home anywhere in JD.

Reid would never fucking forgive me.

I glance over at Reid and Mav, who are still locked in battle with three Devils, but despite being outnumbered, they seem to have it under control. In fact, I'm pretty fucking sure that Reid is smiling. Twisted motherfucker.

"JD?" I bark, needing to know if he's okay as he gets into it with Shadow.

That cunt might be old, but he's brutal. I saw his power time and time again inside. He might prefer to get his minions to do his work most of the time, but when it really matters, he's not afraid to get his hands dirty.

"End him, Bowman," he demands as he takes a swing that Shadow dodges.

Running on pure adrenaline, I reach down my bloody, battered hand and pull my knife from my ankle, marching toward where JD and Shadow are battling.

Our eyes connect over Shadow's shoulder as JD manages to turn him away from me before he slows his assault, allowing him to get the upper hand.

He pins JD up against the wall, wrapping his hand around his throat.

"Is this really all you've got, old man?" JD wheezes out, taunting Shadow as I loom closer.

Tightening my grip on my knife, I lift it, ready to finally do what I promised myself I would in prison when I watched him and his minions end my brothers.

"This ends here, Shadow. It's been a long time coming."

His eyes widen as I sink my blade into his throat, red hot blood spilling over my hand and soaking into his shirt.

The pop of two bullets from the silencer Mav twisted onto the end of his piece before we left the house manages to break through the ringing from the previous shot before the thud of two bodies hit the floor.

"So much for no deaths," Reid mutters just as Shadow loses his fight, releases JD, and drops to the floor, clutching his throat.

"I could say the same about your well-planned job," Mav quips.

The four of us stare at each other for a beat before footsteps race our way.

Reid, Mav, and JD all lift their weapons, ready to put an end to a few more Devils should the need occur, but they all quickly relax when a guy dressed entirely in black steps into the doorway.

"Word's got back. We need to move out."

"Fuck," Reid hisses. "They knew, didn't they?"

"I'd say so, boss," the guy agrees before disappearing once more.

"Let's go," Reid barks, pulling his cell from his pocket, hitting call to someone, and barking more orders that involved getting snakes deeper into the Devil's ranks to leak back intel on when the inevitable hit is going to come.

Mav follows his lead, talking in low tones to someone else, although I don't manage to catch any of his conversations as he emerges from the building to that familiar darkness.

"You good, man?" JD asks, throwing his arm around my shoulder.

"Yeah. Of course."

"You wanna tell that to your face?" he teases.

"Nothing a good shower won't fix," I assure him, although

I can't lie, as the adrenaline begins to fade, the pain starts to set in.

The second we've all piled into Reid's entirely black SUV—it's a beast of a vehicle, not that I'd expect anything else of him—the engine rumbles to life and he shoots off into the night, leaving the Devils to find their fucked-up warehouse and soldiers when they return.

"Where to, Bowman?" Mav asks after long, silent minutes, dragging me from the memory of pushing my knife into that cunt's throat.

I promised him—both out loud and silently—during our time in Iron Marsh that I would be the one to finally end him. Pride swells within me that I managed to follow through on that promise. That and the fact that I've clearly still got what it takes to be a part of Reid's inner circle, even if I am a little rusty.

"Maddison," I say before rattling off Tristan's address.

There's only one person I want to celebrate this success with, even if she won't understand it.

Today, I severed my ties with my five years in prison, and I fucking intend on embarking on life as a civilian again—even if it's a life affiliated with one of the state's most feared gangs—in style.

Reid chuckles as he turns toward my destination instead of heading home.

"You're gone for her, huh?"

"Always have been. And don't even think about trying to rip me for it, not when the three of you are just as bad."

"Bro," JD says beside me, holding his hands up in surrender. "We're not saying a word. Just wanna know if you've tag-teamed her yet."

"J," Mav warns.

"What? You can't tell me that you don't want to know."

Mav laughs. "I really fucking don't. Got enough of my own sexploits to worry about."

"A-fucking-men to that," JD booms.

I shake my head, pain shooting down my neck, desperately trying to keep JD's suggestion out of my mind.

Fuck, if that wouldn't top off my night watching my girl scream and writhe for me... for us.

My cock swells, my need for my girl after what we've achieved tonight at an all-time high.

The second Reid pulls up out the front of Tristan's place, I have my fingers tucked around the handle and I'm ready to leave them behind.

"Call me tomorrow, yeah?" Reid says before I suck in a breath and prepare to haul myself to my feet.

"Sure thing, Mom," I tease, shooting a look. I'm barely able to contain my eye roll when I get a shot of his perfect face. There's not even a fucking scratch on him, and here I am, dripping in fucking blood. Granted, most of it came from that fucker's carotid artery.

Without another word, I swing the door closed and pull my keys from my pocket, which now include exactly what I need to get inside this building unnoticed.

That fucker seriously shouldn't have underestimated me by failing to change the locks. The first thing I did the day I stole his keys was to make copies. Obviously.

Holding my ribs, I stare up at the mountain I need to climb before my eyes snag on the elevator in the darkened corner of the entrance hall.

"Yes," I hiss, shuffling over and jamming my finger into the button

In only seconds, I'm rising through the building. My heart pounds steadily in my chest as I think about Violet. They're home—I saw both their cars as we pulled up and the lights are on.

I try my best to be discreet, but the second I push the front door open, I stumble, and the thing goes crashing back against the wall as a groan of pain rips up my throat.

My ribs smart, my face aches, my knuckles burn.

I'm a mess. But it could be worse. I could be Shadow with a one-way ticket to hell.

But all of that is forgotten the second I round the corner and find the person I've been yearning for.

All the air rushes from my lungs when I find her sitting on Tristan's face, her body beautifully bare and right on the cusp of release.

My body slumps and I have little choice but to lean on the wall for support.

Her eyes widen in shock just before my name falls from her lips, and then she falls into the most stunning orgasm, screaming out Tristan's name as he continues eating her, probably totally unaware of my arrival thanks to her thighs pinned to his ears.

"Knox, shit," she gasps once she's come back to herself.

She scrambles to her feet, although, unsurprisingly, Tristan isn't having any of it.

"Baby girl, what are you—"

He tilts his head back, and his eyes lock with mine.

"Fuck," he barks, moving as quickly as Violet, but I'm distracted from him as Violet steps up to me and cups my face gently.

"What happened?"

# 36

# VIOLET

I'm pushed aside by Tristan as he throws Knox's arm over his shoulder and drags him down toward the bathroom.

"Sit," he instructs, pointing to the bench beside the shower.

"Violet, there's a first aid kit under the sink in the main bathroom. Can you grab it?'

I hesitate, standing there still totally naked with my eyes locked on Knox's face and the sheer amount of blood that's covering him.

"It's not mine, Firefly. Well, not most of it, anyway," he tries to assure me.

"Violet," Tristan prompts, his voice a little short, but I'm sure that's got something to do with the dramatic cockblocking that just happened.

Twice in a few hours... that can't be good for his balls.

"Shit, sorry."

I rush out of the room, fear making my heart pound and blood race past my ears as I search for the box.

"Here," I say, running back into the room.

"Arms up," Tristan demands with his hands wrapped around Knox's black hoodie.

“I just need a shower, man. I’ll be good as new.”

“Shut the fuck up,” Tristan barks, glaring right back at Knox.

“Fine,” he hisses, finally lifting his arms somewhat gingerly.

I gasp the second Tristan peels the fabric up his body and takes in the dark bruises already blooming around his ribs.

“Knox,” I breathe, stepping closer and ghosting my fingers over the angry skin.

“I’m okay, baby. I promise. The old man here is overreacting.”

“Fuck off,” Tristan grunts, ripping open the first aid box and rummaging around inside.

“As entertaining as it is watching you play nurse, Carver, I much prefer the idea of my girl doing it. Especially while she’s naked.” His eyes drop down my body, his attention immediately making my nipples pebble.

“Here, put this on.” Tristan grabs a shirt from fuck knows where and thrusts it at me.

I wrap my fingers around it as Knox growls, “I don’t fucking think so.”

Despite looking like he was only minutes from hitting the deck earlier, he manages to get to his feet remarkably fast.

“Shower with me, then I’ll be a good boy and let you patch me up after. But,” he teases, "I want your undivided and special attention.”

“Unlikely,” Tristan scoffs.

“I could have died tonight. I think I’m owed a little time with my girl. Ow,” he gasps when I reach out and slap what I hope is an uninjured part of his body.

“Don’t fucking joke about that,” I hiss.

“There was no chance of me dying tonight, Firefly.”

“Arrogant much,” Tristan mutters behind me.

“I don’t care. Don’t joke about it. Especially not when you’re covered in—”

"Get me naked, baby," he demands, cutting off my words. "I want to feel your hands wiping that sadistic fuck's blood from my skin."

"Who was he?" I blurt, unable to keep my curiosity inside.

"Some corrupt fuck I had the misfortune of spending time with inside. Trust me, he deserved it."

"Jesus Christ, I can't believe you're bringing this shit into the middle of our lives," Tristan mutters.

"It happened the day daddy dearest decided to try to give us both a normal life. You were just too naïve to see the reality, Carver."

"Stop it. Both of you," I snap. "Fight tomorrow if you have to, but not now."

Stepping forward, I rest my brow in the center of Knox's chest and just breathe him in.

The reality of just how dangerous his life is hits me full force.

I might have no idea what happened tonight, but I know it was bad. His injuries are evidence of that alone, but there's more. There's something in his eyes.

He was scared tonight. And that is not something I ever want to see.

"Tris, can you give us a minute?"

"No," he states.

"What's wrong? Don't you trust me, bro?"

I don't need to look back to know that Tristan is grinding his teeth in irritation.

"Unfortunately, yes. I do," he confesses. "What I don't trust right now is that your legs won't give out and you'll crush her like a fly as you go down."

"Tristan," I hiss, appreciating the gesture but needing a moment with Knox.

"Fine," he concedes. "But I'll be right outside the door."

I pop the button on Knox's ripped jeans as Tristan leaves, the heat of Knox's stare setting my blood on fire as I shove the fabric of both his pants and boxers over his hips, but it's nowhere near enough to override my concern.

Dropping to my knees, my eyes lock on his inked, erect cock. Precum glistens at the tip, and the temptation to lick it up is strong. But Tristan is right—Knox doesn't need to be standing any longer than necessary right now.

Dropping my hands to his feet, I tug his sneakers off and drag the fabric free.

"Come on, let's get you cleaned up."

Leaning into the shower, I turn it on before taking his hand and drawing him inside gently.

The groan that rips from his throat when the warm water cascades over his skin, almost instantly running red at our feet, is pure filth.

I stare at it swirling down the drain with my heart in my throat.

This man. This beautifully broken, conflicted man killed someone tonight.

Someone he says deserves it.

Attempting to swallow that lump down, I look up into his eyes, hating the fear that lingers.

"Talk to me, Knox," I urge.

He shakes his head, refusing to let out whatever is eating at him.

Sliding my hands gently up his chest, I cup his jaw.

"Nothing you can say to me right now will scare me off," I promise. "You say he deserved whatever you did tonight, then I believe you. You're a good person, Knox. I—"

"I almost fucked it all up. Put everyone at risk."

"I'm sure that's not true," I assure him.

"I wasn't fast enough. I'm out of practice, and it could have gotten everyone killed." His eyes darken with disappointment with each word that passes his lips.

"Is that what they told you? What Reid told you?"

"N-no, but I know. I felt it." His eyes rip from mine, and he stares blankly over my shoulder.

"Did you... did you lose anyone?" I ask, totally out of my depth with this conversation.

"No. But my need for vengeance is going to bring war to Reid's front door."

"He's not stupid," I assure him. Truthfully, I have no idea if that's true. But he's taken over one of the most deadly and respected gangs in the state, so logically, you'd like to think he wasn't just a bloodthirsty idiot. "Reid will have weighed up the risks with whatever you did tonight."

"I know. Fuck, I know," Knox barks. "I just... fuck. Prison fucked me up more than I'm willing to admit, Firefly. I'm a fucking mess."

Stretching up on my toes, I close the space between us.

"It'll take time," I say. I don't have even the slightest clue about what he might have gone through inside, but I hope one day that might change when he feels ready to talk about it. "But I'm right here, and I'll remain here as you work through it all."

"I don't deserve you," he breathes, dropping his brow to mine.

"But you have me."

I press my lips to his in a chaste kiss that I'm desperate to deepen, but I refuse and quickly step back.

"Violet," he growls.

"Let's get you washed and then into bed."

"Bed?" he asks, his eyes lighting up.

"Don't get ahead of yourself, bad boy. I've got a few Band-Aids to slap on your body before we even think about anything else."

Grabbing the sponge and Tristan's shower gel, I set to work washing the blood from Knox's skin, careful of his injuries which I discover aren't as bad as I first feared, and doing my best to ignore the way his cock bobs temptingly between us.

The second I'm done, I cut the water and just about manage to slip out of the stall before he drags me back inside.

"Firefly," he groans as I thrust a towel at him.

"Do as you're told, Knox Bowman," I warn, placing my free hand on my hip and glaring at him fiercely.

Although, from the way his lips kick up at the corners, I think I might have missed the mark somewhat.

"You're sexy when you're bossy."

"She's always sexy," a booming voice comes from the other side of the door, making me jump.

"Something we can agree on, Carver," Knox says before looking back down at the towel. "Baby, he is not going to want me wrapping his white towel around me right now."

"The dark ones are tiny," I say, looking back into the closet where they're all neatly folded.

"Good thing I have every intention of you making the most of my nudity then."

Unable to argue with him, I grab one of the hand towels and watch intently as he dries himself off the best he can before walking toward the sink and looking in the mirror.

He hisses through his teeth as he stares at his battered reflection.

"I've looked better, huh?" he mutters, pushing his fingers through his hair to drag it back from his brow.

My eyes lock on the huge hawk wings which are spread across his shoulders, the feathers ending on his upper arms before dropping down his muscular back and to his ass.

"I don't know, some girls love the bad boy look."

"Some girls?" he asks, his eyes drilling into me and forcing me to look up to meet them in the mirror. "What about my girl?"

"You know I do. That's how you ended up corrupting me."

"Mmm. And it was so fucking good."

"Come on," I say, leading him from the bathroom, both of us still butt naked.

Tristan spins around from his position staring out the window at the dark night sky at the sound of our approaching footsteps.

His eyes widen and his chin drops. And I know exactly why.

"Didn't that fucking hurt?" he asks, studying Knox's cock a little more intently than I'm sure he intended.

"It was more than worth it," Knox teases, shooting me a heated look. "Get a little closer and you might understand why."

I swear every muscle in Tristan's body stiffens at Knox's suggestion.

"I'll find you something to wear," he offers, taking off toward his closet.

"Don't bother. I have no shame."

And to prove his point, he falls back on Tristan's bed, making himself at home against his pillows.

"Jesus, couldn't you at least cover your ass before rubbing it on my sheets?"

"Evidently not," Knox quips teasingly before turning his eyes on me. "I'm yours, baby. Do your worst," he offers, holding his arms out to his sides.

Tristan's eyes capture mine, and I'm held motionless in his stare for a few seconds before his long legs close the space between us and his fingers twist in my wet hair.

"Patch him up, then we're finishing what we've started twice tonight. And I don't give a fuck if we have to do it with him watching."

I gasp, his confession rocking through me.

"I need you, Pip. And nothing else is going to stop me from having you."

His lips slam down on mine, his tongue plunging into my mouth, forcing me to submit. My body melts against him, the hardness of his cock pressing against my belly, making my thighs clench.

"You want him to watch again, baby?"

"Oh God," I moan as he cups my ass in one hand and my breast in the other while kissing down my throat.

"Hell yeah, this is what I'm talking about," Knox growls from the bed, making the most of the show we're putting on.

But before I can fully get into it, he releases me, grabs one of his shirts from behind him, and tugs it over my body.

"Tristan," I whine like a horny little bitch.

"Clean up the man bleeding all over my bed, Pip. Then you're mine," he states, his eyes lifting over my head to lock with Knox's. "He's already stolen plenty of your time today."

"I'm injured, man. Don't you think I'm owed a bit of—"

"No," Tris barks, the fierce expression on his face making me laugh. "You get ten minutes," he states before marching from the room.

"I don't need more than ten minutes to have our girl screaming," Knox bellows, rubbing that salt in ever deeper.

"I'm cleaning you up and then you're resting. End of."

"Pfft, you used to be fun. Remember that time when—"

"Nope, nope, nope," I sing, walking into the bathroom to collect the first aid kit. "We're not going there. I've got a job to do."

With the box in hand, I crawl onto the bed and sit beside him while rummaging around for what I need.

Ripping open an antiseptic wipe, I fold it ready to clean him up.

"This is probably going to sting," I warn.

"I think I can handle it, baby."

Reaching out, I press the wipe to the cut on his lip as Tristan's footsteps return, his presence behind me making my skin tingle with awareness.

Knox's hiss rings through the air, and Tristan chuckles.

"Oh yeah, just look how hard you are."

"She took me by surprise," Knox argues. "But I know what will make it better."

I shriek the second he wraps his battered hands around my waist and lifts me onto his lap with a grunt of pain.

"Knox, your ribs," I argue, fighting to get away, but all I seem to achieve is grinding my pussy against his more-than-ready cock.

"If you're gonna move like that, Firefly, at least put me inside you first."

"Clean him up, Pip. The only man getting inside your cunt tonight is me."

I swallow down a wave of desire as Tristan's words roll through me and Knox's length grazes my sensitive skin.

"Oh fuck, man," Knox grunts. "Keep talking. She just fucking gushed for you."

"That's because she knows I'm a far superior fuck than you."

"Sure, whatever you say. Yet, I'm the one who could slide into her right now. Ow," Knox complains when I press the wipe to his brow.

"Sorry," I smile sweetly while rolling my hips, making both of them groan for very different reasons.

"Baby girl," Tristan warns.

"What?" I ask, shooting a sultry look over my shoulder at him.

He's leaning against the doorframe with his muscular arms crossed over his chest and his sweats riding low on his hips. The fabric doesn't hide anything from me, and my mouth waters as my eyes linger on the tent.

"Behave, Violet. And if you're a good girl, you might get what you want."

"You can be bad with me and you'll still get everything you crave," Knox counters, making my head swim with lust.

"I think you both know what I want," I murmur, pulling some closure strips from the first aid kit for the deepest split in his eyebrow.

Silence follows my statement, and when Knox's eyes shift

from mine to look over my shoulder, I swear I hear the silent conversation that happens around me.

Whatever it is they argue about, Knox clearly loses, because his hands fall away from my waist before his heated eyes return to mine.

"Done?" he asks.

"Yeah, but you're going to need some ice for—" My words are cut off by a squeal as another set of hands circles my waist and I'm hauled back.

I come to a stop on my hands and knees astride Knox's long-ass legs.

The shirt I'm wearing is flipped up over my ass, exposing me to the impatient man behind me before his palm collides with my skin.

I howl like a wild beast as the sting blooms a beat before Tristan's hand is there, soothing me.

"I told you to be a good girl, Pip."

"I think you prefer me bad," I purr, burning up from his simple touch alone.

"You just gonna stroke her like a dog, or are you actually going to—"

"Shut the fuck up, Bowman," Tristan hisses, wrapping his fist in my hair and tugging me up until I'm on my knees.

Tristan's shirt is ripped from my body and discarded somewhere on the floor, leaving me bare for them.

"Oh God," I breathe, my skin tingling with their attention, my body hotter than I think it's ever been before with these two men looking at me, touching me with such reverence, with... love?

"Look at what you do to him, baby girl," Tristan whispers in my ear, his lips brushing my skin, leaving me aching for more.

My eyes hold Knox's blazing ones before I rip them away, taking in each and every one of his injuries. He looks better than he did when he first stumbled inside, but while the blood might be gone, the bruising is darkening, showing the level of pain he has to be in.

When my eyes find the firefly tattoo over his heart, I push aside his injuries in favor of his ink and ultimately end up at his rock-hard cock.

My mouth waters, my tongue swiping across my bottom lip as I imagine tasting him again, running my tongue over the firefly he had inked just for me.

I gasp when Tristan's hands move, cupping my breasts, putting on a show for our injured spectator.

"Tristan," I groan when he pinches and twists my nipples.

"Feel how wet she is, bro," Knox encourages, his voice so deep it vibrates through me, ending up right at my pulsating clit.

"Is that what you want, baby girl? You want me to make you come while Knox watches?"

My chest heaves and my head spins with desire.

"Yes. P-please. I need—"

"Give her what she needs, man."

Following orders, Tristan's hand slips down my belly until he finds my swollen pussy.

"Oh shit," he groans, his fingers gliding through my juices. "She's fucking soaking."

"Told you." Knox smirks. "That's just how badly she wanted my dick."

Tristan scoffs. "That rotten looking th—"

"Stop," I beg, my voice thick with desire. "Just sto— yesss," I hiss when Tristan sinks two thick fingers inside me. "Yes."

"Fuck, baby. You look so good right now," Knox groans, his solid length resting well up onto his stomach while Tristan's presses against my ass.

"I-I need you. B-both of you," I gasp.

"Let Carver get you off and we'll see what we can do."

Knox widens his legs, forcing my thighs farther apart and opening me up even more for Tristan's talented fingers.

"That's it, ride his fingers, baby."

"Come for me, Violet. Show Knox just how good my fingers feel inside you. Show him how beautifully you fall for me."

His thumb presses against my clit at the same time Knox reaches for his cock, fisting the length until a filthy groan rips from his lips.

"Oh fuck," I breathe, free-falling over the ledge between them.

My entire body convulses as my release crashes through me.

I cry out both of their names as I ride it out.

Tristan's movements never falter, playing me through every second.

When I come back to myself, I find that Knox is motionless before me, his eyes locked on me, his jaw ticking and his muscles pulled tight.

Tristan's hot breath tickles my shoulder, the air rushing over my chest and ensuring my nipples stay pebbled.

"More," I whisper. Because as earth-shattering as that release might have been, I need more. So much more.

Tristan's fingers dig into my jaw as he twists my head around, slamming his lips down on mine.

I kiss him as if I'd drown without it, and his hunger easily matches mine.

But then, he stops as quickly as he started, placing his hand between my shoulder-blades and forcing me to bend over.

My hands land on Knox's thighs, stopping myself from face-planting him.

I barely adjust to the sudden change before Tristan's tongue runs up the length of my sensitive flesh.

"Tristan," I cry, forcing my ass back, offering more of myself to him.

"Oh shit. How's she taste?" Knox grunts, his hand slowly working his cock once more.

Tristan's grip on my hips is brutal, stopping me from going anywhere as he eats me with all the skill and precision I've become used to from him.

But it's not enough.

"Slide down," I beg, although it sounds more like a needy plea when it falls from my lips.

"Fuck, yeah," Knox quickly agrees, sliding down the bed until his cock is in reaching distance.

His face twists in pain, and while I might feel guilty about causing it, I hope that in about five seconds, I'll be able to forget all about it.

Wrapping my fingers around his shaft, I hold his eyes as I stick my tongue out and lick the precum beading the tip.

"Firefly," he grunts as Tristan's fingers dig into my hips, letting me know that he's aware I'm being bad.

But I don't give a fuck. Because if we're doing this, then we're really fucking doing this.

Knox's fingers twist in my hair. His grip tightens in warning—a warning I don't listen to, because I don't sink down onto him like he wants. Instead, I continue licking him, teasing him, holding off from taking all of him.

"Baby, I need your mouth. I wanna watch you swallowing my dick while Tristan eats your pussy."

Tristan groans against me, the vibrations shooting through my body, bringing my release almost into touching distance.

The image Knox's words conjures up is something I can't deny, and I give him what he wants and sink down on his length.

"Holy fuck, baby," he chokes out as I take him to the back of my throat.

His taste floods my mouth as Tristan sucks on my clit and slides two fingers into me.

I groan around Knox's length before pulling back and teasing the head once more, tracing the thick vein that runs along his underside and kissing my firefly tattoo.

"You gonna come while you're sucking my cock, baby?" he asks once he's fully inside my mouth once more and I nod, moaning my agreement and making him hiss.

Tristan ups the ante on my pussy, grazing his teeth against my clit and curling his finger against my G-spot.

"Yes, Tristan," I cry, releasing Knox with a pop. "Yes. Yes, I'm gonna—" I don't get a chance to finish that sentence because I crash, crying out as my release slams into me once more, turning me into a quivering wreck.

But apparently, we're not done, because Tristan moves back after dropping a kiss on my ass cheek. The sound of rustling fabric hits me before I look back over my shoulder and find him throwing his sweats in the direction of the laundry basket before prowling toward me with his cock in his hand.

Lifting my eyes, I find his blazing with need.

"I need you," I whisper.

"Not as much as I need you," he says, loud enough for Knox to hear every word.

"Ain't that the fucking truth," Knox mutters, clearly pissed about being out of action with his injuries. Not that I think they'd actually stop him from doing anything he really wanted, but so far, he seems to mostly be listening to us.

"Put your lips back around Bowman's cock, baby girl. You're not going to get to come again until he's shot his load down your throat."

"Now that is something I can get on board with," Knox groans, holding himself up for me once more.

Tristan steps up behind me, his hand skimming up the length of my spine, sending a shudder racing through me before he fists my hair.

"Suck him, baby girl. Make him lose his goddamn mind and show him what he's been missing with his right hand in prison."

"Asshole," Knox scoffs.

"Be nice," Tristan teases. "I don't need to be sharing right now."

"You fucking love it."

"I know someone who does," Tristan states as the head of his cock presses against my entrance. "And she's gonna be a good girl and suck your cock, aren't you, Violet?"

I don't get a chance to respond because Tristan thrusts forward, filling me up and forcing me down on Knox's cock at the same time.

It. Is. Fucking. Everything.

Tristan keeps hold of my hair, taking control of my body and all our pleasure as he fucks me like a savage.

The sound of skin colliding and our groans of pleasure fill the room as another wildfire begins to burn inside me.

"Your mouth is heaven, baby," Knox growls. He cups my cheek as I work his cock, his thumb tenderly brushing under my eyes and wiping away the tears from my lack of oxygen as I'm forced to take him deeper and deeper every time Tristan slams inside me. "You want my cum, don't you?"

I nod—well, as much as I can.

"You gonna swallow it all down for me, baby? Show us what a good girl you are?"

Again, I try to nod, sucking him harder, making him groan in pleasure as his length thickens against my lips.

"That's it, just like that."

Tristan complies, holding me down on Knox, forcing me to take him deeper.

"Fuck. Yes. Fuck. Violet," Knox booms, his cock jerking in my mouth as he spills his seed down my throat.

Tristan holds me there until Knox gives him a nod, then his focus turns straight back to the two of us. His hand slips from my hair in favor of my clit, and in only a few more seconds, he pushes me over the edge, falling into his own release right behind me, filling me up with hot jets of his cum.

My limbs give out, but he doesn't allow me to fall into a sweaty, sated heap because he sweeps me into his arms and marches us straight into the shower, much to Knox's irritation.

# 37

# TRISTAN

Violet's back presses against the tiles as I reach for the dial, but before I get a chance to turn the water on, Knox's deep voice rumbles through me.

"You're a selfish cunt, Carver."

"Don't give a fuck, Bowman. Listen to her scream while you lick your wounds," I demand, finally turning the powerful jets on and drowning out whatever his argument to that comment was.

"You're mean," Violet groans when I drop my lips to her neck and kiss a trail down her heated skin.

"That's what happens when you get cockblocked twice in one night. Thought my balls were going to explode."

"Tristan," she moans when I shift us slightly, lining my re-hardened cock up against her entrance.

"Already?" she gasps.

"Always," I breathe.

Pulling back from her neck, I stare into her heated eyes. There are a million questions swirling around in her green depths.

"W-was that... were you..."

Reaching out, I cup her jaw, resting my brow against hers and staring down into her eyes.

"Does it feel like I wasn't okay with it?" I ask, assuming where this is going.

I thrust my hips, the tip of my cock slipping in easily with her arousal and my cum that's dripping out of her.

"Oh God," she moans, her head tipping back against the tiles as her muscles ripple around me.

"It was hot," I confess quietly. "I'm not gonna lie, I've had my share of wild nights in the past—"

"I read about most of them in the trash mags," Violet quips.

"Vi," I groan, knowing how much shit those things are full of.

She shrugs, tilting her hips forward and forcing me to fill her deeper. "I wanted you. It was the closest I could get to the real thing."

"None of those girls saw anything real, baby girl. They got a fake side of me that I barely even remember now. But you," I say, twisting my fingers in her hair and tilting her head back so I can nip down her jaw, "you get all of me. Every raw and dirty inch."

I finally thrust forward, filling her to the hilt and making her cry out.

"Do I want you all to myself? Yeah, you fucking know I do. But also, I see how he feels about you every time he looks at you. I'm fucking kicking myself for not seeing it sooner. And... I guess... I can get on board with whatever our lives might be like with him in them too."

"You really mean that?" she forces out between my low, deep thrusts.

"Yeah, unless you're expecting the two of us to—"

"No," she says with a laugh. "I'm a selfish bitch and I want all your love and devotion directed right at me."

"Good to know," I say, feeling a little tension loosening in my shoulders.

"I mean, it would be hot and all—"

"You're trouble. How about I show you exactly why you want all my love and devotion all to yourself?"

I drop her lower, holding her ass in my hands before pounding into her.

"Fuck, yes. Tristan."

"Louder. I bet he's out there jerking himself off listening to you, baby girl." In all honesty, I'm amazed he hasn't stumbled inside to try and join. Maybe he's not a complete dick, after all—that or he actually is in too much pain.

I banish any kind of guilt that threatens to creep in. He knew the risks of walking into whatever he did tonight. I don't have enough brain space right now to worry about him as well as everything else in my life.

Violet's nails claw at my back, scratching me up in the best way, and I push everything else aside to focus on feeling her clenching tight around me and hearing my name rip from her lips over and over.

---

After finally letting Violet's feet hit the floor once more, I take my time cleaning her up, covering her body in fluffy white bubbles, stealing as much of her time as I can.

Eventually, though, she calls me out on my possessive issues and turns the water off, forcing me to grab us both clean towels and get out.

I rub the water out of my hair before tucking the towel around my waist, dropping a kiss on her bare shoulder as she stands at the sink with the cupboard door open, revealing all her products that have been increasing since she moved in.

"I love having you here," I say when her eyes meet mine in the mirror.

My heart thumps in my chest trying to force me to tell her the truth. It's not just having her here that I love. It's way more than that, and this thing with Knox has only made me realize just how strongly for her I feel.

Her eyes glitter with happiness. "I love being here too. Even more so now you've got furniture."

"Take your time. I'll make sure the patient is okay."

I heard the rumble of his deep voice a few more times as I fucked our girl into oblivion in the shower, but I couldn't make out the words—not that I tried very hard.

With another lingering kiss on her skin, I march toward the door and pull it open.

Knox's eyes narrow on me the second I emerge, and I bite down on the inside of my cheeks to stop myself from barking out a laugh.

"I hate you."

"Funny, I thought the exact same thing when you stole my girl from sleeping beside me and then sent me a fucking video."

He smirks. "Ah, good times. She fucking loved it alfresco."

I shake my head muttering, "Why am I not surprised?" as I walk out of the bedroom.

With three bottles of water and a bottle of painkillers in hand, I make my way back only a few minutes later, the sight of another naked man lying in my bed making me question my life choices.

They soon evaporate, though, when Violet steps into the room wearing just a towel, her face clear of makeup but her body still bearing the marks of what we did earlier.

"Here," I say, ripping my eyes from Violet and focusing once again on Knox.

"Aw, and here I was thinking you didn't care," he quips when I place the waters down and twist the top of the pill bottle, ready to shake a couple into his hand.

"Careful, next time I might not let her suck your cock."

"Let her, puh-lease," he scoffs. "You love it, don't you, baby?" She smirks over her shoulder at him, silently telling both of us everything we need—and possibly don't want—to hear. But I can't lie, seeing so clearly that she wants us both equally does settle some of the jealousy issues I'm battling with.

Pulling my closet door open, she studies the contents for a few seconds before untucking the towel from around her, allowing it to pool at her feet.

A groan rumbles deep in my chest as I run my eyes over her curves.

She reaches in and pulls out a white t-shirt.

"No," I snap, rushing forward and swiping it from her hand. "This one," I say, pulling out another tank with my name stamped on the back.

The second I pull it over her head and let it hang around her body, Knox barks a laugh.

"You've got issues, man."

Violet twists around in the mirror. "I like belonging to you, Tristan Carver."

Pulling her into my arms, I grab handfuls of her ass, crushing her against me.

"You own me too, baby girl," I confess quietly.

"What about me?" Knox sulks, making Violet chuckle.

"Aw, feeling neglected, bad boy?" she asks, releasing me and stalking toward the bed, her hips swaying temptingly, her body barely covered in my huge tank.

Lifting her knee, she crawls up to the bed toward him, making my cock swell once more beneath my towel.

"Not so much anymore. You're fucking beautiful, Firefly."

"You've looked better," she counters, settling on his waist.

Watching my girl with another man shouldn't get me this hot, but fuck.

"Does it hurt?" she asks, reaching out and gently brushing her fingers across the dark bruise that covers the side of his face.

"Nah, nothing I can't handle."

"Sure," she murmurs. "You need to rest."

"What do you think I've been doing while Carver was balls deep in your pussy, baby?"

"Pondering your life decisions and trying to stop yourself from storming in?"

He chuckles, but it's quickly followed by a hiss of pain, his hand landing on his ribs.

"Do you think they're broken?"

When Knox doesn't answer, she looks back over at me.

"I don't think so," I say, finally dropping my towel and moving closer.

Throwing the covers back, I slip inside, trying not to think about the fact I'm naked in bed with another man.

It won't be the first time we've crashed together. We hung out enough as kids, went wild camping as well as attending football camps together where we got up to all sorts of shit, like me losing my V card that fateful night. But we never did it fucking naked before.

Violet watches me get settled before looking back and forth between us for a few seconds.

"I hope you both realize you're living out my ultimate fantasy right now," she says, heat coloring her cheeks.

"Us lying in bed together is your ultimate fantasy?" Knox asks before I get a chance.

"Well, no. Not just lying here. But having both of you."

"You've got us, baby," Knox whispers. "Now all you've got to decide is what you want to do with us."

Her teeth sink into her bottom lip, but despite the lust dripping from Knox's words, all she does is slide off his lap and slip between the two of us beneath the covers.

"Right now, I want you to rest. It's late, and Tristan gets up at the ass crack of dawn, so..." She snuggles deeper, and when she turns her back on me, I'm powerless but to curl around her, tucking her ass against my cock.

"You want to cuddle?" Knox asks curiously.

"Yep. Get down here, bad boy."

He stares down at her for a beat while I make the most of having her to myself.

After a couple of seconds, he slides lower, although he remains on his back, probably due to his ribs.

Violet entwines one of her legs with mine and the other with his before reaching out and wrapping her arm around his stomach.

"Okay?" she asks, checking she's not causing him any pain.

"Yeah, Firefly. Everything is perfect."

We fall into a comfortable silence, and despite the tight squeeze in my queen-sized bed, I find myself drifting off to sleep freakishly fast.

"Shit, the light," Knox murmurs, making me jolt awake in a panic.

"No, leave it on. Violet doesn't like—"

"It's okay," she says sleepily between us. "Nothing can touch me while I'm in the middle of both of you. There's nothing to be scared of."

---

I'm nowhere near ready to wake up when my alarm starts going off the next morning. And I'm in such a deep sleep that it's not until Knox groans in irritation that I even remember there are three of us in bed.

Shutting the thing off before it wakes them both fully, I roll onto my back and blink up at the ceiling as images from last night race through my mind. The three of us...

Jesus.

I scrub my hand down my face.

Is this my life now? The girl of my dreams by my side, and her other boyfriend.

It's insane. Utterly fucking insane. Everyone will think we've lost our minds. And yet, I don't think I actually care.

My biggest concern is the press. I might have mostly fallen off the radar after coming back here, but I'm not naïve enough to think that, once the season starts up and the Panthers rise to the success they're capable of, I'm going to be thrown back into the middle of it all.

And where will that leave Violet?

Her image will be plastered all over the headlines as her life with an ex-NFL player and a gangster is exposed to the world.

"Stop it. I can hear you thinking from here," a deep voice whispers.

"Sorry. I'm just—"

"Freaking out?"

"No." Yes. "Yeah, a little."

"You ever fucked a girl with another guy before?" he asks as if Violet isn't still sleeping between the two of us.

"Y-yeah, actually."

"Ah, I forgot about your celebrity status. You must have fucked your way around the country in those two years."

"I wasn't that bad. But no, I wasn't often lacking offers."

"You?" I ask, immediately realizing my mistake.

"Oh yeah, every night of the fucking week," he deadpans.

"Sorry, I—"

"Prison was..." He trails off, and when I glance over, I find his eyes are glassy as he thinks back. "It was hell, but at least I was never reduced to three-ways with two other dudes."

"Every cloud and all that," I mutter, at a loss for what to say. "How are you feeling?"

"Sore," he admits.

"You taken any more pills?" He shakes his head. "You should."

"They make me sleepy, and I don't want to miss anything. Five years was enough."

"Knox, you're not going to miss anything. She's right there... I'm right here."

He sighs, the weight of everything he's been through pressing down on him.

Finally, he looks over at me.

"I appreciate that, man. And this," he says, glancing at our sleeping beauty. "When I first discovered you two, I didn't think I stood a chance. I don't deserve to have a chance."

"Fuck off, bro. You gave away five years of your life for her. You deserve it and you know it. Why the fuck do you think I'm allowing this?"

"Allowing this?" he teases. "I think you're more than allowing it. You were well fucking into it last night."

"It's her. You make her happy, and that's all I want."

Reaching out, he tucks a lock of her hair behind her ear.

"Same, man. Same. She's the only thing that got me through the past five years. The promise of having this again is what kept me alive."

"I'm glad you made it," I say honestly before silence falls once again, the elephant in the room that we can both clearly see only getting bigger. "What are we going to do this weekend?" I ask, hating to even talk about it but knowing that we can't just ignore it.

"I don't know. Distract her with our dicks?" Knox suggests.

I mean, it's a solid idea, and certainly one I've come up with in the past despite being unable to follow through.

"We should take her away somewhere," I suggest. "I've got a game Friday night, but we could go straight after."

"Getting out of town is good. Any ideas where?"

"Nope, that's something you're going to have to figure out."

"Me?" he balks.

"Yeah, I've kinda got my hands full right now, and from what I can figure, other than running around playing gangster, you're as free as a bird."

"I could have died last night," he mutters.

"Yeah, but you didn't. And unless you've suddenly found

yourself a job, I'm thinking you've got time to plan a break for our girl."

"Fine, but don't fucking whine when it's not fancy enough for you, Mr. NFL."

My brows lift. "I'm not—"

"Yes, you are. You've seen this place, right?"

"If you don't like it, you know where the door is."

"Dude, I fucking love it. I'm just pointing out a fact."

"Just find something you think she'll love."

Throwing the covers off, I march to the bathroom and close the door quietly.

"Fuck," I hiss, hating that Violet is going to be forced to relive it all over again in just a few days. She's already been through it enough recently. But with Roman's birthday on Thursday and then the anniversary of the fire Saturday night, she's going to have little chance of forgetting about it anytime soon.

When I emerge once more, Knox is exactly where I left him, staring up at the ceiling with Violet curled around him like she's terrified he might get up and leave.

"Here," I say, passing him a couple of pills. "She needs you fixed."

He stares at the two white pills in my hand before looking down at Violet.

"Fine," he huffs, throwing them back and allowing me to squirt some water into his mouth from the sports bottle on the side. "Asshole," he hisses when I 'accidentally' spray him in the chest.

"Whoops."

"Fucking whoops. You could have got her wet."

"I should fucking hope I do," I quip, making him smirk.

"I'll make sure you find out when she wakes up. You want evidence again?"

"Fuck you, Knox."

I chuckle, grabbing the books I need from my shelves and shoving my feet into my sneakers.

"She's got class later. Don't make her miss it."

"As if," he gasps. "I might need nursing all day, though."

"Right," I mutter, marching toward the door, but I pause when I get there. "Knox?"

"Yeah."

"You need to tell her the truth. We can't move forward while she's still being dragged down by the unknowns of her past."

"I know, I just... I don't want to hurt her."

"I don't either. But it's time."

With those ominous words hanging in the air, I walk away, hoping like hell he'll figure out a way to do the right thing.

# 38

# KNOX

Almost as soon as Tristan left the apartment, I fell back to sleep.

Having Violet right there curled up beside me made it easier to drift off than I ever remember. I'm pretty sure the pills helped with that, too.

I was awake and staring at the ceiling long before Tristan's alarm started going off. The painkillers had worn off, and the pulsating pain coming from my ribs where Violet was holding me ensured I was fully awake and suffering—not that I was in any rush to lift her arm from me.

I've been dreaming of having her right beside me again for so long that I intend on soaking up every second of having it again, even if it hurts.

And when I wake again, it's to the most amazing feeling.

"Violet," I groan, my body coming back to life long before my head registers why that feels so fucking good.

"Hey, bad boy," she purrs, the raspy lust in her voice making my eyes pop open.

I find her sitting beside me, naked with my hard cock in her hand, stroking me slowly.

"Now this is what I call a good morning," I groan when she

rubs her thumb over my tip, collecting up the precum that's beading there.

"I thought about waking you up by sinking down on your cock, but I wasn't sure if your ribs could handle that."

"They can handle it," I confirm so quickly it makes her laugh.

"I don't want to hurt you."

"Not being inside my girl for twenty-four hours is hurting me."

Her hooded eyes hold mine and she mouths, 'You're sure?'

"Fuck me, Firefly. Use my body and make yourself come. Start your day off as all days should."

"Well, if you insist," she teases, crawling onto my lap and lining my cock up with her entrance.

We both groan loudly as she sinks down on me.

"Fuck, Violet."

"Missed you so much, Knox," she confesses, making my heart clench. "I fucking hated you, but still I missed you."

Her eyes close, severing our connection before her head falls back and she lifts her hands to her tits, giving me a fucking great show, and she bounces up and down on my cock.

I don't move other than to rest my hands on her hips, to help her grind on me. I just let her take complete control. And before long, her moans are getting louder, her walls tightening around me as she finally succumbs to her release, dragging me right along with her.

"You're right," she confesses through her ragged breaths. "Every day should start with that."

She climbs off my dick and collapses beside me before reaching over to cup my cheek and pressing her lips to mine.

"Did Tristan leave already?"

"You really thinking about him right now, Firefly?" I tease.

"Last night..." she starts, staring into my eyes as if they're going to give her the answers she craves.

"Was fun. Shame I was mostly out of action, or it could have been even better."

"Even better?" she asks, testing the waters.

"Yeah, baby." Rolling over, I swallow the pain from my ribs and trail my fingertips down her spine, smirking when she shudders. "We both know what you really want is both of us filling you up at the same time."

She gasps when my finger gets to her ass, circling her entrance.

"Knox."

"Anyone been in here before, Firefly?"

She shakes her head, her eyes dilating as I add a little more pressure.

"I can't believe I'm about to say this, but Tristan should be your first."

Her brows jump up in shock.

"I-I thought you'd want—"

"I do, baby. More than you could possibly imagine. But I already stole enough of your firsts. It's only fair that Tris gets this one."

"That's very... friendly of you."

I shrug. "We are friends. More than friends, seeing as we're both in love with the same girl. We're... boyfriends-in-law?" I ask, feeling stupid for even blurting that shit out.

"Boyfriends-in-law?" she repeats with a laugh. "That sounds... serious. As far as I'm aware, nothing here is official, let alone involving in-laws."

"You're mine, Violet. How much more official do you need than me telling you that I'm never ever going to let you go again? If you need a ring then—"

"Whoa, Knox. Back up a little. I don't need a freaking ring, I just... I don't know. This is..." She gestures to Tristan's bed. "It's unconventional and—"

"I'm in, baby. I'm all fucking in. And something tells me

that Tristan is too, and not just because he's too fucking stubborn to let me have you to myself."

She nods, biting down on my bottom lip.

"My mother would have shit bricks."

"Maybe it's for the best she never got to find out that both your stepbrother and brother's best friend have spent all their lives imagining fucking you, then."

"Yeah, maybe. Although I'm pretty sure Roman would have had a bigger issue."

"He'd have killed us," I blurt, regretting the words the second they fall from my lips.

"Or me," Violet adds.

"Nah, never you. He loved you too much."

"He had a funny way of showing it."

Sadness descends around her as she thinks about her brother.

This week is going to be hard enough already, I don't need to be adding to the stress.

"He was an addict, baby. If I had any idea then I—"

"Stop. Just stop," she begs, sitting up and wrapping her arms around her legs. "None of us ever spoke about our father. You had no reason to know he was at risk."

"I'm still sorry."

A heavy sigh leaves her lips. "No one forced anything on him. He did all that himself. He was old enough to know better."

"Just think how different things could have been if your mother never saw something redeemable in my father."

"No, I refuse to even go there." Her hand finds mine and she twists our fingers together. "If they never met, then we never would have met, and despite the past five years of bullshit, you're one of the best things in my life. I wouldn't be the woman I am now if it weren't for you."

"Nah, baby. There's no way that's true."

"It is. You saw what I was like at school. I was Roman's shy little sister that everyone overlooked. I wasn't sporty, or overly intelligent, or pretty or—"

"Okay, that's enough," I argue, forcing myself to sit up so that I can cup her face and stare into her eyes. "You're the most beautiful girl I've ever seen. You were back then and you still are now. You take my breath away. Violet, you're—"

"I wasn't actually searching for a compliment, but I appreciate it."

"Good. I mean it."

She smiles at me, the shadows from talking about our past still lingering in her eyes. "I was just saying that... you found me, Knox. You dug me out from the shy girl I was hiding behind. You showed me a part of life I never knew existed. You made me feel special, loved, sexy—"

"I love you, Violet," I blurt like an idiot for the second time in two days, only this time, I don't give her an easy way out by kissing her. I just sit there, staring at her as I bleed out my feelings all over another man's bed.

"Knox," she breathes, making my heart knot up. "I—"

I panic, pressing my fingers against her lips. "Don't say anything. I don't deserve to hear it."

"You deserve it, and more. But—"

"There it is," I joke in the hope it covers the hurt.

"But..." she repeats, "you're still hiding things from me. I need all your truths, Knox. If I'm ever going to fully trust you again, I need everything."

I open my mouth to say... fuck knows what, but I'm too slow. She's already off the bed and heading for the bathroom.

She closes the door behind her, and I fall back on the bed with a groan.

"They're not my truths to tell though, Firefly. I just wish I could find the motherfucker who has all the answers you deserve."

---

"Can I drive you to class?" I ask, leaning against Tristan's kitchen counter and drinking his coffee. It's a fuck load better than the shit the Harrises have. It makes me wonder if I could just move my shit in—not that I have a lot of it—and if Tristan would even notice. From what Violet has said, he's not here much. And I sure as shit don't want to go and rent an apartment on my own. The thought of living by myself now... no. Just fuck no.

I've spent five years away from those I love. I don't want to waste another minute.

Violet pauses sorting her purse out on the counter opposite me.

"You drove here in that state last night?" she asks in concern.

"No, Reid dropped me off."

"Okay, good," she says, breathing a sigh of relief. "So—"

"I'll drive your car."

Her eyes crinkle in amusement. "You want to drive my car? You've seen my car, right? You'll look like you're driving a go-cart."

I chuckle at the image her words conjure up. "Could be worse."

"And what are you going to do with my baby while I'm in class?" she asks curiously.

"I need to go and see Reid."

"And you're going to turn up in my car?"

"Yeah, why?"

"N-no reason. I just thought you might want to retain your gangster bad boy image, that's all."

"I think my rep is strong enough to pull it off."

"Sure, if you say so," she quips, smothering a laugh. "Come on then, let's see if you even fit inside it."

"Lead the way, Firefly."

I follow her out, shamelessly watching her ass sway in her tight jeans. "What time are you done later?"

"I only have morning classes today. You can pick me up for lunch if you want."

"That sounds like an offer I can't refuse. I've got a few things I want to do with you."

"Oh yeah?" she says, spinning around the second she's in the elevator, looking up at me through her lashes.

"Yeah, I think it's time I went and bought my own car, and I could do with some clothes that don't belong to Devin."

"Hmm... shopping trips with my boys seem to be becoming a habit."

"I can go on my own if you don't—"

"I'm in. We need to make sure you look fly, after all," she teases.

"Fly? Really?" I toss back. "And don't be thinking you can dress me up like Tristan with his fancy polo shirts and chinos. I'm gangsta, remember?"

Her lips twitch as she fights her smile.

"You can take the boy out of Harrow Creek, but you can't take the Creek out of the boy?" she asks.

"Something like that, baby. And you wouldn't have me any other way."

"You know, I don't think I would. So no polo shirts or football jerseys or chinos?"

"I might be swayed on the chinos. I'm going to need something decent to take you out on a date."

"You're taking me on a date?" she asks curiously.

"Many, hopefully. I want to do all the things we never got to do when we were sneaking around, and all the things that were stolen from us when I went down."

"Aw, Knox. You say the sweetest things to me."

"You're my everything, Firefly," I say quietly, wrapping my hand around the side of her neck and staring down into her eyes. My mouth waters to kiss her, but the elevator dings and I never get the chance.

Despite her owning the world's smallest and girliest car,

it's actually not too bad to drive, thank fuck. Although, it's not exactly Devin's Mustang, but whatever.

The drive to campus is short, too fucking short, and long before I'm ready, I've killed the engine and I'm walking Violet across the parking lot in the direction of her first class.

"You really don't need to walk me. I'm more than capable of—"

"Violet," I growl. "Do you really think this is a fight that you're going to win?"

"Probably not," she confesses. "Come on then, bad boy."

Twisting her fingers through mine, she lets me carry her bag as she navigates through campus to the building her first class is in.

"So, what do you think?"

"What do I think of what?" I ask, pulling her into my body and looking down at her.

"Of college. I'm assuming it's the first time you've been here."

"It is, but the only thing I'm seeing is you."

"Such a smooth talker," she says with a smile, reaching up on her toes so she can steal a kiss.

What was meant to be a simple, chaste moment to say goodbye soon turns heated, and in only minutes Violet finds herself backed up against the wall.

I lose myself in her now just like I did when we were kids. The rest of the world falls away, and it's just the two of us.

That is, until a loud throat clearing behind me finally cuts through the haze of lust.

"Violet, is that you beneath that giant of a man?" a female voice teases, making my girl laugh into our kiss.

"Give him a break, he's had something of a dry spell recently," a deep, familiar voice says.

"Jesus," I groan, forcing myself to pull back from Violet.

Resting my forehead against hers, I take a moment to suck in a breath. It'll never be enough time to sink my boner, but I give it a good go as I attempt to think of unsexy thoughts about Tristan's mom.

When I've finally got myself together, I spin around with a malicious smile on my face.

"Kane Legend at college. What the fuck is the world coming to?"

Kane's stone mask finally cracks on my last two words, and he breaks into a smile.

"Knox Bowman. It's been a while, man. How's it going?"

I glance down at the girl standing at my side and smile.

"Yeah, it's good, man. Really fucking good."

He nods, looking genuinely happy while his eyes linger on the cuts and bruises on my face.

"You remember Letty, right?" he says, choosing to ignore them and pulling his girl into his side.

"I do. I'm still trying to get my head around how you managed to do…" I wiggle my finger between the two of them. "This. She's way too fucking good for you."

Kane laughs. "Yeah, man. She is. But I could also say the same," he teases.

"Are you guys coming in?" one of the guys I recognize as one of Violet's old housemates says, pointing at the building before us.

"Shit, sorry. West, Brax, this is Knox, my—" She cuts herself off in a panic.

"Boyfriend," I finish for her. "What?" I ask when she looks back up at me. "Would you prefer I introduce myself as your stepbrother?"

"Good God, we'll be inside. Good to meet you at last, Knox," West says politely before the two of them duck into the building, leaving us with Kane and Letty.

"What the hell went down last night, man?" Kane asks, his eyes on my injuries once more. "Heard news of a Hawk invasion on Devils' territory."

I shake my head, a smirk playing on my lips. "No idea what you're talking about."

"You always were full of shit," Kane laughs.

"We got what we went for," I mutter, giving him a little more.

"Yeah, I heard there was a little Shadow hunting. Good work on that asshole."

"Seriously?" Letty balks. "You're both going to stand here and talk about this like it's normal?"

"Is it normal," I argue.

"Vi, we need to get in there," she says, ignoring me and turning to my girl.

"I'll see you later, yeah?"

"You got it, Firefly. I'll be here waiting."

After giving our girls a quick kiss, we both watch as they walk into the colossal building beside us.

"Pretty sure we might be two of the luckiest motherfuckers in the world. You're aware of that, right?"

"Yeah," I say with a laugh, rubbing at the back of my neck. "I've definitely had worse luck."

"She came to talk to me about you, did she tell you?" Kane asks.

"I think she was coming to talk to your girl," I tease. "But she got you instead."

"Yeah, all right. No need to look so smug about it."

"Thanks for... well..."

"You got it, man. So, do you have plans or do you wanna grab a coffee?"

"Don't you have class?"

"Nah, not until later. I was just walking my girl in."

"Sure. And actually, I need some help with something."

Kane laughs, clearly having a private joke to himself about something.

"What?"

"Nothing, man. Nothing. But no judgment here if you forgot how to fuck after five years out of the game."

"Fuck you, there is nothing wrong with my moves. Just go ask my girl."

"So what's the plan now, then? You sticking with Hawk life, or are you going after more?" he asks as we round a corner and the lights of a coffee shop emerge.

"I'll always be a Hawk, and not just because I owe Reid my life. It is my life."

"Fair enough."

"That's not to say it's all I want, though. But right now, I'm just taking each day as it comes."

"So, what do you need from me?" he asks as we join the line.

"I want to take my girl away this weekend. I have no idea where to start. Was wondering if you know of somewhere, I don't know, secluded or something. Off grid. Just the... just the three of us."

Kane chuckles again.

"Fucking wondered when you were going to bring Carver into this."

# 39

# VIOLET

I sit in class two days later, staring at the professor as he talks, but I don't hear any of the words falling from his lips.

Everything is a blur. Everything apart from the grief and loss that I've been failing to deal with this week.

Tristan and Knox can see it, and they've been doing everything they can to try and help, but honestly, there isn't anything they can do.

Tristan has been busier than ever this week, mostly leaving me to hang out with Knox, not that either of us is complaining. But I crave them both, and not just in the hours of darkness when Tristan slips into bed with us and wraps me up in his arms.

I hate feeling vulnerable, but it's impossible not to when it feels like my heart is being pushed through a meat grinder once again as the anniversary of the day I lost everything rolls around.

Each year, I say it's going to be different, that I'm going to handle it better. But I've never achieved it.

Just like always, I'm a mess, quickly and quietly falling apart at the seams.

I'd usually party like it's going out of fashion this weekend, anything to help drown the pain and force me to face that my big brother would be a year older, that he should be celebrating, and instead, I'm here alone—okay, not actually alone, but missing all my family—suffering, grieving just as much as I did five years ago.

I've always been told that it gets easier. But I call bullshit on that.

It doesn't get easier.

If anything, every year is harder.

My memories fade and my guilt over the fact increases.

With a sigh, I fall forward on the desk, resting my head on my arms.

A warm, supportive hand lands on my back, and I glance over to see Ella watching me closely with concern in her eyes.

"I'm okay," I whisper.

She smiles at me, but it doesn't meet her eyes. Despite not knowing the truth, she's always been there for me at this time of year while I mourned the loss of my family. But now she knows, I feel her support more than ever.

"Wanna go get drunk after class?" she offers, making me feel all warm and fuzzy inside.

"Thanks, but I think I'm just going to head home."

"Vi—"

"I'm okay, honestly. Give it a few days and it'll be all over again."

"You can't keep doing this," she says, probably thinking of my epic annual alcohol binges as I've tried to deal with this shit.

"I know. I won't. I just... I need them," I say honestly.

"I know, sweetie. Will Knox be home?"

I nod, although I have no idea if that's true or not. I know Tristan won't. The Panthers have their first game of the season tomorrow, and they're all practically working around the clock to ensure the team is ready. Which of course, they are. They're going all the way this year, I just know it.

I don't realize that our professor has brought the lesson to a close until everyone around me starts moving. I still have no idea what it was even about, but I follow their lead and close my unused notepad, dropping it and my pens into my bag.

"Call me if you need anything. Even if you don't want to talk but just need someone."

"I will."

Ella glares at me as if she knows I'm lying. "Promise me, Vi. I hate not being there for you."

"You are," I assure her, reaching for her hand. "You've been nothing but there for me since we first met. I need you to know how much I appreciate it."

"Anytime. Whatever you need," she promises me. "Now go home and make use of that sexy man. I want to hear that you spent the rest of the day being fucked six ways from Sunday, you got it?"

"I'll see if I can talk him into it."

"Talk him into it," she scoffs. "As if. From what I've seen and heard, that man could not be more into you if he tried."

"Making up for lost time," I offer with a shrug.

"Then make up some more this afternoon. If you're not walking funny tomorrow, I'll be having words."

"You got it," I laugh, squeezing her hand once more and taking off toward the parking lot.

The second I'm alone, the darkness begins to press in around me, making each breath harder than the last.

By the time I'm in my car, my chest is heaving as memories from Roman's birthday when we were kids play on repeat in my head.

Tears burn my eyes as I remember that sweet little boy. Growing up, he was everything I could have asked for in a big brother.

All my friends at school used to complain about their

siblings, and it used to make me feel like the luckiest girl in the world to have a brother who I considered my friend.

It's just a shame it never lasted.

I blink back the tears, desperately trying to keep them in, but it's futile, and after only a few seconds, I lose my fight.

Reaching up, I swipe the wetness from my cheek, wishing that I was stronger. Wishing that I could just hate him for leaving me and forget about how much I used to love him. How much I still love him. Because no matter what, he'll always be my big brother. The one who taught me to ride my bike, to play football and basketball—despite me being terrible at it. He used to share his Lego with me and wouldn't get angry when I messed up his models.

As if he knows I need him, my phone dings, and Tristan's name lights up my screen.

**Tristan: Miss you, baby girl. How are you holding up?**

A sob rips from my throat as I stare down at his words, wishing he was here and wrapping me in his strong arms, keeping me from shattering all over the place.

**Violet: I'm okay. Just finished class.**

**Violet: I miss you too. x**

**Tristan: I'm sorry this week has been so crazy. I'll make up for it this weekend, I promise.**

**Violet: I get it. You have nothing to apologize for.**

**Tristan: I still hate not being there with you. Make sure Knox looks after you.**

**Violet: I'm sure he has a few creative ideas to keep me distracted...**

**Tristan: I can assure you he does. As do I. This weekend, yeah?**

**Violet: Are you suggesting what I think you're suggesting?**

My stomach knots and my thighs clench as my imagination begins to run away with itself.

**Tristan: You'll just have to wait to find out. *angel emoji***

**Violet: Tease.**

**Tristan: Shit, my professor just caught me. See you later, baby girl. *kiss emoji* *heart emoji***

**Violet: Caught texting a girl in class. You're meant to be my good boy, Carver.**

**Tristan: *devil emoji***

Despite the tears on my cheeks, I can't help but smile. Even during my darkest days, Tristan was able to lift me out of it. It's why I always wanted more, because I knew, I just knew that one kiss, one touch from him would change my entire world.

And I was right. It did.

I just wasn't expecting Knox's touch to do the same thing after all these years.

Starting my car, I find a playlist I made on my cell a few

years ago that only comes around their anniversary and hit play.

Songs from our childhood fill my speakers as I pull out of the lot and head across town.

The afternoon sun sits low in the sky, blinding me as I drive.

I should head straight home, but I can't resist a pit stop on the way.

If what Tristan has said is true, then I might not get a chance to visit this weekend, and there's no way I'm going to forget just because I'm being distracted by two glorious cocks.

Sorry, Mom.

A tear-filled laugh bubbles up my throat as I think about what her opinion about all of this would be.

She was always dreaming about the day she'd get to choose my wedding dress with me, watch me walk down the aisle, and welcome her grandkids into the world.

Her hope for my future was always very traditional. Hell, before all of this with Tristan and Knox, I had a traditional future in my head for myself too.

But the reality is that what we're doing is anything but that.

I pull over with a heavy sigh, wipe my tears from my eyes, push the door open and walk toward the florist with a very familiar ache in my chest.

"Good afternoon," the happy woman sings the second a little bell above the door dings, alerting her to my entrance.

"Hi," I squeak, not making eye contact with her, instead, scanning the array of flowers to find what I'm looking for.

I come to a stop in front of the peonies, memories of the jug in our kitchen that was always filled with them hitting me.

"Can I help you with anything?" a soft voice says to my side.

"Y-yes. Please could I get twelve?"

"Of course. Anything else?"

I shake my head, not strong enough to speak any more without bursting into tears.

"Okay, let's find you the prettiest ones then, shall we?"

I stand silently as she selects the best blooms and walks over to her desk to wrap them.

Thankfully, she lets me leave with a quiet thank you after paying and in only minutes, I'm back in my car with the familiar scent filling my nose.

The drive to the graveyard on the other side of town takes longer than I was expecting, but eventually, I pull my car to a stop once again and climb out with the flowers tucked into the crook of my arm.

Summer might be over, but the grounds are still beautiful, with colorful flowers attempting to cheer the place up lining the path as I walk toward where Mom now spends her days.

She was buried beside Knox's dad, something I wasn't overly happy with seeing as he played a part in all of this. Knowing for sure that the fire was a hit directly on him for whatever he did to piss Victor Harris off doesn't make it any better.

But Mom loved him despite everything, and I guess that's something I need to come to terms with.

After all, aren't I doing the exact same thing with Knox?

I've told myself for years that I'd never go anywhere near a Hawk, or a member of any gang. Yet, one look at him and I've fallen straight back into his trap.

I come to a stop in front of Mom's headstone and stare at the words carved there.

*Loving mother to Roman and Violet, and wife to Joseph Bowman.*

My eyes linger on Roman's name, tears making the letters blur as I place the flowers down.

He'd have been twenty-five today.

My cell buzzes in my pocket, but I ignore it, too lost in the moment.

Dropping to my ass in front of Mom, I try to imagine what he might look like now. Would his hair be short and perfectly styled like it always used to be, or has he grown it out? Would he be freshly shaven or rocking a beard? Would he have made it to the NFL with Tristan, or was it always inevitable that he'd have fallen prey to the same illness that stole our father from us?

I let out a heavy sigh, the weight of all my unknowns pressing down on my shoulders until each of my breaths are ragged and filled with so much pain I can barely stand it.

"I miss you," I whisper. "Both of you, so much."

Nothing but birdsong and the rustle of the leaves in the trees surrounding me can be heard as I sit there.

"If you're watching down on me, then I guess you know what I've been up to," I mutter, my cheeks heating with the thought. "You think I'm crazy, don't you?"

Unsurprisingly, no answer comes.

"It just feels right though, Mom. I can't even describe it. When I'm with them, everything, all my messy and broken parts just seem to slot into place. It's intense when I'm with one of them, but when I'm with both..." I hang my head, thinking of the two of them. "I love them, Mom. Both of them. I know most people would expect me to choose, but there's no way I can do that. There is no choice. It's just... it's them. It's us."

I fall silent once more, my heart aching in so many ways, but it's the pain and loss as always that takes precedent.

That is, until a shiver of awareness races down my spine.

I try to ignore it, assuming that it's just some other mourner visiting a loved one somewhere behind me. But as the minutes pass, my skin continues to prickle and unease trickles through my veins.

Glancing over my shoulder, I scan the trees, or more so the shadows beneath them.

The sun has descended behind them, leaving pockets of darkness for someone to hide in.

But when I find nothing, no people, no movement, I shake my head and tell myself to stop being so pathetic.

I sit there for a while longer, thinking about nothing and everything as I drown in grief once again.

My cell continues to buzz in my pocket, letting me know that Knox is probably waiting. I didn't give him a firm time that I'd be home this afternoon, aware that it wasn't going to be a good day, but he probably expected me back by now.

Pulling it out, I find that I'm right.

**Knox: Baby, where are you?**

**Knox: I'm getting worried. Just let me know you're okay.**

**Knox: Please, Firefly.**

**Violet: Just putting some flowers on Mom's grave. Be back soon. x**

**Knox: I could have come with you.**

Emotion burns up my throat as I think about the fact that he's never been here. He was locked up long before we got to have the funerals. Hell, he might not even know his dad is here. If he wants to see him.

Guilt washes through me that I didn't even consider offering for him to come, and another tear falls.

It's been easy to think that I was the only one to lose those I loved that day, but the reality is, Knox lost his only parent as well. Hell, he lost his life. Or at least five years of it. I might have been here with just Tristan and his family to pick up the pieces, but Knox had no one, nothing. And I hated him.

Fuck. His life must have been hell. He willingly walked away from everything. Why?

To protect me, he says.

But why? Why would he need to protect me, and from whom?

I barely get to the end of that thought when a thick black glove wraps around my mouth, cutting off the scream that rips up my throat as another strong arm bands around my waist, pinning my own arms to my sides and stopping me from fighting. Not that I don't try.

"GET OFF ME," I scream, although it's totally pointless as it gets lost in his hand.

My heart pounds so hard I can feel it in every inch of my body as my feet leave the ground and I'm dragged back into the shadows that were making me nervous not so long ago.

I kick and thrash, doing everything I can think of to make him let go, but it's clear that I don't have anywhere near the strength I need to overpower this man.

I continue to scream. It's pointless, I know that, but the noise attempts to rip from my throat regardless.

A grunt leaves him when my foot finally collides with his shin, but his hold on me never falters. And it's not until we're hidden in the dark cover of the trees above that he finally speaks.

"Calm the fuck down, Violet. I'm not going to hurt you."

# 40

# TRISTAN

My body aches with exhaustion as I slump back in my chair in the office after practice has finally let up.

The guys are ready. More than ready. But Coach wants more than that, obviously. I mean, so do I. But my need to get home and pull my girl into my arms is stronger.

The week has been tough. My classes are getting harder, my assignments longer and more demanding, the pressure of the season starting is growing, and the few chances I've had to look into my girl's eyes is a stark reminder of everything she's battling with.

I want to be there for her, but I also have to be here.

It's fucking ripping me in two.

I pack my shit up, more than ready to get the hell out of here, all the while wishing I never sat down because now I've stopped, I really don't want to start again.

A shadow falling over the entrance to the office sure doesn't make things any better.

"Carver," Winters grunts.

I nod in his direction, not having the time or energy to deal with his irritating ass.

"Your wide receivers ready?" he taunts. "They didn't look entirely on point this afternoon."

"How about you focus on your issues instead of trying to point out problems that don't exist with our offense?"

"Defense is on point and you know it."

"Whatever," I mutter, not having the time or patience to put up with his constant need to one-up me.

Spinning around in my chair, I wake my computer up before closing everything I have open and powering it off.

"I'm out," I say, although fuck knows why. I don't owe him an explanation.

Stuffing everything into my bag, I pull my cell out and attempt to bring it to life, but the irritating little empty battery icon just flashes at me.

I'm rummaging around for my keys when heavy footsteps pound down the hallway outside our office before the door swings open, crashing back against the wall.

"Whoa, what the fuck do you—" Winters starts but is quickly cut off.

"Have you seen Violet?"

The second I look into Knox's panicked eyes, my heart sinks into my chest.

"N-no. Last time I spoke to her, she was heading home."

"She hasn't come home."

My head spins as my brain refuses to believe what he's saying.

"Are you sure?"

"Yes, I'm fucking sure," he booms, his own panic overtaking his cool façade. "She messaged me when she was leaving the graveyard, but she never came home."

"Maybe she's still there?"

"She's not. I've been there. There's no sign of her."

My heart pounds as I fight to come up with a sensible suggestion.

"You are aware that non-students aren't allowed in here,"

Winters sneers, clearly ignoring the fraught expressions on both our faces.

"Fuck off," I grunt.

"Oh, I'm sorry," he gasps. "The rules are made for a reason. Just like the one about not fucking undergrads. You really should leave her to this gangs—" Winters' words are cut off the second Knox's fist collides with his jaw.

"You really shouldn't have done that," I hiss.

"Prick doesn't get to talk to you like that, bro. Let's go, we need to find our girl."

He grabs my bag from me before striding from the room.

"Shit," I breathe, getting a grip on myself. "Have you tried calling her friends?" I ask, running to catch up with Knox.

"Yes. No one has seen her. Get the fuck in," he barks, nodding at an idling car outside the training facility.

He rips the passenger's door open first, leaving me with no option but to drag the back door open and climb inside.

"Nothing?" a guy asks in the driver's seat.

"No, he hasn't seen her."

"You know she's probably just at a bar getting wasted, right? Probably just trying to catch a breath after being smothered by you two."

"Who the fuck are you?" I growl, not needing a fucking stranger to give me advice on a girl or a relationship he has no fucking clue about.

"Tristan, this is Devin Harris. Feel free to take his advice with a pinch of salt. I do," Knox grunts.

"Right. Where the fuck are we going?" I ask, my heart pounding so hard in my chest, blood rushes past my ears. "Have you tried calling her?" It's a stupid question, I'm more than aware of that, but it seems it needs pointing out.

"This guy, really, Knox?" Devin teases.

"Shut the fuck up, Dev, and drive faster."

"Will you tell me what the fuck we're doing," I demand, wrapping my hands around the headrest and sitting forward.

"We're going to Dev's house. Ellis and Micah are hacking into the graveyard CCTV so we can try and see what happened."

"M-Micah?"

"Yeah, her housemate, my brother's geeky friend," Devin drawls like I'm an idiot.

Geeky friend... right.

I sit back, my hands shaking and my head spinning with fear.

"Do you have an iPhone charger?" I blurt, needing to know if there's anything from Violet sitting on my cell.

"Here." Knox passes a cable back and I rush to plug it in.

"Fucking hurry up," I growl as nothing happens for long minutes.

But when it does finally load, all I get are some memes from a group chat I'm in with some of the Titans and a ton of emails.

"Nothing?" Knox guesses.

"Nope."

"Well, let's hope these two have had more luck."

The engine dies and both Devin and Knox jump out, leaving me lingering like a fucking moron.

"Didn't think you were coming," Devin teases when I catch up with them.

I glare at him but keep my mouth shut as we storm into the house, Knox shoving him out of the way to get to the living room first.

"Anything?" he barks the second his eyes land on the two guys huddled around laptops.

"We're getting there," the one I don't know says. "The church has freakishly good security."

"You can hack it though, right?" Knox asks in a panic.

The guy finally lifts his eyes from his screen. "Does a bear shit in the woods, Bowman?"

"Fuck you. Just find her."

"We will," Micah assures us.

I walk around the table and stand there, staring at the screens which seem to have Devin's brother and Micah enthralled. But all I see is gibberish.

"What the fuck is—"

"Trust us, Tristan," Micah begs. "We'll find her."

"Here, drink this and chill the fuck out," Devin demands, pushing a beer into my chest as Knox takes a seat beside Micah.

"Wait... you know what you're looking at?" I balk.

"Yeah. Ellis is much better than me. He wasn't locked in a cell for five years without a computer."

My eyes widen at his confession.

"What? Didn't you have me down as a nerd, Bowman?"

My lips part to respond, but a triumphant shout comes from Ellis.

"Do you have it?" I ask in a rush, moving closer as a grainy video begins playing on the screen.

"What time was she there?" Ellis asks.

"She messaged me at six to say she was leaving."

"At six?" I bark, horrified. "And it's taken you until now to raise the alarm?"

"I assumed she was stuck in traffic or something, stopped at the store on her way back. The second she was five minutes later than I expected, I didn't immediately jump into action, no," Knox growls.

"But two hours?" Pain lashes at my insides as images of all the things that could have happened to her in two hours play out in my mind.

Ellis fast forwards the video, and the second someone appears on the screen, he slows it once more so we can see if it's her or not.

My heart sinks into my feet when we quickly discover it's not.

We continue stopping and starting the video for a while

until, finally, someone that I would recognize anywhere walks down the path.

"That's her. That's Violet," I shout a beat before Knox does.

Ellis hits pause for a beat before he turns the speed back to normal and we sit and watch as she continues. Headstones spread out on either side of her, but I know exactly which one she's heading to.

"Is that where our parents are?" Knox asks, his voice deep and raspy with emotion.

"Yeah. Violet chose the spot so her mom could watch the sunrise and the seasons change in the trees."

"Shit," he hisses. "I fucked up, doing what I did, didn't I?"

No one says anything, and I can only assume that's because they're all aware of the truth.

"Too late for regrets, man," Devin eventually says, finally saying something helpful.

"I know, but I should have been there beside her while she went through that."

"So should Roman."

Silence hangs heavy around us as we all focus on the screen, the past and all the mistakes we've all made pressing down on our shoulders.

"Fuck, I hate this," Knox barks as we watch Violet obviously cry as she sits in front of her mom's headstone. I've seen her do it in person, and while this might pale in comparison to that, it's still hard to watch.

My fists curl, my need to pull my girl into my arms, to hold her and tell her that everything is going to be okay is overwhelming.

But I can't, because we don't know where the fuck she is.

"What time was this?" I ask.

"Three hours ago," Micah mutters, his eyes glued to the screen just like the rest of us.

"Speed it up a bit," Knox demands. "We don't have time to watch her just sitting there."

Ellis does as he's told, and the second she turns to look over her shoulder, I shout for them to slow it again.

My heart is in my throat as we watch her climb to her feet, her eyes scanning her surroundings more than once as if she senses that something is about to happen, that someone is watching her.

"There," Knox booms, and I'm so focused on Violet as she walks back toward the camera that I jump out of my skin at the sound of his voice.

That fear only gets worse when a dark, hooded figure seems to step out of nowhere and grab our girl.

"NO," I bark, aware that I sound like a pussy but not giving a shit. "No, no," I chant in disbelief.

"Motherfucker," Knox grunts, but there's something in his tone that makes me rip my eyes from the screen in favor of him.

"You know who it is?"

"And you don't? Fuck, Tris," he mutters sounding utterly exasperated with me. "Follow them," he demands of Ellis and Micah.

"They've gone into the trees. They could go anywhere."

"Well, fucking find them. And track her cell. He's smarter than to allow it, but there's always a chance."

Before I get a chance to say anything, Knox blows through the house, the back door slamming loudly.

"We've got this," Ellis assures me. "We'll find her. Just go and make sure he doesn't do anything stupid."

"Fucking hell," I mutter, combing my fingers through my hair and stalking after Knox.

The second I step through the back door, I find Knox standing in the middle of the backyard with his fingers tugging at his hair, his face tipped toward the sky as if he's praying.

"Knox," I whisper, slightly afraid of what he'll do if I startle him.

"I need a cigarette."

"Y-you don't smoke anymore, do you?"

"No, I quit inside, but I fucking need something, Tris."

"No," I state—a little more fiercely than I think he was expecting, if the expression on his face is anything to go by when he wheels around on me.

"No?"

"Exactly. No. I'm not letting you poison yourself because you're scared. It's not going to happen."

His jaw tics as he snarls, "Can you stop being so goddamn noble? You're not fucking perfect, Tristan. Stop expecting me to be."

"What? I don't think— Fucking hell. Us going at it isn't going to help. Who's got her, Knox? I swear, if you've got her in the middle of some fucking gang war then—"

"Roman."

My tirade halts the second he interrupts me with that one single name.

"What?" I eventually ask when all he does is stare at me. "How could you possibly know that?"

He shrugs. "I just do. There was something about him. That motherfucker," Knox spits, his fury coming back stronger than ever. "I've been searching for him for five fucking years, and he was right here under our fucking noses."

"You don't know that. It could be any—"

"It's him. I know it is. And this is because of me. Because I'm here, because I'm with her."

"Okay, so say you're right," I mutter, following along with him despite my reservations. "What the hell does he want with her?"

"To warn her off me? To keep her away from anything to do with the Hawks?"

"Nah. Come on, Knox. If he cared enough about what she

was doing, he'd have popped up years ago. She hasn't exactly lived the life of an innocent angel."

His teeth grind as I say those words.

"I wouldn't know. I wasn't here," he forces out.

"We just need to find her. We'll deal with the rest. With him." If it even is him. "Once we've got her back."

"They could be anywhere."

"Yeah, I agree. But he wouldn't hurt her." Although as I hear my own words, my confidence begins to drain.

I don't know Roman anymore. I haven't known him for a long time. He could be capable of anything these days.

A shiver of fear races down my spine.

Roman proved five years ago just how deadly he could be. We would be stupid to underestimate him.

# 41

# VIOLET

He doesn't say another word, and I'm too shocked to keep up my fight as I'm led through the woods and bundled into a car.

My body still trembles as fear continues to take hold, but that voice in my ear sure helped to calm me.

Although, it probably shouldn't.

I haven't even seen his face. He's kept his hood low, remained hidden, and I can only assume that's because of the CCTV that surrounds the grounds of the graveyard.

"W-what do you want?" I eventually ask when we're heading farther out of town.

His body tenses, his grip on the wheel tightening.

"I won't hurt you," he says again.

"You're not exactly filling me with confidence here," I quip.

"I-I'm sorry. I just... I just need to talk to you."

"Don't you own a cell?" With each biting response, my fear begins to fade and my anger over this bullshit begins to burn red hot. "You can't just come back from the dead and kidnap me."

"I'm not— That's not—"

"Jesus, have you even thought this through? When I don't come home, they'll come for me," I say with complete confidence. Knox might be the one who will burn the world to the ground the moment I don't return home like I promised, but I've no doubt that Tristan will be right at his side.

I squeeze my eyes closed and think of both of my boys.

They'll come for me. They'll find me and—

"Shit. Have you got an actual fucking death wish?" I bark.

The jolt that rocks through his body tells me he hasn't. But what the fuck is he doing? He can't really think this is fucking normal behavior.

"No, that is the opposite of what I have, actually."

His reply stuns me into silence, and instead of responding, encouraging this insanity, I sit back and study my surroundings. That's the sensible thing to do, right?

I know where we are, although I'm not all that familiar with this side of town.

Eventually, he pulls into an old and run-down motel and brings the car to a stop.

"Wow, you couldn't really get much more cliché than this, huh? Young woman killed in a motel room by her deranged older brother," I mutter, putting on my best news reporter voice.

"Violet, I already told you. I'm not going—"

"To hurt me. Yeah, I got that, but you just fucking kidnapped me in the middle of a graveyard, Roman," I screech. "That is not fucking normal behavior."

He kills the engine and pushes the driver's door open.

"Just come with me. Please?" he begs, his voice softer, more like the one I remember this time.

I want to say no. I should say no. But I don't, because my curiosity gets the better of me.

The second he opens my door, I climb out.

But I still don't get to look at him. He keeps his hooded

head lowered, and the second I'm on my feet, he swings the door closed and marches in the opposite direction.

I trail behind him like a pathetic little puppy, falling straight back into old habits and hating myself for it.

I'd have followed him to hell if he led me in that direction. It was pathetic.

I am pathetic.

Unease hits me after he lets himself into one of the downstairs rooms and disappears inside. I hesitate in the doorway, still not entirely convinced that he doesn't want to hurt me.

But in the end, my need to know is too much to deny.

I step inside and close the door behind me.

Roman is standing on the other side of the room, hood still up and shoulders slumped in defeat.

"What's going on, Roman? Why have you brought me here, and—" He spins around and finally knocks his hood down. My gasp of shock rips through the air.

The scar that runs along the length of his cheek makes my heart ache, but it's only made worse by the look in his eyes.

Pure, unfiltered fear stares back at me, and it makes my stomach drop into my feet.

"Roman," I breathe, taking a stop forward.

But he stiffens, and I instantly stop.

"Start talking," I demand, staring into a pair of green eyes that are so much like my own, it's a little unnerving. Something we both inherited from our father.

The air between us turns thick as his silence continues.

"Sit down," he finally growls. My legs instantly follow orders, and I find myself sitting on the edge of the bed while Roman drags the chair closer.

His eyes scan every inch of me so intently that I have to wonder if he's committing me to memory, as if I'm never going to see him again after he walks out of this room.

"Roman, please. You're scaring me."

"It was me."

His words throw me for a loop, and I shake my head in confusion.

"What was you? I don't understand."

He sucks in a deep breath. "The fire, Violet. It was me."

His confession hits me like a bat to the chest, yet all I do is blink at him, my body rejecting the words.

"No. It was one of Victor's soldiers. It was a hit on Joe. It—"

"It was me, Violet. I was the soldier."

"No," I wheeze, but as the words finally settle, I know they're true, and I'm fucking furious with myself for not realizing it sooner. Sure, the thought had hit me a time or two. But Roman was my big brother. He might have made some mistakes, but I didn't truly believe he could—

My stomach turns over and I bolt toward a door opposite the one I entered through in the hope of finding a toilet to vomit in.

Betrayal burns through me, poisoning me from the inside out.

It was Roman.

He started the fire.

He was the Hawk Victor sent.

He was the one Knox was covering for.

I retch again, bringing up everything I've eaten today, which admittedly hasn't been much.

Roman's presence lingers behind me, but he wisely doesn't come any closer.

Good to know he hasn't entirely lost his fucking mind.

"I should have known," I mutter, flushing the toilet and watching the water swirl around the bowl and disappear, just like my life did that night. And all because of my brother.

He doesn't say anything. Not that I think there are any words that can be said right now.

My stomach convulses once more as I think back to the fallout after that night. The pain, the grief, the loss.

"I fucking mourned you, you asshole," I whisper. "I thought you'd run because you couldn't cope. I thought you were dead. I never even considered it was because you couldn't cope with the guilt."

With a surge of red-hot anger spurring me on, I jump to my feet and fly at him.

I hit and kick him with everything I have, and he doesn't so much as try and stop me as I unleash the past five years of hate, anger, and loneliness on him.

My chest heaves, sweat covers my body, tears paint my cheeks, and my fists scream at me to stop, but I don't. I can't.

With a roar of determination, I fight on, needing him to experience even a hint of the pain I have.

He left me.

He left me here to deal with all this shit.

Alone.

"I'm sorry, Violet. I'm so fucking sorry."

"Not good enough. It's never going to be good enough," I scream so loudly I wouldn't be surprised if someone starts hammering on the door any minute to make sure we're not killing each other.

"You killed her. You fucking killed her," I scream, losing any kind of grip I had on reality.

My arms continue to flail around, hitting him wherever I can make contact, but eventually, my hits get lighter and I give in to my exhaustion and my heartbreaking sobs.

My legs give out and I stumble forward, more than prepared to hit the floor, but a strong pair of arms wraps around me long before that happens.

I'm swept off my feet and carried back to the bedroom.

I want to fight, I want to refuse his support, his warmth, but as much as I might hate him right now, I've also missed him so much.

My head and my heart war as I sit there, weak, with tears soaking my shirt, trembling in his arms.

I've got no idea how much time passes as I sit there, breaking all over again just like I have every year since I lost both of them.

His scent wraps around me, taking me back to better times, happier times. Times when I thought I'd always be able to rely on him. Times when I was convinced he would stand by my side and fight whatever was thrown at us together.

"You left," I whimper, ignoring the main issue here and focusing on what I'm able to process. The thought of him lighting that match is just too big right now.

"I was sick, Vi. I'd fucked up, I knew that. But I couldn't see a way out. I was a pussy. I ran. I let you down. I—"

"Knox went down for you," I interrupt. "H-he... th-they protected you. How could you? How could you let us all do that?"

"I didn't ask them to."

I scramble from his lap. "And you think that makes this any better? Jesus, Roman. I—"

At some point during my breakdown, he shed his hoodie, leaving him now in a black t-shirt that exposes his arms.

"Holy shit," I gasp, my eyes locked on the scarring there.

Most from needles, but plenty more that can only have come from blades.

"Roman."

My knees smart as they hit the hard floor of the motel room, but I barely feel it as I reach for him.

"They're not important, Violet," he rasps, his voice full of pain and regret.

I run my thumb over one of the roughest, ugliest scars that runs up the length of his forearm, right along the vein.

My stomach turns over once more, and I look up at his eyes, my heart bleeding for what he's been through.

He stares down at me, tears swimming in his own eyes.

"Knox took the fall because he felt guilty," Roman explains. "He took me to Harrow Creek, introduced me to a world that I should have stayed far, far away from. I thought I could handle it. I didn't think I'd fall into the same darkness that took Dad away. But the parties got wilder, and things just escalated.

"I told myself it was just a bit of weed on the weekends. That Coach would never know. But soon, that wasn't having the effect I craved. So I tried the next thing, and the next.

"Knox tried to stop me. But I fell down the rabbit hole so fast, I don't even remember falling until I hit the bottom.

"Knox blamed himself, but I never did. I blamed Joe. Knox was as innocent as us in all this. Born into it beyond his own choice. But Joe? He chose to raise his son in that world. And then he tarnished our lives with the same bullshit.

"I was doing everything I could to hide how much of a fucking mess I was, but cracks were starting to show. Tristan was noticing my focus on the field slipping, and my grades were going the same way.

"I hated everything. But more than anything, I hated myself for being so fucking weak. For not being the person Mom needed, not being the brother you deserved. I was a fucking mess, and I couldn't see a way out."

"Roman," I sob as tears drip from my jaw, soaking into the denim covering my thighs.

But my reaction to his story doesn't stop him.

"Then I heard about the hit on Joe. I figured if I could take out the person responsible for bringing this on us, then it could get better. Knox could be set free, and I could put it behind me and focus on the future I should have.

"Mom told me that you were both having a night away, so I put everything into motion. I didn't even think about where we'd live, I just needed him out of our life. He was poison. I hated him with every sense of my being. And that hatred clouded everything. It turned my sole purpose in life into getting rid of him. I convinced myself that he would poison you and Mom next, and I refused to allow that to happen.

"I didn't check before I started that fire. I should have gone upstairs to make sure you really weren't there. But instead, I started it and ran. And then, when Knox called me to tell me what was happening, I turned up feeling so fucking smug that I was the one to get the job done. But then there he was, carrying your lifeless body out of the burning building a-and I j-just..." His words trail off.

"I fucked up so fucking bad, Violet. And I know it'll never be enough, but I'm sorry. I'm so fucking sorry."

His tears finally fall, and it breaks my heart to see him shatter.

He was always my strength, my rock. My incredible big brother and—

"Tristan and Knox, they took one look at me, and they just knew. Fuck knows how. They'd both been watching me slip deeper into my addiction and not had a clue what to do about it.

"I didn't even have to confess."

He drops his head, our eye contact finally breaking as he drowns in memories from that night. From a time I have no recollection of because I was unconscious.

"Knox told me to leave. It was all him. He told me that he'd sort it with Victor, get someone who deserved it to take the fall, and demanded that I go and sort my shit out because you needed me.

"I promised them. Fucking swore to them that I would. And I fully intended to, Violet," he chokes out, lifting his head once more and finding my eyes. "I really fucking believed I could do it and that in a few weeks, a month even, that I could come back and the four of us would be okay.

"But the reality was nothing like that." He shakes his head. "Shit got bad, Violet. Really fucking bad. The grief, the guilt. I just wanted to die. I almost did, a number of times.

"All of it was my fault.

"You'd lost everything. Knox was forced to put his life on pause..." He blows out a breath. "At least Tristan got his dream. If only for a little while."

"Why, Roman? Why are you doing this now? You've had five years to come and tell me this."

"Honestly, I thought you'd have known by now. I never expected them to keep the secret they promised they would."

"You underestimated them," I mutter, both loving and hating the depths of my boys' loyalty.

"Yeah, I did."

Pulling one of his scarred hands from mine, he pushes it into his pocket and pulls his wallet out.

He tugs a small square of paper from inside and stares down at it for a beat, his expression softening before he hands it over.

I suck in a sharp breath at the image before me.

"Roman," I breathe.

"Lilly Rose Brady," his says, his voice rough with emotion and pride.

A lump so huge clogs my throat as I stare down at the precious little baby before me.

"Your niece, Violet. My savior. Her and her momma."

The photo flutters to the floor as I drop my head into my hands and let my ugly sobs of grief, anger, and relief free.

# 42

# VIOLET

"Here," Roman says, handing me a cup of takeout coffee he's just collected from a guy who knocked on the door.

"Thanks," I mutter absently, cupping both of my hands around it and lifting it to my nose to inhale the familiar scent.

It's been about thirty minutes since his confessions and neither of us has said anything that hasn't involved the coffee order Roman placed.

I don't know what to say. What does he expect here, exactly?

Forgiveness?

I might be relieved to see him, to know he's alive and that clearly, he's found a way to get his life together. But can I forgive him?

That's a really big fucking question. One that's too big to answer while his concerned stare burns into the side of my head.

"Where have you been?" I ask, finally feeling the need to end the silence.

"To start with, I couldn't even tell you. I hopped from town to town, mostly crashing anywhere I could find shelter, stealing anything I could to put food in my belly and poison in my veins.

"I made a few attempts to get clean in the early days, but I wasn't ready. The darkness, the grief, the regrets. I wasn't ready to deal with them.

"It wasn't pretty, and if you really want to know some of the worst of it, I'll tell you. I'll tell you all of it. But I don't want you to think that my stories are a way to make you feel sorry for me, to force you to forgive me. That's not why I'm here."

"You don't want my forgiveness?" I ask, a deep frown forming across my brow.

"What I want and what I deserve are two very different things, Vi," he says sadly.

"I managed to move back closer when I was having another attempt to get clean. I'd heard of a decent program a few towns over and thought it might be worth a shot. Plus, it would allow me to check in with you."

"You were going to come see me?"

"No," he says so fast it almost gives me whiplash. "I never would have turned up like I was then. Hell, I probably shouldn't even be here now, but there we go. I didn't want you to see me like that. I was weak, sick. You probably wouldn't have even recognized me.

"I was just planning on searching you out, checking you were okay."

"You knew I was still here?"

"I followed you on social media when I could. It made me happy to know you were living your life, that you'd got into college and were happy."

"I'm not sure I was truly happy," I confess.

"Happier than me."

My lips part to respond, but he beats me to it.

"Long story short, I met Imogen at the program, and things started to click into place. Being close to home once again and seeing you gave me new hope, I guess."

"You've been close for a while?"

"Yeah. That's how I knew I'd find you at the graveyard at some point over the coming days."

"You were just going to hang out in the trees waiting to kidnap me?" I ask, my brow quirking.

"I haven't..." He lets out a pained breath. "You can walk out that door at any time, Violet."

I glare at him. "You do know that they will hurt you for this?" I don't mention their names, but from the lack of reaction on my brother's face, I'd hazard a guess that he knows exactly who I'm talking about.

"I knew about you two, you know?"

"What?"

"You and Knox."

"What?" I gasp.

He shrugs. "I saw him sneaking out of your room one night. Smug motherfucker."

"You let that slide?" I ask. Back then, I was convinced that Roman would have hurt anyone who came near me, but the pain he would have caused Knox or Tristan after warning them off me would have been on another level.

"Fuck no. I beat the loving shit out of him for it. Never told him why, though. But then... it wasn't too long later I saw the wrecked expression on his face as he carried you from that house, and I knew that you'd be better off with him than me..."

"I wasn't better off though, Roman. I didn't have either of you. Tristan was left to pick up the pieces."

"He would, though. That sap has been in love with you since he was about eight years old."

All the air rushes from my lungs. "You really should have told me all this," I mutter, thinking how much easier everything could have been.

"So you could have shacked up with both of them sooner?"

"You're still stalking me, then. Good to know," I deadpan.

"I've seen you with both of them recently, yes."

"And?"

"And what? It's your life, Violet. I am in no position to have an opinion on what you do or who you see. I lost that right the second I turned my back on you."

"Damn right you did."

"There is just one thing, though," he says, pain flickering through his eyes.

"Give it a shot."

"They're both good to you, right?"

A laugh falls from my lips as images of my time with both Knox and Tristan recently flicker through my head. "Oh yeah," I confess. "Your best friend and our stepbrother treat me real good, Roman."

It's a low blow, but fuck if the way all the blood drains from his face doesn't make me feel just a teeny bit better about all of this.

"Fucking hell," he mutters, dragging his hand down his face. "You're really with both of them?"

"Yeah. I mean, it's all new and crazy and... yeah. It just works. I dunno how to explain it really."

"As long as you're happy. You could be with the entire football team, for all I care."

"Don't have enough holes for that."

Coffee sprays from both Roman's mouth and nose at my comeback.

"Fucking good luck to them putting up with you."

"Hey," I complain. "They were your best friends once."

"Yeah. Once," he says sadly. "I don't have any crazy idea of anything ever going back to how it was."

"We can't go back, Roman. We can only move forward."

"Don't I fucking know it."

He sits forward on the bed, his elbows resting on his knees, and the way the moonlight filters into the room illuminates the scar on his cheek.

"How did you get that?" I ask, my heart hurting at the evidence of his past being so visible and permanent.

"This one?" he asks, pointing at his cheek.

"There are more?" I gawp. That and the ones on his arms are shocking enough, but more?

"Yeah, Vi. So many more. But the most painful ones are on the inside."

Lifting my legs up, I wrap my arms around them, curling in on myself in the hope it makes everything hurt less.

No matter what he's done, Roman will always be my big brother, and I will always hurt for him, with him.

Should I be calling the cops right now and explaining that they had the wrong man with Knox, that this broken, almost unrecognizable person from my past is actually responsible? Maybe. I'm sure plenty would.

But hasn't he already been through enough?

What's done is done.

Nothing I—we—do now is going to bring Mom back, or bring the relationship back I once had with Roman.

But he's here. He's alive. And fuck, has he suffered.

Is it enough, though?

Is that justice for taking two lives? One of them innocent?

I blow out a long, pained breath.

"I don't remember," he finally says, making me frown.

"R-remember what?"

"How I got this," he says, pointing at himself again. "Woke up in the hospital with it one day."

"Fuck."

"I woke up. Gotta count your blessings, right?"

"Tell me about Imogen and Lilly Rose."

The most incredible smile curls at his lips, and for a second, I forget all the bullshit and just remember the boy who used to be that happy every day.

The way he talks about them, the all-consuming love he has for them makes me tear up again.

It would have been so easy for everyone to turn their back on him when he was lost to his addiction, but it seems he might just have found an angel in Imogen.

"I'd really like for you to meet them one day. If it weren't for Imogen, then I'm not sure my recovery would have stuck this time, either."

"Maybe," I whisper, not willing to commit to anything right now.

All of this, it's been a lot. I have so much to think about, to process, and all on top of the grief I was already drowning under.

"I'm sorry, Violet. I truly am."

I nod, accepting his apology because what else can I do?

That's the easy part.

"They're going to be freaking out that I never made it home."

"I know. I just didn't know how else to do this. I needed to talk to you alone, and I knew that you'd turn me away if I just walked up to you."

Would I?

I think on that for a beat, and I really don't have an answer.

He pushes to stand and shoves his hand in his pocket.

"Here," he says, revealing my cell that I didn't even realize he had. "I took it when I dragged you to the car."

"Yeah, thanks for that."

"I knew they'd follow you. Knox has contacts who'd track that if it were on in a heartbeat, and I just needed an hour."

My brow lifts, vaguely aware that he's stolen more than an hour from me this evening.

"Or a few. Turn it on, call them. Get them to come and get you."

"What about you?" I ask, my fingers trembling as I take my cell from him.

He pulls something else out of his pocket and hands it over.

It's just a scrap of paper with a phone number on it.

"If you want to talk to me again, call me. Anytime."

I nod, emotion burning the backs of my eyes once more.

"I've got a new life now, Violet, and I'd love for you to be a part of it. But I also understand if all of this is too much, if too much time has passed and that you've found yourself a new family now."

"Roman," I sob.

"Just take some time, see how you feel. I'm not going anywhere. I've got too much to live for."

Before I manage to come up with any kind of response to that, he tugs me from the chair and wraps me in his arms, tucking his face into the crook of my neck, squeezing me hard.

"I missed you so fucking much, Vi. And I'm so proud of the woman you've become. Mom would be, too. Now call them, and let them help you through this, okay? And, please don't be too hard on them about all this. All of us only wanted the best for you. It was probably misguided, but we were young, naïve, and scared. If I've learned anything, it's that life is too short for resentment. Take it by the balls, Violet, and live every day like it could be your last."

He marches out of the room while those words still ring in my ears.

"Holy shit," I breathe, rushing toward the window and watching as Roman drops into his car and backs out of the space. He looks up just before he turns away, and his eyes light up when he finds me watching him.

A smile curls at his lips and he gives me a small wave before he heads back to his new life.

Stumbling back, my legs hit the edge of the bed and I fall down onto it with my cell clutched to my chest.

My head spins, my emotions still warring within. The relief, the disbelief, the anger all rage, but Roman's final words override all of them.

*"Life's too short. Take it by the balls."*

## 43

## KNOX

The second my cell buzzes in my hand, my heart jumps into my throat and I lift it.

"It's her," I say at the same time Micah barks, "We've got her."

Relief like I've never experienced before rushes through my body and my knees give out, leaving me on the Harrises' couch a beat before Tristan lands next to me, pressing himself right against me.

"Answer it," he demands as I fumble like a fool.

Swiping my finger across the screen, I lift my cell between us so Tristan can hear as well as I can.

"Firefly, where are you? Are you okay?"

"I-I'm fine," she stutters, her voice rough from what I hope is crying and not screaming. "Can you come get me?"

"Yes, baby. Anything. Where are—" My question is cut off when Micah slides his computer onto my lap, allowing me to see the map where her little red dot is flashing. "Don't worry, baby. We've got you. We're coming right now. We'll be..." I look up at Micah for the answer.

"Thirty minutes max," he says.

"Twenty minutes, baby. Come on, let's go," I say to Tristan as I jump up, full of determination to go rescue my girl.

Our girl.

"Are you okay, baby?" I ask, fear dripping through my veins that she might not be.

"Yeah, I'm fine," she says, her voice weak and not at all convincing. "It was—"

"Roman, I know.'

"H-how?"

"Are you really okay? Has he hurt you in any way? I swear to God, if he has hurt so much as a hair on your—"

"I'm fine, really. We just talked. I know, Knox. I know everything."

Ice drips through my veins as Tristan's stare turns on me, his eyes wide in panic. A panic I feel right down to my core.

"Shit, Firefly. I—"

"Just come and get me, yeah?"

"Y-yeah, we're getting in the car now. Just hang tight."

"Okay."

"Do you want us to stay on the li—" The call cuts as Devin's car comes to life.

"Shit," Tristan hisses.

"We did say that she needed to hear it from him," I reason.

"I know, but this wasn't exactly what I had in mind. I swear, if he's hurt her—"

"He won't have."

"You're seriously optimistic about someone who burned his own house down and killed his own mother."

Tristan's mouth opens again to reply, but I don't give him a chance.

"We don't even know if he's sorted himself out. He's been off grid since he walked away. For all we know—"

"You heard her, she's okay."

"She sounded like she'd been crying."

He sighs, aware that he's not going to win this argument. He might have known Roman better than me as a kid, but he doesn't know him as an addict. And that makes him unpredictable, volatile, and possibly violent. I've grown up around enough to know that you never really know what to expect.

I just pray he's sorted himself out. Because if he hasn't and he's hurt our girl in any way other than just telling her the truth, then I won't stop hunting him until I know he's no longer a threat to her.

"Knox, chill the fuck out, yeah?" Tristan demands after a growl I soon realize came from me rips through the air around us.

Lights flash in my mirrors, and when I look back, I find Ezra following us with Devin, and I assume Ellis and Micah in the back, probably with their eyes still glued to screens.

The drive across town seems to take forever, which only increases my anxiety about what we're going to find when we get there.

What if it's a trap?

"It's not," Tristan barks, making me realize I asked that question out loud. "Just put your fucking foot down."

The second the motel sign comes into view, my heart jumps into my throat.

I'm out of the car before it's even fully come to a stop with Tristan right beside me.

"Where?" I ask, scanning the long row of doors leading to the motel rooms.

"Over there." I follow Tristan's outstretched arm to see a door open.

We barrel toward it, but despite his dodgy knee, he's faster and slips inside a beat before me.

His arms wrap around our girl, who's standing just inside the room, but I don't get a chance to look at her, to check her over.

"It's okay, baby girl. We've got you," Tristan says as I join the huddle, wrapping my arms around her waist, forcing Tristan to back up a little as I tuck my face into her neck, breathing her in and reassuring myself that she's okay.

"I'm okay," she says, but the way her entire body trembles as she says those two words doesn't fill me with confidence.

"What do you need, Firefly? Tell us and it's yours."

We both release her, giving her some space to breathe, but we don't take our eyes or our hands from her body.

"Take me home."

"You've got it."

Tristan tugs her forward. "We've got you, Pip."

"Wait," I bark.

Grabbing her other arm, I turn her my way and run my eyes down the length of her.

Her eyes are red and puffy and her cheeks are stained with dried tears, but other than that, she's okay. Perfect, actually.

"Firefly," I breathe, my relief palpable as I just stare at her.

"I'm so sorry, Knox. I'm so sorry you had to go through all of that because of him."

Before I get to say anything, she throws herself into my arms, slamming her lips down on mine.

She kisses me as if she might die without it, her tongue licking deep into my mouth.

She trembles in my arms as the saltiness of her tears mixes with our kiss.

"Baby girl," Tristan groans, stepping up behind her, pinning her between us. "We've got you."

"Tris," she moans, ripping her lips from mine and twisting around so she can kiss him.

I'm already hard as fuck, but watching them devour each other while I'm right there only makes the situation worse.

"Oh shit. She's okay, then," a sheepish voice mumbles from the door.

Tristan and Violet break apart as I look over, keeping Violet's ass pinned against my crotch so no one gets an eyeful of what they don't want, and my eyes lock with Micah's half-concerned, half-amused ones.

Violet relaxes when she sees who's standing there.

"I'm fine, Micah. Thank you for… for whatever you did."

"It was nothing."

"We're good here," I say loudly, knowing that the Harrises are going to be loitering right behind him. "And thank you."

"You got it, man," Devin barks. "Enjoy your night."

"Shut the fuck up," Ellis, I think, hisses before Devin complains about something.

"Let's go home," I whisper in Violet's ear, sending a violent shiver racing down her spine.

With both of our hands locked with hers, we walk out of the motel room, leaving behind whatever might have happened inside.

We come to a stop at Devin's car as the taillights of the Harrises' departing one disappear around the corner.

"What are you waiting for?" Tristan barks. "You were driving, remember?"

I look at where my fingers are twisted with Violet's and then toward the driver's door.

"Motherfucker," I grunt as he reaches for the back door with a smirk and gestures for Violet to go ahead of him.

"Try not to get too lonely up there."

"I hate you."

"Yeah, yeah, so you keep saying," he teases, slipping into the back with our girl and immediately pulling her into his arms.

"I am okay," Violet assures him as I join them.

"I know, baby girl. Pretty sure it's me who isn't. You were gone… for hours. Do you know how terrifying that was?'

"I'm sorry," she whispers so quietly I barely hear it over the roar of the engine coming to life.

"It wasn't your fault, Firefly. We saw the footage in the graveyard, we know you didn't go willingly."

"You were fierce, Pip. You should be proud of yourself."

"Didn't get me very far though, did it? If he were..." She trails off, and my stomach knots at the thought of things ending a very different way. "If it weren't my brother, then I could be—"

"Don't," I bark, unable to hear whatever was about to follow those words.

"I should be more prepared," she says absently. "I never, ever want to go through that again."

A smile twitches at my lips as an idea pops into my head. "I can train you," I state, finding her eyes in the mirror.

"Knox," Tristan growls, clearly unhappy with the idea.

"What's wrong, Carver? Worried I could turn your girl into a bigger badass than you?"

"No, I'm just not sure I want you to train her to fight dirty. If she wants to protect herself, she should do self-defense classes."

"Firstly, I take offense to you judging my fighting style. And secondly, I'll have you know that I can teach Violet everything she needs to know to have maximum effect and cause more pain than any man who attacks her can cope with."

"I don't need to cause pain," she argues.

"Anyone who touches you without our permission deserves a whole world of pain, Firefly."

"He's not wrong," Tristan begrudgingly agrees. "You're ours, baby girl. And only ours."

I glance back just in time to watch him tuck his fingers under her chin and tilt her face back so he can claim her lips.

I forget what I'm meant to be doing as I watch them again and only come back to myself when someone—possibly the oncoming car on the side of the road I'm not meant to be on—blasts their horn at me.

"Fuck," I bark, swerving just in time to avoid the collision and risking possible death when I have to tell Devin what I'd done to his baby.

"Please try not to kill us," Tristan demands before pulling Violet onto his lap so that she's straddling him. "I've got plans for when we get back."

"Tristan," she moans as he kisses down the length of her throat.

"Fuck's sake," I hiss, tugging at my pants to give my dick some more space. "Don't let her fall."

"Demanding asshole," Tristan mutters.

"You want her begging for our cocks, don't you?"

"Oh God," she whimpers, proving that the images playing out in her mind match mine.

"Gonna help you forget all this shit real good, Firefly."

"We were gonna wait until the weekend," Tristan tells her. "But it seems someone decided we should start the party early. That good with you, baby girl?"

"Anything. Just give me more," she begs, her raspy voice making my cock weep for her.

I'm pretty sure the drive back to Tristan's apartment takes even fucking longer than the one to get our girl with her mewls and moans filling the air as Tristan works her into a frenzy. And by the time I pull the car to an abrupt stop in the first space I find, I'm craving her touch, her kiss, her everything like a fucking junkie needing his next hit.

I jump out while Tristan is still distracted and pull the door open.

"What the fuck?" he barks the second I lift Violet off him and wrap her legs around my waist instead.

"This is all about sharing, ain't that right, Firefly. And now, it's my turn."

Tristan is hot on my heels as I race into the building, and he manages to hit the call button for the elevator before I get a chance.

"You fucking scared us, baby girl," he whispers, pressing his powerful body against her back and turning us around, giving me little choice but to back into the car when it arrives.

My breath leaves me in a grunt when I collide with the handrail, but with Tristan crushing Violet's body against mine, I quickly forget about the discomfort in favor of losing myself in my obsession.

Releasing her ass, I cup her cheek, staring into her glassy eyes.

"I love you, Violet," I tell her, my voice rough with emotion.

"Goddamn you, Knox," Tristan grunts.

"If anything had happened to you tonight, if he had touched you, I need you to know that I'd have raised hell."

"I know, Knox," she says softly. "I know. But you don't need to. I'm fine. I'm—"

I cut her words off by slamming my lips down on hers as we climb through the building. I can only assume that Tristan hit the button for the top floor—that or we're about to spill out onto the unsuspecting residents of this building who are waiting for it.

A wanton moan rumbles up Violet's throat as I continue to kiss her, wiping out my previous thoughts, and when I flick my eyes open, I find Tristan attached to her neck.

"Bedroom," I grunt into her kiss. "I need inside you, Firefly."

She moans again, her hips rolling, her pussy grinding against my length.

The second the elevator dings to announce our arrival, we stumble as one unit through Tristan's front door, and we don't pause for even a second.

As soon as I feel the bed against my calves, I fall back, taking Violet with me.

A shriek of fright rips from her lips as she plummets through the air.

"I'll catch you, baby. I'll always fucking catch you."

She stares down at me, her eyes blown with lust, her lips swollen from both of our kisses. It's almost enough to distract from her previous distress, her tears, but not quite enough. Not yet, anyway.

"Arms up, baby girl." Tristan's deep growl rumbles through the air before his fingers wrap around Violet's shirt and drag it up her body.

My temperature spikes again as he reveals her flawless skin to me.

"More," I growl, staring at her black lace bra as if it's personally offended me. I mean, it has. It's hiding her insane tits from me.

"Yes," Violet cries as Tristan sucks on the sensitive skin of her neck, his hands disappearing behind her back to unhook her bra.

A moan rumbles up her throat as the fabric falls from her body.

Tristan tosses it aside, but by the time his hands come back to her, he's too late.

"Knox," Violet cries as I cup her needy breasts, pinching her nipples and making her grind down on my dick. "Kiss me," she begs.

Her lips are stolen by Tristan as he twists her head around to him, so instead, I drop my mouth to her breasts, licking, nipping and sucking until she's crying out into Tristan's kiss.

"More?" I growl.

"Yes," she pleads, twisting her fingers in my hair and dragging me back to her.

"Greedy girl," I murmur before giving her what she needs.

Tristan claims her lips once, cutting off her response as his hands drop to her waistband, flicking open the button on her jeans and slipping his hand inside.

"She wet for us?" I ask as his knuckles brush against my aching dick as he searches for her clit.

I swallow my grunt, not wanting to turn him off, equally wanting to ignore the fact I'm so far fucking gone that it felt good.

"So wet. You wanna feel Knox's cock stretching you open, baby girl?"

My eyes meet Tristan's, a silent understanding passing between us.

"Yes, yes," Violet cries. "Tristan," she screams when he pushes his hand lower, I assume tucking two fingers inside her.

"Get his pants off him then, Pip."

In a rush to do as she's told, Violet's hands press against my chest, shoving me back.

I comply, falling onto my elbows to watch as she tugs open my fly and Tristan lifts her off the bed so she can free me of my pants and boxers after I've kicked my sneakers off.

She stares down at me naked before her with desire in her green eyes and her lips parted, allowing her increased breaths to escape.

"You want him, baby girl?" Tristan asks, tucking his fingers under her waistband and pushing her jeans and panties over her hips.

"Yes." She licks her tongue along her bottom lip and my cock jerks, desperate to feel her touch.

"What about me?" he asks, although there is no jealousy in his tone, and when his eyes meet mine again, I can read his filthy thoughts.

"I want you too. I want both of you."

"Crawl to him. Give him your mouth and me your cunt."

Violet sucks in a sharp breath at Tristan's crass words. Something tells me she's not used to hearing him talk like that. I'm sure as shit not used to it, and my eyes widen in surprise.

"I'm not just some NFL golden boy, Bowman," he grunts at me as Violet follows orders and crawls up the bed to me.

"I'll believe it when I see it. You wanna play with the bad boys, I'm going to need more evidence than wanting our girl's cunt," I tease.

Ripping my eyes from his when he scoffs a laugh and

begins undressing, I find Violet's wide eyes as she moves closer.

"Fuck me, baby. You're a goddess," I say, reaching out and cupping her cheek with one hand while my other grips my cock, lifting it from my stomach to her in offering.

She dips down, licking around the tip, lapping at the precum beading there.

"Shit, baby," I groan, my cock jerking in its need for more.

The bed dips at my feet as Tristan joins us.

"Suck Knox's cock, baby girl. But don't let him come."

"Demanding asshole," I mutter.

"Feel free to shoot your load like a teenage boy, Bowman. I'll happily take your place and fill her cunt with my cum instead."

"Boys," Violet chastises.

"Eat her pussy, Tris."

"And I'm the demanding one," he quips, gripping Violet's ass cheeks and pushing her forward onto my cock as he licks her.

She cries out around my dick, taking me deeper and making my eyes cross.

"Fuck yes. Fuck. Baby, your mouth is everything."

She sucks me like a pro as Tristan does whatever he does down there that has her trembling for release in seconds.

Fuck. I need to know his secrets.

"You gonna come for us, Firefly?"

"Tristan. Knox," she cries, barely releasing my cock.

"Come all over Tristan's face and then we'll fill you up. You want that, baby?"

"Yes, yes. Everything."

"Goddamn, you blow my fucking mind."

"TRISTAN," she suddenly screams, her back arching, her eyes falling closed and her jaw dropping as her release crashes through her.

"Breathtaking," I mutter as Tristan gets to his knees

between my parted legs, drags her up by her hair, and slams his lips down on hers, letting her taste herself on him.

He stops abruptly, his eyes catching mine. "Let Knox taste how sweet your cunt is, baby."

He slaps her ass, sending her shooting up the bed.

Grabbing her waist, I haul her up, dropping her over my lap and dragging her lips to mine.

The second I lick into her mouth, her taste hits me. It might not be as strong as I crave, but with her soaked pussy grinding down on my length and her lips on mine, I find it hard to care.

"So fucking sweet, baby. Did Tris eat you good?"

She nods, a coy look flashing through her eyes.

"Are you ready for my dick now?"

"So ready," she breathes.

Reaching between us, I line my cock up with her entrance.

"Sink down on him, baby girl," Tristan encourages, watching everything.

Our cries of pleasure mix together as one as she does as he says and drops down onto me, her cunt so slick that she takes all of me with ease.

"Shouldn't like watching my girl with another dick in her this much," Tristan mutters absently to himself as he shuffles closer.

"It's a headfuck, isn't it?" I force out as Violet clenches beautifully around me.

"Yeah, just like knowing you let some motherfucker anywhere near your junk with a needle."

"Get over it, pussy. I wanted its owner branded on it."

"Wait, what?" he asks, his brow wrinkling.

"I'll let you study it after our girl's finished."

"Stop fucking talking," Violet gasps between my slow thrusts up into her body.

With one hand on my stomach, she reaches back for Tristan, needing a connection with him too.

"You want Tris to take your ass, Firefly?" I ask, holding her hips and forcing her to move with me.

"Yes. Fuck yes. I want you both."

Tristan's eyes widen, and he stills behind her.

"You're not an ass virgin are you, Bowman?" I tease.

"I-I... uh... We don't have any—"

I roll my eyes at him over Violet's shoulder.

"Fucking amateur," I mutter. "Top drawer, golden boy." I jerk my chin in the direction of his nightstand.

It takes a beat, but he reaches over and pulls out a massive bottle of lube.

"Christ," he grunts.

"First rule of becoming a Hawk. Always be prepared, my friend."

"That's the fucking scouts, you prick."

"Whatever. You gonna take our girl's anal V card or what?"

"Tristan, please," Violet begs.

Eagerly, he untwists the top and squirts some of the lube onto his fingers.

"Oh fuck," Violet gasps when he presses his fingers against her ass.

"Am I gonna be the first one in here, baby girl?"

Her cry of agreement rings out around us as Tristan finishes his question by pushing into her tight hole.

"Thought it was only right you get to claim a first too," I taunt.

Tristan ignores me as he pumps his fingers deeper.

"Fuck. She's so fucking tight," I groan as his invasion of her body causes her pussy to contract.

"Tristan. Knox," she cries as we both fuck her slow and deep.

"Tell Tristan what you want, Firefly."

# 44

## VIOLET

My head spins, my nerve endings sparking with pleasure as Tristan stretches my ass in preparation for his dick.

"Fuck, what are you thinking about, Firefly? You just gushed around my cock."

"Tristan, I want you inside me."

I've never done anal before, and fuck am I glad I haven't, because this right now... it's everything.

Knox was right the other day. He stole one—most—of my firsts, and Tristan certainly deserves this one.

"Jesus. You sure, baby girl?"

"Tristan," I whimper when Knox circles his hips, hitting that deep place inside me that makes me see stars.

"Shit," he hisses, pulling his fingers free.

"Come here, Firefly," Knox says, reaching up and wrapping his hand around the back of my neck and dragging me down against his chest. "Give Tris some space."

His lips find mine and he kisses me, as the squelch of lube behind me lets us know that Tristan is taking my demands seriously.

"Relax, yeah?" Knox urges as Tristan's hand skims up my

spine before wrapping his hand around the back of my neck and nudging the head of his cock against my ass.

"If this is too much, tell me and I'll—"

"Tristan," I bark impatiently, arching my back and offering myself up to him as much as I can with Knox's dick deep in my pussy.

"Fuck. Shit," he groans as he pushes inside me.

"Tristan," I scream as my body fights to adjust to his size.

"Oh shit. Fuck. So fucking tight," Knox joins in as Tristan keeps going, pushing into me slowly until he's fully seated.

"Oh my God, that's—"

"Fucking incredible?" Tristan groans.

"Mind-blowing," Knox adds. "Move, Tris. She can take it."

"Please," I whimper, desperate to feel them bring me to ruin. To forget everything that's happened tonight and just focus on them. On how incredible it is when the three of us come together.

Knox thrusts up into my pussy, and the second he pulls out a little, Tris thrusts forward.

"Oh my God. Oh my God," I chant as they embark on a rhythm that makes my head spin and my body sing.

I'm so fucking full of them, almost too full, but at the same time, it's nowhere near enough.

"Yes," I cry as Tristan wraps his fist around the length of my hair and pulls me up from Knox's chest, changing the angle and making it even better.

"Holy shit," I gasp. "This is—"

"Heaven, baby girl," Tristan forces out before crashing his lips to mine in a wet and dirty kiss that only makes me fly higher.

A loud groan rips from my throat when Knox presses his thumb to my clit.

"Don't you dare swallow her scream when she falls for us, asshole," Knox warns Tristan as my release surges forward.

"Nah, she's going to scream our names so loud the rest of

the building will hear her, isn't that right, baby girl?" he growls, his lips brushing over my ear.

"Yes. Yes."

They up their pace, sensing that I need that little more, and with only three more thrusts from each of them, I throw myself over the edge, free-falling for long, blissful minutes as they drag every single ounce of pleasure out of me.

"Fuck, Violet. Fuck," Tristan grunts as I come back to myself, his cock jerking deep in my ass and filling me up as Knox groans.

"Fuck, I can feel that."

"Violet, fuck. I love you. Fuck. I fucking love you."

My chest heaves and my heart swells as I fall back into him, melting into his kiss as Knox barks out his own release.

Finding his hand, I twist our fingers together before releasing Tristan and falling over Knox to kiss him as Tristan pulls out of me and collapses onto the bed.

Despite just shooting his load inside me, Knox's cock barely softens, and when I finally release his lips and fall onto the mattress in a sweaty, sated heap between them, little aftershocks shoot around my body.

"No," he complains. "I need to go again."

"Fucking born again virgin," Tristan mutters, twisting into my body and wrapping his arm around my waist, dropping a kiss on my shoulder.

"It's always been like this with my girl. Ain't that right, baby?" Knox asks, also rolling my way, twisting his leg with mine and peppering kisses along my jaw.

"Mmmm... a girl could get used to this," I murmur as they lave me with attention.

"You don't need to get used to it," Knox confesses. "You can have it every day if you want it. I'm yours, Firefly. I always have been, and I'll be here as long as you'll have me."

Heat floods through my veins and my pussy contracts,

desperate to feel one of them inside me again despite the mind-blowing orgasms they just gave me.

They turn me into a shameless whore. And quite honestly, I am fucking here for it.

"Tris?" Knox nudges, kicking him in the shin when he doesn't say anything.

Twisting around, I look over at him with concern twisting up my insides. If he's regretting what we just did then—

My fears diminish the second my eyes find his. Love and adoration ooze from them.

"I'm yours, Violet," he says, his voice thick with emotion. "We're both yours, if you'll still have us."

My brows pinch as I rack my brain for why I might not want them. It takes a couple of seconds for everything to come back to me, but when it does, the memories and pain slam into me like a truck.

"Fuck," I breathe, collapsing back onto the bed and squeezing my eyes closed. Although, I regret that instantly when the image of Roman and his scars fills my mind.

"What happened, baby girl? What did he say?"

I suck in a shaky breath, not wanting to relive it all again, but knowing that I'm going to have to.

"He told me that you both knew it was him, th-that you... that you covered for him all this time."

They share a look over my head, the strength of their old friendship coming back full force.

Tristan cups my cheek, forcing me to look at him.

"You'd already lost too much. We knew that the second Knox got you out. It would have been a miracle if your mom got out too.

"We didn't want you to lose Roman too. We, somewhat stupidly, thought that the shock of what happened might be enough to drag him from the destructive path he was on and give him some kind of focus."

"You needed him, and we hoped that might be enough," Knox adds.

"We were wrong," Tristan surmises, unnecessarily.

"But you took the fall. You ruined your life because of him," I say, twisting to Knox, searching his eyes and seeing nothing but love there.

"No, Firefly. Because of you."

"Th-that's—"

"I'm sorry, Violet. We fucked up. All of us. But we truly thought that Roman would pull his head out of his ass and be what you needed. He loved you so much but—"

"He was already too far gone," I say sadly. "You should see his arms. He... he's been in a really bad place."

When I look back at Tristan, I find his jaw is ticking with frustration.

"What?"

"Shit, Pip. I just—"

"Just tell me. It can't get any worse than what I'm currently dealing with."

He lets out a pained sigh and rips his eyes from me. "I'm glad, that's all. It's awful and makes me a terrible person, but after the way he promised to return and be there for you, I'm glad his life hasn't been all sunshine and roses. Not when you've been fighting every day to try and move past it all."

Silence falls around us at Tristan's confession.

No one speaks for the longest time and I just lie there, soaking up their strength and support while fighting not to drown. The things Roman told me are enough to haunt me, and I know that he only touched on the least painful part of his time since he left Maddison County.

"Are you angry at us, Firefly?" Knox asks hesitantly, breaking the silence.

I suck in a breath. I should be angry with them. I should be furious at them for keeping that huge secret from me.

But what's the point?

What's done is done. No amount of anger will bring Mom back. It won't stop Roman from falling so deep into his addiction that at times he thought the only way out was death. It won't stop Knox's time in prison haunting him for the rest of his life. And it won't do anything for any of our regrets. It won't take the pain away.

"Honestly?" I ask quietly.

"Always honestly, Pip. That's the only way this will work."

"No more secrets," Knox promises. "And no more trying to be God in the hope of protecting those we love. Especially when we know that she's strong enough to deal with everything that can be thrown at her."

"Okay then. Honestly..." I say, sitting up and turning around so I can look at both of them. They both stare back at me anxiously, waiting to hear my thoughts on all this. "I'm tired of hurting, I'm tired of always looking back and wondering 'what-if.' I want to look forward, make a future that's not shadowed with the pain and loss of my past. Roman is alive, and he's doing well. And I've got you two." I take their hands in mine and squeeze. "Yeah, you fucked up. It was naïve and misguided, but I understand. It was a decision made out of love and I get that, b-because... I love you too, both of you. So fucking much that I wonder if I'm actually losing my mind. But there it is."

"Shit, Pip," Tristan gasps, sitting forward so fast it actually startles me. "I love you," he whispers before claiming my lips as Knox's arm snakes around my waist, waiting to steal his time with me.

When it doesn't come fast enough, he grips my hair and physically pulls me from Tristan's lips.

"I love you too, Firefly. I always have."

His kiss is all consuming, and add in Tristan's roaming hands and I fall under their spell way faster than I probably should.

"S-so," I stutter, pulling back from Knox's kiss to look

between them. "Does that mean we're really doing this? The three of us?"

"Yeah, baby girl. I think we're really doing this."

"And there I was, thinking you didn't want a label."

Tristan smiles at me. "It didn't feel right before. And it turns out that was because someone was missing. I just didn't know this fuck already owned half of your heart."

"Don't worry, I was trying to forget about that back then, too. Hey," I squeal when Knox tickles my ribs.

"You couldn't forget about me even if you tried, Firefly," he teases.

"Sadly, that's true."

"Holy shit," Tristan suddenly gasps, making our amusement falter as he stares down at— "It's a firefly. You've got a fucking firefly tattooed on your cock."

Knox barks out a laugh while I follow Tristan's line of sight and take in Knox's impressive, inked-up dick. Fully hard, obviously.

"Hell yeah. My firefly took ownership of my heart and dick long before she even realized it. It only felt right to have a permanent reminder while she couldn't be there with me."

"You're fucking certifiable," Tristan scoffs, although still staring.

"Dude, I know it's pretty and all, but shit. If you're that enthralled, at least show it some appreciation with a quick suck."

"Jesus, Knox. I said I'd put up with you, not that I'll go anywhere near you," Tristan mutters, finally ripping his eyes from Knox's dick.

"You just don't want firsthand experience of how much bigger it is than yours. I can imagine your disappointment when you wrap your hand around your skinny girth after having a handful of mine."

"You motherfucking—"

"Children, please," I say with a laugh, although, quite

honestly, they are more than welcome to continue this little alpha macho argument while both of them are naked for as long as they want. I could just do with some popcorn for the show.

The thought of popcorn makes my stomach growl loudly, and it distracts the guys from their dick measuring.

"Hungry, baby?"

"Yeah, I need a shower and food."

"Now that, we can do. Knox, go get the shower started. What do you want, Pip?" Tris asks, reaching down for his pants to grab his cell.

But my eyes once again fall to Knox's cock as he saunters past me to do as he's told.

"Food, Violet. Although, I don't think either of us will have any issues with you swallowing us before it arrives."

I scoot closer to him, trailing one fingertip down his chest.

"If you want me to suck your cock, Carver, all you've got to do is ask. I'm all about equal opportunities."

"Let me clean up and you're on. I might even be willing to share again."

The image of them both standing before me, hard and proud fills my mind as the remnants from our previous session continue to run from me, coating my thighs.

"Fuck it, I'll order after." Throwing his cell to the bed, he grabs my hand and drags me toward the bathroom, shoving Knox into the shower. He's not expecting it and stumbles, slamming straight into the wall.

"What the fu—"

"Violet wants to suck our cocks," Tristan barks as if it makes up for the extra bruising he just caused to Knox's face.

"Uh..." He looks from Tristan's excited eyes to mine. A smile curls at my lips and his eyes drop to it before dipping lower and taking in my naked body. "Is that right, Firefly?"

I swallow before licking my lips.

"You'd better get on your fucking knees then, baby."

# 45

## KNOX

I woke when Tristan's irritating fucking alarm went off this morning, but I didn't wake up for an early morning chat. Instead, I reached out for Violet and tucked her into my body, seeing as that asshole had stolen her away from me.

"I've got her," I mumble, although honestly, I've no idea if it came out as anything more than an exhausted groan.

He must have been happy with whatever he heard because he quickly disappeared—well, that or I passed back out with Violet's soft body curled against mine and her sweet scent in my nose.

Heaven.

Fucking heaven.

I swear only a couple of seconds pass before another fucking alarm is going off.

I've had five years of early rude awakenings. I am more than ready for a few lazy lie-ins with my girl with nothing to do or nowhere to go. Seems life isn't that fucking fair.

Or maybe it is, I realize, when Violet reaches over me for her cell and kills off the incessant music before snuggling back into my side, resting her head on my chest and holding me tight.

I stare down at her beautiful face and messy hair, my heart pounding beneath her cheek.

There were so many times over the last few years when I didn't think I'd ever get this chance again that being here now is the biggest headfuck there is.

"Stop thinking so hard. Go back to sleep," she murmurs, her voice rough from slumber.

"Don't you have class?" I ask, trying desperately hard not to be as selfish, as much I really want to be.

"Not going. Staying here." She holds me tighter and presses a kiss to my pec.

"Fuck, baby."

"Yeah, we can totally do that too," she agrees, making me chuckle.

"Firefly, I—"

"Shhh." Her hand lifts, her fingers pressing against my lips to stop any other words from coming out.

When she's confident that she's won, she tugs her arm back down and wraps it around my waist.

"I could get used to this, Firefly," I confess, sinking a little lower in bed and fully entwining our bodies.

Surprisingly quickly, Violet's breathing evens out as she drifts back off to sleep, but I'm not that lucky and find myself lying there, watching her sleep until I can't ignore my need for a piss any longer.

Trying my best not to wake her, I untwist my body from hers and slip out of bed.

Glancing at my pile of discarded clothes on the floor, I almost reach for my boxers to cover up, but then I think, *Fuck it*. We more than christened Tristan's apartment last night, and he's had more than a good look at my dick, so why shouldn't I let it all hang out here as if it's my own place?

With a smirk on my lips, more than aware that I've

basically just moved myself in, I pad toward the bathroom to do my thing.

Violet is still out of it when I return so I slip out of the room in favor of coffee that she's no doubt going to want when she does wake again.

The second I step out in the hallway, the closed doors catch my eye and I can't help myself but have a snoop.

The first one I open reveals probably the most lavish bathroom and the biggest tub I've ever seen. Images of Violet sitting in it surrounded by bubbles fills my mind. I'm pretty sure I'd even fit in there with her. That thought steers my fantasy in a whole other direction. I wonder just how pissed Tristan would be if we flooded the room while she rode me in there.

My teeth sink into my bottom lip as I consider the mess it could make and my cock jerks. Fuck what Tristan thinks, his wrath would be totally worth it.

Closing the door—for now—I continue my exploration, but I quickly discover only disappointment greets me when I open the final two doors and find mostly empty rooms. One has unpacked boxes inside, but that's it. One thing is for sure though, Tristan definitely has room for all three of us. And I'd sure prefer to just stay here than have to find a place of my own and what... share Violet with him like we're divorced parents with shared custody of the kids? No fucking thank you. I want to be right where my girl is, and if that means I have to force myself on him too, well that's just something he's going to have to deal with, because nothing short of death is going to rip me from my girl now.

Finally, with two mugs of coffee in my hands, I head back to Violet, and when I turn the corner, I find her sitting up with the sheets clutched to her chest, watching me with sleepy yet heated eyes as I walk around the bed naked. My cock instantly hardens, knowing she's bare beneath those sheets.

"Is that for me?" she asks, lust dripping from every word as her eyes move from mine to the mugs and then down to my dick.

"All of it's yours, baby. Which would you like first?"

"Mmm... I think I'm going to have to take the coffee first."

"Saving the best for last, I like your style," I tease, passing her a mug and placing the other on the nightstand so I can crawl back into bed with her.

"Tristan has good coffee," she breathes after blowing across the steaming liquid and taking a cautious sip.

"He always was a snob," I deadpan, making her laugh.

"He is not," she argues.

"Yeah, well, I guess not everyone can grow up somewhere as... unique as Harrow Creek."

Her humor fades off into nothing, the atmosphere around us changing. We didn't push her to talk last night, and I think she was grateful for that after the evening she'd had, but that didn't mean we weren't desperate to hear every detail of her time with Roman.

"Whatever you want to say, I'm listening, baby," I say, intertwining our fingers as she continues to stare at the wall ahead of us.

"I— I've got a niece."

"What?" I blurt. Of all the things I thought she was going to say, that wasn't it.

"Roman, he's... he's got a little girl. A baby."

"Oh shit, really?"

"Yeah. I think he's really turned it around. Said he met his girlfriend at a rehab group."

"She an addict too?"

She pauses for a beat. "I don't know, he didn't say. I mean, yeah, I guess maybe she is, was... What?" she asks when she looks up at me. "Why do you look so scared?"

I shake my head, forcing a smile onto my face. "Just the reality that we're old enough to look after a kid. Kinda hit me upside the head."

"You're nearly twenty-three. I hate to break it to you, Knox, but you're an adult."

"I guess I am. It's just easy to forget that the last five years happened and pretend I'm still seventeen."

"If only we could get a do-over," she mutters quietly.

"If you could, would you take it and risk not being here right now?"

Her lips part but no words come out.

"I know the past few years have been hard. Trust me, I do. But imagine all that didn't happen and we ended up on different paths, that we didn't get this chance now." My heart aches at the prospect alone.

After a few seconds, she nods. "Everything happens for a reason, right?"

"So they say," I agree.

"Who exactly is they?" she muses before sipping her coffee.

"So what happens next? Are you going to see him again?"

"I don't know," she says honestly. "Right now, I have no idea what to do for the best. Everything inside me is all twisted up and confused. Standing in front of him, seeing him again, I realized just how much I missed him. But then I listened to everything he had to say, his confession about starting that fire, about killing Mom and ruining your life, and I was so angry. No, that doesn't even begin to describe how I felt. But then he talked a little about what he'd been through, and I started to learn how much he'd suffered, and then I just kinda felt bad for him.

"He's been through hell. But so have you. Hell, so have I. And it was all his fault."

"I'm not sure it's fair to say it was all on him. I never should have taken him to the Creek. I—"

"You weren't to know he had an addictive personality and that it would be the beginning of a series of events that would be entirely out of our control."

"But if I knew about the hit on my dad then—"

"Then what? You'd have done it yourself?"

"If it would have spared your mom and ruining all our lives then yes, in a heartbeat."

"Knox, you can't—"

"I can. My father wasn't a good person, Firefly. He was a gangster, and a brutal one at that. He brought me up to believe that violence was normal, that watching your father beat other men to death was okay. That running around that shithole we used to call a home pretending that he was God was okay."

"What was my mom thinking?" Violet breathes, shocked by my words.

"He wasn't always that man. Maybe he really wanted to get out, wanted to live a better life with your mom. He did seem to genuinely love her."

"Do you think he really thought he could get out and live happily ever after in the next town over?" Violet asks.

"I have no idea. Not finding out the truth about his intentions is one of the things I regret the most." I shrug, reaching for my coffee. "We'll never really know the truth. Everyone with all the answers is gone, leaving us behind to always wonder what-if."

"I'm sorry you felt you had to go through everything you did," she whispers into her mug.

"You've nothing to be sorry for. I'd give my life to keep you safe, to protect you. I—"

"No," she spits venomously. "No. You're never going to do anything like that again."

"But—"

"I get that you want to protect me, Knox. Hell, I want to protect you too. But if we're going to do this, then we need to be a team. We make decisions together, even the hard ones."

I nod, unable to argue with her when she looks at me with those pained yet determined eyes.

"I can handle the hard stuff."

Placing my mug down, I pluck hers from her fingers and put it next to mine before tugging her down the bed, making her squeal.

"I know you can, Firefly. You're the strongest person I know."

Before she gets a chance to respond, I capture her lips as I settle myself between her thighs.

The second my cock brushes her pussy, she arches for me, moaning into our kiss.

"Can't get enough of you, Firefly."

"Same," she groans, raking her nails across my back and sending a violent shudder of need racing down my spine. "Fuck me. Please."

"Whatever happened to my sweet and innocent little Violet?" I tease, kissing down her throat and skimming my hands down her sides.

"You happened, Knox. You corrupted me and shattered my heart."

I sit up instantly at her words and stare down at her. "Fuck, baby. I—"

Her fingers find my lips again, cutting off my words.

"I know, Knox. I know, and I get it. How about you just show me how good it is to have you back instead of dwelling on the past."

She pushes her fingers past my lips and I eagerly suck them into my mouth, sinking my teeth into her skin just enough to send a bolt of pain up her arm.

"Knox," she moans, just like I was expecting. Her hips grind in the hope of finding the friction I'm withholding from her.

"You're so beautiful, Firefly. You stole my breath when we were kids, but you fucking consume me now."

I press a kiss to the palm of her hand before making my way down her arm.

"I am fucking addicted to you. All I've thought about for

five years. Loved you since I was sixteen, and I was trying to make myself stay away, and I only love you more now. You're everything, Violet. Fucking everything, and I'm never ever letting you go again." All these confessions and more spill from my lips as I kiss down her body, taking my time to enjoy her, taste her, tease her.

"Knox, please," she moans when I brush my lips over the soft skin of her inner thigh.

"What do you need, baby?"

"Your mouth, Knox. Please, I— YES," she cries when I suck her clit into my mouth.

Her fingers twist in my hair, holding me in place as I lap at her juices.

"So wet for me, Firefly."

"Tristan fucked me before he left," she confesses.

The reality of that statement makes me pause long enough for her to look up, and her eyes burn into the top of my head.

"Problem?" she taunts as my brain tries to compute what the fuck is going on here.

Is there a problem?

Dipping lower, I lick up the length of her, forcing her to fall back and cry out.

"No problem," I state happily before spearing my tongue inside her just to prove a point.

Do I want to be eating Tristan's cum? No, not really. I certainly wouldn't do so straight from the source, but from Violet's cunt? Hell yeah.

"I was lying," she gasps out. "I didn't even hear him leave."

A smirk curls at my lips as pride for my girl's fire burns through me.

"Oh, you're going to pay for that, Firefly."

I attack her clit, giving her everything I have until she's right on the brink of release.

"Yes, yes, yes," she cries before... "No. Knox, what the fuck are you—"

"You're not the only one who can play dirty, baby."

"I-it was a joke."

"So is this," I say, flicking her clit lightly with my tongue. "Funny, isn't it?"

"Asshole."

"Every day of my life, Firefly. You love it."

I cut off her response by diving for her once again, bringing her right back to the edge once more before pulling back.

I do it over and over, loving how angry she gets every time I stop her from falling.

"I'm going to kill you," she growls, her grip on my hair so tight I wonder if she'll come away with a handful as she tries to drag me back to her once more.

"There's only one place you're coming right now, Firefly," I tell her, slipping out of her hold and sitting up on my knees.

With my hands on her waist, I flip her and drag her up onto all fours.

*Crack.*

My palm collides with her ass, making her howl.

"And that is on my cock."

Before she has a chance to process those words, I push inside her.

She's dripping from my mouth, so I fill her to the hilt instantly, making her cry out again.

My hand massages her ass cheek as I pause for a beat before I bring it down again and begin to fuck her.

Skimming my hand up her spine, I twist my fingers in her hair, pushing her face into the pillow as I slam inside her.

The only sounds that can be heard are her whimpers, my heaving breaths, and our heated skin colliding with every powerful thrust I deliver.

That is, until a door slams and footsteps race in our direction.

If she hears then she doesn't care we're about to have an audience, and to be fair, nor do I.

"Motherfucker. I should have fucking known," Tristan barks the second he rushes into the room.

"Good timing, bro," I tease, not bothering to look over at him.

"Tristan," Violet moans, noticing our guest behind me. Stretching out her arm, she reaches for him.

"I-I-I forgot my—"

I circle my hips, ensuring I hit Violet's G-spot, and she cries out.

"Shit," Tristan grunts.

"Tris, please.

"I don't have time, baby girl."

"I want you in my mouth," she begs.

Finally, I glance over my shoulder, and apparently, the expression on my face says everything my mouth doesn't.

"What? I can't just—" I quirk a brow. "Fuck. Fuck. Fuck it. All your fault when I fail, Bowman," he mutters as his bag hits the floor with a loud thud and he marches over, ripping open his jeans and shoving them over his hips.

A low chuckle rumbles deep in my chest, but Tristan doesn't miss it.

"What?" he snaps, wrapping his fingers around his length and moving closer to our girl.

"I do hope your self-control is better in other aspects of your life," I tease.

"Fuck you. Like you could ever say no to our girl."

"I wouldn't have even tried. I'd already be inside her."

He narrows his eyes, but I help him out by releasing my grip on Violet and allowing her to push up onto her hands and knees.

"Make it quick, Firefly. Tristan has other places to be."

"Asshole," he hisses, but anything else he might want to say is quickly cut off when Violet wraps her lips around him. "Fuuuuck."

"That's it, baby. Make Tris forget about the stick that's

shoved up his ass. Show him that it's okay to break the rules every now and then."

He shoots me a look, but he says nothing as Violet takes him to the back of her throat.

I slow my thrusts as she works him, but while I might tease Tristan about his lack of self-control, when it comes to Violet, mine is non-existent and I find my speed increasing in only a few minutes.

She moans around his length, her hips pushing back against me for more.

"Our girl's desperate, Tris. Been edging her for teasing me. Should I let her come?"

His eyes flash with dark intent.

"Not until I've come down her throat."

Violet tenses between us, but she doesn't release Tristan's cock to complain. Instead, she just takes him deeper. His eyes roll back in his head as he grips her hair. His hips begin to move as he fucks her and my balls ache with my need to let go.

"Do you know how fucking sexy you look right now, Firefly? Taking both of us like a bad, bad little girl."

A moan vibrates through her, making Tristan grit his teeth,

"He's close, baby. You're gonna make Tristan blow like a twelfth grader peeping in on the girls' locker room."

"I never did that," he grits out, making me laugh.

"Sure you didn't," I tease.

"Fuck, baby girl. You suck me so good," he groans, forcing her to take him deeper.

Reaching out, he wipes her cheek, collecting up the tears that I assume are streaming.

"Fuck, I bet she looks hot as hell right now."

"You've no fucking idea, man," Tristan says, his voice full of awe and rough with need as he stares down at her. "I love you, Violet. I love you so fucking— fuck," he groans as his body stills and he comes down her throat.

Violet doesn't pull back until he's spent, and when she

does, she licks at the head of his cock, cleaning him up and taking every drop of his cum for herself.

"Fuck, Firefly," I groan, my own cock leaking as I bottom out inside her.

"My turn," she begs, shooting me a pleading look over her shoulder.

"So bossy. Sit down, Tris. Let me show you how it's done."

His eyes flash with indignation and the need to argue. But wisely, he drags his chair over and falls back into it, his pants still around his thighs and his semi on display.

"Go on then. Let's see if you can make her scream as loud as I can," he taunts, his fingers wrapping around his dick again as he watches our girl.

"Come on then, Firefly," I growl, dragging her up so she's facing him. "Let's give the audience a good show. Fuck," I grunt. "She just gushed around my cock."

"You like that, baby girl? You like me watching Knox fuck you?"

"Yes," she breathes as she clamps down on my length, the change of position meaning I hit that spot that drives her crazy with every thrust.

"Play with those tits then, baby. Really give him something to watch as you come all over my cock."

Violet moans at the same time Tristan groans as if he's in pain the second she follows orders.

My hand that's not twisted up in her hair once more slips around her body to find her clit.

"You love this, don't you? Being a filthy little girl for us."

"Yes."

"Look how hard he is again for you already. You do that to us, Firefly. You've ensnared us in your web, enchanted us with your beauty, and fucking ruined us for anyone else."

"Holy shit," she pants.

"Damn, bro. That was... romantic as fuck."

"I'm not just a gangster."

"Knox," Violet cries, her body trembling for the release I've withheld from her.

"Let her go, Knox," Tristan demands.

"Yes, yes. Knox. Tristan. Fuck," she screams before her entire body convulses in my arms as her release rocks through her.

She squeezes down on my dick so hard, my own orgasm surges forward, but not before Tristan gets to his feet and climbs onto the bed with his dick still in hand.

His eyes meet mine and I read his intentions loud and clear.

"We fucking own you, Violet. You're ours."

"Ours," Tristan agrees as I thrust one more time and finally let go, growling out her name, filling her up as he comes over her tits.

"Fuck yeah," I pant.

Twisting her head to the side, I slam my lips down on hers before releasing her abruptly and allowing Tristan to do the same, because I'm a fucking team player like that.

He kisses her for long minutes while I slip out of her and grab a washcloth.

"I really need to get going," he says reluctantly. "Shouldn't you be in class?"

"I wasn't feeling it," Violet confesses, pulling back from him so I can wipe away the mess he made of her.

"You're coming to the game tonight though, yeah?" he asks, his expression softening.

"No need for the puppy dog eyes, Tris. We'll be there cheering you on."

"You missed your chance at cheering me on, asshole."

"It doesn't matter that you're not playing, Tris. The win will be just as epic," Violet tells him.

I watch his reaction, wondering how he's really coping with all of this. I'm pretty sure he told me that he'd be in the NFL on the first day I met him. I'd never experienced anyone with a dream as powerful as his. Hell, I still haven't. But I don't see any bitterness or regrets in his eyes.

"I know. I can't wait. I just want you there," he says, cupping Violet's face and giving her one more lingering kiss. "I guess your boyfriend can come too," he teases.

# 46

# VIOLET

"What. The. Fuck?"

Knox chuckles beside me as he pulls the car through a set of gates completely hidden from the road.

I thought he'd lost his mind when he turned off the side road and toward what looked like a hedge, but it turns out, I'm the idiot, because there is a fuck-off mansion behind those hidden gates that looks like it belongs to Satan himself.

I didn't want to come here when Knox first mentioned it, but then he suggested that I could wait at home and I thought better of it.

I didn't want to be alone, so I pulled up my big girl panties and agreed to go over the border into Harrow Creek.

It's somewhere I swore I'd never go after the fire, but then I guess I'd also sworn off Knox back then as well.

And now, everything is different again, and I figure that if Knox is going to be a part of my life again—which he is—then I need to find a way to come to terms with the fact that he's a Hawk, and that he'll always be a Hawk.

"It's something, right?"

"It's... I've never seen anything like it. It's... terrifying."

"It's all a façade. He's a huge fluffy teddy bear really," Knox deadpans.

I can't help but snort. "Oh yeah, I'll believe that when I see it."

"Okay, so that might be pushing it, but Reid isn't his father. He's a good person, a good businessman, and a solid friend. I wouldn't be here right now if it weren't for him."

"I know, I know. It's just—"

"His surname," Knox finishes for me. "Things are different now. And I promise you, we can trust him."

"I hope you're right," I whisper. "And I hope he doesn't steal you away from me again," I confess even quieter.

He reaches over and twists our fingers together as we get closer to the house of horrors. "That's never going to happen."

The door opens ominously as we pull to a stop, but no one appears.

"It's haunted, isn't it?"

Knox laughs again as if my fears are totally unfounded.

"Even if it is, it's daylight, and I'd never let a ghoul or goblin lay a finger on you."

"A goblin?" I ask in amusement.

"Yeah, right there, look." When I glance over, I find a guy now lingering in the doorway. He looks about the same age as us, but just like Knox, he has an air of danger around him.

"Julian, my man. Meet my girl."

The guy's handsome face twists in anger, making him appear even more deadly. But then it morphs into a smirk.

"Oh, look who's all brave and shit with his girl in tow," he teases.

Knox laughs, and it sends a rush of tingles through me.

I used to see him hanging out with Roman and Tristan often, but I never saw him with his friends back home, and even from here, I can sense the connection between them.

It makes all of this a little bit easier and helps me to think that he might be right. That just because they've all got the same tattoo spread across their backs and have probably seen more blood than I'd like to in a lifetime, it doesn't mean they're bad people.

"Violet this is Ju—"

"JD. The name's JD, darlin'. Don't go listening to any of the bullshit this prick here tries to tell you."

"Uh... okay. It's nice to meet you."

"Bro, what have you been saying to your girl about me? She's terrified," he says with a wide smile.

I can't help but swallow roughly as I consider if he's just teasing or not, because I'm trying really fucking hard not to make it look like I want to bolt should Knox release my hand.

"I haven't told her anything but the truth."

"Damn, you should hold some of that back until she gets to judge for herself. Honestly, Violet, I'm as soft as a bear."

"I thought that was Reid," I deadpan, making his eyes widen before he barks out a laugh loud enough to echo through the entire building.

"Oh, bro, I like this one," he says, clapping Knox on the shoulder. "Come on. Boss is making coffee. You wouldn't want to miss witnessing him being all domesticated and shit."

"It's been a while since I've seen him work his magic in the kitchen," Knox confesses, pressing his hand to the small of my back and urging me forward.

Reid cooks? Well, if this trip isn't full of mind-boggling information.

And the headfuck doesn't stop there, because after walking through the colossal front door, I find that the house inside is really quite normal. I'm not entirely sure what I was expecting. Maybe floor-to-ceiling black and skeletons hanging in every corner. But the reality is, it's just a home.

"Hey," Knox says the second we follow JD into a huge kitchen. "How's it going?"

Now, I've seen photographs of Reid over the years. I've even seen him in real life a couple of times when he's been in Maddison

County visiting Kane. But nothing could have prepared me for seeing him in his own home, in his own kitchen looking relaxed and... happy. I didn't think that was an emotion he ever felt.

I stand there staring as their deep, rumbling voices float around me, but I don't hear any of the words as all the stereotypes I've been clinging onto when it comes to Reid Harris and everything he represents begin to fall away, shattering at my feet.

My skin tingles as they all stare at me, but I can't drag myself out of my frozen state.

"Uh, Knox, is your girl okay?" Reid asks before walking over to the refrigerator and pulling out a carton of cream.

My eyes drop down his body. He's wearing a white wifebeater and gray sweats. It's so relaxed and normal. Like he's just one of the guys.

It makes me realize just how much of a monster I've made him out to be in my head. It's his father's fault, I know that, but I still tarnished him with the same brush.

"Vi, you okay, baby?" Knox asks, cupping my cheek and dragging my eyes to him.

"Y-yeah, I-I just... Is there a bathroom I could use at all?"

I sense Knox and Reid have a silent conversation over my head before Knox leads me from the room and farther down the hallway.

He guides me into a modest bathroom before closing the door on us.

"Firefly?" he asks, ducking down to look into my eyes. "Are you okay?"

I blink at him a couple of times, my head spinning. "Yeah. Sorry, I'm good."

He frowns at me, and I hate the confusion I see in the depths of his eyes.

"This was a bad idea. We should go."

"N-no, it's okay."

"No, it was stupid of me to think this was okay after only seeing Roman yesterday. I know how much you hate all of this, I—"

"Knox, stop," I say, running my hands up his chest and linking them behind his neck. "They—Reid—just shocked me, that's all. He's so... normal. Inside here is so..."

"They're good guys. No different from me or Kane, maybe even Micah, if you ever discover what's really going on there. They're just closer to the action, have a bigger part in making the decisions."

"Yeah, you're right. I just wasn't really expecting to walk into a home."

Knox lowers his head, resting his brow against mine.

"I love you, Firefly," he breathes. There's so much emotion in those four words, it makes my chest ache in the best possible way.

"I love you too. Now, shall we try all of that again? I want to meet your friends."

"Yeah?" he asks, his eyes brightening at my suggestion.

"Yeah."

He smiles down at me before dropping a chaste kiss on my lips, twisting our fingers together and tugging me back out of the bathroom.

Both Reid and JD watch us closely as we return.

"Sorry about that, I—"

"Forget it," Reid says. "You want cream in your coffee?"

"Yes, please," I say, smiling at him, still utterly confused by the enigma that is the Hawks leader.

"Where's your girl?" Knox asks. "I'm starting to think you're making her up."

"She's out with Mav."

Knox looks between the two of them suspiciously. "Are you sure it's not just a cover and the two of you are really hooking up?"

Not expecting Knox's accusation, Reid sprays coffee all over his pristine kitchen.

"No, we're really fucking not," he argues.

"Your loss. I'd be the best you ever had, and you know it," JD teases.

I look between the three of them with a smile on my lips.

Yeah, maybe they're not actually that bad.

"Anyway," Reid says, gesturing toward the couches on the other side of the room.

"Anything from the Ravens or the Devils?" Knox asks the second our asses hit the cushions.

Reid glances at me, silently asking if I want to be involved in this, and I just nod.

Seems a little late to back out now I've accepted that my future is at Knox's side. Like it or not, this is my life now just as much as it is theirs.

"Everything is suspiciously quiet, but we've got eyes on them. You don't need to worry."

Knox remains tense beside me. "I'm not sure if that's reassuring or not."

"Bro, seriously. I know you're in, I've never doubted that. But take as much time as you need. Enjoy your girl, your freedom. We'll always be here, and if we need you, we'll call you."

"I'm not sure how much use I am these days," Knox mutters, allowing his friends to see just a little bit of his vulnerability.

"You'll figure it out. We've got your back."

Finally, Knox sits back and throws his arm around my shoulder.

"So, are you heading to the game tonight?" he asks.

"You know it. Need to see our boy in action. They're going to kill it this year," Reid says, looking oddly excited for someone I never thought would care about college football.

And just like that, all talk of gangs and vendettas and

whatever else they do is forgotten, and I may as well just be hanging out with the guys in our old dorm.

A strong wave of nostalgia hits me as I think about our little family. I still haven't heard anything about our house. But even if Micah were to say it's ready, I can't imagine moving back in.

I've found a new home now. No, more than a home. A future. One that I have zero intention of walking away from.

---

We stayed at Reid's place for a couple of hours before heading back out. I thought we were heading back home, but Knox quickly announced that we had two other stops to make.

And that was how I ended up spending time with all of the ominous Harris brothers in one day.

I knew Ellis fairly well from all the time he's spent at our place over the last couple of years hanging out with Micah, but I've never had anything to do with the rest of them.

When we left, Knox was carrying a couple of duffel bags, and instead of getting into Devin's car, I found an Uber waiting for us.

He took us straight to the shop Knox had bought his new car from, and after grabbing the keys, he threw everything he owned in the world in the back and we headed for home. Okay, so technically it's Tristan's home, but something tells me he's going to have a hard job getting rid of the two of us now.

"Have you warned him about this?" I ask as Knox dumps his bags on the bed and pulls open Tristan's closet as if he's about to make a third of it his own.

"No, why would I do that? He said he's all in, baby. This is what that means."

He looks so serious as he says it that I can't help but laugh. "Still think you should have mentioned it."

"Fine, I'll tell him tonight," he concedes.

"You'd better hope they win," I tease. "You might totally ruin his night."

Knox is on me before I even realize he's moved. He sweeps me off my feet and places my ass on Tristan's desk.

"Nah, he loves me really."

"Sure. And anyway, what's the alternative? Do you really want me living elsewhere?"

Resting my arms over his shoulders, I look up at him, studying every inch of his face.

"Nope. I want you right here. Both of you."

"So that's it, then. Tristan will just have to share his place as well as his girl."

"Everyone is going to think we're crazy, you know that right?"

"Baby, I really don't give a fuck what anyone else thinks. All I've wanted from the first day I laid eyes on you was you. You're it for me, Firefly. I'd put a ring on it right now if I could and seal the deal."

"Jesus, Knox," I gasp.

"I want it all with you, Violet. I want to make up for lost time and never stop."

"Can't argue with that," I confess, reaching up to claim his lips, desperate to spend the rest of the time we have alone doing exactly what he just suggested.

---

"What time do you call this?" Ella barks when we finally get to the Panthers' stadium for tonight's game.

"Sorry, sorry. We were... distracted."

She rolls her eyes at me before glancing back at Knox over my shoulder.

"Sure you were," she drawls.

"What did we miss?" I ask, watching the guys down on the field as they get into place, ready for the game to start.

"Not a lot. Pretty sure Tristan has been looking for you, though."

"Shit," I hiss, guilt washing through me that I was so consumed by Knox that we missed even a second of tonight. I know how badly he wanted us here.

I scan the sidelines where the coaches are all congregated and my heart flips over in my chest when I spot him in a heated discussion with another guy.

"We're here now, Firefly," Knox murmurs, stepping closer and tugging me into his body. "And I'm sure you can make it up to him later."

"Not the point," I sulk, hating that I might have let him down for even a second when all he's done is support me.

I keep my eyes on him, begging him to look up and see that we're here, but he's still too lost, the discussion seeming to get more heated.

"That guy is a jerk," Knox mutters.

"Who is it?"

"The other GA. Had the pleasure of meeting him last night when I went to the training facility to see if you were just hiding under Tristan's desk, giving him a blow job."

Ripping my eyes from Tristan, I stare up at Knox in disbelief.

"Tell me you didn't really think that was where I was?"

"It was the best option I could come up with."

"Jesus."

"Anyway, the guy was a prick. Pretty sure he's just jealous. If you look closely, you'll see a black eye, courtesy of yours truly."

"You didn't," I gasp.

"You would have too if you heard the way he spoke to Tris," Knox says as if it's the simplest thing in the world.

Turning my attention back to Tristan, I watch as he throws his hands up in frustration but finally turns away from the guy, his eyes jumping straight to where we are.

His entire expression changes the second his eyes land on me. My blood instantly heats under his intense stare as his lips curl up in a smile.

Lifting my hand, I give him a little girly wave that makes his smile even wider.

"See, all he needed was his girl," Knox murmurs.

'Good luck,' I mouth.

'I love you,' he mouths back.

"Oh, be still my beating heart," Knox teases.

"Shut the fuck up," I bark, making him laugh as the whistle is blown for the start of the game.

My eyes shoot around the field, finding Brax and West, and then Luca, Leon, and Kane, and my heart swells as I watch them all kill it in the first few minutes of the game while everyone around me screams encouragement.

Even Reid and JD throw themselves right in the middle of the excitement as we make our first touchdown, sending the entire crowd crazy.

# 47

## TRISTAN

The high from the win surges through me as I make my way toward the exit where all the crazed Panthers fans will be waiting for their beloved players, but it's nothing compared to the thrill of knowing that she's going to be waiting for me.

Whenever she came to see me play, whether it was here when I was a Panther and she was still in high school, or when I was a Titan, all I wanted to do after the rush of a win, hell, even the disappointment of a loss, was to walk out of the stadium and wrap my arms around her, lose myself in her.

And this time, I can.

I'm not sure I've ever felt the level of disappointment I did when I looked up to where all her friends were waiting for the game to start, and she and Knox weren't there. It really wasn't what I needed as Winters continued to drone on about... whatever the fuck he was droning on about.

I forget about the fact almost everyone waiting on the other side of the double doors is anxiously awaiting the team and push through. I probably should have gone around the other side, but my need for my girl is too strong to wait any longer.

Those few minutes I had with her earlier when I popped home to grab some books were nowhere near enough. If anything, it was just a giant tease.

A roar of excitement goes up, but it quickly dies when they see me. It's a massive kick in the teeth. If I were still a Titan and emerged victorious from the locker room then...

No.

I slam that thought down, because it's not my reality anymore.

I'm here, and it's exactly where I'm meant to be.

Thankfully, there is one person who is as desperate to see me as I am her, and her small body collides with mine not a second later.

She jumps into my arms and wraps herself around me like a koala.

Tucking my face into her neck, I breathe her in, but her scent makes me laugh and confirms everything I already knew.

"What?" she asks.

"You were late, Pip," I point out.

"Uh... yeah, we lost track of time."

"Right well, you're mine tonight. He's stolen enough of you today."

"Mmm, I'm sure I can get on board with that," she murmurs, kissing my neck as I carry her away from the crowd and toward a smug-looking Knox standing on the outskirts.

"You're driving home alone," I tell him. "I'm taking Violet. If I'm lucky, she might give me a celebratory blow job on the way home."

"I'm sure it can be arranged," Violet whispers in my ear, tightening her legs around my waist as her pussy grinds against my quickly swelling length.

"I don't fucking think so," Knox barks, his voice getting all dark and dangerous. "I'll fucking kill you before you put her in danger like that."

"Whatever, Bowman. Like you'd turn down her mouth mid-drive."

His lips press together and his jaw tics as he considers my words.

In the end, he doesn't bother arguing. Instead, he steps up beside me, twists his fingers in Violet's hair and turns her to face him.

"Be a good girl, Firefly. We'd hate to leave you out of the surprise we've got planned."

She tenses in my arms. "Surprise?"

---

"Are you going to tell me yet?" Violet asks, just like she has all the way back from the stadium.

"Just get the hell in the car, Firefly," Knox barks, unmoving from the driver's seat of his new ride.

"Bossy asshole," I mutter, throwing the bags that were in the trunk of mine into his instead.

"Wait, we're going somewhere?" Violet asks, watching me.

"For the whole weekend, baby girl. What do you say?"

"Just the three of us?"

"Just the three of us."

"I say it sounds like heaven," she breathes, her eyes getting a little glassy.

She might look okay, like she's dealing with everything, but I can see the shadows hiding deep in her eyes. I refuse to let her break, not again, and I know that the guy in the front of that Ford Mustang feels exactly the same.

This weekend is about proving to her that we're here for the good, the bad, and the ugly. That we'll strive to be everything she needs, even when she's not aware of what that is herself.

"Good. Now get in the back, you owe me a car blow job," I tease.

"Oh, hell fucking no. When I want my car christened, it'll be me who's blowing his load into our girl, not—"

"Shut the fuck up, Bowman. What did you really expect when you insisted on picking your car up today so you could drive?"

"I was expecting my girl to ride shotgun so I could finger her on the way."

"Well, sucks for you. I'll make sure she screams loud enough to ensure you know what you're missing, though."

Violet shrieks as I drag her into the back of the car with me and instantly place her on my lap.

"Tristan," she gasps when I tug her close enough that she has no choice but to feel how badly I need her.

"This skirt was a good choice tonight, Pip. Did you put it on with ideas of one of us making use of the easy access?"

"I fucking hate you."

"Nah, man. Don't hate the player, hate the game," I tease. "You've had her all day. Now, she's all mine."

"Surprised she's got any energy left," Knox teases as he pulls away so quickly we almost go crashing into the door.

"Be careful, asshole," I hiss, grazing my lips across Violet's jaw before tasting the sweet skin of her throat.

"Tris," she breathes, her hips rolling against me.

"How fucking long is this drive?"

"Plenty long enough to get what I need, and to ensure our girl gets hers a few times over."

Knox's unimpressed growl rips through the air before a low chuckle rumbles in my chest.

"You're mean," Violet whispers, although she doesn't even attempt to move.

"I walked in on him fucking you earlier. I think it's only fair."

"He let you join in," Violet points out.

"Oh, he's more than welcome to jerk off listening to you."

"You're wicked."

"For you, baby girl. Only for you. Now, let's see," I say, walking my fingers up her thigh. "Did you remember to put panties on under this skirt earlier?"

"Oh shit," Violet hisses the second my fingers collide with her bare skin.

"Fuck, baby girl. You really did come out looking for some fun tonight, huh?"

"Motherfucker," Knox barks.

"Rookie mistake there, Bowman. You should have checked on this situation hours ago. Snooze you lose, I guess."

"Tristan."

"Oh, and she's so fucking wet for me, aren't you, baby girl."

"It's me," Knox happily announces while Violet laughs as if they're having some private joke.

"Is that right, baby girl? Has Knox filled you up so well today that it's still dripping out of you?"

"Yes," she cries when I push two fingers deep inside her.

"You're a filthy, filthy little girl for walking around like this," I warn as their juices drip down my fingers.

"No," she moans when I suddenly rip them from her body and lift them to her lips in an offering.

"Here. Tell me how the two of you taste."

But unlike I'm expecting, her lips don't part.

My brow quirks.

"Are you being a naughty girl, Firefly?" Knox asks, his voice deep with lust as we head out of town and toward the mountains.

He refused to tell me what he'd booked for the weekend, and I've been too busy to really grill him about it. He told me to trust him, and that's all I can do. If he thinks it's good enough to help our girl get out of her own head this weekend, then I'm fully on board with his plan.

"I'll taste it off your tongue," she challenges, wicked intent filling her eyes.

Wrapping her fingers around my wrist, she lifts my hand toward my mouth.

Shock covers her face when my lips part and I lean forward, taking my fingers into my mouth.

"Oh shit," she gasps when I hold her eyes.

"Dude," Knox grunts.

"You taste like heaven, baby girl," I confess before twisting my fingers in her hair and dragging her lips to mine, letting her do what she suggested and licking deep into her mouth.

Grabbing her ass with my spare hand, I close the final bit of space between us, needing as much of her as I can get.

"Are you going to scream for us, Violet?" I ask when I eventually release her lips.

One quick glance out of the window tells me that I lost myself in my girl's kiss for way longer than I thought.

"You've got twenty minutes to make this the best journey of her life," Knox informs me.

"I thought you were against us christening your car?"

"I'm against you getting off in my car. I'm all for hearing my girl scream."

"Now that sounds like a challenge I can't refuse."

"And we all know you can't turn those down."

His eyes meet mine in the mirror, a silent question filling them.

"You tasted good, man," I say, "but don't get any ideas."

His eyes almost pop out of his head.

"What?" I ask, amusement filling my tone while Violet chuckles. "It was okay for you to rib me last night, but you can't take it back? I'm ashamed, man."

Knox shakes his head. "Just focus on the job at hand, yeah? You're down to fifteen minutes."

"You think it'll take me fifteen minutes to get her off?" I scoff.

"Prove me wrong," he taunts.

"All day fucking long," I promise.

---

"Violet," I whisper, thinking she's fallen asleep on my shoulder after the two mind-blowing orgasms I gave her only five minutes after Knox dished out my most recent challenge.

"I'm awake," she murmurs, nuzzling my neck.

"We're here, Firefly," Knox says softly.

Truth is, we've been here a while. To start with, I assumed Knox was waiting for her to notice, but then he never said anything, and nor did I.

It was nice. Peaceful.

Of course, it helped that we were surrounded by nothing but trees and a pretty sweet log cabin.

Color me impressed by his find.

After a beat, Violet sits up. Her eyes meet mine before she looks out of the window and sucks in a sharp breath.

"Where are we?" she asks.

"Nowhere. Want to get lost with us, Firefly?"

"Oh my God," she gasps, continuing to look around at our surroundings. "This is... wow."

"Ready to go explore?" I ask.

"More than ready." She scrambles off my lap, just about managing to miss kneeing me in the balls as she rushes for the door that Knox opens for her.

He sweeps her up into his arms and crushes his lips to hers, but she doesn't allow him to linger. Instead, she pushes him back and darts toward the front door of the cabin.

"Come on, losers," she calls as she collides with the front door that thankfully opens for her when she twists the handle. She disappears inside a second before the two of us take off after her.

"Holy shit," I gasp the moment we're inside and find that the entire back wall of the cabin is glass, allowing for almost panoramic views of a valley beyond. "How the hell did you find this?"

Ignoring me, Knox stalks forward and wraps his arm around Violet's shoulder where she's stopped just before the huge window, staring out to the vastness of nothing beyond.

I follow soon after, stepping up to her other side and wrapping my arm around her waist.

A contented yet pained sigh falls from her lips.

"Thank you," she whispers. "For everything."

# 48

# VIOLET

*Two months later...*

I stand in the middle of the kitchen, my version of the one Mom had installed all those years ago.

I might have modernized it when I had the place rebuilt, but I kept her essence here. It was her favorite room in the entire house, and I understand why: the huge windows that give incredible views of the gardens let so much light stream in.

A smile curls at my lips as I remember her sitting in this very window seat with a coffee and a book, watching Roman, Tristan, and me playing in the yard.

And just like back then, I have the crazy urge to make those exact memories but with my own young family.

When I originally decided to make this place my home once again, it wasn't with the intention of having a family of my own. I didn't even have a boyfriend back then. But since finding myself with two, my mind wanders to the future more often than it ever has.

Yes, it's still early days. We've only really been officially a throuple for a couple of months, but I've no doubt that this is it for us.

I don't think I have ever been as happy as I am when I'm with them. Either alone or together. Everything about the three of us is just... right.

Both of them continue to bicker at the most inappropriate times, and it brings a smile to my face every time, despite how exasperating they are.

I loved Knox when I was a kid, and I thought it was all-consuming and intense. I mean, it was. But what we have now. It's... it's everything.

He's hot-headed, irrational, adventurous, and spontaneous, mostly the opposite to Tristan, who is my rock. He's predictable—outside of the bedroom—reliable, strong. And together, they complete me in a way I never knew I was missing.

Everyone's reactions to us announcing our relationship has probably been one of the most amusing parts of all of this. Our friends, while thinking we're insane, have accepted it without question. Okay, no, not without question, they all had more than a few questions about how it works, mostly in the bedroom, and just how friendly Knox and Tristan actually are. I'm still yet to work out if people are relieved or disappointed when they explain that they're both here for my pleasure.

Tristan's parents were incredible when the three of us visited them. He was worried in the days running up to it, I could tell. But as ever, Mommy and Daddy Carver were cool and chilled out, and his mom just announced that as long as there was a way for her to still have grandbabies in the future, she didn't care who he was in love with. It was kinda perfect, and I'm sure the reaction that thousands of people wish for when they have to confess to a more-than-conventional way of life.

I continue sipping on my coffee, looking out at the yard

that's mostly covered in leaves that fall left behind, when voices and footsteps start moving my way.

My boys' laughter fills my heart so full, I swear that it'll explode one day. I listen to them joking around, butterflies erupting at the thought of seeing them as they close in on the kitchen. It's a feeling I really hope never leaves me.

I turn toward the door a second before they spill through it. They've spent the morning working out in the basement that Tristan has been turning into the gym of his dreams.

We might officially live in Tristan's apartment most of the time, but any weekend we can escape—or more so when Tristan can escape—we come out here so we can shut ourselves off from the rest of the world.

We finally got word via Micah that our house wasn't going to be habitable until at least the new year. Thankfully, the landlord let us out of our contract and they have all managed to find a new place for the four of them. Poor Ella is now in a house full of testosterone, not that she seems to care all that much.

Knox and Tristan's laughter trails off when their eyes land on me, and their happiness is replaced by concern.

"Are you sure about this? Tristan asks, a frown marring his brow.

"Yep," I say confidently.

It feels like I've spent every minute of the past eight weeks thinking about what to do for the best here, but in the end, I think there really is only one answer.

"That's good because I can hear a car," Knox says, stalking closer. "Last chance to change your mind, baby, and we'll go scare him off." The wicked sparkle in his eye tells me that he's not entirely joking.

"Nope. Pull up your big boy boxers. We're doing this."

I hop up and take Knox's face in my hands.

"You'll feel better once it's done," I assure him, aware that he's about as anxious about this meeting as I am.

"Come on, kids. Let's not keep our guests waiting. Ow, asshole," Tristan hisses when Knox punches him in the shoulder as he passes us.

"It's going to be just like old times, isn't it?" I mutter, taking Knox's hand and following Tristan through the house.

I pause for a moment as we walk down the hallway, looking at the photo that used to sit on my nightstand of Mom, Roman, and me all those years ago. It's surrounded by others from our past that Tristan's parents managed to dig out for us. Although looking at them hurts, they also remind me of something different every time I pass them, and that's something I never want to lose.

With one final look into Mom's eyes, I take off again as the doorbell rings through the house.

Tristan is already there, but he doesn't reach for the door. He waits for me.

"You've got this, Pip."

"And we've got your back, no matter what," Knox promises.

Blowing out a long breath, I reach for the door knob and twist.

My heart is in my throat as I pull it open, but the second my eyes land on a pair that mirror my own, I instantly relax. Despite all the unknowns between us, there will always be an inseverable connection between us.

But the second a small noise comes from someone else and I look down, I swear my heart literally explodes right there on my own doorstep.

"Roman," I breathe, emotion clogging my throat. "She's—"

"She looks just like you as a baby, Vi," he says, looking down at his daughter and then back up at me.

My mouth opens and closes but no words come out as I stare at the little bundle of pink in his arms.

After a few silent seconds, movement over his shoulder catches my attention, and when I look up, I find a pretty blonde standing there with a deep V between her brows as she watches this scene play out.

"Hi," I squeak like an idiot.

I have no idea what she sees on my face, but her expression immediately softens and a smile appears on her lips.

Without a word of warning, she ducks around Roman and throws her arms around me.

"It's so good to finally meet you," she whispers in my ear. "You've no idea how much he talks about you."

The lump in my throat only grows at her confession, and by the time she pulls back, my tears are barely holding onto my lashes.

The second my eyes collide with my big brother's again, a sob rips from my throat.

"Here," he says, holding my niece out toward me. "She's a great cuddler."

"Oh my God," I gasp, taking her from him and tucking her against my hip. "Hey, baby girl," I whisper, tears now freely cascading down my cheeks.

She smiles up at me as she reaches for a lock of my hair and I just melt.

"I guess you'd all better come in," Tristan says from beside me, reminding me that I'm currently being protected by my boys. His voice is deep and holds a warning I'm not used to hearing, but I can't deny that his protectiveness of me does things to my insides that are entirely inappropriate in front of my big brother.

Stepping back, I allow Roman and Imogen to enter.

Roman's eyes are everywhere as he walks in.

"Violet, this place is amazing," he breathes.

We've spoken since that night he stupidly decided to abduct me, but it's mostly been through messages and the odd call. But seeing him again is as surreal as it was that night—even more so with us back here.

"W-would you both like coffee or—"

"Coffee would be great, thank you," Imogen cuts me off.

"Come and help me make it?" Tristan says, giving her a reason to escape so that Roman, Knox and I can talk alone for a few minutes.

"Uh... sure." She turns to me. "Do you want me to—" I clutch her cute daughter closer, and she laughs. "Just shout if she starts causing trouble."

With a smile, she follows Tristan to the kitchen.

"Everything is in the same place," I tell Roman when he hovers like he doesn't know which direction to turn.

But even still, he doesn't make a move until I do.

I lead them both through to the living room, and the three of us stand there somewhat awkwardly as Roman focuses on the décor and furnishing over having to look at Knox.

Eventually, though, he finds some inner strength from somewhere, and finally, he turns and stares Knox dead in the eyes.

"I know it doesn't even come close to making everything okay, but... I'm sorry. I'm truly fucking sorry for everything I put you through."

Knox nods before wrapping his arm around my shoulder and dropping a kiss to my temple.

"I'd do it all over again in a heartbeat for this one," he confesses. "I just wish—" He cuts himself off and shakes his head. "So many things. But we're all here now, so... shall we try and start over? We've got a lifetime to live with our regrets and pain."

"Fucking hell." The breath Roman releases is so big, it makes me wonder if he's been holding it since he stepped over the threshold.

"Don't worry," Knox warns darkly. "I can kick your ass if it's what you really want. I have a gun right out in the hallway."

"N-no," Roman stutters, looking more than a little horrified. "I'm good with the whole starting over thing."

Lilly starts to wriggle in my arms and I walk her farther into the room and lower us to the rug in front of the fireplace.

"Here," Roman says, following us and dropping a bag to the floor beside me. "There are toys and things in there."

"Thank you."

I sit Lilly in front of me, hesitating when she wobbles a bit.

"She's okay," he assures me. "She's a strong little thing, just like her auntie."

"Damn it, Roman," I hiss when my tears start up again.

Knox moves over and takes the seat behind me, leaning forward to rest his hand on my shoulder supportively. If I were to look back, I've got a feeling that he'd be watching Roman very closely with a more-than-obvious threat in his eyes.

Knox might be saying all the right words to help bridge the gap between Roman and me, but it's going to take time for him to work through everything that's happened and be okay with this new version of my brother sitting before us. Hell, I'm not exactly expecting it to be a walk in the park for me, either.

But I want to do it.

I want him, Imogen, and Lilly Rose in my life.

They're my family, and having lost so much of that already, I want to hold on to everyone I can.

No one more so than my boys.

By the time Tristan and Imogen rejoin us with a trayful of coffee and cake, Lilly is giggling like a little demon on the rug as I tickle her pudgy belly and Roman and Knox are attempting to have a conversation about the Panthers' season, although it's strained at best.

Imogen takes the tray from Tristan when he pauses just inside the room and watches us with concern in his eyes.

"Come and meet Lilly," I say, knowing how good Tristan is with kids from seeing him with his own nieces and nephews.

He drops down beside me and takes over the tickling while Imogen watches us with love in her eyes.

I look up and our eyes collide. No words are said between us, but there is so much understanding.

'Thank you,' I mouth, needing her to know how grateful I am for everything she's done for Roman.

She shakes her head, a soft smile playing on her lips as she drops down beside my brother and places her hand on his thigh.

Happiness shines in both of their eyes, and it fixes one of the many cracks that have been left behind from that night.

"So Ro, have you been watching us this season?" Tristan says, picking up on his and Knox's previous conversation.

"Hell yeah, I have. Your boys are killing it. Going all the way this year, yeah?"

"I sure fucking hope so," Tristan says, grabbing a stuffy from Lilly's bag and teasing her with it.

Sitting back, I watch as my boys push aside everything that has happened in the past five years and attempt to work toward moving past it all. I don't want to say forgiving, because there is a chance that none of us will ever truly forgive Roman. But equally, I refuse to dwell on it.

All of us have experienced enough pain. It's time we found out if there really are any happily ever afters out there, and this house is going to be a home for the next generation.

# EPILOGUE

Violet

*Eighteen months later...*

"You know, I thought I'd feel a lot more glamorous than I do right now," I complain to Ella as I attempt to make the mortar board sit straight on my head.

"You look hot. Your boys are going to lose their shit when they see you."

"Oh shush, I might as well be wearing a garbage bag," I moan, pulling the shapeless fabric from my body.

"You have seen what it's hiding though, right? That dress is going to cause arguments," she teases.

Yeah, okay, so maybe I did buy the dress with the exposed zipper up the back with the idea of making my boys fight over who's going to get to pull it down later tonight.

"You're wicked," Ella teases, seeing my true intentions written all over my face.

"Whoever doesn't get the zipper can work on the bottom layer." I wiggle my eyebrows suggestively.

"That good?"

"That good."

"Fucking hell, I miss sex," Ella whines, flouncing down on the chair behind her where we're waiting to be called, ready to head out on stage to get our moment in the spotlight.

"From what I've heard, you've had more than a little action recently."

"Fucking boys," she moans. "I remember when we used to be the biggest gossips in our house."

"So what's really the issue?"

She folds her arms over her chest and pouts before mumbling something that I don't catch with the low rumble of other conversations flowing through the room.

"What was that?" I ask, moving closer.

"It's him, okay? It's always fucking him."

"Ella," I sigh, hating that she's still hurting over Colton fucking Rogers.

He entered the draft last spring and then went skipping off into the sunset a few months later.

Despite them never having anything serious, and her being adamant that it was fine, for the best even, we all knew she was lying.

Colt stole a piece of her heart long ago despite Ella knowing it would end in disaster. She couldn't help herself and just kept going back.

I want to hate him for it, for stringing her along. But the truth is, he did. He was open and honest with her from the get go. His career came above all else, and while he was more than down for having some fun, no girl, no matter how magical, sweet, and special she was, was going to distract him from his end goal.

Part of me wishes that he could have given her a chance, but then ultimately, that would have hurt even worse.

Maybe Ella is the one for him, maybe they are written in the stars or whatever, but Colt certainly isn't ready even if that is the case.

I guess, it probably would have been a similar story with Tristan a few years ago. The NFL was his endgame, and I remember just how focused on that he was. As far as I know, he's never had anything long-term with a girl before me, so there is a very good chance he was similar to Colt back in the day.

"I know, I know. I just... I miss him."

With a sigh, I step closer to her and wrap my arms around her.

"You're going to meet so many more awesome guys once you step out into the world that's waiting for you outside MKU."

"Yeah, I know. I just... I don't know if I'm ready."

Graduating and watching our family break apart even more than it already has is hard. I get that. But it was always inevitable. West and Brax are heading off to embark on their own football careers, both of them scoring incredible teams for their first season in the NFL. Micah is staying in Maddison County and enrolling at MKU as a grad student while working with Reid and the guys. Not as a Hawk, because just like he promised me that day, he isn't one. Not that the truth when it came out was all that much better, but I've learned over the past couple of years to put my hatred and distrust of gangsters behind me, because actually, they're some of the best people I've ever met. And Ella, well, she's heading back down south to spend a bit of time with her family in the hope she can make a decision about what she wants to do. She's lost, and as much as I might want to help her figure it all out, I know I can't. That's for her, I just have to hope she finds whatever it is she's looking for sooner rather than later, because I hate seeing her so unsure of herself.

"Everything is going to be okay. Just wait, you'll get off the airplane in a few days and walk straight into the love of your life."

"We can all hope, huh?" she says sadly.

"Violet Brady," a voice calls from the other side of the room, dragging my focus from Ella.

"Come on, Titch," West says, throwing his arm around my shoulders. "Let's not hold everything up," he teases.

When I glance over, I find him, Brax, and Micah all dressed the same as us and ready to get the show on the road.

"Look at you guys," I sigh, emotion burning up the back of my throat.

This is it. The day we've all been waiting for but equally terrified of."

"First day of the rest of our lives,'" Brax muses.

"Violet," Micah warns. "Please don't cry, you know we can't cope with tears."

"Sorry. I'm sorry. I need to go."

"Violet," Ella calls before I manage to get away.

Spinning around, I find her on her feet in the middle of the guys.

"Thank you. You're right, everything is going to work out."

I can't help but smile when Micah throws his arm around her shoulders.

Things might have gotten a little weird between them, and I won't lie, when she confessed what happened, I was worried. But despite the odds, their friendship has blossomed since. It's incredible to see.

"Of course it will. And if you get bored down south, you know there's always a home for you here," he says.

"Or wherever we are," West also offers.

"You guys," she sobs before they all close in around her.

Reaching an arm out, Brax tugs me into the huddle, and everything other than my family is forgotten.

---

The second I step out on stage, I put everything we just talked about and the sadness of our family all going in different directions aside as I search for my boys.

The crowd is full of parents. I mean, those two tickets we were allocated probably were intended for everyone's moms and dads and not their two boyfriends. But fuck it.

The second I find them, everything inside me relaxes, because while one part of my life might be coming to an end, I know, no matter what, that I've got the two of them ready to pick me up and hold me together.

'I love you,' Tristan mouths, making my heart soar while Knox blows me a kiss.

Lifting my hand, I press it to my heart as it pounds just for them.

I keep my eyes on them for the entire ceremony, even when they try to mortify me by making more noise than anyone around them when my name is announced. It doesn't work though, I'm so far from being embarrassed by either of them, too full of love to care about what anyone else thinks about our setup.

It's unconventional, yes. But who gives a shit? The three of us are happy, so fucking happy.

After taking a few months off to get back to normal life, Knox started working more and more for Reid again. Although, he hardly ever gets his hands dirty like the night he needed to deliver some retaliation on the man who made his life inside hell. Instead, he prefers to be sitting behind a computer, doing surveillance and intel gathering with Ellis and Micah. He loves it, he thrives on the challenge, while I mostly sit beside him, having literally no clue as to what all the codes and shit on the screens mean.

Tristan has now finished his graduate degree and will be graduating in just over a week's time. Despite being offered numerous jobs at a number of colleges across the country, he's decided to go back to his roots, and he's accepted a coaching position at our old high school. It wasn't the move anyone expected him to make, and I think a few of his colleagues are a little disappointed, but I see the excitement in his eyes every time he talks about training the NFL players of the future and I know wholeheartedly that he's making the right choice.

And as for me? Well, who knows. Honestly, I'm about as lost as Ella right now. But I'm okay with that. I'm going to take some time to just enjoy life, enjoy my boys, and then we'll see where it all goes from there. Between us all, we've got enough money that we don't need to worry, and I'm hoping that the freedom that gives me will help lead me to what I should be doing next with my life. Here's hoping, anyway.

---

"I'm so fucking proud of you," Tristan says, sweeping me off my feet and spinning me around while I squeal in delight.

The second he puts me down, I'm wrapped up in another pair of arms, but Knox is a little less polite given we're surrounded by everyone else's friends and family, and he slams his lips down on mine in a hot and heavy kiss that leaves us both panting and ready to leave this place behind.

We have a drink with everyone, and Tristan and Knox graze their way down the buffet table despite the fact we're meeting Roman and Imogen for a meal in just over an hour's time.

The time with my friends passes all too soon, and before I know it, I'm having to say goodbye to West and Brax, who are only back for a few days. They're heading back off this evening so they don't miss any training time with their new teams. Ella is hanging around for a few more days before she heads back to her parents. Thankfully, Letty has decided to stay on and do her master's, seeing as Kane still has two more years before he can graduate, and Micah will still be here. But still, I hate knowing that there is going to be so many miles between us all.

When we finally walk away, I've got tears freely flowing down my cheeks while both Tristan and Knox try to distract me from my sadness as we head toward Knox's Mustang.

"Come on, baby. We hate seeing you crying," Knox says, a deep V marring his brow.

"I'm sorry. I'm okay."

"Dude, stop making her feel worse," Tristan chastises. "I've already booked the flights to go and watch their first games of the season."

"I know. And it's going to be amazing. It's just... the end of an era."

"I know, baby girl."

"I'm excited about the new one we're starting."

Tristan drags me into the back of Knox's car, much to Knox's displeasure.

"So am I, baby girl."

After the academic year finished, the three of us officially moved into my house. Tristan still owns the apartment, and Kane and Letty are going to move into it, seeing as their landlord gave them notice on their place.

I love being in the house with my boys. I love the space we have, the ability to spend days out in the yard and finally make use of the pool I never had finished off when I rebuilt the place, thinking that it would be a waste. I especially enjoy our naked late-night pool parties. They are the best.

The restaurant where we're meeting Roman is only a short drive away, but I don't get a chance to see any of it, because the second Tristan closes the door behind him, he's on me, his tongue delving into my mouth and distracting me from my tears and thoughts of my friends flying halfway around the country by the end of the day.

"You're gonna want to do something about that boner before we walk in there to see Violet's big brother," Knox taunts from the driver's seat once he's pulled the car to a stop. "I wonder what your mom looks like naked," he muses, making me snort a laugh.

"Fuck you, asshole."

"Do you think she wears slutty lingerie for your dad?"

"Tristan," I shriek when he surges forward and punches Knox in the shoulder.

"Worked, didn't it?"

Tristan scoffs. "I had it under control," he mutters, sliding across the seat and pushing the door open.

"I'm sure Roman is more than aware of what the two of you do to me on a daily basis."

"Yeah, makes you wonder why we're both still breathing, doesn't it?"

"He deserves it," I state, following Tristan out of his car just in time to catch him rearranging himself. "Problem?" I ask, quirking my brow at him.

"Nothing that wouldn't be fixed with you on your knees and my cock in your luscious mouth."

A shot of lust shoots straight through me, turning my blood to lava.

"Now that sounds like something I can get on board with," Knox murmurs as he steps up behind me, pressing the front of his body against my back and letting me know that Tristan isn't the only one battling his own body. "We know how much you love getting on your knees for us."

I close my eyes for a beat, remembering a couple of weeks ago when they both stood before me, gloriously naked and ready for me.

"You're wet for us, aren't you, baby girl?"

Knox doesn't give me a chance to answer, not that I really

need to give them one. They know just as much as I do that I'm soaked for them.

"You know, I think she might have bought this dress just to tease us," Knox says over my shoulder.

"You want us to unwrap you like the most precious gift we've ever received later, don't you, baby girl?"

Knox teases me with the zipper at the base of my neck while Tristan undresses me with his eyes.

"I thought you might like it," I whisper, burning up with need for them.

"We do, Firefly. We more than like it."

Looking up, I meet my brother's impatient eyes as he stands in the entrance of the restaurant with my gorgeous niece at his side.

"Rain check," I say before rushing forward.

"Sorry," I say in a rush to Roman before dropping to my haunches to meet the more important of the two of them.

"Hey, gorgeous girl. What have you got there? I ask, noticing that she's strangling a stuffy in her arms.

"It's meant to be for you," Roman confesses with a laugh, "but she's a little attached to it."

"Aw, can I see?" I ask, holding my hand out.

Her huge green eyes stare into mine, silently assessing if she can trust me.

She must like what she sees, because, after a couple of seconds, she releases the toy and passes him over.

"Ongratulaton," she whispers.

I take in the bear that's dressed up in its graduation gown and my heart melts even more for this little girl.

"Thank you, Lilly. I love him. Could you do me a favor though?"

She nods eagerly.

"Could you look after him while we eat?"

"I will," she agrees quietly before I pass him back and lift her into my arms instead.

"Don't feel too guilty," Roman whispers when I stand in front of him once more. "Imogen took pity on her and bought a spare."

I can't help but laugh.

"Congratulations, kid. I'm proud of you."

---

I fully expect to just head home after our meal with Roman, Imogen, and Lilly, but much to my surprise and irritation, the second we climb back into the car, a blindfold is slipped around my face, blocking my view of everything.

"You have to be kidding me," I hiss, lifting my hands to remove it but quickly finding both of them locked in a large pair of hands.

Two low chuckles fill the enclosed space around me, making a shiver of desire run down my spine.

"If you wanted to play kinky games, all you had to do was say."

"Oh Firefly, we have plans. But right now, we just need you to sit back, relax, and trust us."

"While blindfolded?" I confirm.

"Will that be a problem?" Tristan asks.

I pretend to think for a few seconds, but the reality is that I trust them both with my life, so there isn't really a question to consider.

"It better be worth it," I mutter, pretending to be pissed off. Really, my body is buzzing with anticipation for what they've done.

"Firefly, we promise you, it's going to be worth it."

The car rumbles to life beneath me and Tristan complains from the back seat about being lonely and the blindfold not being necessary if I were just back there with him as Knox pulls away.

I have no concept of time as I sit there in the dark. Even

the songs playing out of the speakers begin to blur into one, making me lose any sense of time. And eventually, the exhaustion of the day begins to get the better of me and I find myself drifting off to sleep with Knox's hand locked around my thigh and my new stuffy in my lap.

I come to a few times, but the second I realize that we're still driving, I let myself drift back off, hoping the energy will come in useful once we get to wherever we're going.

A loud moan finally wakes me, and I quickly realize that it ripped from me. The next thing I discover is that I've got lips on me.

Cool night air rushes over my skin as someone kisses along my jaw and another grazes his lips over my collarbone.

"Could get used to this kind of wake-up," I murmur, my voice thick with sleep.

"It's just the beginning, baby girl."

Tristan's deep voice makes the rest of my body wake up, and I arch off the seat, needing more of them.

"Such a filthy little girl, Firefly," Knox groans. "Get her out, Tris. But don't let her—"

"I know the plan, asshole."

In a flash, I'm out of the car with Tristan's large hands on my waist, keeping me steady as the blindfold remains in place.

The air is fresh, fresher than what we left behind, and birdsong fills the air. Other than that, there's silence.

An idea pops into my head, and excited butterflies fill my belly at the prospect.

Tristan guides me forward, and after climbing some stairs which confirm my previous thought, he walks me through a building until we're outside again.

He releases me and steps around my body, leaving me cold without his touch.

Silence fills the space between us. The only thing I can hear other than the birdsong is my own racing heart.

"Take it off," Knox demands.

It takes me a second to move, but eventually, I do and pull the blindfold from my eyes.

"Oh my God," I gasp when I find us standing exactly where I thought, only on the deck where we spent so long on that weekend they first brought me here.

Those few days were hard. I was still drowning in grief, and it made me realize that even five years on, I hadn't really dealt with my loss.

Knowing Roman was alive helped, but that weekend with my boys really made me see things more clearly. They held me while I cried and listened as I reminisced about the past.

Being back here now, celebrating, hits me in a very different yet equally powerful way.

Soft fairy lights illuminate the space along with flickering candles. The hot tub is sitting off to the side, waiting for us along with a couple of bottles of chilled champagne. But by far, the most mesmerizing sight is the two men standing before me.

"Violet, you changed our lives long before you even realized," Tristan starts.

"The light in your eyes, the excitement in your smile. They ensnared me the moment I saw them. And despite knowing that you were far too good for me, I couldn't stop myself," Knox adds.

"I did the right thing for as long as I could, trying to keep misguided promises and secrets that I long should have forgotten about, because no matter what, my mind always returned to you, Pip. You're the only girl who's ever stolen my heart, and you're the only one who will ever own it."

"I swore years ago that I would always protect you, that I would do the right thing by you, even if that meant having to let you go.

"I stand by what I did, but there won't be a day that I won't regret losing time with you. There also won't be a day where I forget how fucking lucky I am that you forgave me and gave me another chance."

I sniffle as both of them bear their hearts to me.

"We know what we have is unconventional, and it stops us from doing some things officially, but that isn't going to stop us from wanting the world to know that you're ours," Tristan explains.

"If you'll have us," Knox adds as Tristan reveals a small black jewelry box and flips it open.

"Oh my God," I gasp again. "It's beautiful."

"Three bands," Knox says. "One for me," he points to the silver, "one for Tris," the gold. "And the center one with all the diamonds for our girl. Our heart."

A sob rips from my throat as I look from the ring and up to them as my tears fall once more.

"Will you be ours, Violet?" Tristan asks.

"Because we're yours. Forever."

"Always."

"Yes. Yes," I cry as Knox plucks the ring from the box and slips it up my ring finger. "It fits."

"Of course it does, we're not amateurs, Pip," Tristan teases before I launch myself at both of them. They catch me like they always do and hold me up as I try to show them both just how much I love them before we find out who wins and gets to pull the zipper down my back, revealing the gift I have hiding beneath. Not that that lasts long, and we all end up naked in the hot tub enjoying each other the best way we know how.

Now. Always. Forever.

Want to know more about Reid, JD, & Maverick? Read their story, Merciless, Book #1 in the Harrow Creek Hawks Series.
GET YOUR COPY NOW!

Keep reading for a sneak peek of Merciless!

# MERCILESS
## SNEAK PEEK

### Alana

I'm stronger than the men who run this town. I can do this.

My body trembles with fear, exhaustion, and hunger, but I forge on.

The sight of the 'You're Leaving Harrow Creek' sign illuminated ahead makes my heart beat wildly and my stomach flip with excitement.

I'm going to do this. I'm going to defy all the odds and get out.

Without looking back, I emerge from the darkness and pick up speed.

Once I get to the other side of that sign, everything is going to be easier.

Everything is going to get better.

Everything is—

My steps falter when headlights ahead get brighter, lighting me up like a fucking homing beacon.

I swallow nervously, tugging my bag up higher on my shoulders, and will my legs to just keep going. I lower my head, hiding from the driver.

But this is me, and my luck just isn't that good.

The car slows, and I immediately take off running in the opposite direction and into the trees.

Darkness engulfs me once more as I stumble over thick tree roots and rocks.

The bang of a car door slamming startles me, and I pinch my lips closed before a scream of terror can rip from my throat.

*Just keep running. Just keep running.*

*Your life isn't going to be worth living if they catch you.*

White noise fills my ears as I run. My bag slows me down, especially when it gets caught on a branch, but I refuse to abandon it.

I can't.

Just when I begin to think I might have outrun the man in the car, my bag is yanked backward. I scream as an arm wraps around my waist, restraining me while a large, hot hand covers my mouth.

"Nice try, Doll," a deep, deadly voice whispers in my ear.

Ice-cold fear rushes through my veins as I fight to drag the air I need through my nose.

I was so close. So fucking close.

Want to know what happens next? Grab your copy of MERCILESS now!

# ABOUT THE AUTHOR

Tracy Lorraine is a *USA Today* and *Wall Street Journal* bestselling new adult and contemporary romance author. Tracy has recently turned thirty and lives in a cute Cotswold village in England with her husband, baby girl and lovable but slightly crazy dog. Having always been a bookaholic with her head stuck in her Kindle, Tracy decided to try her hand at a story idea she dreamt up and hasn't looked back since.

Be the first to find out about new releases and offers. Sign up to my newsletter here.

If you want to know what I'm up to and see teasers and snippets of what I'm working on, then you need to be in my Facebook group. Join Tracy's Angels here.

*Keep up to date with Tracy's books at*
www.tracylorraine.com

## ALSO BY TRACY LORRAINE

**Falling Series**

Falling for Ryan: Part One #1

Falling for Ryan: Part Two #2

Falling for Jax #3

Falling for Daniel (A Falling Series Novella)

Falling for Ruben #4

Falling for Fin #5

Falling for Lucas #6

Falling for Caleb #7

Falling for Declan #8

Falling For Liam #9

**Forbidden Series**

Falling for the Forbidden #1

Losing the Forbidden #2

Fighting for the Forbidden #3

Craving Redemption #4

Demanding Redemption #5

Avoiding Temptation #6

Chasing Temptation #7

**Rebel Ink Series**

Hate You #1

Trick You #2

Defy You #3

Play You #4

Inked (A Rebel Ink/Driven Crossover)

**Rosewood High Series**

Thorn #1

Paine #2

Savage #3

Fierce #4

Hunter #5

Faze (#6 Prequel)

Fury #6

Legend #7

**Maddison Kings University Series**

TMYM: Prequel

TRYS #1

TDYW #2

TBYS #3

TVYC #4

TDYD #5

TDYR #6

TRYD #7

**Knight's Ridge Empire Series**

Wicked Summer Knight: Prequel (Stella & Seb)

Wicked Knight #1 (Stella & Seb)

Wicked Princess #2 (Stella & Seb)

Wicked Empire #3 (Stella & Seb)

Deviant Knight #4 (Emmie & Theo)

Deviant Princess #5 (Emmie & Theo

Deviant Reign #6 (Emmie & Theo)

One Reckless Knight (Jodie & Toby)

Reckless Knight #7 (Jodie & Toby)

Reckless Princess #8 (Jodie & Toby)

Reckless Dynasty #9 (Jodie & Toby)

Dark Halloween Knight (Calli & Batman)

Dark Knight #10 (Calli & Batman)

Dark Princess #11 (Calli & Batman)

Dark Legacy #12 (Calli & Batman)

Corrupt Valentine Knight (Nico & Siren)

**Ruined Series**

Ruined Plans #1

Ruined by Lies #2

Ruined Promises #3

**Never Forget Series**

Never Forget Him #1

Never Forget Us #2

Everywhere & Nowhere #3

**Chasing Series**

Chasing Logan

**The Cocktail Girls**

His Manhattan

# Her Kensington

Made in the USA
Monee, IL
09 March 2024

54717467R10319